It's Been a

Brian Johnston joined the BBC's Outside
Broadcasts Department immediately after the
war and worked first on live radio broadcasts
from theatres and music halls all over Great
Britain. He was one of the first broadcasters to
work both for television and radio and began
his long association with cricket commentary in
the summer of 1946. Between 1948 and 1952 he
also presented the live feature 'Let's Go
Somewhere' for the popular Saturday night
radio programme *In Town Tonight*.

From 1946 until the end of the sixties he
covered all the televised Test Matches for the
BBC and was a member of the television
commentary teams for the funeral of King
George VI, the Coronation and the wedding of
Princess Margaret.

He became the BBC's first Cricket
Correspondent in 1963 and held this post until
his retirement in 1972. Since then he has
continued as a regular member of the *Test
Match Special* team and, until 1987, as
presenter of the long-running radio programme
Down Your Way

Brian Johnston is married with three sons
and two daughters and lives within strolling
distance of the Lord's Cricket Ground in
north-west London.

BRIAN JOHNSTON

It's Been
a Piece of Cake

*A Tribute to my Favourite
Test Cricketers*

Mandarin

A Mandarin Paperback

IT'S BEEN A PIECE OF CAKE

First published in Great Britain 1989
by Methuen London
This edition published 1990
by Mandarin Paperbacks
Michelin House, 81 Fulham Road, London SW3 6RB

Mandarin is an imprint of the Octopus Publishing Group

Copyright © Brian Johnston 1989

A CIP catalogue record for this title
is available from the British Library

ISBN 0 7493 0293 3

Printed in Great Britain
by Cox and Wyman Ltd, Reading, Berks.

With all my love to
Pauline,
who, more than anyone,
deserves a tribute

Contents

Illustrations

Acknowledgements and thanks for permission to reproduce photographs are due to Patrick Eagar for illustrations 25, 33, 34, 35, 38, 39, 41, 49, 50, 51, 52, 53, 56, 57, 59, 60, 62, 63, 64, 65, 66, 67, 69, 70, 71, 73, 74, 76 and 77; Ken Kelly for illustrations 12, 15, 21, 27, 28, 31, 37, 40, 47, 48, 54, 55 and 58; Sport and General for illustrations 1, 2, 3, 5, 7, 10, 14, 18, 24, 29, 30, 32, 36, 46, 61 and 68; The Hulton – Deutsch Collection for illustrations 13, 20, 22, 23 and 43; All-Sport – Adrian Murrell for illustrations 72 and 75; the MCC for illustrations 4 and 26; David Frith for illustration 45.
Illustrations 6, 8, 9, 11, 16, 17, 19 and 42 are taken from Denzil Batchelor's *The Book of Cricket*, Collins (1952); illustration 44 is taken from *Trevor Bailey's Cricket Book*, Frederick Muller (1959).

Acknowledgements

I would like to thank Christopher Falkus,
who first conceived this book with me,
and Ann Mansbridge and Alex Bennion,
who have nursed it and put it to bed.
Finally, I am extremely grateful to
Ann Nash for providing such
a beautifully typed manuscript from
my scribbled thoughts on paper.

Author's note

All Test and career records are taken from
the end of the 1988 England cricket season, and I would like to
thank Bill Frindall for his usual kind help and advice.

Introduction

I suppose most of us from time to time sit back and reflect on our lives. I know I do, and every time I feel a little ashamed that the game of cricket has played such a large part in mine. First of all following the scores in the papers, then reading some of the many books. Playing it, of course, and merely watching it as a spectator, and finally for well over half of my life earning some of my living by commentating on it. All that time spent on just a game! Or is it something more than that? Many of us believe that it is. More than anything else in my life it taught me to try to work and play with others, and to be a member of a team. I was taught the importance of improving my own performance by practice, dedication and discipline; and to accept the umpire's decision, to win or lose gracefully and to take the inevitable disappointments with a smile. These are the ideals and I am not boasting or pretending that I have ever lived up to them, but they do explain the phrase 'it's not cricket'.

Far more indelible than memories of games played or watched are the happy recollections of countless friendships resulting entirely from a mutual love of cricket. I was lucky to collect a growing band of friends as I progressed through life. School, university, business, the war and club cricket provided many of them. And then, beyond my wildest dreams, when I joined the BBC in 1946 and became a commentator Test and county cricketers gave me *their* friendship. I shall always treasure this. Here was I, a humble (?!) club cricketer accepted by the greats in the game. It has made my time in the commentary box a supremely happy one, and I shall always be grateful to them, and to all my colleagues in the commentary box.

One great bonus which cricket has given to the world is its humour and its literature. More stories are told about its characters, and more books have been and are being written about it, than of all other games put together. It is something which makes it unique in sport and enables those of us past our playing days to relive matches and to meet and learn about all the players which cricket has produced.

I have just completed my forty-third season in the commentary box, and the Sri Lankan Test at Lord's in 1988 was the 250th on which I have commentated either on television or on radio. So I feel the time is right for me to try to portray, and to pay tribute to, some of the players and characters, and to try to recapture the tremendous pleasure which their skills and performances have given to me. With four exceptions I will only write about those on whom I have personally commentated. They are my own personal choice, and inevitably other people's favourites will be left out. I don't suppose they will mind, but if they do I am sorry. There is a limit to the size even of a cricket book, however.

I have chosen seventy-seven – one for each year of my life to date. I am very conscious of the fact that I have left out many fine players, especially from overseas, and I have also had to leave out some of my good companions on tours, who provided so much fun and laughter as we travelled round the world together – people like David Brown, Robin Hobbs, Raman Subba Row, 'J.T.' Murray, Peter Parfitt and Peter Richardson.

Finally, the title of the book. It is not meant to sound conceited, as if I am boasting that my commentator's job has been easy. It merely refers to the somewhat bizarre association that I have had with chocolate cakes. It all started some ten years ago when a kind lady sent me a chocolate cake on my birthday, during a Test match at Lord's. I perhaps unwisely thanked her over the air. Since then gifts of all sorts have flooded into the box: bottles, sweets, biscuits and of course cakes galore – usually chocolate. On some occasions they are works of art. For instance, last year I was given by some friends in Cardiff a colour reproduction in icing of the famous picture of Lord's in the early 1900s, which hangs in the Memorial Gallery at Lord's! It depicts a rather rotund fielder stopping a ball in front of the small stand which used to be on the left of the pavilion, where the Warner Stand now is. Walking on the edge of the boundary is King Edward VII with Queen Alexandra on his arm, and sitting in the stand is the easily recognisable figure of Lily Langtry!

So what do we do with all the cakes? Some we eat, or share with our television colleagues, our engineers and our many casual visitors to the box. The one I have mentioned above was too good to eat, and it is still in my freezer in St John's Wood. I am also glad to say that we often send those we cannot eat to local children's hospitals. With my thanks to the many hundreds of people who have sent in cakes, I hope they – and you too – will now appreciate the title!

The first I can remember of anything to do with cricket was when I was aged about six, and an old Oxford blue called H. G. Tylecote lived in the village of Offley where we had our home. He used to come and coach my eldest brother Michael on our tennis court, and I was allowed to do a spot of fielding. Two years later I went to boarding school at Eastbourne, and it was there that I 'became' Patsy Hendren. My brother was J. W. Hearne (young 'Jack'), and we used to play needle matches in the nets. So I think it makes sense to give my hero pride of place in the batting order of my favourites, and he is one of the four exceptions of the seventy-seven on whom I never commentated.

I have always regretted that I never commentated on a Hendren innings. This also applies to other great cricketers whom I watched before the war – not that I did much watching in the years from 1921 to 1939. Whenever I could, I preferred to play instead, but I was lucky to be at school in Eastbourne from 1921 to 1925, and we used to go to the Saffrons to see H. D. G. Leveson-Gower's eleven against both Oxford and Cambridge. I remember famous names like A. P. F. Chapman, the three Ashtons (G., H., C.T.), Rev. F. H. Gillingham, R. H. Bettington, G. E. B. Abell, the two Gilligans (A.E.R., A.H.), T. C. Lowry, M. D. Lyon, G. T. S. Stevens, K. S. Duleepsinhji and F. B. R. Browne.

The latter had the nickname of 'Tishy', because just before he delivered the ball he crossed his legs. The 'Tishy' came from a mare of that name who used to cross her legs when jumping and, not surprisingly, fell a number of times. There was a rather rude joke at the time which said that she had crossed her legs and fallen at Becher's in the Grand National because she had spotted the Rector of Stiffkey in the crowd on the other side of the fence. Stiffkey was a village in Norfolk and there was a *cause célèbre* involving the Rector and a number of London prostitutes. F.B.R. was a master at St Andrew's school, which could also boast of J. L. Bryan on its staff. Naturally they were always a good side and normally beat us except when D. R. S. Bader (the famous Douglas) was in our eleven. He could be relied on to make a hundred more often than not. This great airman-to-be was a popular figure at my school, Temple Grove, because whenever he *did* make a hundred we were excused evening prep. Writing down all these names reminds me of a fairly useless skill which I have always had. I am very bad at remembering names but I'm a wizard at initials and would gladly choose 'Initials of First-Class Cricketers' as my specialist subject in 'Mastermind'.

But I digress. Back to the Saffrons, where I seem to remember a number of fancy caps, including the Harlequins. I must have seen Yorkshire play there once, because I distinctly remember Herbert Sutcliffe with his sleek black hair hooking a six over long leg.

From 1923 we lived in Dorset for a couple of years, before moving to Herefordshire. In July 1924 our tutor took me and my brother in the sidecar of his motorbike to watch Hampshire play Notts at Bournemouth. We sat by the sight screen and watched a bald, red-faced Arthur Carr, in a cream silk shirt with a knotted handkerchief round his neck, driving with great power. Alec Kennedy, the fast-medium bowler, had a beautifully smooth run up to the wicket, and standing at mid-off was the considerable figure of Lionel Tennyson. I was especially interested in the wicket-keeper Livsey, who in addition to keeping wicket was also Tennyson's butler. Personally, after six hours crouching behind the stumps, I wouldn't have felt like waiting at table! On this occasion I didn't see Philip Mead bat. I only saw him walking from slip to slip at the end of each over with his shambling farmer's gait. I was lucky enough to see him bat a few years later and can confirm this classical description of him by a very dear friend – the late 'Crusoe', R. C. Robertson Glasgow:

> Having settled his whereabouts with the umpire, he
> wiggled the toe of his left boot for some fifteen
> seconds inside the crease, pulled the peak of a cap
> that seemed all peak, wiggled again, pulled again,
> then gave a comprehensive stare round him as if to
> satisfy himself that no fielder, aware of the task
> ahead, had brought a stick of dynamite. Then he
> leaned forward and looked down at the pitch, quite
> still. His bat looked almost laughably broad.

Great stuff. Can you wonder that Crusoe was my favourite cricket writer? I met him first at a dinner at the Club in Trinity, Oxford, in 1933, when he gave his famous rendering of 'Eskimo Nell'. No one has ever done it better!

I once played with Lord Tennyson when, through Alec Dunglass (Lord Home as he is now), I was asked to play for the Lords and Commons against Westminster at Vincent Square. Tennyson came into the dressing-room with an enormous portmanteau. He opened it up and revealed a batch of bottles – whisky, gin, wine etc. 'Help yourselves, gentlemen, and if you care to give me an order afterwards I shall be only too pleased that it is delivered to your house.' The only other person I know who used to sell his wares in the dressing-room was Godfrey Evans, who would bring a small case full of attractive marcasite jewellery in which he was financially interested. And whilst on the subject of jewellery, there was a splendid character who used to haunt the Yorkshire grounds. He carried in his pocket a small soft leather bag full of the most priceless jewels. Goodness knows what they were worth, but he used to come up to our commentary box and display the dazzling rings and bracelets. Why he was never mugged I don't know. Perhaps he was – I haven't seen him for over twenty years. He always used to have a good story, and once told me: 'I'm very worried about the three Ms.' 'The three Ms?' I asked. 'What on earth are they?' 'Oh,' he said, 'the Missus, the maid and the mortgage. They're all three overdue!'

Whilst still in Dorset I had a tremendous thrill – I actually saw the great Jack Hobbs play, alas the only time that I did. It was in a charity match at Bridport in 1924, and so far as I can remember he made 17. I can still picture one magnificent square cut which he played, though my vision was somewhat clouded by the smoke of a foul-smelling pipe smoked by either J. T. Brown or J. Tunnicliffe, the great Yorkshire opening pair. They were sitting in front of me and I don't know which one was the offender. But they were first-class cricketers and I forgave them anything.

After the war I was lucky to meet Jack, and no nicer nor more modest man can ever have played cricket; he had a delightful sense of humour and a twinkle in his eye. I used to visit him when he retired to Hove.

In 1925 we moved to Herefordshire, so were in easy reach of Cheltenham and Worcester. In 1926 I saw my first ever touring team, and got my first sight of those baggy green Australian caps. They were playing Gloucestershire at Cheltenham. I had read a lot about the fast bowling of Jack Gregory and was duly impressed with his speed and long run up to the wicket. A chap called Ellis was keeping wicket in place of Oldfield, and one ball from Gregory was so fast that he could only get his left hand to it and his glove came off. The crowd were cheered by a lively second innings of 32 by their burly captain, Lt-Col. D. C. Robinson. Brig.-Gen. Poore of Hampshire (1898–1906) was once asked in the 1930s how he would have dealt with Harold Larwood. 'I'd have charged him,' he replied. Well, Lt-Col. Robinson obviously had the same idea as he advanced down the pitch to meet Gregory's expresses. He missed some, snicked some and hit some, but it was highly entertaining while it lasted. I have fleeting memories of Dipper, Sinfield, Parker, and Goddard, but none of Hammond because he didn't play for Gloucestershire that year. He had picked up a virus in the West Indies and was in a nursing home throughout the summer.

We were lucky to see the Australians batting, and it was the small figure of C. G. Macartney – green floppy cap pulled low over his eyes – who caught my attention with his late cutting. And I realise now how lucky I was not only to see Gregory, but also the gnome-like Clarrie Grimmett with his round-arm action spinning out the Gloucestershire batsmen. (He took 11 wickets in the match.) I met him and interviewed him in the 1960s at Adelaide. He was obviously very bitter that he had not been selected to tour England with Don Bradman's team in 1938. On figures alone he had reason to be. In the winter of 1935–6 he had toured South Africa and in five Tests took 44 wickets for 14.59 apiece, which still remains the highest for Australia in any Test series. The following winter Gubby Allen's team visited Australia and, surprisingly, Grimmett did not play in a single Test, his place being taken by another leg spinner, F. A. Ward, and later by the left-arm chinaman bowler L. O'B. Fleetwood-Smith. Both these were selected to tour England in 1938 with very limited success, Ward taking 0 for 142 in the one Test in which he played, and Fleetwood Smith 14 wickets – but at a cost of over 50 runs per wicket. So it does seem strange that Grimmett didn't come. It's even stranger when the records show that Grimmett was highly successful in the Sheffield Shield in the season when Bradman's team was picked. He actually took 30 wickets in Sheffield Shield matches from South Australia in *both* the seasons of 1936–7 and 1937–8 – 15 more than Ward in 1936–7 and 5 more in 1937–8, and 5 runs an over cheaper. So it rather looks as if there was a clash of personalities somewhere.

We paid quite a few visits to the lovely Worcester ground nestling in the shadow of the Cathedral. It was the time of Major M. F. S. Jewell and M. K. Foster, one of the seven Foster brothers who all played for Worcestershire. My special favourite was Tarbox (C. V.) because of his unusual name. And of course there was Fred Root with his new leg theory bowling – giant in-swingers with a posse of fielders in the leg trap. He was no more than fast-medium so was never as dangerous as Larwood. My stepfather decided to copy him, and you should have seen the looks on the Much Marcle village side when he directed six of them to crowd round the bat on the leg side. They were not only in danger from the usual village sloggers but also from my stepfather's 'deliveries', which tended to stray wide of the leg-stump and head straight for the cluster of short legs. He was soon persuaded to give it up!

I also paid two visits to Taunton: the first time in 1925 to see Yorkshire play Somerset. I can remember nothing of the game except that during the lunch interval I saw Abe Waddington and Maurice Leyland walking across the ground to the lunch tent. I rushed after them to get their autographs and to my great disappointment they refused. I inwardly cursed them at the time but I now realise why they did so – and it's a tip I would pass on to all young autograph-hunters. Never ask a cricketer for his autograph when he's on the way to lunch. He only has forty minutes and his mind is concentrated on only one thing – his stomach!

My second visit was far luckier. It was in 1932 and I saw K. S. Duleepsinhji make 90 in what was I think his last first-class innings. I can picture him now – dark, slim, rather frail but with exquisite timing. J. C. (Farmer) White was wheeling away over after over at one end with his accurate slow left arm, but time and time again Duleep danced down the pitch and hit him over or past mid-on. A sight to treasure.

Tuesday, 1 July 1930 will always be a red-letter day in my cricket life. It was the day I saw my first Test match. It was the fourth and last day of the second Test match against Australia at Lord's. Some of the 'twenty-two' (second eleven) at Eton were entertained in one of the old Tavern boxes by an old blue called 'Sonny' Mugliston. He was a remarkable and rather unique sportsman. He got a cricket blue at *Cambridge* in 1907 and 1908 and also played seven matches for Lancashire during that period. But here comes the unusual part. At soccer he played left back for *Oxford* and the Corinthians and also represented *Oxford* at golf. How he divided his time between Cambridge and Oxford is not revealed.

Anyway, he was a friendly and generous host and we arrived in time for an excellent lunch. We then saw the second half of Percy Chapman's great innings of 121. At lunch England were 262 for 5, still needing 42 to make Australia bat again, and with a slight chance of saving the game. Gubby Allen was batting with Chapman but was lbw to Grimmett for a hard-hit 57. Chapman, who might have been out before he had scored (a skier dropped between V. Richardson and Ponsford), proceeded to hit out at everything and hit three sixes off Grimmett bowling from the Nursery End. I can still see them – towering on-drives into the far corner of the Mound Stand. There was tremendous excitement when he reached his first – and only – Test hundred. And then a short time afterwards he was facing Fairfax from the Pavilion End when he snicked a ball to Oldfield behind the stumps. Believe it or not, he told our cricket master, Nick Roe, whom he later saw in the pavilion, that he had swallowed a blue-bottle! Enough to get anyone out! Otherwise he might have gone on and saved the match, but as it was Australia only needed 72 to win, and after a short panic when they lost 3 wickets for only 22 runs they won by 7 wickets. Walter Robins put on early and took 2 quick wickets, but the one I can remember is D. Bradman caught Chapman bowled Tate 1. It was really a hat trick for me as it was the first time I saw Bradman bat, the first time I saw Tate bowl, and it was the best catch I had ever seen up to then. Bradman had made a brilliant 254 in the first innings and we were all longing to see him bat. He tried to cut a ball from Tate, however, and although he hit it right in the middle only inches off the ground, Chapman scooped the ball up in the gully. Naturally we were disappointed at not seeing more of Bradman, but it really was a tremendous catch.

Chapman at the time was at the peak of his career – as captain of England he had regained the Ashes at the Oval in 1926, followed by his successful 4–1 tour of Australia in 1928–9. He was the ideal schoolboy's hero – tall, with curly hair and a chubby smiling face, and a brilliant hitter and fielder with enormous hands. I had seen him playing at the Saffrons for Cambridge against Leveson-Gower's eleven, and he was usually in the covers, swooping in on the ball.

From that day at Lord's, although he made 45 in the next Test, things began to go wrong for Chapman. To the general surprise he was dropped from the fifth Test at the Oval, Bob Wyatt taking over as captain. No one was more surprised or disappointed than Chapman himself. The *Daily Mail* published an article by him which hit the headlines: 'Why have I been dropped?' by Percy Chapman. He had a point because he had averaged over 40 in the series and Wyatt had never played against Australia. One phrase in Chapman's article sticks in my mind: 'My friends are good enough to say that my batting is still as good as ever.' But typically he sent a telegram wishing Wyatt good luck.

That winter he captained England on an unsuccessful tour of South Africa, both for England and for himself. He had been selected for the tour before he was dropped at the Oval and this must have made things very awkward for him. He continued to play his type of attractive cricket throughout the early thirties, proving a popular captain of Kent until he gave up at the end of 1936. He was becoming more and more involved in his job of selling whisky, and it gradually dragged him down. The debonair smiling personality, the born leader, the striker of sixes and the outstanding fielder of his generation became a sad figure. I used to see him after the war at Lord's. I would pass the time of day but I never got to know him well. Quite one of the saddest days of my life was when I saw him being carried to a taxi outside the back door of the pavilion. I try to shut out that memory and just remember that July day in 1930 when he scored his only Test hundred at Lord's and gave immense pleasure to a schoolboy who looked on him as a god-like figure.

But cricket in general has only happy memories for me, so let's start on the tributes to my chosen seventy-seven players who have given me so much pleasure during my commentaries in Test matches.

Patsy Hendren

After I 'became' Hendren in 1921, I noticed one day an advertisement in a paper. It showed a picture of Hendren batting, and underneath said: 'Why not take Wincarnis like Patsy Hendren of 26 Cairn Avenue, Ealing W5?' Just think of putting Ian Botham's private address in a paper for all to see! Anyway, there it was, and I immediately wrote off asking Patsy for his autograph, neglecting to enclose a stamped addressed envelope. After a few days, back came a piece of foolscap paper with three of his autographs. They looked something like this:

E. Patsy Hendren.

Note that the t was not crossed, and the two lines under the n. His kindness made a deep impression on me. My signature today is still

Brian Johnston.

My next indirect connection with him was in 1926 after England had won the Ashes at the Oval. There was no commentary point over the radio then, so at the end of the match Patsy was rushed by taxi to Broadcasting House to give a summary of the game. I can still remember the words in which he described the exciting scenes in front of the pavilion: 'The crowd was real glad and all was merry and bright.'

From then on I followed his career closely until he retired in 1937. Each morning I would find the sports page and see how many he had made. He seldom let me down. Early in his career, before I adopted him, he had had some hiccups in Test matches and was said not to have a Test match temperament. But he finished up with a Test average of 47.63 – just .09 behind Boycott (!) and ninth in the batting averages of all England Test batsmen. In other areas of first-class cricket there is no question as to where he stood. Altogether he scored 57,611 runs, beaten only by Hobbs and Woolley; 170 hundreds, beaten only by Hobbs; and an overall average in his career of 50.80, with only six other batsmen averaging more. So what was so special about him both as a player and as a man?

1 Patsy Hendren

He had every stroke in the book from the late chop or cut, the square cut and an off-drive between cover and extra cover. He drove fiercely and was the best hooker of his time. He was – as befitted a professional footballer who played on the wing for Brentford – very fast between the wickets and always tried to take a quick single off his first ball. He was small by modern standards, with very strong wrists and forearms, and his twinkling feet and magnificent 'arm' made him an outstanding fielder in the deep. In later years he fielded closer to the wicket, either at slip or crouching at short leg with his hands cupped and his bottom sticking out.

As a man he was cricket's most lovable clown, who never went too far. When batting he seemed to be in permanent conversation with the wicket-keeper, judging by the laughter of all those lucky enough to be fielding near to the wicket. He had an ugly pug-like face and made remarks with a deadpan look. His favourite expression when telling a story was, 'Oh dear, oh dear.' He enjoyed pulling the leg of batsmen and would often chase a ball and stoop to pick it up when still ten yards or so short of it. He would even turn round and pretend to throw the ball. When he saw the batsmen hesitating he would run on and pounce on the ball, throwing it back low and fast over the top of the stumps.

He also once pulled Alf Gover's leg with considerable success. As I've said, he was a great hooker and liked nothing better than short fast balls. In 1929 Alf was a new boy at Surrey when they went to play Middlesex at Lord's. Patsy had heard something about this new young fast bowler, so before play started he wandered into the Surrey dressing-room. In a kindly way he talked to Alf, bade him welcome to Lord's and hoped apprehensively that Alf wouldn't bowl too short at him when he came into bat. He said something about the 'peepers' not being able to pick up the ball so quickly these days. Anyhow, as soon as Patsy came in Alf remembered this conversation and immediately bowled a succession of short bouncers which Patsy promptly hooked for four or six into the Tavern. At the end of the over Jack Hobbs asked Alf what on earth he was trying to do. 'Oh,' said Alf, 'Mr Hendren doesn't like short bowling these days. He told me so himself.' What Jack said I don't know, but from then on Alf pitched the ball up!

After the war I used to go and sit with Patsy when he was scoring for Middlesex. He told me once of the occasion on Arthur Gilligan's tour of 1924 when Patsy was fielding out in the deep just under the Hill. A batsman hit a steepling catch to him. Up and up it went and Patsy tried to position himself underneath. As he did so a voice from the hill shouted: 'If you drop that catch, Patsy, you can sleep with my sister.' I asked him what happened. 'Oh dear, oh dear,' he said. 'As I hadn't seen his sister, I decided to make the catch.'

He also told me that he was once sitting in a train when a very pale man with a white silk scarf wound round his neck got into the carriage. He looked so ill and miserable that Patsy took pity on him and asked him what was the matter. 'Oh,' croaked the man, 'it's terrible. My club side was playing in the final of a competition. The opposition, with 1 wicket in hand, needed 2 runs to win off the last ball of the match. The batsman shied it in the air and it came to me at deep mid-on. They had run one by the time the ball came down – it was an absolute sitter – and I dropped it. They then ran another and won the match. My team mates will never forgive me.' 'Oh,' said Patsy jocularly, trying to cheer the poor man up, 'if I'd done that, I'd have cut my throat.' 'I have done,' whispered the man hoarsely.

I'm not sure if I believe that one, any more than I do the one when he had a day off in Australia, and took a car into the outback. He stopped to watch a game of cricket which was just about to start. A man came up and asked him if he played cricket, and if so would he like to make up one of the sides. Patsy thought it would be fun and agreed. His side fielded first and he was placed straight out in the deep behind the bowler. The wicket was on a high plateau and Patsy was right out of sight at the bottom of a hill. He could hear occasional shouts and applauses, but no one bothered him and he must have been there for over an hour when he suddenly saw the ball in the air coming over the hill. He ran up and caught it and held it aloft for his fellow fielders to see. 'I've caught it, I've caught it!' he cried. 'You silly b——,' said one of the batsmen. 'We've bowled the other side out and that's our number one batsman whom you've caught.'

As with Fred Trueman, many stories about Patsy are obviously not true. But this one definitely happened. In 1929 Middlesex were playing Derbyshire at Lord's. It was a wet wicket drying in the sun, and T. B. Mitchell was causing havoc with his leg-breaks. Patsy was playing a masterful innings, and with Middlesex 7 wickets down he was joined by Walter Robins. Robbie had got into the habit of charging down the pitch to slow bowlers, and if he missed the ball he never tried to get back into his crease. He just tucked his bat under his arm and, without looking round, would make his way back to the pavilion. Mitchell was bowling from the Pavilion End and tossed one up in the air to tempt Robbie. Robbie charged down the pitch, missed the ball by miles and, without looking round, continued his way back to the pavilion. This was too much for Patsy. 'He's missed it,' he shouted. Robbie turned in his tracks and flung himself on the damp pitch with his bat outstretched towards the batting crease. He heard a roar of laughter from the fielders and the crowd. He looked up and saw Harold Elliott the wicket-keeper tossing the ball from hand to hand with the bails lying ominously on the ground. He picked himself up, his white flannels covered in mud. Even Patsy wouldn't reveal what Robbie said as he passed him on the way to the pavilion. But it is said that, from then on, Robbie never charged down the pitch without looking back if he missed the ball.

Patsy was a lovable man, who gave pleasure to thousands both with his antics and performances on the field, and with his humour and sense of fun off it. He was my first real hero. I think I made a good choice.

Don Bradman

Back now to that July day at Lord's in 1930 when I saw for the first time the greatest run-making machine cricket has ever known. Early in the afternoon I had seen his brilliant running, picking up and throwing from the deep. Then, when Australia batted, down the pavilion steps he came, in green baggy cap walking ever so slowly with measured strides – using his bat as a walking-stick.

2 Don Bradman

Whenever I saw him bat after that he invariably did the same, sometimes looking up at the sky – accustoming his eyes to the light. He failed on this occasion and it was not until 1938 that I saw him bat again – at Lord's in the second Test when he made 102 not out and in the third Test at Headingley, 103.

Why was he so great? Before I try to answer that, I'll stagger you with some of his outstanding figures. He only played in 52 Tests, and in 80 innings scored 6,996 runs with 29 hundreds at an average of 99.94! He only needed to score 4 in his last Test innings at the Oval to give him an average of 100.00 exactly, and his 7,000th run in Test cricket.

Of these 52 Tests, 37 were against England, with 5 home Tests each against South Africa, the West Indies and India. The only *overseas* Tests he played were against England. Just imagine what his Test record would have been had he toured the other countries, and had Australia played New Zealand, Pakistan and Sri Lanka as they do today.

His overall figures are even more astonishing: 338 innings for 28.067 runs at an average of 95.14 with 117 hundreds – in other words, he made a hundred every three times he went in. His 117 hundreds include 452 not out, 4 other scores over 300, and 30 double-centuries. Enough said. I hope you feel duly staggered!

So what had he got, that set him on a plane above all other run-getters both past and present?

First, I think his character. He was a perfectionist. Whatever he did, he wanted to achieve as near 100 per cent perfection as possible. He was not ashamed to learn from others. In fact, he will tell you that he was never coached but used to watch and copy the great Australian and English batsmen he saw as a young man. Then there was his insatiable love of batting and making runs, rivalled only in our day by Geoff Boycott. People like Jack Hobbs often used to get themselves out after they had made a hundred, but not Bradman. And to help him he had the sort of dedicated concentration which is necessary to achieve the really big scores. Like Hanif, Gavaskar and Boycott, he could shut himself away from what was going on around him.

He had an amazing quickness of eye, which enabled him to see the ball that fraction earlier, and so enable him to get early into position and play the ball that much later than most batsmen. I believe that when he had his eyes tested his eyesight proved to be excellent but not phenomenal. Incidentally, I always regret that the portrait of Bradman in the pavilion at Lord's has him wearing spectacles – as he does today.

Then there was his general athleticism: he was a fast runner and mover with a boxer's footwork. The combination of his eye, concentration and his footwork meant that he could play *all* the strokes. He was strong, with powerful forearms, so was especially good off the back foot with his cutting and hooking. Equally, he would dance down the pitch and drive the ball, but very seldom in the air. He decided early on that by keeping the ball along the ground he would eliminate one way of getting out.

He was a great placer of the ball, a good judge of a run, and always ran his first run very fast. He told me once in an interview that he attributed much of his successful placing of the ball to his memory. Before each ball he would glance quickly round the field and note where each fielder was positioned. He would then – *before he received the ball* – decide where if possible he would hit it – no matter what its length – either on the offside or onside. In other words, he memorised the empty spaces. No wonder he kept the score-board ticking over so fast. In fact – and I'm sticking my neck out – I would say that he must have been the fastest scorer of all the great Test batsmen. The main difference between him and someone like Geoff Boycott was that Bradman's aim was to dominate the bowlers and to get on top. He wanted to dictate the play. Boycott, on the other hand, was prepared to 'sit it out' and concentrate on *not* getting out.

There was otherwise a certain similarity between the two in that cricket came first in their lives. They were both loners who would be happier in their hotel rooms, conserving energy and resting, rather than being 'one of the boys' and enjoying a gay social life.

A justifiable criticism of Bradman was that he was not as good a player on bad wickets as Hobbs, Sutcliffe, Hammond and Hutton had been. To this he used to reply that Walter Lindrum did not make his big breaks on bad billiard tables. He expected and got the best. So it could be fairly said that Bradman was not prepared to get 'stuck in' and try to defend against the turning ball on a rain-affected wicket. A perfect example of this was the second Test at Lord's in 1934 where Hedley Verity took 15 wickets for 104 runs in the match. Bradman proceeded to take the whole thing rather light-heartedly and for once even hit the ball in the air, actually hitting 7 fours in his first innings of 36.

His success, and the adulation and extra money that came his way, did not always make Bradman popular with his fellow players (you could say the same about Boycott), but I met Bradman many times, especially in Australia, and found him a cheerful, friendly and outspoken character. He was quick to argue his point and, what's more, knew all his facts and figures. When I first commentated for the Australian Broadcasting Commission at Sydney we used to have a small box in the Noble Stand and immediately below our open window was a row of seats reserved for the Australian selectors. He could hear every word we said and would often turn round and laugh or gesticulate at any comment with which he did not agree.

In another more recent interview I asked him whether, if he were playing today, he would have worn a helmet, and to my surprise he said yes. I pointed out to him that he had never worn one against Larwood, but he stuck to his point. Personally I think he was merely trying to be kind to the modern batsmen, but he denied this.

He was seldom caught out in conversation, though in his admirable researches Irving Rosenwater worked out that Bradman was caught out *on the field* in 58 per cent of his dismissals, compared with 26 per cent bowled. Anyhow, on Peter May's 1958–9 tour, as so often happens with a losing touring side, England were critical of one of the Australian umpires. He had got excellent reports during Len Hutton's tour in 1954–5, but had obviously fallen away since then. A great friend of mine, Tom Crawford of Kent, was talking to the Don about umpiring. He pointed out – quite rightly – that in England most of our first-class umpires are retired players who have played not just first-class cricket but quite a few Test matches as well. In Australia I cannot ever remember seeing an old Test player as umpire, and very few, if any, have ever played Sheffield Shield cricket. Tom argued to the Don that the English umpire knew the players and what it was like out in the middle of huge crowds. In fact, one of the features of our county cricket is the good relationship between players and umpires. If a player is transgressing in any way, the umpire will often have a quiet word with him before applying measures demanded by the Laws. In Australia this could not happen, and however well they knew the Laws and had good judgement, they could never be such good umpires as ours. The Don became indignant at this. 'What about so and so?' he asked, mentioning the umpire who had been criticised. 'He played for South Australia until his eyesight went!' He immediately realised what he had said, but on this occasion a Pom won the argument!

Finally, of course, Bradman was a fine leader of men and one of the greatest tacticians ever. He captained Australia twenty-four times, and to my mind there has been no better Test match captain.

To end I must go back to just before 6 p.m. on 14 August 1948 at the Oval for the fifth Test against Australia. From the pavilion emerged Don Bradman to play his last ever Test innings. In the TV commentary box Roy Webber had advised us that the Don only needed to make 4 runs to bring his Test match average to exactly 100.00. He was given a tremendous and emotional reception by the packed crowd, who stood and cheered him all the way to the wicket. As usual he walked to the wicket ever so slowly. As he approached the square Norman Yardley called for three cheers from his England team, who had all gathered on the pitch. Some shook him by the hand.

Bradman quietly took his guard, apparently unmoved by all the emotional scenes. There was a hush from the crowd as Hollies ran up to bowl from the Vauxhall end. Bradman played the first ball quietly on the off side. The next pitched on a perfect length on or just outside the off-stump. Bradman pushed forward as if to play it as a leg-break, but it was a perfectly disguised googly. It touched the inside of his bat and he played on. Bowled for 0 in his last Test innings. The cheers as he turned and walked slowly back to the pavilion were as loud as when he came in. Not, I like to think, because the crowd were pleased that England had got his wicket, but rather as the best way possible to say goodbye to the greatest run-getter of all time.

Just three final comments on this dismissal:

1. A film was made of the series and showed Bradman being bowled by Hollies with Hollies bowling *round the wicket*. This he did *not* do on this occasion. I believe that what happened was that the camera got Bradman being bowled, but had not shot Hollies as he ran up. So they must have gone to the film archives and found an old shot of Hollies who happened – bad luck to them – to be bowling round the wicket. I don't think many people noticed it. But I had to do the commentary on the film and was very conscious of a fake picture.

2. In interviews in later years I asked the Don whether he had missed the ball because his eyes were full of tears at his tremendous reception. He denied it emphatically, but then he would – he was nothing if not tough. But I still don't believe that he could have been unaffected.

3. The other question I asked was whether he knew that he only needed 4 more runs to bring his Test career average to 100.00. He told me with a twinkle in his eyes that he had had no idea, but

that if he had done, he might perhaps have taken a wee bit more trouble!

The cricket world celebrated his eightieth birthday on 27 August 1988, and he still lives in his lovely house in Adelaide with his adored wife Jessie. Neither of them have had good health over the past few years, but needless to say he still follows cricket whenever it is played and writes long letters in his own hand to many friends in England. It is not, I hope, revealing a secret, but I would say that he is slightly disillusioned today by some of the cricket and some of the happenings both on and off the field. He set a high standard of play and sportsmanship. He's just sorry that these standards have been lowered throughout the world today.

Wally Hammond

I was lucky enough to see Wally Hammond play. I saw him make his superb 240 against Australia at Lord's in 1938, and his 76 in the Headingley Test in the same year. As a commentator I was also privileged to describe two of his innings against India eight years later in 1946. Unless you saw Hammond it is difficult to comprehend how great a player he was, though his figures prove a certain amount. In all first-class cricket: 50,551 runs, average 56.10; 167 hundreds; 732 wickets and 819 catches. In Tests: 7,249 runs, average 58.45; 22 hundreds. He also took 83 wickets and made 110 catches.

The simple fact is that he was head and shoulders above his contemporaries in England. He dominated English cricket throughout the late twenties and the thirties. Even after the war he headed the batting averages in 1946 with an average of 84, for the eighth season in succession – an all-time record.

He was a marvellous athlete and successful in whatever game he played. He had a commanding presence and there was an aura of majesty in the way he walked to the wicket. 'Like a ship in full sail,' R.C. Robertson Glasgow once wrote. He was strong and beautifully built, and like a boxer was light on his feet. His most famous stroke was his square cover drive, and his back strokes, even in defence, were dreaded by fielders at mid-off and mid-on.

He played with a light bat, so was a perfect late-cutter, and also produced an unorthodox stroke down to long leg, more of a paddle than a sweep. They used to say that he was not so strong on the leg side, but it must be remembered that in his day most bowlers bowled a line on off-stump or just outside, so he didn't get all that much practice! He was, though, to prove occasionally vulnerable to Bill O'Reilly, who with his bounce concentrated on Wally's leg-stump.

3 Wally Hammond

As a bowler he was not unlike Maurice Tate, with a good action and plenty of pace off the pitch. He took a short run but bowled at a brisk medium pace. At first slip he was in the top class alongside names like Woolley, Gregory, Miller, Simpson, Cowdrey, Sharpe, Chappell (Greg) and Botham. He made it all look so ridiculously easy. I don't ever remember seeing him fling himself at the ball. He just seemed to stand there and pouch the ball – often putting it in his pocket after he had made the catch.

When he became an amateur in 1938 he captained England twenty times, including two overseas tours to South Africa and Australia. He was an efficient captain on the field without being great. Off the field – especially on tours – he tended to go his own way, and rather left the team to their own devices. As I have said, I was the TV commentator for the two London Tests against

India. It's difficult to believe it now, but I never spoke to him nor interviewed him during that time. It just didn't happen in those days. No interviews on the prospects of a match, at the close of play nor even at the end of the game. Like actors and actresses of that era, cricketers were more remote from their public and not as over-exposed as they are today.

For one who had dominated the scene for so long, the twilight of Hammond's career was rather sad. He had that very successful post-war season in 1946, followed by an unsuccessful tour of Australia both for himself and his team, but he did score 79 in his final Test – against New Zealand in Christchurch. He then, except for two appearances in 1950 and 1951, retired from first-class cricket, and eventually settled in South Africa, where he became coach at the University of Pietermaritzburg. It was in Durban in 1964 that I spoke to him for the very first time. I was covering Mike Smith's MCC tour for the BBC and one day went down to the Kingsmead ground in Durban to see them practise. I spotted a lone figure leaning over the back of a stand which was alongside the nets. He was looking down on the players practising below. I recognised him immediately and introduced myself. He couldn't have been more charming and quite obviously still took a great interest in cricket, especially in the MCC team. I alerted Mike Smith, who immediately asked Wally to come down to the nets, where he remained with the team for the rest of the practice.

That night in the lounge of the hotel I saw the great man surrounded by the MCC team, who were hanging on to his every word as he reminisced about the past. It was a happy ending to what I always felt was rather a sad life after he had given up cricket. The players were thrilled to meet him and it must have given him much pleasure and satisfaction to be the centre of their admiration and obvious hero-worship. That was in December 1964, and he died in July 1965 at the age of only sixty-two. I shall always remember him from a photograph of him playing his famous cover drive, from a yard outside his crease, with his dark blue handkerchief showing out of his trouser pocket, and Bertie Oldfield crouching down behind the stumps. He was in the perfect position for the stroke as he followed through with his bat. It must have been a four.

Gubby Allen

I never commentated on a Test in which Gubby Allen played, but we all knew him at school because as an Old Etonian he had been a frequent visitor. He was a very fast bowler with a superb action, and an amazing follow-through. He propelled himself through the air with his legs trailing behind him. It was as if he was trying to dive through a hoop. No wonder he had so much back trouble. In fact he played remarkably little cricket for Middlesex because of his job in the City. And when he did play – even on a Saturday – if the match was at Lord's he would go into the City first. His constant aches and pains were a running joke, but he got his own back on me once. The Eton Ramblers were playing at Chislehurst and I was their wicket-keeper. Gubby was also playing and as we went out on the field told me that he had a bad back. 'I shan't be able to bowl fast, so you'd better stand up.' This I rather reluctantly did. To my surprise Gubby took his usual long run and bowled a fast ball which started on a line of the off-stump and swung away to leg behind the batsman. I hopefully stuck out my left glove to try to stop it, and just managed to reach the ball and half stop it, but at the expense of a broken little finger! Bad back or not, after that I decided to treat Gubby as a really fast bowler and stood well back. He was also a very fine bat and had he played more regularly would have made many first-class runs. Even so, he made nearly 10,000 and scored one Test hundred against New Zealand in 1931. He can also boast that he topped the first-class batting averages in 1948 with an average of 76.8 for 8 innings.

He had two MCC tours as captain, and a very shrewd one he was. In 1936–7 England won the first two Tests but lost the next three. In the first Test at Brisbane Australia were bowled out for 58 in their second innings. There had been overnight rain after Voce had bowled Fingleton for 0 on the previous evening. Gubby told me once that he had thought that the conditions would be ideal for Hedley Verity, so he put himself on for one over in order that Voce could switch ends, and Verity bowl the next over. But to his surprise Gubby got Badcock and Bradman in his first over. They were both caught by Fagg and both made 0. So not surprisingly Gubby decided to keep himself on and to leave Voce at the other end. Result – Gubby 5 for 36, Voce 4 for 16.

4 Gubby Allen

Walter Robins always told a story about the third Test at Melbourne which Gubby strongly denies! Gubby decided to set a trap for Bradman and placed Robins just backward of square leg. Sure enough, Bradman hit a ball in the air straight at Robins. He was normally a brilliant fielder, but, possibly because he had a sore finger, he dropped the catch. He felt very downcast and at the end of the over went up to Gubby and apologised profusely. 'Don't worry, Robbie, it doesn't matter at all. It's only lost us the series!' As I've said, Gubby denies it, but if he did say it he was right. Bradman went on to make 270, and Australia won that Test and the next two.

Gubby didn't have any better luck when he was persuaded – at the age of forty-four – to captain the MCC team to West Indies. It was a disastrous tour as MCC didn't win a single match, though it is only fair to point out that the top players like Hutton, Bedser,

Compton and Edrich did not go on the tour – though an SOS was sent for Hutton after the second Test. Believe it or not, Gubby was unfit to play in the first Test because he had pulled a calf-muscle when skipping on the deck of the banana boat on the voyage over!

Gubby has been, and still is as I write, a tremendous influence on all that goes on in cricket in England, and indeed all over the world. He was chairman of selectors from 1955 to 1961, and used to say he picked players on their class, and not necessarily on their current form. He was a trustee of MCC at Lord's for twelve years, which meant that he could sit on all the committees. He moved his home from Queen's Gate to Grove End Road with a garden gate into the ground. This meant that he could always be on the job, and had no train to catch at the end of long meetings. When others had to leave he could stay on to the bitter end, and so get his way.

I would say that his influence has been wholly for the good of cricket. With his great friend Don Bradman he has fought to keep the game as skilful and as sporting as it always was. He and the Don may not always have agreed – and alas did not always succeed in stopping some of the objectionable commercialism that has crept in, and some of the less pleasant incidents that have taken place on the field – but, as their frequent exchange of letters would I am sure prove, they both wanted cricket to stay the best game in the world.

Freddie Brown

The famous bread advertisement used to read: 'Don't say brown, say Hovis', so to me Freddie was always Hovis. I daren't tell you what he used to call me! He is an old friend from the pre-war days when, in spite of his distinguished first-class career, he happily played in club cricket with cricketers like myself. Perhaps he thought he would get more wickets that way! But it was typical of his hale-fellow-well-met approach to life. He was bluff, blunt and hearty and would have made an ideal model for John Bull. He was tall, strongly built, with gingerish hair, and had a red-faced, chubby-cheeked appearance. I don't ever remember him batting or fielding without a cap, and as long as I knew him he always had a white knotted handkerchief round his substantial neck. He enjoyed a drink and was good fun at a party, but tended to get into rather heated arguments. When he did, his bottom lip would be pushed out and he would make his points by prodding his 'opponent' in the chest with his more than ample forefinger – rather like a Palethorpe sausage!

5 Freddie Brown

He was a good, loyal friend, however, and made a daring, forceful captain, who led from the front and expected everyone to follow him – which they did to the best of their ability. He set a perfect example with his guts and physical stamina, and whilst his first aim was to take the necessary risks to win, he was equally determined not to lose a match if he possibly could.

He captained England fifteen times and was a selector from 1951 to 1953. In the last year he became chairman and was the only one to play for England whilst still in office. He was persuaded to play in the second Test at Lord's, possibly to lend the captain, Len Hutton, support and counsel against Lindsay Hassett's Australian side. Anyway, at the age of forty-two he played an important part in helping England to draw a match which they seemed likely to lose, until the famous Bailey/Watson partnership. Freddie took 4 wickets in Australia's second innings and scored a total of 50 runs, 28 of them in the last half hour of the match, with a typical attacking innings.

Altogether he had an unusual career, with a large gap in the middle. He was one of several England captains to be born abroad, in Lima, Peru. (Others were Lord Harris, Sir Pelham Warner, Sir George Allen, Ted Dexter, Colin Cowdrey and Tony Greig.) He went to Leys School, Cambridge, upon which James Hilton is said to have based his novel *Goodbye, Mr Chips*. From there he went to Cambridge and got a blue in the two years he was up. He played some matches for Surrey and then at the age of twenty-one was selected to go to Australia with Douglas Jardine's 1932–3 side. This was on the strength of a remarkable season for Surrey in the summer of 1932, when he achieved the double in all first-class matches. For Surrey he made scores of 212, 168 and 135, and hammered some of the county slow bowlers unmercifully. For Surrey alone he took 95 wickets at the amazingly low average cost for a leg-spinner of 15.98. So it was inevitable that he should be selected to go to Australia. What a pity he was not used more. The tour would have been a far happier one had he played in the Tests.

At that time he was a leg-break bowler who spun the ball a lot and bowled at a faster pace than most – not as fast as Doug Wright, but definitely nearer medium than slow. He was also a forceful batsman who believed in hitting the ball hard and high and often. He had already played in three Tests in England, two against New Zealand in 1931 and one against India in 1932 (the only Test they played), but in Australia he was frankly not needed. Jardine had Larwood, Voce, Allen, Bowes and Verity as the regulars plus another leg spinner, Tommy Mitchell, the bespectacled Derbyshire player. So, as far as cricket went he had a pretty miserable time, but being Freddie he enjoyed himself off the field and was tremendously popular wherever he went. For exercise he played golf but this for some reason did not go down well with Jardine, who I believe threatened to confiscate his clubs!

Back in England he played for Surrey throughout the thirties, though not on a regular basis. He was recalled to Test cricket in 1937 for one Test against New Zealand, when he made a spirited 57 and took 4 wickets.

Then came the war, where he was a prisoner-of-war in Italy for three years together with quite a few Australians, so 'Test' matches were soon organised. At that time and immediately after the war Freddie must have thought that his Test career was over. He played occasionally for Surrey until 1949 when, under the sponsorship of

British Timken, who offered him a job, he became captain of Northamptonshire. And what a dramatic year it was for him. He amazingly did the double, which he had last done seventeen years ago. What's more, he took over the captaincy of England from George Mann in the last two Tests against New Zealand. He did the same again in 1950, taking over from Norman Yardley as captain for the last two Tests against the West Indies, both of which incidentally the West Indies won. But by that time he had been asked to captain MCC on their tour to Australia in the winter. Norman Yardley and George Mann were not available for business reasons and Freddie's selection was clinched when he made a magnificent 122 out of 131 in 110 minutes for the Gentlemen against the Players at Lord's. The Players had a useful attack too: Shackleton and Bedser, and, unusually, three spinners – Tattersall, Wright and Hollies.

In addition he took 4 wickets and at the age of thirty-nine was lying in a hot bath with a large whisky and soda when Walter Robins came in – I hope he knocked! – and offered him the captaincy against Australia. British Timken were generous employers so he was able to accept. The only – to me – rather sad thing about his selection was that it meant that he sat down there and then to help choose the team. For some reason or other he and Bill Edrich did not get on and predictably – because the captain usually has the final say – Bill did not go on the tour. I often wonder whether Freddie regretted this decision.

Anyhow the 1950–1 tour of Australia will always be remembered for Freddie's brave, gutsy captaincy. He had a far weaker side than Australia, who won the first four Test matches, though England struggled gamely. For instance, in the second Test they only lost by 28 runs, with Freddie top-scoring for England with 62 and also taking 5 wickets in the match. He did even better in the third Test. He again top-scored with 79 and, because Trevor Bailey had had a finger fractured by Lindwall, Freddie had to share the bowling with Bedser, Warr and Compton during a total of 426. He was then aged forty and he bowled 44 overs and took 4 for 153, whilst Alec Bedser bowled 43 overs and took 4 for 107. Poor John Warr took 0 for 142 in 36 overs, and Denis Compton bowled a mere 6 overs for 14 runs. It was a mammoth performance by Freddie and Alec and a wonderful feat of endurance, stamina and guts in the heat of a Sydney summer.

By this time he had given up his leg spin, and bowled accurate medium-pace seamers which, because of his height and strength, got quite a bit of lift off the Australian pitches.

Freddie became the hero of Australia. In spite of all the defeats he always kept smiling and never gave up, and they loved him for it. There is the old story of the greengrocer selling his lettuces with these words: 'Lettuces – lettuces – with hearts as big as Freddie Brown's.'

During the next Test at Adelaide Freddie had a slight argument with a lamp-post when driving his car home one night. The lamp-post was evidently driving on the wrong side of the road! So he did not do much in that game, but finally had his triumph in the final Test at Melbourne where he took 5 for 49 and England won their first Test against Australia since 1938 at the Oval.

When he returned to England Freddie captained England in the five Tests against South Africa, England winning the series 3–1. He only bowled himself in three of the Tests and picked up 7 wickets. As I said earlier, he played the last of his twenty-two Tests at Lord's in 1953, but went on to manage two MCC tours under Peter May's captaincy: South Africa in 1956–7 and Australia in 1958–9. He also did a lot of radio work, first of all as a commentator for an Australian commercial network during the Australian visit here in 1956, and then for many years as summariser for the BBC's 'Test Match Special' with his old friend Norman Yardley. As you would expect, he was forthright in all his comments but always fair, and as an old England captain was tactically very sound.

A funny thing happened to him once when summarising at Lord's. Robert Hudson was the commentator and had the nervous habit of fiddling with the rubber bands which Bill Frindall used to secure his score-sheets to a wooden board. Robert used to pull them out and stretch them to their limit. One day he accidentally let go and the rubber band shot across the commentary box to where Freddie was sitting. He was in the middle of his summary when the band hit him a stunning blow on the left ear. He let out a yelp but bravely continued talking, unaware whether he had been stung by a wasp or struck by a poisoned dart!

After he retired he devoted much of his time to the welfare of youth cricket as president of the National Cricket Association. He was also president of MCC in 1971 and chairman of the Cricket Council from 1974–9. And goodness knows how many other cricket committees he has sat on. He hasn't been too well in recent years but is still his bluff, cheerful, outspoken self with strong opinions which he sticks to. He has been a great personality in the cricket world and a strong supporter of all the good things which cricket stands for.

Les Ames

My favourite wicket-keeper during the late twenties and thirties was undoubtedly Les Ames. He was a great all round wicket-keeper most famous for his partnership with Tich Freeman, as his number of stumpings will show: a record 418 in his career and 64 in the season of 1932, which is also a record. He three times got over 100 victims in a season, with his 128 in 1929 yet another record. Many of these came of course from standing up to Freeman, but when he played for England Les proved how good he was when standing back to the fast bowlers. He was well built and on the tall side for a wicket-keeper. I cannot ever remember seeing him fling himself at a ball as the modern keepers do. In fact he told me once that 'it wasn't done' to fall over in those days. In other words, players like himself and Bert Oldfield somehow managed to get into position behind the ball by moving quickly across. I will concede that they may not have made all the brilliant catches down the leg side which we see today, but so far as the off side was concerned they left more catches to the slips, instead of flinging themselves right across them to pinch catches which the slips could have caught.

Les was an easy man to pick out on the field. He never seemed to hurry but walked with a rolling gait between the wickets. He had a dark, rather blotchy face which portrayed the Romany blood from which he came. He was the least flamboyant of keepers and his appeals were made in a gentlemanly way in contrast to the high-pitched 'quack-quack' of George Duckworth. On the 1932–3 'body-line' tour he had to stand well back to Larwood, Voce, Allen and Bowes. But I am told that his keeping when standing up to Hammond could not have been better, reminding you that Hammond bowled a similar pace to Tate or Bedser.

It is difficult to compare his skills with those of his contemporary rival and great friend George Duckworth. They were so entirely different. George was chubby and rotund, vociferous and extrovert, and more spectacular in all that he did. He played in 24 Tests compared with Les's 47, and undoubtedly the selectors' vote often went to Les because of his vastly superior batting. He averaged just over 40 in Tests with 8 hundreds. He scored 102 hundreds in his career, once made 3,000 runs in a season, and scored over 37,000 runs with an average of 43.51. How could George cope with that, even though he could play a useful defensive innings when required?

6 Les Ames

Les was a stylish attacking batsman who played straight with all the strokes, but was especially strong in driving. He was particularly light on his feet and delighted in dancing down the pitch. He usually occupied a middle-order position but could well have gone in higher. Back trouble curtailed his wicket-keeping after the war, but he continued to make a lot of runs for Kent until his retirement in 1951. Although he owned a sports business he also managed to play a big part in the administration of cricket. He was the first professional to be appointed as a regular selector, and then later became secretary/manager of Kent for fourteen years.

I was with him on two tours when he managed MCC, first in the West Indies and then in Pakistan, both under the captaincy of his Kent colleague Cowdrey. Whatever the circumstances he was efficient, friendly with the media, and remained calm and outwardly unmoved no matter what happened – for example during the bottle-throwing and tear-gas incident at Kingston in 1968, or a year later in Pakistan when rioting in Karachi caused the tour to be abandoned. On both occasions he had to act as diplomat as well as manager, and his judgement and calmness greatly impressed the British High Commissioners with whom he had to deal and from whom he had to take political advice. In fact I only once saw him outwardly disturbed and that was a slightly less serious occasion during a private tour by D. H. Robins's eleven in South Africa. Derrick Robins had to thank the Mayor of Durban for a reception which he gave for the Robins team. He started his speech with the unfortunate phrase: 'I'd like to ask you all to give the Mayor the clap he so richly deserves.' A deadly silence followed and even Les looked worried.

However, on the two occasions I have mentioned Les was superb. My wife took a photograph of him, Cowdrey and Graveney walking in a dignified manner across the tear-gas-stricken Sabina Park. In Pakistan before he went to play the second Test at Dacca he had to carry out numerous negotiations with politicians, police and even students. There had been crowd invasions and even minor riots in the first Test at Lahore, where the police seemed powerless to control the unruly crowd, many of them students. In the end serious trouble was only averted by Aftab Gul, a student leader who went in first for Pakistan. I remember him being caught by Pocock off Underwood and immediately going across to the most unruly stand, and telling them in Urdu to 'give it a rest' or the equivalent. Anyway, it worked and peace reigned. But MCC were not keen to go on with the tour with so much violence being threatened. They were implored to do so by both Pakistan officials and the British High Commission. So, remarkably, Les agreed to go to Dacca provided that there were no police nor soldiers present on the ground, after he had been assured by the students that they would keep order themselves. This they did and there was no trouble at all over the four days.

We were not so lucky at Karachi, where Les had to organise a quick night flight home to England for all the team and the media. This followed a riot on the third day of the match when Alan Knott was 96 not out and David Brown 25 not out. Before Knotty could make his first Test hundred the crowd swarmed on to the pitch, picking up the stumps and threatening the players and umpires. Knott and Brown would have won a gold medal for the 100 metres at the pace they ran back to the pavilion! I was commentating on Pakistan TV at the time but as I began to describe the crowd setting fire to the various enclosures we were cut off. I made my way hurriedly to the back of the pavilion where I took shelter in the England dressing-room. We were locked in for quite a time with all the uproar going on outside. The rioters were mainly students. They had nothing against the players themselves, but a general strike had been called for that day for some political reason, and they could not see why professional cricketers should be playing during a strike.

Eventually we were all smuggled away in cars – there were at least ten of us in the one I was in. Not many people can boast of having an English cricketer on his knee! Back at our hotel Les got down to work and by a miracle organised a flight home that night, the tour sadly being cancelled. As usual he was calm and efficient and we all owed him a debt of thanks for handling the ugly situation so well.

Les has always been one of the real gentlemen of cricket. In his eighties he still plays golf every day except when it rains. He then goes for a seven-mile walk across country to the village of Elham where he was born. After having something to eat at the pub he does remember his age and actually takes a bus home. He is a fine judge of a player and there is no one better for a young cricketer to go to for advice than Les. We still see him at Test matches and it always makes my day if he greets me with his friendly smile and slightly high-pitched voice.

Len Hutton

In 1952 Len became the first professional to be appointed captain of England in this country. In 1956 he was the first professional to be made an honorary member of MCC and the second professional to be knighted (Jack Hobbs was the first in 1953). And how well he has worn the mantle ever since. He has become the wise old man of cricket, whose judgement and comments are respected throughout the cricket world. For two years – 1975–6 – he served as a selector, but has kept largely in the background except for his presidency of Scarborough CC and the Forty Club.

He is no committee man but can be seen at most Tests in this country, and other big cricket occasions, confidentially whispering words of wisdom into somebody's ear. He has a dry wit and speaks quietly with a twinkle in his eye. He is still a fine reader of the game and a good judge of players. He usually ends his often enigmatic remarks with a 'see what I mean?'.

7 Len Hutton

I only saw him play once before the war, and that was in the Lord's Test in 1938, when he only made 4 and 5 against Australia. This followed his 100 exactly at Trent Bridge and the next innings he played was his world record 364 at the Oval, later beaten by Gary Sobers's 365 not out against Pakistan in 1958. I listened to that great cricket commentator Howard Marshall describing it in his commentary from the Oval. He had a delightful deep burbling voice, ideally suited to cricket, and I can still remember some of his phrases: 'Bradman standing there arms akimbo', 'the Oval sparrows pecking away at the grass by the pavilion gate'.

At that time Len was a lean and rather fragile figure, with a hungry look. Indeed, throughout his career his health was never really 100 per cent. He suffered a further handicap during the war when as a PT instructor he damaged his left arm in a fall, and ever afterwards it was a shade shorter than his right. This *should* have affected his batting, but it never appeared to do so.

He was a complete stylist with every stroke and the most correct of all post-war batsmen, with the possible exception of Barry Richards, who was at least his equal. Unlike most overseas batsmen he was a magnificent player on bad pitches, and his immaculate defensive technique matched that of Hobbs, Sutcliffe and Hammond. He tended to play spinners from the crease, and although he had every stroke in the book, I didn't often see him hook. I remember best his exquisite off-drive, which was pure perfection with everything in the right place. He had a phlegmatic temperament, was determined and, outwardly at least, appeared unaffected by the battering he so often had to face as an opening batsman against the likes of Lindwall and Miller.

The one exception to this was the Lord's Test against Australia in 1948 when he – like most of the others – did not seem to 'relish' Lindwall's short-pitched bowling, and took a lot of knocks on the body. As a result – for the only time in his career – he was dropped by the selectors for the next Test. But when he came back he scored 81 and 57 at Headingley, and 30 (the only double figures in England's 52 all out) and 64 at the Oval – both top scores for England.

Len was one of England's most successful captains. He won the series against India in 1952, regained the Ashes after nineteen years at the Oval in 1953, drew 2–2 against West Indies in 1953–4 and then kept the Ashes in Australia in 1954–5. Captaincy seemed to drain his strength, however. He found the pressures too much, and in the end, on the 1954–5 tour of Australia, it began to affect his batting. When he returned triumphantly to England he was immediately appointed captain for all five Tests against South Africa, but he contracted lumbago, Peter May took over the captaincy, and Len never played another Test. At the end of that season he retired from first-class cricket, having only been able to play in ten matches for Yorkshire because of ill-health. Quite simply, he had had enough.

Not only was Len a successful Test captain but he was also a fine tactician, especially in the way he could detect a batsman's weakness, and set the field accordingly. Probably because of the fierce fast bowling he himself had to face, he always wanted as many fast bowlers in his side as possible. He believed – correctly – that in Tests it is generally fast bowlers who win the matches. One of his ploys in the field was perhaps not so acceptable, however. He was the first to slow down the over-rate as a tactic to spare his fast bowlers. Ever since then the slow over-rate has been the curse of Test cricket, and has robbed the paying spectators of many overs each day. Nowadays, in most Test series regulations decree a minimum of overs to be bowled each day.

Earlier I mentioned Hutton's wit. Denis Compton told me that during a torrid time at Lord's in the 1953 Test, Hutton and he were facing a terrible barrage from Lindwall and Miller. At the end of an over Len beckoned Denis for a mid-wicket conference. 'What tactics is he going to suggest?' thought Denis. All Len said was, 'There must be better ways of earning a living than this,' and then walked back to face the next over.

Once in a charity match at Chislehurst, Colin Cowdrey's eleven played against the England Ladies Eleven. I was keeping wicket, with Len at first slip. 'What do you think about ladies playing cricket, Len?' I asked. He thought for a moment and then with a twinkle in his eye said, 'Not much. It's just like trying to teach a man to knit!'

To sum up, Len was certainly one of the best ever opening batsmen in Test cricket, and was probably the equal of Hobbs and Sutcliffe on bad wickets. And if you ask any cricketer to write out his world eleven of all time, I think you will find that more often than not, one of the opening batsmen will be Len Hutton.

Denis Compton

By 1936 Patsy Hendren was soon due to retire and I was looking for another 'hero' to take his place – preferably from Middlesex. It didn't take me long to make my choice. In the Whitsun match at Lord's that year against Sussex, number eleven in the Middlesex side was a young eighteen-year-old from the Lord's ground staff playing his first first-class match. He had a last-wicket partnership with Gubby Allen, but was finally given out lbw for 14. He tells the story of how Gubby said to the umpire, Bestwick: 'He wasn't out.'

'I know he wasn't, Mr Allen, but I am dying to have a wee!' replied Bestwick.

Young Denis Compton had arrived, and I saw him a week later make 87 against Northants, an innings which even then showed his class and the originality of his strokes.

8 Denis Compton

So I 'adopted' him as my replacement for Patsy, who retired at the end of 1937, when he made a duck in his last innings for Middlesex. In the same year Denis played in his first Test against New Zealand at the Oval, where as a possible augury of things to come he was *run out* for 65. But on this occasion it was *not* his fault – just bad luck that a hard hit by Joe Hardstaff was deflected on to the stumps at the bowler's end, with Denis out of his crease. I didn't see him play in a Test until 1938 against Australia at Lord's, where in the second innings he came in at number seven, with England in real trouble at 76 for 5. He had made a hundred up at Trent Bridge in his first Test against Australia, and here at Lord's he batted with tremendous confidence, and as a twenty-year-old showed all his strokes in an attacking innings of 76 not out. I congratulated myself on making such a perfect choice as my replacement for Patsy.

I suppose that no cricketer of *any* generation could have given more pleasure to more people than Denis did. He was the cavalier of cricket with the dancing feet, unorthodox in attack but strictly orthodox in defence. The highlight of his career was the glorious summer of 1947 when he thrilled the war-weary and cricket-starved crowds with two records which are still unbroken – 18 hundreds and 3,816 runs in one season. Not that he himself worried about statistics. He was the entertainer supreme who just loved to play cricket. He would dance down the pitch to the slow bowlers and sometimes to the fast bowlers as well.

His favourite strokes were the late cut or 'chop', the square cover drive, the on-drive, the hook and his own special sweep down to fine leg. The later got him out occasionally but he made a lot of runs with it. At the Oval once I saw him fall over when trying to sweep, but he still managed to hit the ball for four as he lay flat on the ground. Like Bradman, he did not often hit the ball in the air. During the tea-interval at Lord's in a match against Hampshire someone chided him about this. He promptly went out after tea and hit Derek Shackleton's first ball over mid-off for six into the pavilion.

Two points need stressing about Denis. First of all, his flair and the brilliance of his stroke-play was supported by perfect defensive strokes. So he was the complete batsman, fully capable of coping on a difficult or turning pitch. Secondly, there was his tremendous courage when facing Lindwall and Miller. There were no helmets in those days. He had to rely on a good eye, sound judgement as to whether to duck or hook and, most important of all – guts. The best example of this was at Old Trafford in 1948 when he was struck over the eye by a ball which flew off his bat as he tried to hook a no-ball bouncer from Lindwall. After being stitched up and a short rest he returned to make a fine 145 not out.

His running between the wickets has become legendary. He was certainly the worst judge of a run of any top-class batsman I have ever seen. His partners used to say that a call from Compton was just a basis for negotiation. He once achieved a hat-trick of run-outs in his brother Leslie's benefit match. To make matters worse one of the victims was the beneficiary himself! Denis did go on to make 72 not out on a turning wicket, but he admits that his brother wasn't too pleased with him on his way back to the pavilion.

As one might expect from an outside left who won an FA Cup-

Winner's medal with the Arsenal in 1950, he was a fine fielder and catcher. Had he not made so many runs, he would, I'm sure, have become a more regular wicket-taker with his left-arm chinamen and googlies. Even so, he managed to take 622 wickets in his career, including 25 in Tests. His googly was not all that easy to detect and when I kept wicket to him in charity matches, he used kindly to give me a signal when it was coming.

To sum up Denis: he was – and is – a casual character, forgetful of appointments and sometimes late. He often had to borrow other players' bats, trousers, socks and even boxes, because he had lost or forgotten his. He was handsome and debonair, and the women loved him. So did he the women! For years his face was on every advertising board in the country boosting Brylcreem. In the advertisement his hair was immaculately brushed, though on the field of play it fell all over his face. He nearly missed out on this lucrative contract because he used to receive hundreds of letters which he seldom had time to open. One day an agent called Bagenal Harvey offered to go through the mail and answer when necessary. Amongst the pile of letters he found one from Brylcreem offering Denis the contract.

His vagueness and forgetfulness are legendary. He was invited to a leaving party by J. J. Warr in 1987. The time and venue was 6.30 p.m. at the Royal Exchange on a Wednesday. Denis arrived at 5.30 p.m. at the Stock Exchange on the previous Tuesday!

1988 saw many celebrations of his seventieth birthday including a splendid banquet at the Inter-Continental Hotel. Over six hundred guests were there including 'anyone who is anyone' in cricket and the football world. At the start of the dinner the chairman, George Mann, rose to welcome the guests, with an empty chair on his left. He had just begun his speech when in rushed a rather dishevelled Compton – last man in – late as usual. At least he came to the right place on the right day. There has always been a slight mystery about the exact year of his birth. *Wisden* have got it right now as 1918, but when Denis was fifty a large party was given for him by a number of friends. They were busy drinking his health when the telephone rang and it was for Denis. He went to answer it and came back looking rather forlorn. 'Who was it?' they asked, 'It was my mother,' said Denis. 'She says I am only forty-nine!'

He has a wonderful sense of humour, and for ten years or so on TV he made a delightful companion in the commentary box. As a summariser he was a kind critic, and an enthusiastic advocate of attacking cricket and sporting behaviour on the field.

I have one complaint against him, however. Denis has a wonderful sense of humour and is generally laughing, but unfortunately his laugh was rather loud in the commentary box and often made a perfectly innocent remark sound a dirty one. For instance, once at Worcester I said: 'Barry Richards has just hit one of d'Oliveira's balls clean out of the ground.' Nothing wrong in that in cricket terms, you might think. But a guffaw from Denis Compton completely changed its meaning!

His career was plagued by knee trouble, caused by injuries when he played football for the Arsenal. Unfortunately, he did not have the benefit of today's skilful surgery, which has enabled players like Procter and Willis to continue as fast bowlers minus their knee-caps. Denis had a series of operations which hampered his movements during the later part of his career, and finally caused him to give up altogether in 1958. Undoubtedly one of the greatest players of all time – and one of the nicest.

Bill Edrich

To face top-class fast bowling you have to have guts. It has always been so. Just think what it must have been like for batsmen in the old days with their skeleton pads, inadequately padded batting gloves and largely unprepared pitches.

Today there are more fast bowlers than ever, and they bowl shorter and hurl down more bouncers. The pitches are better, but even so the modern batsman has been forced to wear far more protection – helmets, thigh and chest pads, arm protectors, batting gloves, and that most essential box. After about fifteen years it seems that helmets have come to stay, but before the seventies such protection was rarely, if ever, used. A few batsmen wore caps but many more batted bare-headed. The bowlers were certainly no less fast, but with exceptions they did not bowl so persistently short, nor bowl so many bouncers. During this pre-armour period two batsmen stood out above all others for their guts and bravery under hostile attack by fast bowlers. They were Bill Edrich and Brian Close.

Bill was a doughty fighter if ever there was one. Short in stature but sturdy, with a determined chin and eyes which blazed defiance. He and his three brothers, E. H., G. A. and B. R., were all born in Norfolk, and for many years the Edriches could produce a family eleven to take on all comers. Bill played for Norfolk for five years before qualifying for Middlesex in 1937. He met with immediate success, making 2,000 runs or more in each of the three seasons before the war. He won the first of his thirty-nine caps for England in 1938, in which year he also made 1,000 runs by the end of May.

9 Bill Edrich

The war revealed Bill's true character, and he gained a DFC and a reputation for outstanding bravery when flying Blenheims in low-level daylight raids on France.

After the war his record is legendary, reaching its peak in that glorious summer of 1947, when he and Compton seemed to live permanently at the crease. Compton has perhaps been given most of the accolades for his two records of 18 hundreds and aggregate of 3,816 runs, but it's often forgotten that Bill made 3,539 runs with 12 hundreds. In 1984 Middlesex gave a golden anniversary dinner at the Hilton in London in recognition of their fifty years' friendship and association. I was 'inspired' to write the following poem in the menu:

> Dear Compers and Edders,
> Both several time wedders!
> Incomparable twins
> Brought great Middlesex wins.
> Cavalier, cover drive, elegant sweep,
> DFC gallant, strong pulls to the deep.
> When they were together it brought the sun out
> And, sometimes, I fear, a dramatic run-out.
> They both are my friends and I'm happy to say,
> Edders and Compers, I saw you both play.

A bit of poetic licence there, I'm afraid, as I believe it's a fact that they never once in all their partnerships had a run out.

As a batsman Bill was not a pretty player. He relied more on his good eye and his strength than on his timing. He was a good cutter, a fearless hooker, and scored many of his runs from his favourite stroke, the pull. It would go wide of and often over mid-on. His stroke play was backed up by an immaculate defence and his courage, determination and guts. No game was ever lost while he was at the wicket. Here are two examples of his tremendous courage. In 1946 in the first Test at Brisbane he made 16 in $1\frac{3}{4}$ hours on what *Wisden* described as 'a nightmare pitch'. Violent thunderstorms had made it practically unplayable, with nearly every ball from Lindwall and Miller bouncing shoulder or head high. Bill was repeatedly struck all over the body and was a mass of bruises. 'They shall not pass' might well have been his motto.

The other occasion was during the Middlesex *v.* Northamptonshire match at Lord's in 1954. Frank Tyson was then at his fastest and most fearsome, and he hit Bill in the face. He was rushed off to hospital where he had to spend the night. Everyone thought that he would be out of the match. But, battered and bruised, he turned up the next morning apparently quite unperturbed at the thought of facing Frank Tyson again. He only made 20 but he never flinched.

The amazing thing about Bill's career was the way the selectors persevered with him, in spite of a succession of low scores. He made his Test début against Australia at Trent Bridge in 1938. The Old Trafford Test was abandoned without a ball being bowled, but in the other four Tests Bill made 5, 0, 10, 12, 28, 12. In spite of this he was selected for the following winter tour of South Africa. His scores in the Tests there were 4, 10, 0, 6, 0 and then finally 219 in the last innings of the 'timeless' Test in Durban, which actually ended in a draw.

Forgetting the 219, he averaged 8 runs in 11 innings. How many other batsmen have been given such a long run in an England team after such a bad start? I would say nobody, and Bill really had to thank Wally Hammond for his continuous selection. Wally was captain of England by then, and he said he always wanted Bill in the side because he was so good at 'the bits and pieces'. By that he meant that Bill was a fine fielder anywhere, but especially in the slips. He was also a more than useful tearaway bowler who for a few overs could be genuinely fast. He appeared to hurl himself at the batsman after a furious run-up to the wicket – it's a wonder he never took off. He did occasionally open the bowling for England and finished with 41 Test wickets.

Like Wally Hammond, he played for both the Gentlemen and the Players, becoming an amateur after the war in 1947. Again like Hammond, he was a natural athlete and played football for Tottenham Hotspur. He captained Middlesex from 1951 to 1957 – sharing the first two years with Denis Compton. He always enjoyed his cricket and this showed in his captaincy. He was always prepared to take a risk in order to win, and much preferred a definite result, rather than a draw.

I suppose Bill will be remembered affectionately to his countless friends as a character even more than as a cricketer. He lived life to the full and seemed to need less sleep than most people. Incidentally, I am not good at records so I cannot remember how many times he was married! He loved parties and enjoyed drinking, and was usually the centre of the noisiest section of the guests. He had an encyclopaedic knowledge of popular music and would sing the night away, word perfect in all the hits for the last fifty years or so. He was a great companion and remarkably well informed on almost any subject. He was never afraid to back his opinion with forthright comment, which didn't always endear him to his superiors. What went wrong I don't know, but he should certainly have gone on Freddie Brown's tour of Australia in 1950–1, but for some private disagreement. I was lucky to spend two *Cricketer* holidays with him, and he was the livewire on all occasions. The only nuisance was that I had to hide my posted *Daily Telegraph*, or he would finish the crossword before I had a chance.

On his seventieth birthday Middlesex and the Lord's Taverners gave him a dinner at the Berkeley, the guests being his own selected friends, many of whom paid touching tribute to him. Some, like myself, were also grateful to him for – of all things – his financial advice. He saved many people paying more tax than they needed by siphoning the money into self-employed pension schemes. He took endless trouble and the best advice before recommending anything.

He retired from this business after his seventieth birthday, and was given a leaving dinner. The next day the Middlesex Committee entertained him, to thank him for all the time and energy he had put in to Middlesex cricket. The day after that he attended the St George's Day Luncheon at Grosvenor House. He was picked out in a speech by an Air Vice-Marshal who said that he had served under Bill in the war, and that he was the bravest and best Squadron-Leader he had ever served under. The company rose and gave Bill a tremendous reception. That late afternoon he went home and there had an accident, falling down the stairs and fracturing his skull, possibly as the result of a sudden heart attack.

But, as Bill would have said, 'What a way to go! What an exit!' – with the applause and appreciation of his friends still singing in his ears. He would never have claimed to be a saint in his personal life – but what a character. We could do with a few more like him today.

Norman Yardley

In the early thirties the Eton Ramblers used to tour Yorkshire in August. One of the fixtures was at Escrick, just outside York, against the Yorkshire gentlemen. A young gentleman who played against us was at St Peter's, York, and was called Norman Yardley. He was a class or two above all of us and it was obvious that he was going to 'go places'. He certainly did but, as with so many of his generation, the war interfered with his career. Even so, he played in twenty Tests and captained England in fourteen of them. He became a very shrewd tactician, and an astute reader of pitches. He was exceedingly popular both with the England players, and with the Yorkshire team, whom he captained for eight years. It seems a silly thing to say, but he was too nice to be a great captain. He had all the other necessary attributes but lacked the 'Monty' touch of ruthlessness. He also had to captain England against possibly the strongest Australian team ever in 1948.

10 Norman Yardley

He was a good middle-order batsman with a penchant for the on-side. But, give him a half volley outside the off-stump and he would drive it through extra cover with the best of them. He was consistent enough to score 1,000 runs in a season eight times, and had a Test average of 25.37. He never made a Test hundred but came mighty near it in 1947, when he scored 99 against South Africa. So on figures alone he did not justify a Test place for his batting, but in addition to his captaincy he was an excellent fielder and good close catcher, and became an invaluable breaker-up of stands. He bowled medium-pace swingers and had the knack of wobbling the ball in the air. His greatest achievement with the ball was in Australia in 1946, when he dismissed Bradman three times in successive innings.

When he retired in order to devote time to his wine business he still continued to play an important part behind the scenes as an England selector and a much valued member of the Yorkshire committee. I felt dreadfully sorry for him over the Boycott affair.

It nearly broke his heart. After I left TV in 1970 I got to know Norman well in the radio commentary box. He was an ideal summariser – knowledgeable, fair and kind. Perhaps here again he was too nice, and found it difficult to be too critical of his old colleagues, but he was a cheerful companion and formed a useful partnership with Freddie Brown and Trevor Bailey.

My favourite story of Norman took place at Trent Bridge in 1950. It was our first visit there with TV, as the Sutton Coldfield transmitter had only just come into service. England had won the first Test and West Indies the second at Lord's – the famous calypso Test. In the third at Trent Bridge in reply to England's 223 West Indies lost 3 wickets for 238, and then Worrell and Weekes put on a magnificent 283 runs in 210 minutes for the fourth wicket. They were hitting the England bowlers to all corners of the ground and at about four o'clock in the afternoon I said: 'This is an enormous problem for Norman Yardley. I wonder what he's thinking as he stands there at mid-on.' This was a hint to the camera to pan in on Norman. He filled the TV screen, but unfortunately at that moment he was scratching himself in the crutch. I was speechless for a moment but managed to blurt out: 'It's obviously a very ticklish problem.' He told me later that he got a tremendous rocket from his wife Tony when he got home!

So there you have a very nice man – a Test captain and all-round sportsman, who won a hockey blue and was six times North of England squash champion. One slight mystery remains about him however. His nickname was Lavender, after the famous Yardley toiletries, but how on earth did he come by his third Christian name of Dransfield? I must remember to ask him one day.

Alec Bedser

The 'Big Fella' was the first great English player to emerge after the Second World War. And what an entrance he made on to the stage of Test Cricket – 22 wickets in his first two Tests against India in 1946. Unlike Hutton and Compton, who started their Test careers before the war, Alec only played two games for Surrey in 1939, both against the Universities. He and his twin brother, Eric, were on the ground staff and spent most of their time bowling to members in the nets. As Alec showed such promise as a fast-medium bowler Eric decided to concentrate on becoming an off-spinner. The twins were born in Reading in 1918, Eric arriving just a few minutes before Alec. As boys they were brought up in Woking, where the old Surrey player Alan Peach taught them their early cricket. They used to walk two miles to school every day, where they even sang in the choir! Alec has always maintained that this daily walk gave his legs the strength which enabled him to take 1,924 wickets at 20.41 during his career (1939–60).

11 Alec Bedser

He remained remarkably fit, and except for his shingles on Len Hutton's Australian tour in 1954–5, I cannot remember him missing a Test because of any of the modern ailments which seem to afflict bowlers today – bad backs, sore shins, pulled rib muscles, etc. Alec has always opposed the modern thirty-minute warm-up exercises which take place before the start of play every day. Based on the number of *back* injuries suffered by fast bowlers today, it seems that he is right. I should love to have seen him or Fred Trueman balancing on one leg, as the other was placed on the shoulder of the physiotherapist! – good for the hamstrings, they say. The only way to keep fit as a bowler is to bowl, says Alec. I think he has a point.

He and Eric are identical twins and look remarkably alike. I learnt to identify them fairly early on – Alec has the broader face – but they don't make it easy. They dress alike, wearing the same suit, shirt and tie. Even when they are apart they select the same tie, though whether it's instinct or whether they ring each other each morning I'm not sure. But when they *are* at home they are said to pick up in the morning the first sock or shirt which comes to hand, no matter who wore them the day before.

When they are together they carry on a joint conversation with you, each one picking up where 'the brother' leaves off. Alec had an excellent benefit (for those days) of £12,866. They wisely invested it in an office furniture business which, because of their hard work, integrity and large circle of friends and admirers, prospered. They were able to sell it and remain as consultants to the takeover firm.

Alec has never taken a holiday as such. He has used all the spare time due to him to go on tours (in 1962–3 as assistant manager in Australia, and in 1974–5 and 1979–80 as manager) or to attend Test matches in this country (as selector from 1962 to 1981, and chairman for the last thirteen years of that period). He, like other players of his generation, finds it difficult to comprehend the large sums of money the modern Test player can earn, but in spite of the contrast in financial awards, cricket has brought Alec many useful contacts and a well-deserved OBE. In return, he has put a great deal back into cricket, as selector, committee-man and, finally, president of Surrey.

As a man, Alec has high principles. Honesty, loyalty, hard work and good manners and behaviour come high on his list. He has never been an optimist, and even when things are going well he will find something to grumble at – a typical English trait. To him 'things are not what they were in my day', but it's all said with a gentle smile on his broad face and underneath you realise there is a 'softy', something I am sure that the young England players whom he selected or managed came to recognise.

Finally, what about Alec the player? He was certainly one of the best fast-medium bowlers there has ever been – very much in the Maurice Tate mould. Both of them liked their wicket-keepers to stand up to them and give them something to bowl at. They both seemed to do the impossible – that is, to gain pace off the pitch. An optical illusion, no doubt, but ask Godfrey Evans about the speed with which the ball came into his gloves.

Alec had the perfect swivel bowling action, and with his impeccable length and direction he was, strangely, mainly an *in*-swing bowler. I say strangely because with his perfect action and his delivery so close to the stumps one would have expected him to be an *out*-swinger, but to compensate he learnt to bowl a devastating leg-cutter – drawing his enormous hand across the seam of the ball to produce what was in essence a fast leg-break. His feat of 236 Test wickets becomes all the more remarkable when one considers that for much of the time from 1946 to 1954 he alone bore the brunt of England's attack without support at the other end. Though no greyhound in the field, those large hands of his pouched 289 catches, and like many bowlers he is always happy to talk about his batting – especially his night-watchman's 79 at Headingley against Australia in 1948.

To sum Alec up, he is a lovable person and a good friend who values honesty and loyalty. As a player he gave everything to his county and country. Since he retired he has put a tremendous amount back into cricket – far more than he ever took out. But cricket has been his life and that is certainly one thing about which he wouldn't grumble!

Arthur Morris

Arthur was one of the nicest, most popular, and most modest of all Test cricketers. I cannot remember ever hearing a word said against him. And in addition he was one of Australia's greatest batsman, averaging 46.48 in 46 Tests with an aggregate of 3,553 runs, and scoring 12 hundreds. In Sheffield Shield matches, his average for New South Wales was 65.

He toured England in 1948 and 1953 and became known as 'Bedser's Bunny'. Alec dismissed him as many as eighteen times, but in return Arthur also scored a good many runs off him. He scored 122 and 124 not out against England at Adelaide in 1947 (Denis Compton capped this with 147 and 103 not out in the same Test). Arthur followed this on Don Bradman's tour of England in 1948 with an outstanding series, scoring 696 runs with an average of 87. His consistency was amazing with scores of 31, 9, 105, 62, 51, 54*, 6, 182, 196. It was his partnership with Don Bradman of

301 in 217 minutes which enabled Australia to win a remarkable victory in the fourth Test at Headingley. They scored 404 for 3 in the fourth innings of the match to win by 7 wickets.

12 Arthur Morris

Arthur made his top Test score of 206 against Freddie Brown's team in 1951, but he didn't do so well in England in 1953, despite starting off the series with scores of 60, 67, 30 and 89. However, he reminded Len Hutton and his team that he could still bat a bit by scoring 153 against them in the first Test at Brisbane in 1954.

I have deliberately given all these figures because I feel that Arthur's ability has never been fully appreciated. I rarely hear him mentioned when cricketers discuss great batsmen of the past. Perhaps he lived too much in the shadow of Don Bradman. He was a left-handed opener and was both elegant and stylish, with excellent footwork. He used his feet like a boxer to dance down the pitch, and as a result played slow bowling as well if not better than the quicks.

To be fair, I suppose he was lucky that in the first seven years of Test cricket after the war, he did not have to play against any really fast bowlers, until Statham, Trueman and Tyson reached their peak pace in 1953–4. Frank Tyson in Australia in 1955 was acknowledged to be the fastest bowler any of the current players had seen, and he did capture Arthur's wicket three times in that series.

Arthur was a fine fielder anywhere, with a good arm, and in the middle fifties was probably the most televised bowler in Test cricket. He used to bowl slow left-arm chinamen, and Lindsay Hassett put him on to bowl that famous last over at the Oval Test of 1953.

England needed 5 runs to win to regain the Ashes for the first time in nineteen years. Bill Edrich scored a single off the third ball. Denis Compton then tried to sweep him down to the gasholders for the 4 runs necessary for victory. The crowd were ringing the ground ready to dash on to cheer England's victory. As Denis swept they charged from all directions, but they had reckoned without 'The Claw' – alias Alan Davidson. He was fielding at backward square leg, stuck out his enormous left hand and stopped the ball. So there was a delay as the crowd had to make their way back behind the boundary line. Then Arthur fed Denis's sweep with another chinaman outside the leg stump. This time the ball sped past Alan towards the square-leg boundary. Whether it ever got there no one has ever discovered, as once again the crowd swept on to the ground and surrounded the players as they made a dash for the pavilion. I remember it so well because I was lucky to be commentating on television at the time. All I could do was to shout hoarsely: 'It's the Ashes. It's the Ashes.'

Anyway, Arthur's analysis was 0.5–0–5–0, and because of the tension and excitement of that last over every TV shop in the country seemed to use the film of it for demonstration purposes. You only had to look in the shop windows to see Arthur bowling on about half a dozen sets. He has always been immensely proud of that, and also of the two Test wickets he actually took that year, one against South Africa at Adelaide and the other against England in the third Test at Old Trafford. At a recent dinner at Claridges given in Arthur's honour, J. J. Warr acknowledged in his speech that Arthur had taken twice as many Test wickets as he had!

At the same dinner Arthur told of how he and his old friend and captain Lindsay Hassett played in a charity match some time after they had both retired. It was the traditional Prime Minister's match against a touring team. Arthur went in first and made a few runs. When he was back in the pavilion he met Hassett coming out, who asked if he could borrow Arthur's bat. He played very well with it, and after he was out was surrounded by a cheering crowd of small boys. In a speech at the dinner that night the Prime Minister congratulated Hassett on his innings. 'And,' he went on, 'I'd like to say how typical it was of Lindsay's generosity to give his bat away to one of the small boys in the crowd.' Believe it or not, Arthur and Lindsay are still friends!

For the last twenty years or so Arthur has been an active member of the Sydney Cricket Ground Trust. He devotes most of his time to trying to put something back into the game he loved to play. It is all entirely voluntary and mostly goes unrecognised and unsung – but, being the nice person he is, he prefers it that way.

Ray Lindwall

Whenever I am asked to pick a world eleven from all the Test cricketers whom I have seen, I always pick Ray Lindwall as my number one fast bowler. As to who partners him at the other end, I have to be very careful if Fred Trueman is listening. I just daren't leave him out!

Linders was to me the perfect model for any aspiring fast bowler to follow. His run-up was not too long; it was relaxed and he gathered speed as he approached the wicket. His sideways delivery was copybook, and when he wanted to be he was as fast as anyone, but one of his strengths was his well-disguised variations in pace – the *really* fast ball being kept in reserve and used sparingly. The batsman would be on tenterhooks, never knowing when it would come. He was essentially an out-swing bowler, but after playing league cricket in Lancashire he began to bowl the in-swinger as well. Like so many Test fast bowlers who have played in the leagues, he soon discovered that he would not get many wickets from slip catches – his pace was too much for amateur slip fielders. So he had to learn to hit the stumps! What made him such a class bowler was that he swung the ball so *late*.

Cricket historians always say what a hostile pair Lindwall and Miller were, and of course they bowled bouncers like any other fast bowler, but they did not do so in the abundance we see today. It's interesting to find on talking to the likes of Len Hutton and Denis Compton that, although they rated Lindwall as the better bowler, they would always prefer to face him rather than Miller.

I was lucky enough to keep wicket to Lindwall in a Sunday charity match at Didsbury during an Old Trafford Test in either

1961 or 1964 – I forget which. He was over here as a journalist writing for an Australian paper. I was standing a long way back, although of course he was getting on a bit then, and anyway would not bowl flat out in a charity game. Len Hutton was standing alongside me at slip and I suggested to him that we asked Linders to bowl just one ball as fast as he could. I asked him to do so before the start of his next over, and also warned the batsman to keep well out of the way. Linders then bowled one wide of the off-stump and it came through into my gloves chest high, and nearly knocked me over backwards – and that was when he was over forty. But it proved to me how fast he must have been.

13 Ray Lindwall

Linders was strong and beautifully built, five feet ten inches tall with big shoulders. He was a superb fielder anywhere, and a good enough batsman to average over 20 with the bat and to score a hundred in the third Test at Melbourne in 1947.

Like many fast bowlers, he liked his glass of beer. I am always very careful to have some cans in the fridge if I have any Australian friends coming, as I know how cold they like it, but I committed a terrible crime at a supper party we gave during the MCC Bicentary Match in 1987. We had used up the cans which had been in the fridge, so when Linders asked for some more beer I opened a tin which, although not warm was not, I thought, cold enough. So when I had poured it out, I put some ice into it. You should have seen his face! I might have just hit him for six, and I realised what he must have looked like to a batsman as he ran up to bowl. He soon forgave me, but I now realise that ice *in* an Australian's beer is sacrilege and I shall never do it again.

He has got a slow Australian drawl with rather a husky voice, and he was one of the summarisers for ABC, during Ted Dexter's MCC tour 1962–3. He has a good sense of humour and was good fun in the box. He tells a good story, and at the Lord's Taverners' dinner for Bill Edrich and Denis Compton in 1986 he told this one about two friends of his who stayed for three days in Bangkok on their way back to Australia. On the last day the wife told her husband to go and amuse himself while she went shopping. She asked him to pick her up in a couple of hours.

The husband thought that he would visit one of Bangkok's famous massage parlours. He was given the address of one by the hall porter and duly rang the bell. An attractive Thai girl opened the door and he asked whether he could have one of their massages. She said certainly, and that it would cost him a thousand dollars. 'Oh,' he said, 'I can't afford anything like that. Two hundred would be the most I could pay.' She apologised and said that she was sorry but that was their price and she couldn't change it.

So he went off and visited one of the museums to while away the time before he collected his wife. This he finally did and was walking with her down the street, when he saw the Thai girl from the massage parlour walking towards them. 'There you are,' she said. See what you get for two hundred dollars!'

Trevor Bailey was an old adversary of Linders, but only on the field, where they had many a battle. Off it they were great friends, and this was proved at Sydney in the fifth Test in 1955. Bailey had made 72 and Len Hutton was about to declare. Bailey knew that Lindwall needed one more wicket to reach his hundredth against England, so he allowed himself to be bowled by Lindwall – the only time, I am sure, that he ever gave his wicket away. Cricket can be a tough game, however, especially when England play Australia. Four years later at Melbourne Bailey opened both English innings with Peter Richardson. He bagged a pair – each time falling to Lindwall! Such is gratitude.

Two final facts about Linders, perhaps not generally known by

English cricket followers at least. He captained Australia once against India at Bombay in 1956 and remarkably, for one of the greatest fast bowlers of all time, he now runs a successful florist's shop with his wife Peggy in Brisbane. May his flowers continue to bloom for many years to come.

Keith Miller

People often come up to me and ask: 'Where are the characters in cricket these days?' They then proceed to name a number of 'characters' from the past, and one name which always seems to crop up is Keith Miller. I must say he comes high up on my list.

14 Keith Miller

First of all his appearance: tall, athletic, rugged good looks, imposing carriage and walk, all adding up to a dynamic god-like figure. You couldn't fail to notice Keith. I believe that even in these days of helmets he would have been easily recognisable. His character matched his appearance – he lived life to the full and played cricket because he enjoyed it. He was competitive, as anyone who had to face his bowling would agree, but not to the extent that winning was the only thing that mattered. He had the gift of friendship. Even after bowling a particularly vicious bouncer, he would quite likely ask the batsman at the end of the over if he had heard the winner of the three-thirty. He has more friends round the world than anyone I can think of, and he keeps in touch. On my last birthday the telephone rang and there was Keith wishing me many happy returns. He had rung Sir Leonard Hutton the day before for the same purpose. Other people, like Billy Griffith, who are not too well, may suddenly get a call from Australia just to see how they are.

Somehow he communicated this innate friendliness to the crowds, and how he played up to them. Before running up to bowl he would paw the ground like a horse, tossing his head so that his mane of hair fell over his forehead. If the batsman hit him for six or played an outstanding stroke, Keith would applaud him. In 1956 at Lord's, when Australia won easily and he had taken 5 wickets in each innings, he somehow managed to seize the ball at the end of the match, and as he strode triumphantly from the field he threw it into the crowd, just like a winning golfer does on the last green.

Off the field he enjoyed the bright lights and the company of the female sex. He didn't believe in going to bed too early – even during a Test match – and you might find him at the Royal Albert Hall listening to a concert of classical music, one of his great loves. The other of course is racing, and most years you can still see his handsome figure at Ascot in his grey top hat and tails, attracting more glances from the girls than other more reputed lady-killers. He would sometimes slip away from a match to a nearby course just to watch a horse he had backed. When over here he would make a regular morning call to his great friend Scobie Breasley, the Australian jockey with the bobbing head.

As befits his character, he gave gallant service to the RAAF, during the war, and was over in England for the victory Tests of 1945. He captured the hearts of the spectators at Lord's with a brilliant display of batting in an innings of 185. Rex Alston remembers it well, as Keith seemed determined to break the glass of the old BBC commentary box, which in those days was above the England dressing-room.

He was undoubtedly a great all-rounder, and on his record a better bowler than a bat. He was a powerful driver and a good cutter and hooker, but he often appeared unhappy against spin on a turning pitch. He would get into an awful mess, and often nearly did the splits as he stretched out down the pitch. He was a brilliant fielder, especially in the slips, where behind a casual façade he made difficult catches look easy.

It is as a bowler that he was most feared, however. Lindwall may have been better, but it is surprising how many batsmen of that era have said they would sooner face him than Keith. They never knew what he was going to bowl, and with his height and good action he would dig the ball in, resulting in explosive bouncers. He varied his run-up, sometimes turning round when halfway back and bowling off a short run. I have seen him drop the ball during his run up, pick it up in his stride and bowl it without stopping. He could bowl a variety of balls, as I learnt to my cost when keeping wicket to him once in a charity match at Cranleigh. In one over he bowled six different balls, including a full pitch, a bouncer, a googly, a leg-break, and an off-break. The other I think was just straight on a good length.

I said that to him winning was not the first priority and that he didn't care for statistics and averages. He was a complete contrast in character to his Test captain in 1946 and 1948, and often disagreed with the tactics which Bradman used. In 1948 against Essex, the Australians scored 721 runs in one day, W. A. Brown and Bradman putting on 219 in ninety minutes for the second wicket. When Brown was out Miller strode out to join Bradman. He had had enough of this slaughter of a county attack, and proceeded – I suspect deliberately – to be bowled first ball by Trevor Bailey.

He was a natural cricketer who had little coaching and did most things by instinct. I remember that we were once making a programme about cricket coaching and the producers had booked Keith to explain the various ways of bowling in-swing, out-swing, etc. I asked him in rehearsal to show me the various grips, and he honestly didn't know! He just bowled naturally.

Many Australians say he was the best captain they ever played under, when he led the New South Wales side. He led from the front and played for a result, and was insistent that everyone enjoyed their cricket. Perhaps he was a trifle too devil-may-care to make an ideal Test captain. He was once leading out the NSW team on to the field at Newcastle. He strode majestically twenty yards in front of them, tossing his head as he walked with that long stride of his. Jimmy Burke ran up behind him and tugged at his sweater. 'Nugget, Nugget,' he said, 'we've got twelve men on the field.' Keith didn't look round or stop in his stride. He just gave that peculiar little cough that so often proceeds his speech and said: 'Well, tell one of them to bugger off then,' and went on walking. I think that says a lot about Keith's character.

There is also a story of his days in the RAAF. He had left their station 'somewhere in England' to go down to the local town for a haircut. When he had had his haircut, he saw one of his officers in the street. 'Ah, Miller,' said the officer, who was carrying a bag of golf clubs, 'are you going back to the station?' 'Yes, sir,' said Miller. 'Good. I wonder if you would mind taking my golf clubs back with you.' So Keith slung them across his shoulder and walked back to the station, where he saw his commanding officer. 'Ah, Miller,' he said, 'been playing golf, eh!' 'No, sir,' replied Keith, 'getting my hair cut.' And he was given seven days in detention for insubordination!

Godfrey Evans

Every morning of a Test match before play starts a bustling figure with enormous grey mutton-chop whiskers appears in our commentary box. It's 'Godders' with the latest Ladbroke betting odds for the day's cricket. He is their consultant expert, who assesses for director Ron Pollard the condition and state of the game.

He is always chirpy, smiling and full of quips. I don't ever remember him being put out by anything, certainly never down in the dumps. He is the eternal optimist. This cheerfulness, supported by his tireless energy, was one of the qualities which made him such a great player for England. Even on the hottest days abroad he never flagged. In between overs he bustled from one end to the other, perky little steps, arms swinging – a busy man in a hurry. He would encourage flagging spirits with a reminder that the gin and tonics were waiting in the dressing-room, ice tinkling against the glasses. He would rush from behind the stumps to make a poor return into a full pitch. He would ostentatiously applaud a good ball or a fine piece of fielding. He was a showman whom the crowds loved, and a wonderful support for his captain. He was also a great chatter-up of batsmen, something they didn't always appreciate.

His rise to fame was rapid. As an eighteen-year-old he appeared in a few matches for Kent before the war in 1939. With Les Ames still having trouble with his back, Godfrey became the regular Kent wicket-keeper in 1946, and played for England against India in the third Test at the Oval – the first time I saw him. My first impression was his tremendous energy and flamboyant brilliance as he stood close up to the stumps.

15 Godfrey Evans

He lost his England place in the first Test at Brisbane on Wally Hammond's tour of 1946–7. Paul Gibb played instead, but Godfrey kept wicket in the four remaining Tests. He then kept wicket for England almost continuously until his ninety-first and final Test against India at Lord's in 1959, when he took his (then) record of dismissals to 219. Appropriately, his last victim was a stumping, because in my opinion he was the greatest 'stumper' of all Test wicket-keepers. During the period from 1946 to 1959 he was occasionally not selected because of injury – Brennan, Spooner, Andrew, McIntyre and Swetman replacing him – but in George Mann's tour of South Africa in 1948–9 Billy Griffiths played in the fourth and fifth Tests, taking Godfrey's place on merit.

As a wicket-keeper Godfrey was the man for the big occasion. Like many Test players he was at his best when playing for his country, but perhaps lost some of the incentive when keeping for

Kent. He was the most spectacular wicket-keeper I have ever seen, and also the most brilliant. He did have his occasional off-days, however, the most disastrous being the last day of the 1948 Test against Australia at Headingley, when as a result of many missed chances at slip or behind the wicket Australia made 404 for 3 to win. But normally he was an inspiration to his side. He crouched close to the stumps, balancing on his toes. He stood up to fast-medium bowlers like Alec Bedser, who insisted on him doing so 'because I like something to bowl at'. Alec was basically an in-swinger, and this meant that Godfrey often had to take the ball on the leg side, which he did superbly. I was not there, but am told that in 1950–1 in Australia, when both he and Alec were in their prime, his taking of the swinging new ball on the fast, bouncy Australian pitches was miraculous. So much so, on his appeal of, 'How's that?' when he brought off a fast leg-side stumping in an up-country match all the square-leg umpire could say was, 'Bloody marvellous!'

Of course he had to stand back to the quick bowlers like Tyson, Trueman and Statham, and he hurled himself acrobatically in all directions to take seemingly impossible catches. Perhaps his greatest was when he caught the left-handed Neil Harvey off Tyson wide down the leg side in the third Test at Melbourne in 1955. People who were playing in the match have told me that they had never seen anything like it. In the pre-war days of Oldfield, Duckworth and Ames, the wicket-keepers seldom flung themselves at the ball, and I suppose that Godfrey was one of the first of the great wicket-keepers to hurl themselves like goal-keepers. The crowds love it, and undoubtedly catches are taken which would never have been attempted in the old days.

As a batsman he always enjoyed himself, and with his twinkling feet (he was once a boxer) he ran very fast between the wickets and stole some outrageous singles. He loved to hit the ball, and scored 98 not out before lunch against India at Lord's in 1952. Two years earlier against the West Indies at Old Trafford he made the first of his two Test hundreds, and it only took him 2 hours 20 minutes. In contrast, in the fourth Test at Adelaide in 1947, he took 97 minutes to score his *first* run in a back-to-the-wall partnership with Denis Compton. But no matter what he scored, the cricket always came to life when Godders was batting.

Off the field Godders was always the life and soul of every party –

and still is! His outrageous 'Carmen Miranda' won the fancy-dress prize on all the boat trips to and from Australia. In 1958–9, with Trevor Bailey, Frank Tyson and Raman Subba Row, he founded the 'Bowers Club', of which I had the honour to be elected a member. It was a male-only drinking club, and we would meet once a week and carry out various rituals invented and conducted by Godders, accompanied by the odd glass of wine.

He has always been a gambler at heart, so he is especially happy in his consultancy job for Ladbrokes. Not all his ventures have been successful, however. Most of his benefit money went into chickens, but they all got the croup! As I said he was in the marcasite business, and used to bring samples of his wares to the dressing-room, but I believe his partner 'disappeared'. There was also the little matter of some land development on the Essex coast: unfortunately, someone forgot to obtain planning permission! At one time he was mine host in a pub on the A3 just outside Petersfield. You had to be a bit wary of calling in to see him, as he would greet you warmly and announce to the assembled drinkers that the drinks were on you! He has always been the genial host at the Sportsman's Club, greeting all and sundry as if he had known them all his life. In spite of – or perhaps because of – all his varied activities, I doubt if he will ever become a millionaire, but he will continue to bring fun and laughter to all his countless friends and to every stranger he meets.

He still turns out in charity matches with his mutton-chop whiskers and the glasses which he now wears. He still crouches close up to the stumps and brings off miraculous stumpings, often down the leg side, which was his speciality. He keeps for about an hour and then goes off, having shown to an admiring younger generation what *real* wicket-keeping looks like.

Jim Laker

I knew Jim for a long time first as a player, then later as a commentator, but it wasn't until the last few years of his life that I got to know him as a real friend. For two years we travelled together round England with a cricket show called 'That's Cricket'. It consisted of a number of films and a panel of three people such as Jim,

Freddie Trueman, Tom Graveney, Ray Illingworth, Trevor Bailey, etc., chaired by myself. It had a simple format and played to big audiences. We did about twenty-five shows and filled places like the new Entertainment Centre in Nottingham (twice), the Fairfield Hall in Croydon (twice), and the Palace Theatre in Manchester.

16 Jim Laker

It had been the brainchild of music impresario Raymond Gubbay, who puts on so many concerts at the Barbican. In 1984 he had the Barbican booked for a concert one evening just after Christmas, so he thought, why not use it in the afternoon and have a show which would attract cricket enthusiasts of all ages? And so for three Christmases running we packed the Barbican, and it was a joy to see the wonderful mix of ages in the audience, with a large number of young boys home for the Christmas holidays.

Which brings me back to Jim. I had always known that he had a dry sense of humour, not always apparent in his TV commentaries. He was always a slow, deliberate mover – calm and unhurried. It was the same when he spoke, either as a successful after-dinner speaker or when taking part in our show – his delivery was always slow and deliberate. He had a fund of cricket stories and told them beautifully, with a chuckle in his voice. His timing of the punchline was perfect. He soon became the one regular member of our panel and got tremendous belly laughs wherever we went but, as anyone who ever heard him on television will know, he also had an outstanding cricket brain and great knowledge of the game, based on his own experiences in big cricket. So in addition to the 'funnies' he was a vital member of the panel in the serious discussions which we had about cricket in the programme.

I have unashamedly 'inherited' one of his best stories, and I am sure that he wouldn't mind. It was when he went to India with a Commonwealth team captained by Richie Benaud. The Australian left-arm bowler George Tribe was in the side and he had the Indian batsmen in a lot of trouble with his chinaman (the left-arm bowler's off-break). Time and time again he would force the batsman back on to his stumps and then rap him on the pad with one of his off-breaks. Each time he appealed, the Indian umpire would say: 'Very close, Mr Tribe – but too high. Another inch lower and I would have had to give him out.' Or: 'Sorry, Mr Tribe, but your big spin turned too much,' and so on. After about six of these appeals Tribe trapped another batsmen slap in front of the stumps. 'How about that one then?' he shouted. 'I nearly had to raise my finger, Mr Tribe, but I must give the batsman benefit of the doubt.' At this Tribe lost his temper, turned round and took the umpire by the throat, and, pointing him towards the batsman, said: 'Have another look.' The terrified umpire did take another careful look and after a short pause raised his finger and said: 'You're right, Mr Tribe, he is out!'

Jim of course will always be remembered for his unbelievable analysis of 19 for 90 – in the 1956 Test against Australia at Old Trafford – one record I cannot believe will ever be broken, let alone equalled. It was the more remarkable because, although the pitch did later take spin, England, batting first, made a total of 459. Jim's Surrey colleague Tony Lock then bowled *69 overs* in the match and took *1 for 106*, whereas Jim only bowled *68 overs* for his 19 wickets. Goodness knows what would have happened to Jim these days in similar circumstances – his ten colleagues would have leapt on him, hugged him and kissed him. In 1956, after his final successful appeal for lbw, he just swung round, took his sweater from the umpire, and with head down walked with measured tread back towards the pavilion. There was the odd clap on the back from his team, but basically they were as shattered as he was by sheer disbelief at what had happened. They formed an avenue for Jim to lead them back into the pavilion, where ten minutes or so later I rushed across to get him to come to our television scaffolding to do an interview. I always remember the scene in the English dressing-room. There was shouting and jubilation and the popping of champagne corks, but Jim himself was sitting quietly alone in a corner, sipping something which looked strangely like orangeade. He came and did his interview, still in a daze, and unable to explain why he had taken so many wickets and Lock only one. I think he did go so far as to say he wouldn't mind taking the pitch around with him for the rest of his career, but he was too modest to admit that it was his superb bowling and their lack of technique in playing spin which really caused the downfall of the Australian batsmen.

There was no M6 in those days and, still in a state of shock, he drove slowly down the A34 on the five-hour drive to London, where, believe it or not, he had to play in a match the next day for Surrey at the Oval. And guess who it was against? The Australians, of course, in the second match of the tour against Surrey. In their first match in May, Jim had taken 10 for 88 and 2 for 42. In this second one he was a comparative failure with 4 for 44 and 1 for 17. This meant that at the end of the summer Jim's total number of wickets against the Australians was 63.

To return to Jim's drive home: he stopped at a pub in Lichfield for a snack and quite unrecognised, sat quietly in a corner and watched the television recording of his amazing feat. No one even offered him a drink. It's just as well he *wasn't* recognised, since he was driving.

He must be a candidate for the best off-spin bowler ever, but I suppose the great Sydney Barnes would take precedence, even though he did not bowl only off-spin. It was a joy to watch Jim bowl, but from the spectator's point of view, not the batsman's. I can also give a wicket-keeper's opinion of his art. In a charity match in Surrey I was lucky to keep to Jim. He was extremely difficult to take because he managed to make the ball bounce. He had such a perfect action – his high right arm brushing his right ear, the swivel as he delivered the ball, the flight, the prodigious off-spin, the accuracy, direction and the away floater beautifully disguised. I was keeping pretty badly, when the batsman went a long way down the pitch. 'Ah,' I said to myself, 'a chance to redeem myself with a leg-side stumping.' So I positioned myself outside the leg-stump and waited for the off-break to curve round the batsman's body into my waiting hands. Alas, it was the away floater and there I was stranded down the leg side, whilst the ball sailed away for 4 byes wide of the off-stump. Yes, I remember his bowling well! Especially that slow measured walk back, and the upward glance to heaven as he swung round to start his short run-up.

His success against Australia must have delighted him since in 1948 they had collared him, and in 1953 he only played in three of the Tests and took just 9 wickets. In fact he did not gain a regular place in the England team until 1956. One final analysis cannot be left out when looking at his records. It's 14–12–2–8 in the Bradford Test Trial in 1950 – an amazing piece of bowling on a drying pitch on a ground just five miles from his birthplace (Frizinghall).

In the field Jim was no greyhound but usually fielded at gully, where he was a safe catcher. With a top Test score of 63 he was a useful number nine and at Headingley in 1953 made 48 in a match-saving partnership of 57 with Trevor Bailey, who batted for 262 minutes for just 38 runs. They were together on the last morning with Jim scoring nearly all the runs. It was a beautifully sunny day and they were desperately playing for time. With two minutes to go before lunch Bailey summoned Laker to a mid-wicket confer-ence. He looked up at the blue sky and dazzling sun and said to Jim who was due to play at the last over: 'Go to Frank Chester at square leg and appeal against the light.' Jim was amazed but Bailey urged him to do so, reminding him that they were then allowed one appeal per session against the light. So, reluctantly, Jim went up to Frank Chester, who asked him what he wanted. 'I'm appealing against the light,' said Jim. Frank stared at him in disbelief but Jim said: 'We are allowed to do so by the present Test regulations, and it means that you must go and consult Frank Lee, the other umpire.' The seconds were ticking by and Frank reluctantly made his way over to the bowler's end. By that time it was almost half past one on the clock, and Lindsay Hassett the Australian captain stormed off the field in disgust. It was not a sporting ploy, but it saved England having to face another over before lunch.

Jim left Surrey in 1959 and went at Bailey's invitation to play for Essex as an amateur. At about this time a ghosted autobiography called *Over to Me* got Jim into hot water with both Surrey and Lord's, mainly because of some criticisms he made of Peter May. However, all was later forgiven and he was welcomed back to the

Oval, where he did much useful work on committees and was always willing to help the young players on the staff with advice and coaching.

In 1970 I left BBC TV as one of their cricket commentators after twenty-four years, and from then until his sad death in April 1986, Jim and Richie Benaud were the main TV commentators. Jim was a match for Richie. He learnt to time his short, pithy comments to match the action and never spoke unless it was necessary. He was an excellent reader of the game, a kind critic and had a sound knowledge of tactics, something he probably learnt from Stuart Surridge, whom he used to say was the best captain he ever played under. Surridge had a gift for leadership and, whereas he would get Tony Lock to do his best by a spot of swearing and an aggressive approach, he always treated Jim gently – a sound piece of psychology.

I must just finish with one other story which Jim used to tell so well on our cricket show, 'That's Cricket'. He would remind the audience that in the 1984 series against the West Indies Pat Pocock was recalled to the England side for the fourth Test at Old Trafford. There he bowled over forty-five overs and took 4 for 121, so justifying his selection, though he did make a pair when batting. At the Oval he didn't get a bowl in the West Indies' first innings, which closed at 190 towards the end of the first day thanks to Botham taking 5 wickets.

Pocock, always called Percy, was told by David Gower to pad up and prepare to go in as night-watchman if either Fowler or Broad got out early. He was naturally very apprehensive at the thought of facing the likes of Marshall, Holding and Garner in somewhat uncertain light. As it turned out, Broad was soon bowled by Garner for 4, and there was panic in the English dressing-room as they couldn't find Percy. After a brief search they found him in the wash-room below the dressing-room, gargling and cleaning his teeth. 'Hurry up, Percy,' they shouted. 'You're in as night-watchman. What on earth are you doing?' 'Oh,' said Percy, as he went up the stairs to collect his bat and helmet, 'I was just rinsing and cleaning out my mouth, in case Bernie Thomas [the physio-therapist] has to give me the kiss of life!' I wish you could have heard Jim tell that story.

George Mann

At my preparatory school in the early twenties we used to have what we thought was a terribly good joke about F. T. Mann, the Middlesex captain. 'F. T. Mann is a hefty man,' was the cry whenever his name was mentioned, which was quite often because of my following Middlesex and Patsy Hendren. I suppose the name naturally encourages a pun. Once in South Africa in 1948 his son, George Mann, was clean bowled by a beauty from Tufty Mann, the South African slow left-arm bowler. As George departed for the pavilion, John Arlott commented with his delightful Hampshire burr: 'Mann's inhumanity to Mann'.

George and his brother John came to Eton just after I had left. They were both outstanding games players and won every sort of colour for different sports. I used to see them once every year when their father F.T. (Frank) brought them to the Eton and Harrow match at Lord's. In those days it was a very well-attended two-day match with coaches dotted round the boundary, men in top hats and tails and the ladies tarted up to the nines. My friends and I used to gather at the top of Block 'G' on the right of the sightscreen at the nursery end. We barracked the Harrow players unmercifully and generally made a number of appalling jokes. For instance, if a Harrovian arrived in an immaculate suit of tails we might shout out: 'Oh, Burtons' have just rung up. Can you be sure to get that morning dress back to them before closing time. They need it for a wedding tomorrow morning.' We used to make so much noise that once Sir Pelham Warner sent over an official to ask the 'young gentlemen' to keep quieter.

I think the two Menn must have enjoyed it all, as they came back year after year. They both played for Eton, and George was captain in 1937. He then went on to get a blue for Cambridge in the two summers before the war. In this he served with great distinction in the Scots guards, winning a DSO and a MC – a rare occurrence. He was a natural leader and throughout his life seems to have been at the head of anything in which he became involved. He was captain of Middlesex and England, chairman of the TCCB, chairman of Middlesex and president of MCC. Indeed, his faculty for leadership made things difficult for him on a number of occasions, with the conflicting interests of TCCB and MCC, and Middlesex and MCC. If he had had three feet he would have had one in each camp!

17 George Mann

On the surface you won't spot the leadership quality immediately. He is quiet, diffident, modest and even shy. He is always friendly and good-mannered and with his charming smile and sense of humour he has had no need for the tough Monty-like approach. There were one or two occasions when I thought he might have been tougher, but his decisions were always based on seeing both sides of an issue, with the good of cricket as his sole aim.

All this may sound too good to be true and make him appear to be a paragon of virtue, but you will seldom find anyone to say a word against him. He had some difficult problems when at the head of the TCCB, but he handled them all remarkably well.

As a player he was a fine forcing bat like his father, and correct in style and execution of all the strokes. He was also a magnificent fielder. His cricketing life was curtailed by the need to work in the family brewery, otherwise he might well have captained England through the early fifties. His tour to South Africa as captain in 1948–9 was a resounding success, not just because of the results – though these were satisfactory enough, England winning two of the five Tests and drawing the other three. His example in the field meant that he had a brilliant fielding side. Off the field he had a disciplined and happy side, not always an easy combination to achieve.

Batting at number six in the Tests he made four scores in double figures under 20, a useful 44 and a splendid match-winning 136 not out in the fifth Test at Port Elizabeth. On his return to England he captained England in the first two Tests against New Zealand, but then came the calls of business. He was an equally popular and successful captain of Middlesex in his two years as captain of the county. They finished third in 1948, and equal top with Yorkshire in 1949.

If you had to debate the merits of the public school system, George would be a perfect example of what it *can* produce. Equally, in a discussion on the pros and cons of the amateur or professional as captains, George would score a definite plus in favour of the amateurs. Like quite a few of them he was not quite good enough to play for England on his cricket ability alone, but his leadership – like Brearley's – was worth a lot of runs. Finally, I cannot believe that the events in Pakistan in 1987 would ever have happened under George's captaincy.

Neil Harvey

He was easy to pick out on the field. Only five feet six inches tall, he moved very fast with small steps, and was a perky, cocky figure in the nicest possible way. Because of his height he always gave the appearance of being very close to the ground, and this helped him to be one of the best ever fielders in Test cricket. He prowled about in the covers, covering a tremendous amount of ground. He was as quick as lightning and his returns to the wicket-keeper came whizzing in over the top of the stumps. In later years he became equally good as a slip fielder. Incidentally, although a left-handed batsman, he threw with his right.

He ranks with Bradman, Greg Chappell and Allan Border as one of the most successful Australian Test batsmen. He started his Test career earlier than any of them, playing in his first Test when only nineteen years of age – the youngest of *any* Australian. He was successful straight away. He made a century in his *first* club match, and a century in his *first* game for Victoria. He scored 153 in his *second* Test against India in 1947, and then a year later at Headingley made a hundred in his *first* Test match against England. For the next fifteen years he was one of the mainstays of Australia's batting, normally going in at number three, occasionally at number four. He played 79 tests and made 6,149 runs at an average of 48.41.

18 Neil Harvey

I give these statistics, but I doubt if Neil himself knows their details. Averages meant nothing to him. He was one of that all too rare breed of Test cricketers who only enjoyed batting when he was playing strokes – and he had plenty of those. I suppose his greatest asset was his nimble footwork. He loved to dance down the pitch to the spinners, and occasionally to the quicker bowlers too. His defensive technique was faultless, and enabled him to play better than his colleagues on a turning pitch. He had all the left-hander's strokes through the off-side, and if he had a weakness it was because he was always prepared to have a go against anything outside the off-stump. He realised that he could have left many of the balls alone, but that to him would have been *boring*. He had what at that time was an unorthodox way of dealing with short balls pitched on his stumps. He would step back to give himself room, and crash the ball through the covers. Nowadays of course in one-day cricket everyone tries to 'give themselves room', resulting in many who do so being clean-bowled. One other feature of his batting was his speed between the wickets. He was one of the best runners I have seen.

He made four tours to England in 1948, 1953, 1956 and 1961. Not many other Australians have done this, though Bertie Oldfield, Don Bradman, Greg Chappell, Rodney Marsh and Dennis Lillee come to mind as some who did. In 1961 Neil was vice-captain to Richie Benaud, and a very happy partnership they made. Richie had shoulder trouble after the first Test, so Neil was captain in the second at Lord's, which Australia won by five wickets. There's a nice story told about him and Alan Davidson. Alan had the reputation of being a bit of a hypochondriac, and was always leaving the field with some 'injury' or other. He used to spend most of his waking hours on the massage table. In England's first innings he had hobbled off after taking one wicket, and when the Australians returned to the dressing-room at lunch there he was lying on the table, groaning about some damage to his ankle. Australia's bowling, robbed of Benaud, was not too strong and relied heavily on Davo to support McKenzie, Misson and Mackay. Davo and Neil got on well together – they both played for New South Wales. So Richie thought he would try to persuade Davo to return to the field after lunch. He pleaded away at Davo without much success until he thought of a subtle ploy. 'This is Neil's first Test as captain. Won't you support him? He needs you badly out there.' Davo thought for a moment and then just as the team were leaving to go out to field, suddenly leapt off the table. 'For the little fellow,' he said, 'I would do anything. For him anything I'd do,' and with that he went back on to the field and promptly took four more wickets in a devastating piece of fast left-arm bowling. He took five for 43 and England were all out for 206 – May, Barrington, Lock and Trueman all falling to the rejuvenated Davo. This was the only time that Neil captained Australia and he's always proud of never having led Australia to defeat!

One interesting thing people may not have known about Neil.

Nowadays – as befits his position as a selector – he looks very imposing in his horn-rimmed spectacles, but he doesn't just wear them for effect. He needs them. I discovered this in 1961 when I took Richie and Neil to see *The Sound of Music* at the Palace Theatre during the Lord's Test. As we took our seats in the dress circle, the lights dimmed and I saw Neil put his hand in his pocket and put on a pair of spectacles. I had never seen him in them before, so afterwards I asked him about them. He then confessed that he had always been short-sighted and couldn't even read the number on an approaching bus. I must say I was amazed – to think that such a superb batsman could not see clearly. How many runs might he have made if his eye-sight had been normal? Even so, in that last tour in 1961 he made Test scores of 114, 73, 53, 35, and in the following year against Ted Dexter's team he made scores of 39, 57, 64, 154. Not bad for a batsman with a white stick.

His biggest disappointment was when he took a pair in Jim Laker's match at Old Trafford in 1956. He may blame the pitch for his dismissal in the first innings, when he was bowled by a turner from Laker. But he had no excuse in the second innings. Colin Cowdrey caught him at mid-on off that rare Laker ball – a full pitch!

Neil is still as chirpy and cheerful as he always was, speaking in short clipped sentences with laughter never far away. I always look forward to meeting him whenever I go to Australia.

Trevor Bailey

I suppose the best exponent of the forward defensive stroke in my time was Trevor Bailey, and ironically he now lives in a road called The Drive! In most people's minds he will always be the dour defender, enjoying far more the minutes or even hours spent at the crease rather than the number of runs he scored. In a sense this is a false picture. In his early days he was a free stroke-maker, and for Essex throughout his career he was always happy to attack, but somehow in Tests the mantle of saviour and rescuer of his side fell on his shoulders. It became expected of him, and goodness knows there were plenty of occasions when England needed to be rescued. So it became a habit with him, and once set in a groove he found it difficult to change his style. He revelled in a crisis and was a great baiter of the opposition. He would wait for a fast bowler to start his run and then step away from his wicket pretending he had a fly in his eye. You had to have guts to do that sort of thing to someone like Keith Miller, but the Boil had plenty of them. And he never batted in a helmet, and seldom in a cap – just curly black hair to protect his head.

19 Trevor Bailey

I must explain about his nickname 'Boil'. It was not one of my nicknames. It came about when he was playing football for Leytonstone in the East of London, and a cockney voice yelled out: 'Come on, *Boily*.'

He enjoyed causing aggravation and frustration to his opponents – especially Australians! A good example of this was his 71 in four and a quarter hours at Lords' in 1953 when on the last day he and Willie Watson's partnership for the fifth wicket of 163 saved England from certain defeat. A later occasion was at Brisbane in 1958 when for Peter May's side in the first Test he scored 48 in 7 hours 38 minutes! But at Brisbane in 1954 he had actually hit a six clean out of the ground off Ian Johnson. This proved two things: firstly, that he *could* hit the ball when he wanted to and, secondly, that an incentive can work wonders. A local businessman had offered £100 to the first batsman to hit a six in the match. The Boil had got to hear of this and decided to have a go. £100 went a long way in those days and it provided a spectacular party for the England team at Lennon's Hotel.

Trevor was basically a middle-order batsman, but in fact enjoyed going in first and on the 1958 tour opened the innings in four Tests. Even today when he is in the commentary box, a gleam of appreciation comes into his eyes if he sees a batsman play a correct defensive stroke – head still, eyes on the line of the ball, bat slightly angled down, making contact with the ball just in front of the left foot. More than any other batsman the Boil used to 'smell' the ball.

He was a genuine all-rounder, and was one of the few Test players who could get into the side *either* as a batsman *or* as a bowler, supported by his magnificent fielding and catching close to the wicket. He did the double 8 times, scored a thousand runs 17 times and took 100 wickets 9 times. In 1959 he even made 2,011 runs and took 100 wickets, admittedly with a little help from a successful Scarborough Festival.

I first saw him bowl at Lord's in 1945 when, as a strapping young man in the Royal Marines, he played for the Royal Navy against the Army. He and his side-kick A. W. H. Mallett – also from Dulwich – both took three wickets. He was then fast and lively with a beautiful high action. As he developed he settled for accurate fast-medium with swing and movement off the pitch, and because of his action could extract bounce from the pitch. He took 132 Test wickets and for five years was the main support for Alec Bedser and Brian Statham. Undoubtedly his best bowling performance was on a shiny shirt-front pitch at Sabina Park, Kingston in 1954. He opened the bowling with Trueman and took 7 for 34 in 16 overs, which, coupled with Len Hutton's 205, enabled England to win by 9 wickets and so square the series 2–2.

I mentioned earlier his fine close fielding, and against Australia in 1956 at Lords' I saw him make one of the best catches I have ever seen. Trueman was bowling at his fastest from the Nursery End to Neil Harvey the left-hander. A ball pitched on Neil's leg-stump and he hit it really hard round the corner. The Boil was at backward short-leg and flung himself at full length to his right, making a brilliant one-handed catch inches off the ground.

Essex should be eternally grateful for their local Westcliffe boy.

In addition to his all-round performances for the county he did sterling work as captain (1961–6) and secretary (1954–67). In those days Essex had their travelling circus of mobile scoreboard, and lorries carrying chairs, tents, etc. They played on at least six different grounds, and you can imagine the organisation required to prepare each ground for a first-class match. I have seen the Boil selling tickets at the gate, dealing with members in the secretary's tent, going out to toss and on occasions helping to mop up flooded marquees. But somehow he coped with it all, and in between his various duties – he would then go out and do his bit on the field. Luckily he has always had a great sense of humour – sometimes slightly wicked – and so he took everything in his stride.

Besides cricket he has had a versatile career. He got a soccer blue for Cambridge, played for Leytonstone and won an FA Amateur Cup medal. He is – or certainly was – a fanatical cinema-goer and on tours or in the evenings of county matches used to slip off to the local flea-pit. He is a tremendous party-goer and enjoys his food and drink.

Australia 1958–9 was my first tour and the Boil made me welcome and helped me a lot. It was all new to me, but he was an old campaigner and knew all the ropes. I remember that when MCC were playing Victoria he was not selected, so he took me up to the outback, where we visited a snake farm. We were both visibly shocked because the snakes were fed with live mice!

Anyway, it was lucky for him that he was not playing because there was a heatwave, with the dry hot wind from the Northern Territories making the Melbourne ground like a cauldron. It was difficult to breathe and all the cars, railings and seats became red-hot to touch. Out in the middle it was unbearable. The players had ice-cooled scarves round their necks, drinks were tucked away behind the stumps or hidden under caps and, uniquely, I should say, Colin Cowdrey, who was captain instead of Peter May, gave Trueman, Loader and Tyson one-over spells. Poor John Mortimore had to bowl twenty overs and as a result was sick on the pitch. He had been flown out as a reinforcement with Ted Dexter. This led to the lovely story of the two old members reading their papers in a St James's Street Club. 'I see MCC have asked for reinforcements and they are sending out Dexter and *Mortimore*,' said one of them. 'What's that you say?' said the other. 'How many did you say they were sending – forty more?'

Since he stopped playing, the Boil has had a number of interests – public relations, importing German wines and countless other mysterious businesses, all of which, knowing the Boil, have been highly successful. He has been cricket and football correspondent for the *Financial Times*, and has shown his deep knowledge of both games with his critical descriptions of play.

He is now best known, however, for his long association with 'Test Match Special' on Radio 3. He is the doyen of the commentary box, as he made his first broadcast in 1965 when I was still with television. He is a splendid person to have in the box, 100 per cent reliable and professional, and able to fill in at a moment's notice and keep talking during any crisis. These sometimes occur when the rest of us get an attack of the giggles and are incapable of speech, and then the Boil takes over until we recover. He has a slight nasal drawl and as a summariser is fair but not afraid to speak his mind. If he is critical of bad cricket he is equally quick to praise the good things; He has a dry sense of humour and a chuckle is never far away; he tends to talk in short staccato sentences like Mr Jingle in *The Pickwick Papers*: 'Fine bowler – keeps good length – strong, wiry – like him in my side.'

Because he has a good sense of humour he is a good feed for some of my worst puns. I asked him once: 'What do you call a Frenchman who is shot out of a cannon?' The answer was 'Napoleon Blownaparte', which got the accolade of a groan from the Boil. He has other uses too. People are very kind and send us up the odd bottle to the commentary box. The Boil is a great silent remover of corks, so that listeners don't hear a loud pop in the background. You can always tell when he is in the box because several times a day he produces a high-pitched sneeze, which is usually repeated six times.

To sum the Boil up: he was a great and genuine Test all-rounder, who could have been an excellent England captain with his knowledge of tactics and techniques, but he broke his contract with MCC by writing a book about Len Hutton's West Indian tour and he was never forgiven. He is a splendid companion and colleague both in and out of the box, though he is rather like a homing pigeon. After each day's play of a London Test he goes back to his wife Greta, and their home in The Drive. During other Tests he always goes home at weekends. He certainly enjoys his life.

David Sheppard

Not many bishops have captained their country at cricket. I can only think of one, the present Bishop of Liverpool, David Sheppard. Immediately after the war I heard of this very promising young schoolboy batsman at Sherborne, and in the summer holidays of 1947 he played for Sussex at the age of eighteen. He went up to Cambridge and gained a blue in all three years from 1950 to 1952. In his last year he was captain, and it is interesting that he was chosen rather than a certain P. B. H. May, later to captain England more times than anyone else. To cap it all David made 127 in the University match that year, the first hundred in the match since the war. Ten years later he was to make another hundred at Lord's – for the Gentlemen in the last Gentlemen *v*. Players match.

Before these two hundreds, however, this amazing young cricketer had already played for England at home, and toured Australia with Freddie Brown's MCC team in 1950–1. His first Test was against the West Indies at the Oval in 1950; he then played in two more in Australia, and one in New Zealand the following winter. He didn't trouble the scorers too much in these four Tests, but his performances while he was up at Cambridge were outstanding. In his three years he scored 3,545 runs, 1,281 of them (with 7 hundreds) in 1952. In that year he even topped the national batting averages with 2,262 runs at an average of 64.62, and also made his career-best score of 239 not out. This meant that he was selected for the last two Tests against India, and in his current form he inevitably scored his first Test hundred at the Oval. Incidentally, during his Cambridge days he shared in two enormous opening partnerships with John Dewes of 343 against the West Indies at Fenners, and 349 against Sussex at Hove.

So what sort of batsman was this young accumulator of runs? He was not naturally athletic, and because he was heavily built he always seemed to me to be a bit cumbersome and slow-moving, but he had been well coached and played straight with an especially powerful off-drive. He also had a good defensive technique. His early successes were due largely to his character, however. He was dedicated, determined, and competitive and quite simply enjoyed making runs – lots of them. I was lucky to see all his three Test hundreds, the one against India in 1952 and two against Australia.

20 David Sheppard

There was his 113 in Jim Laker's match at Old Trafford in 1956 and yet another 113 at Melbourne in 1963. He was run out going for the winning run, England beating Australia in both these matches. Altogether, he played in 22 Tests with an average of 37.80, and there is no knowing what he might have achieved had he not taken holy orders in 1955. It was as a newly ordained clergyman that he made his hundred at Old Trafford – and also his hundred for the Gentlemen. It was this innings, incidentally, which was largely responsible for his being chosen to go to Australia for a second time – with Ted Dexter's MCC side.

This tour was not an unqualified success for David, in spite of scores of 31, 53, 113, 30 and 68. He had always been a fine close fielder in his Cambridge and early Sussex days, but when he left cricket temporarily to enter the church his fielding became a little 'rusty'. He found it difficult to regain his former safe catching, and unfortunately dropped quite a few catches on the tour. This was wretched for him and was the source of several stories. For example, there was a young couple who had recently migrated to Australia, and during the tour, the wife had a baby. 'Great,' said her husband. 'I've got a wonderful idea. We'll get the Rev. David Sheppard to christen it.' 'Not likely,' replied the wife quickly, 'he'd only drop it!'

There was also Fred Trueman's famous remark after David had missed yet another catch. 'I don't understand it,' he said. 'The Reverend should have a better chance than any of us when he puts his hands together.' There was also a funny but rather sad climax to it all. In the Adelaide Test he was fielding in the deep and a ball was hit to him hard and high. He got underneath it and to his immense joy caught the ball and flung it in the air. His joy was, however, short-lived as Brian Statham shouted out to him to throw it back quickly as it was a no-ball, and the batsmen were still running.

Off the field he had a tremendous success with his preaching, and every Sunday filled cathedrals and churches wherever MCC happened to be playing. People flocked in from the outback to hear him and there was a full house every time. At Adelaide he was preaching on the Sunday at St Peter's Cathedral, so Colin Cowdrey, John Woodcock of *The Times* and I went to hear him preach. We knew that he felt he had to give 'good value for money', as so many people had travelled so far to hear him. We therefore decided to have a sweep on how long he would talk, and we all opted for something between twenty and thirty minutes. It became very exciting as he passed the twenty mark, and at one point soon afterwards he paused and we thought he had finished. Two of us passed our money to the winner (I can't remember which of us it was), when suddenly David cleared his throat and went on: 'Finally, there is one more point which I would like to make . . .' He then continued for another ten minutes or so and passed the thirty mark quite easily. We got quite hysterical, but as none of us had got the winning time right, we called off the bets. Of course we shouldn't have behaved like this, because David was really a superb preacher and the Australian congregations lapped it all up and thoroughly enjoyed it.

He played no more first class cricket after 1963 and devoted himself to his vocation. He ran the Mayflower Family Centre in the

East End, and as its Warden did a wonderful job for both the young and the old. In 1969 he became Suffragan Bishop of Woolwich and six years later started his highly successful career as Bishop of Liverpool, where he still displays great powers of leadership.

I think that he can thank cricket for playing a not unimportant part in his rapid rise to the top of the church. He is tall, good-looking and became a familiar figure as he played for England and Sussex. There was a glamour about him which made him especially attractive to the young. He is obviously a born leader, and this was proved when he captained Sussex in 1953 and took them from thirteenth place in 1952 to the position of runners-up to Surrey. He was firm, fair and led by example, and created a team which played above its real form. Some people may also forget that he captained England twice. It was against Pakistan in 1954 when Len Hutton was ill, and he got off to a good start, England winning by an innings and 129 runs at Trent Bridge. So he reached the top in cricket by captaining his country. I wonder if he will end up by captaining the Church of England as Archbishop of Canterbury. I wouldn't be surprised.

If he does I wish him better luck than he had in the apocryphal story which was told in the fifties. Evidently the Roman Catholics challenged the Church of England to a needle cricket match at Lord's. The Archbishop was very keen to win and ordered David Sheppard's ordination to be hurried through so that he would be qualified to play. This was duly done and David played at Lord's. The Archbishop rang up during the luncheon interval to find out the latest score. 'Oh, your Grace,' said the canon in charge of cricket, 'we are not doing very well. We won the toss and batted and at lunch are 55 for 5.' 'Oh dear,' said the Archbishop, 'that's bad. What happened to David Sheppard?' 'He had back luck, your Grace. He had to retire hurt at 0. He was knocked out by a bouncer which hit him on the head. It was bowled by a fast bowler the Roman Catholics had called Father Trueman!'

The four W's

Yes, I know it's normally the three W's, but I am cheating slightly. I am adding Wes to Worrell, Walcott and Weekes. My excuse is that everyone calls him Wes, so that the Hall becomes superfluous. He is also such a great personality and was such a magnificent fast bowler that he merits joining the ranks of the three musketeers. Together they form a perfect contrast in character and skills, and during their playing time were the driving force which took the West Indies to the top of the International League. There are and were many other fine players who contributed to the successes of the West Indies – I have already included Sobers, Lloyd and Richards – but space prevents me from naming them all. It would make a book in itself.

Of my four, Sir Frank Worrell during his short life had more influence on West Indies cricket than possibly any other West Indian. He was the first black man to captain them, and welded together the various islands with all their differences into a team. He was dignified, calm, friendly and had that indefinable attribute of charisma. He was captain in 15 Tests, winning 9, losing 3, drawing 2 and tying 1, and his behaviour both on and off the field was always impeccable. He could have played in more Tests had he not decided to study economics first at Manchester University, and later in Jamaica, where he went to live and became a senator in their Parliament. He was, like the other three, born in Barbados but for some reason was unhappy there. The highlights of his captaincy were undoubtedly the famous Brisbane tie in 1960, and the dramatic last-over finish at Lord's in 1963 which ended in a draw. On both occasions it was his calm leadership which controlled the natural exuberance of the West Indian players. The 1960–1 Australian tour ended with an unprecedented tribute to him and his team. They paraded through the streets of Melbourne in a motorcade cheered by an estimated 500,000 people lining the route. His own personal accolade came in 1964 when he was knighted by the Queen for his services to the game. He retired after the 1963 tour of England and sadly died of leukaemia at the early age of forty-two. Again, uniquely for a cricketer, a memorial service was held for him in Westminster Abbey. It was a tribute and recognition, not just of his captaincy and prowess as a cricketer, but of his outstanding qualities as a man.

The emphasis on his captaincy and character tends to overshadow his skills as a player. He was a graceful batsman with plenty of strokes, good footwork and immense powers of concentration. He played in 51 Tests, scoring 3,860 runs with the remarkably high average of 49.48 and scored 9 hundreds. He enjoyed playing a long innings, as scores of 261 and 197 not out against England will indicate. He was also a useful left-arm bowler, sometimes slow but more often fast-medium, and took 69 Test wickets, though they were fairly expensive at 38.72 apiece. I shall always treasure the memory of keeping wicket to him in a charity match in Kent. I remember standing up to him, so he must have been bowling his slows. Sadly I cannot remember whether I caught or stumped anyone off him, but the odds are that I didn't!

Clyde Walcott was a complete contrast to the feline grace of Worrell. He was six feet two inches tall, burly, immensely strong and one of the hardest hitters the game has ever known. There was never much competition to field at mid-off or mid-on when he was batting. He drove with great power off both the front and back foot and, as if this was not enough, was a fierce square cutter and hooker. In 74 Tests he scored 3,798 runs at the high average of 56,68, eleventh best of all Test cricketers. Like Worrell he enjoyed going on after reaching a hundred. He scored fifteen hundreds in Tests, including 220 and 168 not out against England. Perhaps his best ever achievement was in the West Indies against Australia in 1955. He was at the pinnacle of his career and in 5 Tests scored 827 runs at 82.70, including 5 hundreds, and twice scored two hundreds in one match – a Test record. This was a tremendous feat against bowlers like Lindwall, Miller, W. A. Johnston and Benaud. He must also hold another unusual record. In a Test against India at Bridgetown in 1953 he had scored 98 when he was given out (lbw) by his uncle (J. H. Walcott)!

He was a versatile cricketer. In spite of his height and bulk he was a more than competent wicket-keeper, especially to the slows, but I cannot quite remember seeing him flinging himself about as

21 *left* Frank Worrell

22 *below* Clyde Walcott

23 Everton DeCourcey Weekes

24 Wes Hall

Dujon has to do today. He eventually gave it up after slipping a disc and having his nose broken. At a pinch he could also bowl, medium-paced in-duckers or off-cutters – whatever they were, he did take 11 Test wickets. He has continued his versatility since he retired from Test cricket in 1960 and went to live in Guyana. He has been cricket organiser and coach, commentator, manager of the West Indies side to England in 1976, and is now president of the West Indies board – a just reward for a big friendly man.

Everton DeCourcey Weekes has the broadest grin in cricket, and was the most prolific scorer of the three W's. He played in 48 Tests and scored 4,455 runs with an average of 58.61, putting him seventh in the list of Test averages, 0.06 behind Ken Barrington but above Hammond, Sobers and Hobbs. He was smaller than Walcott but seemingly equally powerful, with every known stroke in the game. Words like 'plunder', 'murderous', 'savage' and 'thrash' are constantly used by writers describing some of his innings, and he could be quite merciless in the way he tore into even the strongest attacks. He had two special assets: nimble footwork and guts.

People who played against him in the Test at Lord's in 1957 say that his 90 in the second innings was one of the best and bravest innings they have ever seen. Trueman, Bailey and Statham were exploiting the famous ridge at the Nursery End, and the ball rose sharply every time they hit it. Weekes suffered a cracked bone in a finger of his right hand. In spite of this – and he was obviously in great pain – he attacked the bowling for two and three-quarter hours and hit as many as sixteen fours in a superb innings – a tremendous display of guts. I am sure that Godfrey Evans was sorry to have to appeal when he finally caught him off Trevor Bailey.

Everton's most prolific spell of batting came in 1948–9. He scored 141 against England at Kingston in the fourth and final Test of Gubby Allen's tour in March. The following November the West Indies toured India and in the first three Tests he scored 128, 194, 162 and 101. In the fourth Test at Madras he was run out for 90! I suspect that just for once there was no grin on his face! He might have gone on to score many more Test runs but he was forced to retire early because of a bad thigh injury. Since then his chief claim to fame has been as a world-class bridge player – appropriately enough, since he was born in Bridgetown. But he is always there to welcome visitors to Barbados, and is an equally welcome visitor whenever he comes over here.

Lastly, the intruder W. Wes Hall. One of the fastest ever Test bowlers, with probably the longest run-up to the wicket. I remember being in the commentary box at Sabina Park and Wes starting his run from just below us. If we had had longer arms we could very nearly have patted him on the head. He was tall (six feet two inches) and gangling with long arms and legs. In spite of his long run he had tremendous stamina and could bowl for long spells. In 1963 at Lord's in England's second innings on the last day he bowled for nearly three and a half hours unchanged. This of course meant a very slow over-rate, which made England's task much harder. If you were a spectator it was a joy to watch him as he ran up, gaining pace and lengthening his stride as he approached the stumps. The batsmen, I am sure, held a different view, as they waited for the ball to be hurled at them at something like 90 m.p.h. He could move the ball in the air but it was primarily his pace which won him most of his 192 Test wickets at 26.38 apiece. He had a lovely action as he delivered the ball, left arm high in the air, right arm stretched right back, rather as if he was about to throw a javelin. He followed through a long way down the pitch, often ending up a few yards from the batsman. He could – and did – bowl a fearsome bouncer, but though batsmen feared and hated him *on* the field, he was one of the most popular cricketers *off* it.

He became a smiling gentle giant, witty, friendly and a superb mimic. He seldom stopped talking and he is reported to have told a reporter when he first became a senator in Barbados: 'if you think my run-up was long, wait till you hear my speeches!' He has now progressed from senator to minister in charge of tourism and sport, and has selected a most suitable assistant – Gary Sobers. Wes works tremendously hard to supply tourists with more facilities than just the sun and the beaches.

It was a coincidence that on the occasions of both the Brisbane tie and the 1963 draw at Lord's he was the bowler to bowl the last over. In Brisbane Australia needed 6 runs off an 8-ball over to win with 3 wickets still to fall. At Lord's England needed 8 runs to win with 2 wickets to fall. Wes, under the calming influence of Frank Worrell, kept his head on both occasions, and made certain that he did not bowl a no-ball.

Like most bowlers, he fancied himself as a batsman and there was fierce competition between himself and Charlie Griffith as to who went in above the other. In fact, at the Brisbane tie Wes made his top Test score of 50, and on Colin Cowdrey's tour in 1968 he saved West Indies from defeat in the first Test at Port-of-Spain. He put on 68 for the ninth wicket with Gary Sobers, and batted throughout the final session. As a batsman he had, and played, all the strokes – many of them brilliantly spectacular. The only trouble was that on most occasions he failed to make contact with the ball!

He will always remain one of the greatest characters of cricket, and I treasure the memory of him running up to bowl with the gold crucifix hanging from his neck, glistening in the sun. Like so many West Indians he was always passionately fond of horse-racing, and has had shares in racehorses in Barbados. What I didn't know until the other day was that it had been his ambition as a boy to become a jockey. With his six-foot-two-inch frame and well-built body I bet the horses are glad that he didn't.

Brian Close

Once when Yorkshire were playing Gloucestershire, Brian Close was in his usual position at forward short leg, only a few feet away from the batsman, who was Martin Young. Ray Illingworth bowled a shortish ball which Martin pulled really hard. The ball hit Brian on the forehead over the right eye. From there it ricocheted to Phil Sharpe at first slip, who took an easy balloon catch. Blood poured from Brian's forehead, but except for the occasional dab with a handkerchief he just carried on regardless, still only a few feet from the bat. At the interval as he walked up the pavilion steps, a member stopped him and said: 'Mr Close, I know you are very brave but you really must not stand so close to the bat. It's far too dangerous. Just think what might have happened if it had hit you in the *middle* of the forehead.' 'It would have been caught at cover,' was Brian's reply.

In 1963 at Lord's against the West Indies, he stepped down the pitch to play the fast bowling of Hall and Griffiths. If he missed the ball, he deliberately let it hit him on the body, and knowing him he would not have been wearing any protective clothing. I'm also pretty sure that he was batting bare-headed.

He made 70 before charging down the pitch once too often. When he got back to the dressing-room his body was a mass of purple bruises. I'm told he looked rather like a dalmatian dog – spotted all over. It was one of the most courageous innings I have ever seen, but he rivalled it thirteen(!) years later when he was recalled at the age of forty-five to the England side against the West Indies at Old Trafford. After Greenidge had made his second hundred of the Match Clive Lloyd declared just after tea on the Saturday, setting England a victory target of 552! Brian and John Edrich opened for England with a combined age of eighty-four, and had to face eighty minutes of the fastest and most hostile bowling I have ever seen. It was a travesty of what cricket is meant to be. Bouncer followed bouncer unchecked by the umpires. Both batsmen defended bravely and grimly, not attempting to score. Roberts and Holding were the chief culprits, backed up by Daniel. They were quite uncontrolled and even Lloyd had to admit afterwards that 'our fellows got carried away' (what is a captain for?). It finally took three bouncers in succession from Holding to Close before Bill Alley warned him. Both batsmen held on bravely until the close, by which time Brian had yet to get off the mark, but it was the most gallant nought I ever saw in a Test match.

I hope these three examples will give you some idea of Brian's courage. Add to this a grim determination to win every game, never giving up until the last ball was bowled. He had all the Yorkshire qualities of honesty, obstinacy and guts, qualities which got him into quite a few brushes with the authorities. He always spoke his mind and said exactly what he thought, no matter to whom he was speaking. His honesty cost him the England captaincy for the West Indies tour of 1967–8. It happened like this. He was recalled to the captaincy of England in the fifth Test against the West Indies in 1966. They were already 3 up in the series, but under Brian England completely outplayed them and won by an innings and 34 runs – an utter contrast to what had gone on in the earlier Tests. This ensured Brian being given the captaincy the following summer – a joint tour by India and Pakistan. He could hardly have done better, winning all three against India and winning two with one draw against Pakistan.

By mid-August he was a certainty to take the MCC side to the West Indies in the winter, but there then came what proved to be a watershed in his career. Yorkshire played Warwickshire at Edgbaston in mid-August, and only saved the game by some dubious delaying tactics. Warwickshire had to make 142 to win in a hundred minutes. For the first eighty-five minutes Yorkshire bowled 22 overs, a slow over-rate of about 15 per hour, but the last fifteen minutes were even worse. There was some drizzle, during which Yorkshire left the pitch to the batsmen and umpires. There were also various other time-wasting ploys so that only *two* overs were bowled, leaving Warwickshire nine runs short of victory.

25 Brian Close

It was blatant gamesmanship of the worst kind and even York-shire writers like Bill Bowes and Jim Kilburn deprecated it. Brian was censored on all sides and was summoned to Lord's, where the selectors were meeting to select the captain for the MCC tour of the West Indies. It had appeared to be a formality, with Brian having such a successful summer against India and Pakistan. There was still the Oval Test to come, for which of course he had already been appointed captain, but the selectors were worried by the volatile situation in the West Indies and how their crowds would react if similar gamesmanship was employed out there in the Tests. They asked Brian to give his assurance that he would never employ such tactics on the tour of West Indies. As I've said earlier on, Brian was obstinate and also honest, and felt he could not give this assurance. He knew that his career as England captain was at stake, but he also knew that in similar circumstances in order to save a game he would not hesitate to waste time. So in spite of entreaties from his friends, and advisers like Brian Sellers, he refused to give the guarantee the selectors required. Colin Cowdrey was appointed captain for the tour in his place. One cannot help admiring Brian's honesty. He could so easily have said – with his fingers crossed – that he would comply with the selectors' wishes.

It was all a great pity because from 1963 to 1970 Close proved a fine captain for Yorkshire. He was as tough as you make them and a strong disciplinarian. He wouldn't tolerate non-triers and demanded high standards both on and off the field. He left Yorkshire for Somerset in 1971, where he continued his reign of tough captaincy, always leading from the front. He even showed that he could handle a promising young player called Ian Botham.

His departure from Yorkshire was acrimonious and sudden. He had led them successfully to four Championships in seven years, plus winning one Gillette Cup. This was ironic, as it was because of his openly stated dislike and contempt for the one-day game that Yorkshire summarily sacked him.

One quite good story is told about when he captained Derrick Robins's eleven in South Africa in 1974–5. On one occasion, to his disgust, they were soundly beaten after he had declared. He locked the dressing-room door and berated his team for all the inefficient things they had done wrong. After about half an hour of cataloguing the reasons for their defeat, he asked if anyone could think of any other reason why they had lost. One member of the team was Lancashire wicket-keeper John Lyon. He was a shy and reserved person who had hardly spoken a word to anyone on the tour, but he plucked up courage, held up his hand and said: 'Yes, skipper. You declared too bloody early!'

As a player Brian never fulfilled his early promise. In 1949 at the age of eighteen he was the youngest person ever to do the double, he was the youngest player ever to gain a Yorkshire cap, and the youngest ever to represent England, which he did in the third Test against New Zealand at Old Trafford. He then went to Australia with Freddie Brown in 1950–1. He made 108 in the first match, but after that he had a miserable tour. He made 0 and 1 in the only Test in which he played, and found himself left out in the cold by the other more elderly members of the team.

He was tall and strong, had a good technique and was a hard

hitter of the ball, but although in his twenty-nine seasons he made nearly 35,000 runs, one feels that he should have made more. His close fielding is legendary, and with a high action he was a more than useful off-spinner, taking over 1,100 wickets. But somehow he did not become the really great all-rounder which, with his talents and character, he should have been.

He gained the reputation of being the fastest (and most dangerous) driver on the first-class circuit and he 'enjoyed' quite a few prangs. He was also a good footballer and played for Leeds United, Arsenal and Bradford City. On top of all this he was, and still is, a more than average golfer with the remarkable ability to play equally well either left- or right-handed. This led to the following story about him. Someone once asked him how he decided which way round he would play. 'Oh,' he said, 'when I wake up in the morning if my wife is lying on her right side I play right-handed. If she's on her left I play left-handed.' 'But what do you do if when you wake she is lying on her back?' He quickly replied: 'I ring up the golf club to say that I shall be an hour late!'

J. J. Warr

He wasn't the best fast-medium bowler who ever played for England, but he was certainly the funniest. For many years now – possibly since the death of Lord Birkett in 1962 – he has been the best after-dinner speaker in London. Many broadcasters like myself do a lot of after-dinner speaking, but most of us have an 'act'. In other words we give basically the same speech on all occasions, with minor adjustments. It's like the old music-hall comics, who used the same material year after year as they travelled from theatre to theatre all round the country (television has killed all that, of course). J.J. – as he is always called – is a bit different, however. He matches and changes his material for each dinner, using a basic framework on which to put his topical jokes and stories. His timing is impeccable, he is brief and very witty. He tells a good story about almost anyone, including himself, but is always kind, never cruel.

His witty remarks are legion and quoted far and wide. One of his most famous was when he turned up at the church for Bill Edrich's fourth wedding. When asked by the usher which side of the aisle to put him: 'Bride or bridegroom?' J.J. promptly replied: 'Season ticket.' In the 1950–1 tour of Australia he took 1 for 281 in the only two Tests in which he played, and someone asked him (rather stupidly) how he felt. J.J. referred him immediately to Hymn No. 281: 'Art thou weary, art thou languid . . .' I always quote two lines from Hymn No. 4 to him: 'There comes the promised time when War(r) shall be no more.'

26 J. J. Warr

He and I once took part about twenty years ago in a radio programme presented by Kenneth Horne. Kenneth used to visit and interview people in their houses, and invite them to ask a neighbour in just to talk, or if possible to do a turn. At that time I lived at 1a Cavendish Avenue, and J.J. at No. 14. So I asked him to do a cross-talk act with me consisting of all the old jokes. We rehearsed and rehearsed and at least *we* used to laugh at it. There were the usual dog jokes: 'I call my dog Carpenter.' 'Why?' 'Because he always does odd jobs about the house – you should see him make a bolt for the door.' Or: 'The invisible man is outside.' 'Well, tell him I can't see him today.' And so it went on, and Kenneth Horne was kind enough to laugh, though he must have heard the old jokes before.

Just one more story about J.J. before we talk about his cricket. We were televising at Lord's one day and J.J. was sitting in the grandstand with his fiancée, Valerie. They were looking so close and friendly that we put the camera on to them and said, 'There you are – "Warr and Piece" '.

What sort of cricketer was he? He was tall and strongly built and played for some years for Cambridge as a fastish bowler who didn't 'do' a great deal, but he was always at his best at Lord's and collected 16 wickets in the four University matches. He played all this time as an amateur for Middlesex and began to develop a dangerous out-swinger, so that in all first-class matches he finished with 956 wickets, taking 100 wickets in a season twice. He was not a great batsman, perhaps a bit rustic, but somehow collected nearly 4,000 runs at an average of 11.45, which was about par for his form.

Whilst still at Cambridge he was surprisingly chosen for Freddie Brown's MCC tour of Australia. In truth he was a bit out of his depth, and although he enjoyed himself as a tourist, on the field he was not too happy. As so many first-time visitors to Australia do, he found the bright light difficult and dropped a few catches. The side was not strong in bowling and he found himself selected for two Test matches at Sydney and Adelaide, where in those days both pitches were a batsman's paradise. As *Wisden* says, 'From first to last he tried hard and cheerfully,' but in the two Tests took only 1 wicket for 281. It was really asking too much of an inexperienced undergraduate and at Sydney, because of an injury to Trevor Bailey, he had to share the bowling with Bedser (43 overs), Brown (44) and himself with an analysis of 36–4–142–0. So he only took 1 wicket in his short Test career but, nothing daunted, said to Fred Trueman recently: 'Do you know, Fred, you and I have taken 308 Test wickets between us!'

On his return he continued to play for Middlesex, was captain for three years, and in 1960 led them to third place in the Championship table. He was firm but always cheerful, and once when Middlesex had to follow on after a poor batting performance he told them in the dressing-room: 'Same order, different batting.'

In 1956 he had some revenge for the drubbing which he had received in Australia. When the Gentlemen of England played the Australians at Lord's, he took 4 for 46 with some excellent fast bowling. He was even brave enough to bowl a bouncer at Keith Miller, which hit Keith on the forehead just over the eye. He somehow also managed to hit his wicket, so J.J. got his wicket and could boast that he had given the great Miller a black eye. Luckily for J.J. the match was rained off, so he did not have to go in to bat against Keith. If he had, it might have been 'Two lovely black eyes'.

Since he retired from first-class cricket in 1960 J.J. rose to the top in the Discount Market, and could be seen visiting banks wearing a top hat. He has always been keen on racing, and in addition to being a steward at places like Windsor and Goodwood, he was elected a member of the Jockey Club in 1977. Now, no longer in the City, he has been appointed chairman of The Racecourse Authority.

He has served on various committees at Lord's, has been the representative of Australia on the International Cricket Conference, and crowned his career when Colin Cowdrey selected him to succeed him as president of MCC in 1987–8. So he has his serious side and has many sensible ideas about what is wrong – and right – with modern cricket. You will be a lucky person if you ever attend a dinner where the toast-master announces: 'My Lord's, ladies and gentlemen. Pray silence for Mr John Warr.'

Tom Graveney

I was lucky enough to see Cyril Walters play. He was the most graceful of batsmen and I would gladly have settled for him, until I saw the elegance and grace of Tom Graveney. Old cricketers have also written and spoken of the two Palairet Brothers, L. C. H. and R. C. N., who played for Somerset in the 1890s. They were both famous for their graceful style, but anyone who saw Tom Graveney will have seen at least their equal. From the moment he glided out to the wicket, tugging at the protruding peak of his cap, he looked all that a cricketer should be. Immaculately turned out in spotless white, he had a certain quality which attracted attention. Once at the crease, every movement was of graceful elegance, not just with his attacking strokes but also in defence. Even when he was not scoring runs, he was never boring. Basically a front-foot player, he drove beautifully through the off-side and also amassed many runs by steering the ball through empty spaces between square leg and mid-on. He stroked the ball rather than hit it and was a remarkably consistent scorer. His career spanned the years from 1948 to 1972, and during that time he scored more runs than any post-war first-class cricketer – with one exception, Geoff Boycott. Geoff passed him in his final season in 1986, scoring 48,426 runs against Tom's 47,793. Tom also made 122 hundreds, scored 2,000 runs seven times, and 1,000 twenty times. That makes him sound like a run-making machine, but he was not just that. He was a batsman who compelled you to watch and enjoy the manner of his batting.

27 Tom Graveney

Whereas the cricket public loved him, he was not always so popular with the selectors when it came to playing for England. His Test appearances came in fits and starts. When he was not chosen the reason given was that he was not a grafter. True enough, his elegant stroke-play meant that he sometimes took a risk and got out, and so compared unfavourably with the dour, unattractive defensive techniques employed by some of the top Test scorers. But even so, in 79 Tests he scored 4,882 runs at an average of 44.38 – a useful man to have in your side!

Funnily enough, he scored far more runs against the West Indies than against Australia, off whose attack he only made one hundred – in the fifth Test at Sydney in 1955, when the rubber had been won.

Compare that with his amazing form against the West Indies. In the 1957 series in England he made 258 and 164 against them. Then there was his sensational return when he was recalled at the age of forty to play in the second Test at Lord's. He made 96 and 30 not out, followed by 109, 32, 8, 19 and 165 run out! Two years later at Port of Spain he played a beautiful innings of 118 in the first Test of Colin Cowdrey's tour. So his front-foot style proved highly successful against fast bowlers, as well as against spinners like Sobers and Gibbs.

His career did not run entirely smoothly. Like so many good cricketers he was born in the north-east at Riding Mill, Northumberland, but he went to Bristol Grammar School and played for Gloucestershire from 1948 to 1960, captaining them in 1959 and 1960. There was then a little 'local difficulty' when an amateur, Tom Pugh, was appointed captain in his place.

After a year's break for qualification in 1961, he went to Worcestershire, where he was also captain for three years. It was during his time there that he became an even more accomplished batsman, and his final ten years were the most successful of his career.

As if his Test career had not been interrupted by enough strange selectional decisions, it was to end in an even stranger way in 1969. He played in the first Test against West Indies at Old Trafford and played his usual stylish innings, this time 75. He had, however, promised an organiser of one of his benefit matches to play in a match at Luton during the Sunday of the Old Trafford Test. There was some misunderstanding between him and Alec Bedser, chairman of the selectors. Tom thought he had made it plain that if he were selected to play in the Test, he would have to honour his promise to play at Luton. Anyway, as a result he was dropped and never played for England again.

When he retired in 1970 he played a few more first-class matches in Queensland, where he was player-coach for two years. He then ran a highly successful pub near Cheltenham race-course. Since he gave that up he has become as stylish in his television or radio summaries as he ever was with his batting.

There are two facts about Tom which are not always known by cricketer followers. First, he captained England once – in the fourth Test against Australia at Headingley in 1968 as a result of an injury to Colin Cowdrey. He did not win the match, which was drawn, but he enjoyed the experience. And by coincidence the Australian captain was Barry Jarman, also captaining for the first and only time because of an injury to *his* captain, Bill Lawry.

The other fact not generally known is that in the 1955 Test against South Africa at Old Trafford he actually kept wicket for England. He modestly says that he made 0 and 1 in the match and dropped quite a few catches at slip, so when Godfrey Evans broke his right-hand little finger, Tom was 'chosen' to deputise for him. There were no volunteers for the job, and for a very good reason. Frank Tyson – just back from his triumphant tour of Australia with Len Hutton (he took 28 wickets in the series) – was bowling at his fastest, and everyone at the time said that for two years or so he was the fastest bowler anyone had ever seen. Tom stood halfway back to the boundary and prepared apprehensively to take the first express. It was down the leg side. Tom stretched out to try to take it, and the ball broke *his* little finger. It still looks the worse for wear.

And a final story which Tom tells against himself. He was once sweeping the leaves outside the gate of his house in Winchcombe. Two boys rode by on their bicycles and one shouted to the other: 'Tom Graveney lives there.' 'Which house?' asked his friend. 'Oh, the one where the old man is sweeping up the leaves.'

Peter May

When I became a TV commentator in 1946 I was introduced to the world of first-class cricket. I had been an avid follower from a distance for over twenty-five years, but now I was to meet and work with the first-class players themselves. After six years of war without the county championship there was plenty to talk about, but in most conversations a new name kept on cropping up. There was talk about a new Hutton or Compton, still only seventeen years old but said by George Geary to be the best young batsman he had ever seen. The boy was Peter May, who was still at Charterhouse, where George was the highly respected and much loved coach. Peter had got into the first eleven there when only fourteen years old, and, what's more, headed the batting averages at the end of the summer. Three years later he made a brilliant 146 at Lord's, playing for the Public Schools against the Combined Services.

In 1948 he began his National Service in the Royal Navy as Writer May and made his first-class début for Combined Services. By 1950 he was up at Cambridge, where he gained a blue for the next three years. In the same year, after the university match, he began the first of his fourteen seasons with Surrey. One interesting fact which often traps contestants in sports quizzes: 'Peter May was captain of Cambridge. In what year did he captain them in the University match at Lord's?' The answer is that he never did. He was not captain at cricket but at soccer.

28 Peter May

He played in his first Test match in 1951 at Headingley against South Africa, and inevitably he scored a hundred (138). Alas, I was not there to see it. At that time there was no Holme Moss transmitter, so BBC TV was still unable to cover matches at Old Trafford or Headingley. Peter wasn't so successful in his first encounters with the Australians in 1953. When Surrey played them at the Oval Peter was deliberately subjected to some short fast bowling from Lindwall, Davidson and Archer. They were determined to eliminate this up-and-coming star, and succeeded. He made 0 and 1, and when selected for the first Test he only made 9. He was then dropped until the final Ashes-winning Test at the Oval, where he played two vital innings of 39 and 37. It was tough-going, but from then on he played in the next 54 Tests until the first of his back operations in

July 1959. His highest Test score – and perhaps his most significant innings – was his 285 not out against the West Indies in England's second innings in the first Test at Edgbaston in 1957. His stand of 411 with Cowdrey not only saved the match for England but finally released England from the grip of Ramadhin, who, after bowling 98 overs in the innings and taking 2 for 179, was never again a real threat to England.

How good a batsman was Peter, and did he live up to his early reputation as a future Hutton or Compton? I believe that he is still the outstanding English batsman who started playing *after* the war. There are obviously a few contenders for this title – people like Cowdrey, Graveney and Boycott – but somehow Peter just topped them all. He was technically perfect in both defence and attack. He played very straight and was equally good on the back or front foot. He had every stroke, but his speciality was the perfect on-drive, not the easiest stroke to play, as inevitably the batsman has to play slightly across the line of the ball. He was a stronger and more forceful batsman than Cowdrey, without perhaps the latter's delicate timing. He may not have been as graceful as Graveney, but certainly matched Boycott for temperament, determination and love of making runs.

Not only in his technique, but also in his bearing and appearance, he was an ideal example for young players to follow. He was always immaculately turned out – shirt, flannels, pads and boots all spotlessly white. He usually batted without a cap, and all through his career had a boyish look. He was a very safe catcher and fielder, though for a soccer blue he was not noticeably fast over the ground.

He captained England forty-one times and Surrey from 1957 to 1962, and Richie Benaud reckons that he was the best England captain he played against. He absorbed a lot of his cricket knowledge from Len Hutton and played the game as hard as Len had out in the middle, but off the field he appeared shy, modest and sensitive. Although friendly and co-operative, he was not an easy person to interview. He gave little away and parried questions about tactics or what had happened on the field, usually saying that the boys had tried hard and done their best. He also held the strange belief that it was not necessary for him to tell a Test batsman what to do. He said that anyone selected should know how to react to the state of the game, and did not have to be told to score more quickly or to go on the defensive.

It was a sad day for England when he retired from Test cricket in 1961. He had been captain for six years between 1955 and 1961, and had been forced to leave the West Indies tour in 1960 due to trouble in the lower part of his back. He had previously had an operation which went wrong, and batted in great pain for the first three Tests. It meant that he missed the 1960 Test series against South Africa, but he returned in 1961 against Australia, playing in the last four Tests, three of them as captain. And that was it. He had a promising career in the City with a large insurance firm, and over the years he had become tired of criticism from the press. Strangely, they were often critical of him, especially on the 1958–9 tour of Australia, when England lost four of the Tests, although their team had been heralded as the most powerful ever to leave England.

They were, however, handicapped by a succession of injuries to vital players, and the appearance of two new Australian fast bowlers, Meckiff and Rorke. The former's action was suspect, to say the least, and in the end he was no-balled out of Test cricket. Rorke had an enormous drag and would deliver the ball from something like eighteen yards from the batsman. Cowdrey once said that he didn't dare to play forward, in case he hit him. So from a playing point of view the tour was an unhappy one for May, but even worse for him was the way the press attacked him for having his fiancée with him for part of the tour. She was Harold Gilligan's daughter, Virginia, whom Peter subsequently married. As I've said, he was sensitive and he never really forgave the press.

Since becoming a highly successful businessman, Peter has put a lot back into cricket, both with Surrey and as chairman of the selectors from 1982 to 1988. Once again he had to put up with a lot of flak over Test selections. Obviously the selectors *have* made mistakes, but if one is honest one has to admit that there is not all that much talent from which to select. Peter gave as good as he got to his critics, and although not able to watch as much cricket as he should, he seemed to enjoy the challenge. When he does get any spare time at home he devotes his time to driving a horse box to the various events in which his four 'horsey' daughters take part, but I think he would rather face Lindwall or Miller at their best than get on a horse himself!

Brian Statham

When asked to give the perfect example of what a cricket professional should be, I always choose Brian Statham – or George as he was known to his friends. There are and have been many others who have come near his standard, but he is always top of my list.

29 Brian Statham

He was quiet, modest, loyal, completely free from temperament and a great trier who never gave up. It all sounds too good to be true, but it is. And you can add to all that a lovely dry wit, delivered with a slow smile and a slow Lancashire drawl.

Physically he was wiry, lean, loose-limbed and apparently double-jointed. He had a smooth run-up and a fine action, with his arm so high that it brushed his right ear. He was really fast and he obtained his 252 Test wickets by his accuracy with length and line. He invariably bowled *at* the stumps, on the principle that if the batsman missed the ball, then he was certain to bowl him. He didn't swing the ball in the air but moved it either way off the pitch, and in his Test career proved a magnificent foil to Trueman and Tyson. I suppose that in a sense he was always the junior partner, frustrating the batsmen from the other end. What's more, if there was an uphill slope and a headwind he would be the one chosen to run up it and bowl into it.

Arthur Gilligan told me a story which he swore was true. In a Test match at Perth, Statham had a long spell bowling into the 'Freemantle Doctor' – a stiff breeze which blows up in the middle of the day off the nearby Swan river. At close of play a lady came up to Arthur Gilligan and said: 'Mr Gilligan, would you please give these tablets to Brian Statham.' 'Yes, of course I will. But why?' replied Arthur. 'Oh,' she said, 'I heard you say in your commentary that Statham was suffering from the wind.'

Statham was nicknamed 'the greyhound' or 'whippet' because of his speed in the field. He usually fielded down at long leg or third man, and swooped on the ball and threw with a strong arm into the gloves of the wicket-keeper. He was a left-handed bat and could keep his end up in a crisis. He usually batted at number eleven for England, but occasionally – to his delight – was promoted to number ten or even nine. And once – though please don't spread it around in Yorkshire – he went in *above* Freddie Trueman in the Lord's Test against South Africa in 1955.

I hope I haven't made 'George' sound too perfect, but in addition to what I have already said he was a wonderful tourer, always giving of his best both on and off the field. If journeys or hotels were bad or disorganised – and they often are on tour – he took it all calmly without moaning. And on the field if he missed the stumps by inches, or had an appeal turned down, there were no histrionics. He just got on with the job of trying to get batsmen out.

Just one last thing. He is the only bowler I know who after a long hot day in the field would take off his boots and socks and then talk to his feet – apologising for the way he had treated them!

Richie Benaud

Who is the nattiest-dressed cricket commentator? Who has the neatest coiffure? Who captained Australia in six series, winning five, and drawing one? Who took more Test wickets than any other Australian spinner? Who was the first Test cricketer to make 2,000 runs and take 200 Test wickets? I am sure your buzzers went after the first question, without need of further clues. Yes of course, it's Richie Benaud, who organises every minute of his life more efficiently than anyone I know, helped, I hasten to add by his wife Daphne, or Daphers as we call her.

I first met Richie during the 1953 Australian tour of England, when, to be honest, he was not a great success. He played in three Tests, took 2 wickets for 174, and made 15 runs in five innings, but he finished the tour with a flourish and a warning of things to come. Against T. N. Pearce's eleven at Scarborough he made 135 in 110 minutes, hitting eleven sixes and nine fours, his first hundred in England. He was always a fine driver of the ball, and as his career developed he became a complete stroke-player, which made him into a genuine Test all-rounder.

It was as a leg-spin bowler that he really made his mark, however. He had a fine high action which, especially on overseas pitches in Australia, South Africa and the West Indies, enabled him to get bounce into his deliveries. He was a great one for practising and spent hours in the nets perfecting his mixture of leg-breaks, googlies, top-spinners and flippers. He was not afraid to bowl the latter, which he picked up from Bruce Dooland, and took quite a number of his 248 Test wickets with it. He described it to me as a ball held in the tips of the first and third fingers of the right hand. It is squeezed or flipped out of the hand from underneath the wrist – rather like flipping a cherry stone. The object is to bowl it just on or outside the off-strump. It hurries from the pitch, usually straight but sometimes from off to leg. It is a surprise ball which often traps a batsman who has played back.

Richie was not a big spinner of the ball, but he was always accurate and with his flight, line and bounce was difficult to score off. English pitches did not suit him, but in spite of a bad shoulder he did win the fourth Test for Australia at Old Trafford in 1961 by bowling his leg-breaks round the wicket into the rough outside the leg-stump. His analysis is worth noting – superb figures for a slow bowler: 32–11–70–6.

30 Richie Benaud

The fact that he was a brilliant close-fielder, especially in the gully, made him the complete all-rounder, but it was as a captain that he probably did most for Australia. He was certainly the best post-war captain whom I saw. He had everything a captain needs. He was a natural leader who inspired his teams to play above themselves. He was a motivator and he animated and encouraged them both on and off the field, where he placed great importance on a happy dressing-room. On the field I'm afraid he was really the starter of the hugging and kissing which goes on so much today. I asked him about it once and he said he was prepared to do anything if it helped to take wickets. Tony Lock carried on the habit when he came to captain Leicestershire – so much so that Maurice Hallam normally an excellent fielder, once dropped two catches running down at long leg. When asked why he hadn't caught them, he is said to have replied: 'What, and be kissed by Tony Lock. Not bloody likely!'

Richie was an amazingly good reader of a game, and was quick to spot and memorise an opponent's weakness. He tried to be a positive captain and would attack whenever he could, but he was not prepared to 'play ball' unless the other side responded. A perfect example of this was the fifth Test at Sydney in 1963 against Ted Dexter's side. The series was level, and a thoroughly dull game followed England's desperately slow first innings of 321.

Off the field Richie was the best PRO of any captain I have seen. At the end of each day, however hot and tired, he would meet the press, TV and radio, and answer questions about the day's play. He was not afraid to be candid but was perfectly fair in his assessment of the day's events. It was still *his* opinion as Australian captain, however, and as a result the English newspapers, unintentionally no doubt, would often put over Australia's view of the match.

He took as much trouble to learn to commentate as he did to learn to bowl. When on tour here in 1956 and 1961 he took a great interest in our TV coverage, and managed to engineer a crash course for himself at the end of the 1961 tour. When still captain of Australia he joined TMS for radio commentary on the South African Tests in England in 1960. He soon picked up the tricks of the trade and joined BBC TV when he retired from Test cricket in February 1964. People often ask me why we have to have an Australian on BBC. The answer is simply that he is the best. He has tremendous knowledge of the tactics and techniques of the game, is quick-witted and knows when to talk or not to talk. He is also a very good summariser at the end of the day's play. He is fluent, knowledgeable, unflappable and remembers all the details of the play. What more can a producer ask for?

He also has a dry sense of humour and was great fun to work with in the box. Peter West, he and I always used to call the value of a run as soon as the ball left the bat. Richie was a pretty good judge and normally got it right. I wasn't so good, but if I said 'that's 4 all the way' and only 3 runs were scored I would either blame the slowness of the outfield or praise the speed and skill of the fielder.

I cannot end without explaining why Richie was indirectly responsible for my giving up wicket-keeping. One Sunday he and I were playing in a charity match at the Dragons School at Oxford. I was keeping wicket and he was bowling his googlies, top-spinners, flippers and leg-breaks. I read them all perfectly well, but most of them went for 4 byes. When the last man came in Richie bowled him a terrific leg-break. The man went down the pitch, and missed the ball by miles. It came into my gloves, and with all my old speed – so I thought – I whipped off the bails and appealed. The umpire raised his finger and there was I, an ordinary club cricketer, stumping someone off the Australian captain. No wonder I was looking pleased as I walked off. The bursar of the school confirmed my high opinion of my skill by coming up and saying: 'Jolly well stumped.' He then unfortunately went on to say: 'And I'd like to congratulate you on the sporting way you tried to give him time to get back.' I then realised that it was time for me to retire and hang up my gloves. I never kept wicket again.

In his spare time – which is very scarce – Richie is a dedicated golfer and thinks nothing, during a Test match, of getting up at five o'clock to play a game of golf before going off for a day's commentary. He is also a great connoisseur of food and wine, and at the end of a season he and Daphers sometimes go off for a gastronomic holiday in France. It may seem as if I have eulogised Richie too much, but he is an exceptional person, combining, as he does, his knowledge and experience of Test cricket with the ability to put it over on television.

Fred Trueman

I have lost count of the number of times that people have said to me: 'Where are the characters in first-class cricket today?' And they usually add: 'As there used to be, with people like Freddie Trueman.' His name always seems to be the one to crop up, and he certainly was – and still is – a remarkable character. Larger than life, belligerent, with a quick temper usually matched with a shaft of Rabelaisian wit. Intensely patriotic and strongly to the right in his politics and opinions.

He tells a story as well as anyone I have ever heard. They are usually blue and laced with expletives, but given the right audience they are very funny, and when he retired from first-class cricket he did a round of the clubs as a stand-up comic. Nowadays he's probably 'the most in demand' of all after-dinner speakers. With his cigar and excellent timing he can keep going for well over an hour. He gets over the difficulty of speaking to a mixed audience by saying: 'If any of you ladies want to know what a stag night is then listen to me' – and then proceeds to give his normal act! He enjoys telling stories and one-liners and usually has a fresh one when he arrives at the commentary box each morning – like the time he asked me if I knew about the flasher who had decided to retire. When I obediently said no, Fred said: 'Well, he's decided to stick it out for another year.'

31 Fred Trueman

He was a great entertainer and played to the crowds with his ferocious gestures and expressions. He was tough and physically strong and kept going far longer than the modern fast bowlers. He not only gave his all for England, but also in ordinary county games for Yorkshire, and he regularly took 100 wickets a year. I cannot remember him losing his Test place through injury or strains. He acquired the reputation of being temperamental and difficult to handle, and the press always pictured him as a 'naughty boy', who drank large quantities of beer and made unacceptable remarks to officials or dignitaries on tour. Certainly, one or two captains preferred not to take him on tour, and he is never tired of saying that had he gone on the tours to Australia in 1954–5, and South

Africa in 1956–7 and 1964–5, he might well have taken 400 Test wickets. In fact he was not a beer drinker, and on tour I always found him a bit of a loner. As with Winston Churchill many apocryphal stories are told about him – such as when he was meant to have said to a West Indian official at a dinner, 'Pass the salt, Gunga Din' – but here are two which I believe to be true.

When he came in to bat at number ten in a Test against the West Indies in 1954, Jeff Stollmeyer crowded him with four short legs, a silly point, close gully, and two slips. All the fielders were surrounding the stumps, with Fred glowering in the middle of them. 'If you bring any of these b——s in any closer, I'll appeal against the flippin' light,' he said to Jeff.

The other story Norman Yardley has assured me is true. In the late forties, when Norman first captained Yorkshire, they used to play pre-season practice matches against various club sides. Once they were playing the Yorkshire Gentlemen at Escrick, just outside York. Fred was still in his teens and bowled very fast with a number of vicious bouncers. He knocked out four of the Yorkshire Gentlemen, who were carted off to hospital. They were then 20-something for 6, when a distinguished-looking figure emerged from the pavilion, with I. Zingari cap, white bristling military moustache and silk shirt buttoned up at the wrists. Norman went across to Fred and said: 'This is Brigadier So and So. He's a patron of the club and does a lot for us. Please treat him gently.' So Fred approached the apprehensive-looking Brigadier and said: 'It's all right, Brigadier. No need to worry. I'll give you one to get off the mark.' The Brigadier's face relaxed, only to freeze with horror as Fred went on: 'Ay,' he said, 'and with second I'll pin you against flippin' sight screen.'

Incidentally, this habit of giving one to a batsman doesn't always work out. Colin Ingleby-Mackenzie told me of a charity match in which Hampshire played Lord Porchester's eleven at Highclere. 'Butch' White, the fast bowler, had restrained himself admirably, bowling well-pitched-up military medium at all the club batsmen. When Lord Porchester himself came in, Colin went up to Butch and said, 'Give him one, Butch,' then walked away without seeing what Butch was doing. Butch's eyes had gleamed at the welcome instruction from his skipper, and he hurriedly paced out his usual thirty yards' run. Before Colin could stop him he came charging in at full speed and bowled a terrifying bouncer which nearly removed

Porchy's head. I *believe* the fixture was renewed the next year, but I'm not too sure!

Anyway, back to Fred the player. He was certainly one of the great Test bowlers of all time, and not just because he was the first one to take 300 Test wickets. He did this in the fifth Test at the Oval in 1964 against Australia. He knew he had taken 299, and when Ted Dexter appeared to be hesitating as to whom to put on to bowl Fred seized the ball and measured out his run. I was lucky to be commentating on TV at the time and saw Colin Cowdrey catch Neil Hawke – an old friend of Fred's – at first slip. There were emotional scenes of congratulations and I remember that Colin actually hugged Fred – though I don't think he went so far as to kiss him.

He was genuinely fast and for years was much feared on the county circuit and also by some batsmen in Test cricket, especially by the Indians in his Test début against them in 1952. Later he learnt from Ray Lindwall the importance of varying his deliveries in pace, and not bowling every ball flat out. He had a long curving run, with his ample bottom acting as a thrust to his slightly bowed legs. He bowled from very close to the stumps with a classical swivel body action, left arm high and his eyes looking over his left shoulder. As a result his main ball, which got him so many of his wickets, was the out-swinger, which swung away late. In Tests he could and did bowl bouncers, but used them sensibly as a warning and deterrent to the batsmen. He says today that he never wilfully tried to hit a batsman, only to frighten him. I believe him, but he would not deny that *on* the field he hated batsmen, and if he had been hit or snicked for a four, he would walk back to his mark muttering probably unmentionable words to himself. Sir Robert Menzies once speculated in a speech exactly what it was that Fred did say, and came to the conclusion that he must be reciting Greek Iambics!

As a batsman Fred enjoyed having a crack, and with his great strength and a mighty swing hit the ball for many a six, usually in the region of mid-wicket and long-on. When necessary he had a perfectly sound defence and could play a responsible innings which enabled him to make three first-class hundreds.

He was a fine fielder at short leg, especially leg-slip, where with his cap at a jaunty angle, he picked up many spectacular catches. He also had a good arm from the deep, and varied it sometimes by throwing left-handed.

He tells a delightful story of his last match for the Combined Services, for whom he played when doing his national service in the RAF. The match took place the day after the final Test at the Oval in 1953, where in his first Test against Australia his four wickets helped England to regain the Ashes after nineteen years.

When the Combined Services took the field, as an England bowler he naturally expected to be put on first with the new ball. But the naval lieutenant-commander who captained his side thought differently, and threw the ball to a rather portly army captain. Fred was surprised and, muttering to himself, automatically went to leg-slip where he had been fielding for England in the recent Test. 'What are you doing there, Trueman?' asked the lieutenant-commander. 'Go down to long leg. Major Parnaby always fields at leg-slip and has done so for many years.' So a disgusted Trueman went off to long leg swearing loudly, this time not to himself. He was slightly cheered up when the very first ball went straight through Major Parnaby's hands at leg-slip, and Fred made little effort to save it going for four. At the end of the over he got a rocket from the lieutenant-commander for his behaviour. 'You'll never play again for the Combined Services, Trueman.' 'You're too dead right I won't,' replied Fred. 'I come out of the RAF tomorrow!'

Fred has always been sensitive about the fact that he has never been honoured for his services to cricket. He is apt to reel off a list of far inferior players who have received OBEs or MBEs, and he also used to quote Peter May, who like himself had been overlooked. This was really surprising considering that Peter captained England forty-one times and led a blameless life on and off the field – a perfect example of how a cricketer should behave. Anyway, eventually he was awarded the CBE to join others like Cowdrey, Compton and Evans.

What I believe normally happens is that when the Prime Minister's office decide to offer sportsmen an award, before asking them they have a final check with the governing body of his or her particular sport. The story is that way back in the sixties Harold Wilson, then Prime Minister, decided to give 'the greatest living Yorkshireman' a knighthood. The usual check was made with MCC, who are said to have replied that they thought that a knighthood was perhaps a little too much, and suggested that Fred should be given another honour instead.

So without their approval Fred lost his knighthood, and, sadly, the alternative honour seems to have been forgotten ever since. And here we are in 1989, and he is still without anything after his name. After all, Len Hutton may have been the first professional captain appointed in England, but Fred was also the first bowler ever to take 300 Test wickets.

Anyway, it has always – and I think rightly – rankled with Fred, and unfortunately a few years ago I put my foot in it. I had just had one of my books published and asked my publishers to send copies to everyone on 'Test Match Special'. I signed the copies with the nicknames of the recipients: the Boil, the Alderman, the Bearded Wonder, etc. At that time I used to call Fred jokingly (!) Sir Frederick, which he accepted with a wry smile. So in his book I put: 'To Sir Frederick, with many memories of happy days on "TMS".'

I sent all the books back to my publishers for them to send and thought no more about it. However, one morning Fred was at home having breakfast when the postman ran up the path shouting: 'You've got it, Fred. You've got it at last.' Fred came to the door and took the parcel, which was addressed to *Sir* Frederick Trueman. He looked at it with disgust and cursed me: 'What's this —— Johnners up to now!' What neither he nor I knew until he told me about it was that the girl in the publishers' office, seeing my inscription in the front of the book, had thought that Fred really was a knight, and had addressed it accordingly. I no longer call him Sir Frederick – it might not be wise!

Since he retired Fred has been a much valued member of our 'Test Match Special' commentary team. His earthy wit enlivens the dullest day, and his forthright comments on modern cricket evoke varying reactions. Some people agree with him heartily that things are not what they were. Others think he goes on a bit. But whatever he does, he is never boring and gets a reaction from the listeners. His favourite expression when some tactics puzzle him is: 'I don't know what's going off, out there.'

On one occasion he was saying what a unique game cricket was, because everything was done sideways. 'Remember,' he said to the listeners, 'it's a sideways-on game. Everything should be done sideways – the batsman's stance, the bowler's action, the fielder's throwing and so on.' A few days later he received a letter which went something like this:

Dear Mr Trueman,
I heard what you said about cricket being a
sideways game. I tried it without success the other
day. In the first over I was hit twice on my left
temple, twice on the left cheek of my bottom, and
the other two balls each went for 4 byes. You see,
I am a wicket-keeper! I don't think your theory
works!

He and I are very different people, but we have always got on
famously and pull each other's legs whenever we can. He usually
produces a difficult cricket question, whilst I ask him one of the
many riddles which our young listeners send in for me to try out
on him. It's been a happy time in the box, even with Fred's pipe
and cigars. We always call them his Adam and Eve cigars – when
he's 'ad em, we 'eave. What a character, and what a great bowler!

Hanif Mohammad and Sunil Gavaskar:

the two 'Little Masters'

No book such as this would be complete without a tribute to the
two greatest batsmen from India and Pakistan. They were both
small (Hanif five feet four and Gavaskar five feet four and three-
quarters). They both enjoyed playing long innings and accumulating
runs. Their techniques were remarkably similar and a model for
any schoolboy. They both had the virtues of dedication, patience
and tremendous powers of concentration. They were both extremely
courteous, friendly and polite, and it was a real pleasure to have
them both up in the commentary box during the summer of 1987.

Hanif Mohammad was one of four brothers, all of whom played
Test cricket for Pakistan. They were Wazir, Hanif, Mushtaq and
Sadiq, born in that order. Now to add to them there is Hanif's son,
Shoaib. When Hanif played in his last Test at Karachi against New
Zealand in 1969, it was his brother Sadiq's first Test. This meant
that three brothers played for their country in a Test for the first

and only time since the Graces W. G., E. M. and G. F. played for England at the Oval in the first Test in this country against Australia in 1880. There was another occasion when three Hearnes played in a Test between England and South Africa at Cape Town in 1892, but only two, J. T. and A., played for England. Frank, who had already played twice for England, this time represented South Africa.

Hanif has black curly hair and always seemed to bat bare-headed. He *could* play all the strokes but seldom did, preferring to soldier on and let the runs come with well-placed pushes. For such a prolific scorer he had rather disappointing Test figures. In 55 Tests he scored 3,915 runs with an average of 43.98. He scored 12 centuries, including the third highest individual score in Tests – 337, which he made against the West Indies in Barbados in 1958. It is the longest ever Test innings and the longest in first-class cricket – 16 hours 10 minutes. It's interesting to note that Len Hutton's 364 took only 13 hours 17 minutes, and Gary Sobers's 365 not out a mere 10 hours 14 minutes. This 365 not out was curiously made only just over a month later than Hanif's 337 – in the third Test at Kingston. This says something for the excellence of the West Indian pitches at that time.

Hanif was told an amusing story about his innings. A West Indian supporter watched the first part of it perched perilously on the branch of a tree. He stuck it out for most of the day as Hanif continued relentlessly to add run after run. In the end, either from the heat or sheer boredom the spectator went to sleep, and fell with a resounding crash to the ground, knocking himself out. He was rushed to hospital, where he remained unconscious for some time. When he eventually came round, the hospital nurse told him that he had been 'out' for two hours. Quick as a flash he said: 'I only hope that Hanif has been too!'

One strange thing about Hanif's career was his comparative failure in Test matches in England. He came on three tours, in 1954, 1962 and 1967, and only made one hundred – 187 not out at Lord's in 1967. In the other twenty-two Test innings which he played in England, he only scored 429 runs at an average of 19.50.

He is still credited with the highest score in first-class cricket. In January 1959 he scored 499 at Karachi against Bahawalpur. It took him only 640 minutes – not bad going – and incredibly he was run out off the last ball of the day trying to get his 500th run.

Inevitably, when writing about these two 'little masters', figures and records keep cropping up. The technique which produced all these runs seems to take second place. As I said, their styles were not dissimilar and were both based on the basic rules for batting: sideways on, head down and keep absolutely still. They both got to the pitch of the ball and watched it right on to the bat. They were both equally good against speed or spin.

32 Hanif Mohammad and **33** Sunil Gavaskar

Sunil Gavaskar – or 'Sunny' as he became – exemplified all these virtues. His small compact figure was usually topped by a white floppy hat, underneath which he had his own home-made helmet. His Test record will take some beating – more Tests (125), more runs (10,122), more hundreds (34) than anyone else. Only his average of 51.12 is surprisingly low, and it is exceeded by as many as twenty-one other players. Unlike Hanif he kept more of his big scores for Test matches, and seemed not to worry too much about the other first-class matches in which he played.

It is not difficult to pick out the best innings which I saw him play. It was one of the great fight-backs in all Test cricket, and took place in the fourth Test at the Oval in 1979. England made 305, and India 202. In their second innings England made 334 for eight declared, leaving India with 438 to get to win. Gavaskar and

Chauhan opened for India and by the start of the fifth morning they had progressed to 75 for 0, still needing 363 to win at just over a run a minute. Gavaskar was superb, ably backed up by Chauhan. They never seemed to hurry but the score crept slowly upwards and by tea had reached 304 for one, Botham catching Chauhan in the slips off Willis for a splendid 80. With Vengsarkar as partner Gavaskar increased the pace and masterminded the whole thing beautifully. As they went for the runs wickets began to fall and Gavaskar was finally caught by Gower at mid-on off Botham for 221, which included 21 fours and had lasted just over 8 hours. It deserved to win the match for India, but with England using the regrettable delaying tactics which are now so regularly used in Tests, India still needed 15 to win off the last over. They only got 6 of them, so it was a draw, but none of us would have grudged them what would have been – and so nearly was – a sensational victory.

Another innings of his that I will always treasure was his magnificent 188 in the MCC bicentenary match against the Rest of the World. He had to face an opening attack consisting of Malcolm Marshall and Richard Hadlee, supported by Clive Rice, John Emburey and his fellow Indian Ravish Shastri. He dealt with them all in great style and it was a joy to watch the battle between bat and ball. Although not a Test, it was such a unique occasion before a packed crowd that everyone was trying to the full. During the match Gavaskar announced his retirement from Test cricket, and one wondered why. His batting was such perfection, and he showed the enthralled spectators every stroke in the book. A great innings, on a great occasion and a fitting curtain to his brilliant career. When he came up to be interviewed after his innings, we tried to persuade him to continue Test cricket. He was quite adamant, but it would be nice and for the good of cricket, if he were to change his mind.

Gavaskar had two strange lapses during his career. He put up an extraordinary performance at Lord's in 1975, in the first Prudential World Cup match against England. England had made 334 for 4 off their 60 overs, which admittedly left India with the mammoth task of scoring at a rate of about 5.6 runs per over. Not impossible, but not easy against the England attack of John Snow, Peter Lever, Geoff Arnold and Tony Greig. Anyhow, Gavaskar decided it wasn't on and proceeded to make 36 not out in 60 overs before a 20,000 crowd. Neither they – nor his team – were pleased, especially when he is said to have told them that it was a good opportunity to have some batting practice!

His other equally unaccountable lapse was at Melbourne in 1981 in the third Test against Australia. He had had a bad run of scores in the previous two Tests – 0, 10, 23, 5. He then made only 10 in the first innings of the third, but he found his form at last in the second innings and had scored a good 70 when he was given lbw to Lillee. Whether he had hit it or not I don't know, but he was so angry and upset at the decision that he persuaded his partner, Chauhan, to walk back to the pavilion with him. The game came to a stop, but Chauhan was ordered by his manager to return to the field and all was well. Apologies followed, but it was a strange incident and not typical of 'Sunny'.

Both the 'Little Masters' captained their countries from time to time, and it did not seem to affect their form with the bat, but it is not as captains that they will be remembered. They will stay in my mind as two stylishly correct batsmen who had outstanding powers of concentration and patience and an insatiable desire to make runs – as many of them as possible.

Colin Cowdrey

On 30 July 1946, I went to Lord's to sit in the sun and watch some schoolboy cricket. The previous day in the Clifton *v*. Tonbridge match a thirteen-year-old playing for Tonbridge had made 75 out of 156 and then had taken 3 wickets with teasing leg-breaks. Michael Cowdrey, the papers called him and he was said to be the youngest player ever to play at Lord's. I thought I would have a look at this infant prodigy. I was rewarded by seeing him make 44 in his second innings and then win the match for Tonbridge by taking 5 for 59 with his highly tossed leg-breaks; three times he enticed the batsmen down the pitch and was rewarded by three stumpings. He was small but already had a slightly rotund figure. I enquired about him and was told that his father – a great cricket enthusiast – lived and worked in India and had deliberately given his son the initials MCC. It didn't need an expert to predict a promising future for the young boy, and for once the promise was fulfilled – though not so far as the leg-spin went. Like so many small boys who bowl leg-breaks, as he grew taller they seemed to lose their teasing flight, but his batting got better and better. Three years playing for Oxford University were followed by his selection for Len Hutton's MCC tour of Australia in 1954 at the age of twenty-one. Sadly, his father died before Colin played his first Test, but he did know that Colin had been chosen for the tour and that the MCC gimmick had borne fruit.

34 Colin Cowdrey

From then on Colin was an essential and seemingly inevitable member of the England team: 114 Tests with 7,624 runs, 22 hundreds and 120 catches, captain 27 times, 6 tours of Australia, vice-captain 4 times. An incredible record, and yet somehow it might have been even better.

As a batsman, though heavily built, he was remarkably light of foot with an exceptional eye – two assets which made him such a fine racquets player. He always played straight and had every stroke in the game – and stroke is the right word. He never seemed to hit the ball, but by superb timing seemed to 'waft' it away to the boundary. The late-cut, the off-, straight- and on-drive, and his own particular sweep were strokes I remember best. His sweep was more of a paddle, with the bat vertical rather than horizontal, and played very fine. His defence was as solid as a rock, and he developed –

perhaps over-developed – a skilful use of his pads as a second line of defence. The best example of this was his 154 in a record partnership of 411 with Peter May in the first Test against the West Indies in 1957. It is still the highest fourth-wicket partnership in all Test cricket, and successfully put paid to the mystery spin of Ramadhin. By sound judgement of where his off-stump was, Colin used his pads not just as a second line of defence but also a first line. It proved effective, but wasn't pleasant to watch.

He not only played spin well but was even better against fast bowling. He showed his class by always seeming to have plenty of time to play the ball, and never had to hurry. He often opened for England and played some of his biggest innings when going in first. But he was equally happy and effective batting lower in the order.

I am not the only one to think that, great player as he undoubtedly was, he could perhaps have been the greatest. So what was the flaw which stopped him reaching even greater heights? Strange to say, it was a lack of confidence in his own ability. He would often start off an innings brilliantly and then suddenly for no apparent reason shut up shop and get into all sorts of difficulties. In spite of his tremendous successes he would every now and again begin experimenting with a new grip on his bat or a new stance for his feet. Perhaps too he lacked the final killer instinct. But no matter – he was a great batsman in every sense of the word.

He was in the highest class as a slip fielder, that class including Hammond, Miller, Simpson, Sharpe, G. Chappell and Botham. Of course the quickness of his eye helped, but he believed in practice and you could always see him taking part in the catching sessions round a slip machine. It was the same with his batting. He had a net and a bowling machine in his garden. This not only gave him practice but helped him to coach his sons, two of whom – Christopher and Graham – have followed him into the Kent side, with Chris having also played in six Tests. Colin's wife, Penny, was also a useful bowler and I once convulsed the commentary team by saying that 'her swingers were practically unplayable' (she had taken 5 wickets when playing against Graham's junior school).

This lack of confidence and a killer instinct perhaps prevented Colin from being a great captain, though he was a sound enough tactician and a natural leader of men. On a tour he ran a happy ship and always included the media in this. He was a good communicator and his public relations were superb. Nothing was too much trouble, and he paid innumerable visits to schools and hospitals, as well as striking the right note at all the social functions. If a problem cropped up on or off the field he was strangely indecisive, however. A perfect example of this was the fourth Test in Trinidad in 1968. Sobers had sportingly declared to set England to score 215 in 165 minutes. At tea England had lost Edrich and were behind the clock, but Boycott and Cowdrey were batting well and, with so many wickets in hand, it seemed definitely worth while for England to take risks and go for victory. Colin had to be persuaded that it was possible, his inclination being to play safe. As it was, he and Boycott attacked the bowling and England won with three minutes to spare. But it has taken quite a lot of persuasion by Ken Barrington, in particular, to persuade Colin that he was capable of playing in the way he finally did.

As a character he was kind, caring and sensitive, and was a great one for saying 'thank you'. At the end of a tour, everyone would get a little note thanking them for their support. He didn't always have the best of luck, and Sunday, 25 May 1969 was a black day for him. He broke his achilles tendon during a John Player match at the Mote Ground at Maidstone. I swear I could hear the crack as I sat on the boundary. It meant the end of his captaincy of England just as he had built up his team after the successful West Indies tour, and the more dramatic one in Pakistan. He was naturally disappointed, especially as it had always been his ambition to captain England in Australia. Out of his six tours he was vice-captain four times – 'always the bridesmaid...' – but he had his compensation with his successful captaincy of Kent for fourteen years. He was a great cricketer, a very nice person and achieved perhaps his final ambition when he was elected president of MCC in their bicentenary year. Again he was struck down by bad luck. There were a few 'local difficulties' at Lord's, resulting in a special general meeting, but by this time Colin had suffered from heart trouble and was unable to attend the meeting nor attend the wonderful bicentenary match in August. After an operation and a slow recuperation, he is now happily fit again.

As usual, he showed great courage throughout his troublesome presidency and it is something which he always showed on the cricket field. I remember him well coming down the steps at Lord's in that marvellous Test against the West Indies in 1963. He had had his left forearm broken by Wes Hall, but with two balls left and six runs needed for victory he came out to join David Allen, his wrist in plaster, and the prospect of facing a ball from Wes Hall. If he had had to do so he had decided to bat as a left-hander, with his right hand holding the bat.

Another occasion was at Kingston, Jamaica, during the famous tear-gas riot. I can see him now walking towards the stand from where the crowd was hurling bottles. With his hands held up he advanced into the shower of bottles to try to pacify the angry crowd. He didn't succeed, but he proved what a worthy captain of England he was.

Gary Sobers

Was Gary Sobers the greatest all-rounder the game has ever known? Or was W. G. Grace? Well, to have seen W. G. play first-class cricket you would now be about ninety years of age, as he played his last match in 1908. So there must be some people still alive who were lucky enough to have seen *both* play, and they alone can speak with any authority. But the large majority of us, who never saw W. G., will I am sure select Gary from all the other possible candidates like Hirst, Rhodes, Woolley, Hammond, Botham, Imran Khan, Kapil Dev, Miller, Benaud, Davidson and Hadlee.

It is difficult to think of a more complete cricketer. As a batsman – like all the greats – he had a sound defensive technique, but in attack with a high backlift and perfect timing the power of his strokes had to be seen to be believed. His sizzling drives and crashing hooks were hammered to the boundary, leaving the fielders helpless to stop them. The best example of this was his 254 for a world eleven against Australia in Melbourne in 1972 – an innings which Don Bradman said was the best one he had ever seen in Australia. I was lucky enough to see it too, and shall never forget the speed with which his shots reached the longest boundaries in the world. It was fantastic, with scorching drives, cuts and hooks. Towards the end he went completely berserk and played many unorthodox strokes with his feet nowhere near the ball. The crowd went mad and even the Australian fielders were applauding some of his strokes.

He played fast bowlers and spinners equally well, and like all the greatest players saw the ball early. There were no helmets in his day, and I cannot ever remember seeing him bat in a cap. He also never wore a thigh pad and was able to cut so well because he used a light bat – about 2 lbs 4 oz. Against the spinners he worked it out that if he went down the pitch to hit them, it gave them an extra means of getting him out – stumped. In fact he claims that he was only stumped once in his career, though there was another occasion when a stumping chance was missed by the wicket-keeper. Gary played all spinners from the crease – if the ball was well pitched up he could still drive it. If it was short he had plenty of time to play it off the back foot.

35 Gary Sobers

With his amazing Test record it is remarkable that he batted so often at number six, and I suppose if he had regularly gone in higher up he would have made even more runs. He was naturally an attacking player, but he could discipline himself and by defensive batting got West Indies out of quite a few crises. He played his first Test for the West Indies at the age of seventeen in 1954, and was then regarded as a promising orthodox slow left-arm bowler who could bat a bit. He had to wait four years for his first Test hundred and then (as Bobby Simpson did at Old Trafford in 1964) he obliged with a triple century – his 365 not out, which passed Hutton's 364 and is still the highest individual Test score. A comparison with

Hutton's innings is interesting. Len was just twenty-two years old, batted for 13 hours 17 minutes and hit 35 fours. Gary was still only twenty-one, batted for 10 hours 14 minutes and hit 38 fours. They were both of course knighted by the Queen in 1975, Len at Buckingham Palace and Gary on the Garrison Savannah in Barbados, less than a mile from where he was brought up.

One man will always remember Gary more than anyone else – Malcolm Nash of Glamorgan. He it was who bowled the over at Swansea in 1968 in which Gary hit six successive sixes – a record 36 off the over. (This was equalled by R. J. Shastri for Bombay against Baroda at Bombay in 1984–5.) The one consolation for Malcolm was that at least he has his name in the record pages of *Wisden*. Actually he has got it in twice because Frank Hayes hit 34 off one over from him at Swansea in 1977.

Gary's feat set him on a different plane to other greats like Bradman, Hobbs, Hutton and even W. G. I cannot imagine them ever doing it, though any day now Ian Botham probably will – back trouble permitting.

Gary's great advantage over the other contenders for being the greatest all-rounder ever was that he was a three-part bowler. There was the slow left-arm orthodox with which he started, but which he gradually used less and less once he had learned to bowl the chinaman and googly. His best wicket-taker, however was his fast left-arm-over-the-wicket style, and when I say fast, I mean it. He was deceptive, with a lazy loping run and a perfect sideways action, but when he wanted to he could bowl as fast as anyone. Like Alan Davidson he would run the ball away across the right-handed batsman, and then bowl the deadly – and often unsuspected – ball which swung in late at the batsman and earned Gary a good few lbw's. I suppose of all the bowlers I have enjoyed watching running up to the wicket, Gary and Michael Holding were the two most pleasing. They seemed to glide over the ground.

Gary was naturally a beautiful mover – rather like a cat. He slunk over the ground, giving slightly at the knees, and was light of foot and exceptionally quick in movement and reaction. This is what made him such a magnificent fielder, especially in his later years when he used to gobble up catches at very short leg-slip off Lance Gibbs. But wherever he fielded he caught the eye by the grace of his movements.

He succeeded Frank Worrell as captain of the West Indies for thirty-nine Tests. He perhaps enjoyed cricket too much to make an ideal captain. That sounds cynical but means that he liked a good game of cricket and was prepared to attack and take risks to obtain it. The best example of this was in the fourth Test match at Port-of-Spain against Colin Cowdrey's side in 1968. He declared, giving England the sporting chance of scoring 215 runs in 165 minutes, which they succeeded in doing with three minutes to spare. No modern captain would ever be so generous, and the wrath of the whole Caribbean fell upon him. From being a national hero he became a scapegoat. It was understandable because this one victory gave England the series, but Gary had enjoyed his game of cricket and took it all smiling. He gave the best possible reply to his critics. In the next Test he made 152 and 95 not out, and took 3 wickets in each innings.

I mention his smile because it was never absent for long, and as a person he was modest, had great charm and a delightful sense of humour. He lived a happy family life in Barbados as a young man, and was a good soccer player as a boy. He has two passions besides cricket: horse-racing and golf. He had many opportunities to indulge in the former when he played for Nottingham from 1968 to 1974. I only wish that it had been more profitable for him. He would have made a fine professional golfer, and when his knee began to trouble him thought seriously of abandoning cricket for a belated golfing career. He plays whenever he can and still beats the best. He was a true all-rounder in every sense of the word, and I find it difficult to believe that there will ever be a better.

Ken Barrington

One of the most popular and best loved Test cricketers I ever met was Ken Barrington – or Barrers to me. He had a craggy face, a large hooked nose, an engaging grin and an impish sense of humour. He also had a tendency to malapropisms for example: 'A lion never changes his spots.'

He was also a splendid mimic of movement. He would put on a large black beard, a small cap on his head, skeleton pads on his legs and a towel tucked underneath his shirt to give him a belly. And lo and behold – there was W. G. Grace to the life. You may have seen a film clip of the GOM, batting in a net, with his left foot cocked up in the air, and his jerky strokes speeded up by the old film camera. Barrers copied this to perfection. I once saw him in a Test match in Cape Town in 1965, where the game had reached a stalemate. To liven things up he proceeded to give a lifelike impression of Jim Laker bowling. The joke was that he bowled so well that his analysis read: 3.1–1–4–3.

36 Ken Barrington

He was born in the county town of Reading, where his father was a soldier in the Berkshire regiment. As a result he had a love of the army all his life, and not for nothing did the players call him the Colonel. He gave a marvellous impression of a marching military band by drumming his fingers on a tin tray.

He was an avuncular figure on a tour, counsellor and coach and always ready with sympathy and advice for those in any sort of trouble, either on or off the field. There was always laughter around when he was about, both at his malapropisms and his genuinely funny remarks.

He was very emotional and could become desperately unhappy at unkind criticism by the media. I remember the first Test against New Zealand at Edgbaston in 1965. He made 137 out of England's 435, but it took him 7 hours 17 minutes and, when approaching his hundred, he stayed on 85 for over an hour. Then to make matters worse, as soon as he had completed his hundred, he promptly began to hit out and hit three or four boundaries. He was slated in the press, and on television and radio, and on the surface it did look like a selfish innings. I gave him a lift back to London and he was very upset and downhearted – even more so ten days later when he was dropped from the next Test as punishment. But you couldn't keep him down for long and his chirpy humour soon came back. And so did he. He was re-selected for the final Test and made 163!

It was his emotional reaction to the pressures of modern Test cricket that so sadly brought about his sudden and premature death in Barbados in 1981. He was assistant manager to Alan Smith on Ian Botham's ill-fated tour. All the dramas and crises proved too much for him. He was bowling his leg-breaks in the nets one afternoon, and died in his hotel that night after a heart attack. So England lost a lovable person whose loyalty, determination and fighting spirit had served his country so well.

He started his first-class life as a hard-hitting batsman, and when selected for the first two Tests against South Africa in 1955 he made 0, 34 and 18 before being dropped. He went back to Surrey and had a good think. He realised that in five-day Tests survival was all-important, and he worked out a method which made him one of the most difficult batsmen in Test cricket to get out. He changed his stance and stood almost square-on to the bowler. He cut out all dangerous strokes, and when he was recalled to Test cricket in 1959 he became England's Rock of Gibraltar.

He was a great man in a crisis, of which he had many to face. If he felt any pressure, he never showed it. He strode confidently to the wicket with a determined measured tread, and chin stuck out. Wally Grout once described him as 'trailing a Union Jack behind him'.

In contrast to his rather grim Test style, I twice saw him reach a Test hundred with a six, once in Adelaide in 1963, and again at Melbourne in 1966. Both shots were high pulls over long-on and it's worth noting that his 115 at Melbourne took only 2 hours 29 minutes, uncommonly fast for Test cricket.

In the field he was a safe and sure catcher anywhere, including the slips. He was also a very accurate thrower, ballooning the ball high in the air to drop with a plop right into the wicket-keeper's gloves. He was also a much under-rated and under-bowled leg-break bowler. He got plenty of bounce and break, and learnt to bowl the flipper from Richie Benaud. I saw him take 7 for 40 against Griqueland West in South Africa in 1965. During that tour I kept wicket to him in a charity match near Cape Town. The batsman went down the pitch to a leg-break. He missed it. So did I. It bounced and hit me on my right tit. You should have seen Barrers' face! He never let me forget it. Whenever we met, no matter where it was, his first greeting was always: 'Hello Johnners, how's the right tit?'

I must end by paying a tribute to him as a Test batsman. His figures say it all: 131 innings (15 not out), 6,806 runs, highest score 256, average *58.67*. Only Herbert Sutcliffe (60.73) and Eddie Paynter (59.23) of England batsmen had better averages, though Hammond (58.45), Hobbs (56.94), Hutton (56.67) and Compton (50.06) were all breathing down his neck.

Ted Dexter

The late Rev. John Wilkes, one-time Warden of Radley, once told me that after Ted Dexter had made one of his many hundreds for the school he would go into the chapel and play the organ to relax. I can believe anything of this remarkable character who brought a breath of the past as he strutted across the cricket scene in the fifties and sixties. He was an Edwardian figure. Finely built, a natural ball-player and athlete, he could appear to be aristocratic, haughty and aloof – hence his nickname 'Lord Edward'. But I believe that he was basically shy and realistically conscious of the fact that he *was* a bit different from the other players he was joining in the England Test team. He was also a deep thinker and a dreamer, and he often appeared to be thinking of other matters than those in hand.

He had so many interests outside cricket, and when he took up a new hobby he gave it 100 per cent dedication. He was a per-fectionist and tried to be the best in all he did. He would take up something for a while and then switch over to another craze or hobby. Pelmanism, religion, flying, greyhounds, horses, fast motor-bikes and golf are just a few of the pastimes to which he has devoted himself. And I should also add politics, because he had the audacity to stand as a Conservative candidate against Jim Callaghan in Cardiff in 1964. Needless to say, he lost but he put up a sporting fight. This caused him to lose the England captaincy to Mike Smith after thirty Tests in the job.

37 Ted Dexter

As a captain he perhaps had too many theories. Fred Trueman always says that Ted had more theories than Darwin. He enjoyed experimenting and as a result did do one or two unorthodox things, but because of his great skills as a batsman he could always lead from the front. There have been few better attacking Test batsmen than Ted – especially against fast bowlers. He wasn't always so certain against spin. He played with equal power off the front or back foot, and his 70 against the West Indies at Lord's in 1963 is still the best short Test innings I have seen. The way he stood up to Hall and Griffith and forced them through mid-off or mid-on off the back foot was both majestic and inspiring. It showed that they *could* be mastered. His Test figures show how much he enjoyed batting, and he was quite happy to go on after scoring a hundred.

He was a useful medium-pace change bowler in Tests, and had a reputation for breaking up partnerships. He had a good high action with a last-minute swivel of the body, which resulted in a loud grunt every time he bowled. (The loudest grunter I ever heard was Allan Jones, who shares with Jim Cumbes the distinction of having played for four different counties.) Incidentally, I'm rather proud of my nickname for Jim – it's Cata.

To complete his all-round ability Ted was a very good fielder anywhere, so long as he maintained his concentration. He could often be seen practising golf shots whilst standing in the slips, his mind obviously miles away. There is no doubt that had he been a professional, he could have reached the top at golf. He was – and still is – one of the longest hitters in the game, though whether he could out-drive Ian Botham I don't know. His short game, which needs so much more practice, was not quite so good, but one of his happiest moments was when, after many attempts, he won the President's Putter at Rye.

We could do with more Ted Dexters in first-class cricket. Theories or no theories, he speaks much good sense in his television summaries. There is also need of more players like him who believe that attack is the best policy. He is now wrapped up in a thriving PRO, business and has inaugurated many new features in cricket: the sponsorship of tourists' matches against counties, the Deloitte's Ratings for Test Cricketers, or his noble attempt to find some new fast bowlers. He has lots of good ideas, and much courage. How else could he have decided to fly his wife and two young children out to Australia in his small plane with his wife, Sue, doing their lessons with them at the back, as he sat in the cockpit? He did this in 1970 when he was reporting Ray Illingworth's tour. There is really nothing that he cannot put his hand to, and it would be good for cricket if he could be given some official job to do – selecting, coaching or just being an *active* member of some cricket committee. He is a businessman and might have to be paid for it, but it would be well worth while.

He was good fun on a tour and a great party-goer, but he is also a highly intelligent person who can talk with authority on many subjects. He also has a splendid sense of humour. I shall always remember the occasion when he, John Woodcock of *The Times* and myself were having dinner in a crowded restaurant in Tasmania. Wooders and I are two of only a few people who can tuck their ears in. An old groom of ours taught me the trick and, surprisingly, Wooders can also do it. We were trying to show Ted how it is done, and kept tucking our ears in and flipping them out again. He was roaring with laughter and our table soon became the centre of attention. People all around us were trying to tuck *their* ears in, and failing miserably. So Wooders and I got up and went round the room trying to tuck total strangers' ears in for them. We didn't succeed with anyone, let alone Ted, but it was a hilarious scene.

On another occasion, however, he rather let me – or rather my wife – down. It was during the New Zealand part of his 1962–3 tour when the Duke of Norfolk was his manager. They were both Sussex men and got on very well, though I am bound to say that more often than not it was Ted who did the leading and decision-making, not the Earl Marshal of England! Anyway, I had had to fly home at the end of the Australian tour and my wife, Pauline, went on to New Zealand. On the day she was flying home she had lunch with Ted and then said she would like to have a sleep before she went off to the airport. So Ted said that the Duke was away for the day, and suggested that she should go up to his suite and lie down on the bed which he didn't use in his double room. This she did and fell fast asleep, only to wake up suddenly to see a rather red, podgy face peering round the door and saying: 'Who's been sleeping in *my* bed?' The Duke had come back unexpectedly early. But he took it all in good part and gave Pauline a nice cup of tea before she went off to catch her flight!

Ted had so much natural ability that every game came naturally to him. He didn't have to practise as much as us mere mortals. Proof of this was in 1968. In 1965 he had had an accident on the Great West Road and broke a leg. This meant that he played in no Tests that summer and also resigned the Sussex captaincy. He was laid up for quite some time and Ted's agent, Bagenal Harvey, suggested to BBC TV, that Ted should act as summariser for the Tests. The idea was that he should do it from his bed at home, from a TV set, but in spite of the *coup* of getting the last England captain into our commentary team, the Beeb declined the offer.

Ted then played virtually no first-class cricket until July 1968, when he was persuaded to turn out again for Sussex, then under the captaincy of Mike Griffith. It was a typical cavalier return. Ted picked up where he had left off and on the pleasant Hastings ground proceeded to make 203 against Kent. He even treated Underwood with disdain and hit three sixes and twenty-three fours in a brilliant innings full of his best majestic strokes. He only played once more for Sussex but was promptly selected once again for England against Australia in the fourth and fifth Tests. He made 10, 38, 21, 28, and so ended his Test career, not perhaps with the flourish he would have enjoyed, but at least it was proof of how much he had been missed during the previous two years. Like Peter May he retired too early, but families have to be educated and maintained!

Ray Illingworth

I have always called him Illy, but Yorkshire folk give him his full Christian name of Raymond. He is one of the longest serving cricketers in the modern game, playing from 1951 until 1983. I can only think of Fred Titmus (1949–82) who can beat that. Not even the old-timers like Wilfred Rhodes (32 years), Jack Hobbs (29 years), Frank Woolley (32 years), Phil Mead (31 years) and George Gunn (30 years) can do more than equal him – but remember that their careers contained four blank seasons during the Great War. I concede that W. G. Grace played for 29 years for Gloucestershire and then for another 4 for London County, but for first-class county matches I think Illy is the winner. He was fifty-one when he finally retired, but as I write in 1988 he still plays in the Bradford league.

He has always kept himself remarkably fit and on the field appeared to be completely relaxed and never over-exerted himself. He preferred to field in the gully, where he was a very safe catcher. He had a short run-up, running lightly on his toes. He bowled fairly flat off-spin, with a well-disguised floater. His main assets were his length and direction, he bowled very few bad balls, and could be relied on to drop the ball on a sixpence from the word go. Like Fred Titmus he was not a great spinner of the ball, but his accuracy and reading of batsman's weaknesses brought him 122 Test wickets. He was an effective but rather ordinary-looking batsman, though captaincy of England seemed to inspire him to greater heights and he played a variety of match-saving or match-winning innings for his country.

On the surface, then, a technically efficient all-rounder, but from the moment he became captain of Leicester in 1969 he became a different man – and player. He blossomed in a job which he did exceedingly well both for Leicestershire (1 County Championship, 2 Benson and Hedges Cups and 2 John Player League Cups) and for England (12 wins, 14 draws, 5 losses). He was a shrewd tactician, full of cricket knowledge handed down by past Yorkshire players. He read a batsman's weakness as well as anybody I know, and this was reflected in his field placings. He was a players' captain. They liked him because they knew exactly where they were with him – he spoke his mind, was strictly honest, and would stand no nonsense. He wanted to win and expected everyone to try as hard as he did. They also knew that he would always support them in any brush with administrators and fight for their cause. He appears as a paragon of virtue, and in most senses he was, but he regarded his main job as winning a series and it is *on* the field that matches are won. Off it he lacked some of the social graces and tended to play a low-key role in PR. He was, however, helpful and truthful with the media and was one of the easiest captains I ever had to interview. He gave straight answers, and never waffled.

38 Ray Illingworth

His playing life was divided into three. For seventeen years he played for Yorkshire, but in the end quarrelled with the committee (not the first – nor last – Yorkshireman to do so!) because they refused to give him a three-year contract. Mike Turner of Leicestershire snapped him up and, as captain for ten years, he transformed them as a team.

As he approached fifty years of age his playing career seemed to be ending. After much thought and discussion he accepted Yorkshire's invitation to return as manager to try to restore their fortunes. He didn't have a very happy time there, in what had become a civil war between the pro- and anti-Boycott factions. In the mid-summer of 1982 he took over the captaincy himself from Chris Old and in the following year achieved an ironical result. Yorkshire, the bastion of traditional cricket, were bottom of the County Championship table but won the forty-over frolic of the John Player League. This was achieved largely by Illy relying on the spin bowling of himself and Phil Carrick – his final gesture to prove that spinners can and should play a successful part in limited-over cricket.

Illy is a highly organised person. Like a true Yorkshireman he has made and saved his pennies to give him a secure future. Some of his time will undoubtedly be spent in the TV commentary box, where his dry wit and quick reading of the game have proved invaluable. He turned down the offer of becoming England team manager because he was not going to be given complete control – he wanted to be more like Bobby Robson. The structure of the first-class game has always allowed for selectors chosen by the counties, however, and to put all the power in the hands of one man would have been too big a jump. He'll admit, I think, that on the whole he's been lucky, and in spite of one or two setbacks things have worked out well for him. The highlight of his career would for him undoubtedly have been the 1970–1 Ashes-winning tour of Australia. He – like Hutton – went there with just one purpose and he achieved it in a highly professional manner. It must have been a sweet moment for him when he was carried triumphantly off the field at Sydney by his team.

He had shown his determination and toughness in that final Test when he led his team off the field in protest against the manhandling of John Snow by an angry spectator, and the shower of bottles and tins which were hurled on to the field. I defended his action at the time as I happened to be commentating, and was supported by two old Australian captains, Richie Benaud and Bill Lawry, but many of the English press disagreed. My point was that the umpires should have gone down to the scene of the trouble instead of staying on the pitch. It had also been proved in the West Indies riots that staying on the field merely lengthened the riot, and on at least two occasions play had to be abandoned. But Illy's method made the crowd realise that they would be robbed of any more cricket if they went on throwing things, so, after an announcement, the playing area was quickly cleaned up and play restarted in under a quarter of an hour. Of course, theoretically it was wrong to take his team off without the permission of the umpires, but it needed courage to do so and it worked.

One other feature of his captaincy was that he was prone to under-bowl himself. Cynics – and they may have something – used to say that he didn't much fancy bowling on any pitch which didn't give a spinner some help.

It is nice to have him around us in the commentary area, although he does rather tend to invade the radio box round about tea-time. Like us he has a penchant for chocolate cake – and it's amazing how he sniffs out the arrival of a new one. As I've said, on the whole he's a lucky person, as proved in 1971. After the Ashes victory we wrote a pretty awful song to a delightful old music-hall tune. When we got back to England we recorded it at the Decca studios. Vic Lewis – that most enthusiastic of cricketers and collector of cricket-club ties – organised a wonderful accompanying orchestra drawn from all the top session musicians in London who were cricket supporters. The end product, called 'The Ashes Song', sounded smashing to us, though the public didn't think so. We hoped it would top the charts but in fact our total royalties were £53.86. There was no point in dividing this up, so we decided to have a draw at the Test Trial in Hove in 1973. Who better to make the draw than the England captain? And whose name did he pull out of the hat? Yes, you've guessed it. Raymond Illingworth, none other.

I did pay him out a season or two later when I made a semi-deliberate gaffe about him. 'Welcome to Leicester,' I said, 'where the captain, Ray Illingworth, has just relieved himself at the Pavilion End.'

M. J. K. Smith

A most deceptive character. Tall, fair, athletic, with an owl-like appearance because of the glasses he always wore. He spurned contact lenses. He thought people only wore them out of false pride, and he was not worried about everyone knowing he was short-sighted. When batting he would wrinkle his nose and screw up his eyes, as myopics often do when trying to read something. For some reason too he bared his teeth. That was the view the bowlers got as they ran up to bowl, and must often have given them a false sense of confidence.

39 M. J. K. Smith

It was a completely misleading picture of the real man, however. Underneath was a born leader of men. He captained England twenty-five times, including three tours abroad. He was also captain of his school at Stamford, and of Oxford University and Warwickshire, from 1957 to 1967. You don't get all these jobs as captain unless you have something special to offer. He ran a wonderfully happy dressing-room, and was a great debunker of any bumptiousness or pomposity. He had an ever-present sense of humour with a cackling laugh, and made everyone realise that it was the team that mattered, not the individual. Some captains had difficulty with Geoff Boycott and his slow play. M. J. K. solved the problem with subtle but not unkind irony. He christened Geoff 'fiery', which gave him a feeling of confidence and, on tours of South Africa and Australia under M. J. K., resulted in many fine Boycott innings, *full of strokes*.

In addition to this quality of bringing out the best in people, M. J. K. was brave and always led from the front. His comparative failure against fast bowling was not due to lack of courage, but rather to the fact that at the start of an innings, before his eyes had properly focused, he was vulnerable to pace. But in the field it was he – glasses and all – who took the dangerous positions at silly point, or forward short leg. He would crouch there within feet of the batsman, elbows on knees, one leg slightly stretched out behind him, and of course in those days there was no helmet, nor so far as I know a box! His reactions were remarkably quick. Elsewhere in the field he was a fast mover, as befits an England fly-half. He was one of those rare beings, a double blue and a double international. At rugby at Oxford he had a wonderfully successful partnership with David Brace at scrum-half. They were completely unorthodox, always doing the unexpected with dummies, scissor movements, reverse passes and so on. He then went on to play one match for England against Wales, again at fly-half. Incidentally, although he was so short-sighted, when playing rugby he discarded his glasses and played without them. He didn't wear contact lenses either, but they were not so highly developed at that time.

As a schoolboy cricketer he played three matches for Leicester-shire in the summer holidays of 1951, but not, alas, with great success. In four innings he scored 5 runs with an average of 1.25! After his three years in National Service he went up to Oxford and played for them in 1954, 1955 and 1956, being captain in the last year. He had an incredible record in the University Match – 201 not out in 1954, 104 in 1955 and 117 in 1956.

After Oxford he left Leicestershire for Warwickshire, for whom he became a prolific scorer in county cricket. In one season – 1959 – he scored 3,245 runs, scored 2,000 runs in six consecutive seasons, and made 1,000 or more nineteen times. He particularly enjoyed spin bowling – he wouldn't have much fun today! Technically he was correct but favoured the on side more than the off. He perfected the 'lap', a lofted stroke between mid-wicket and mid-on, and was a very fast runner between the wickets and an especially good judge of a run. This enabled him to score at a faster rate than most other batsmen, though usually after a slow and scratchy start.

I have said what a fine leader he was off the field. On it he was a good tactician, though perhaps not as adventurous as he might have been. Because he played spin so well himself, he tended to neglect his spinners and favour the fast bowlers, whom he found more difficult to play. But he was an inspiring captain, completely unflappable, who expected – and got – the best from his team.

So far as I know only a few people call him Mike – it's always M.J.K. He had a new, more friendly and relaxed method of captaincy, and there was always a lot of laughter and leg-pulling when he was around. He perhaps carried his casual approach too far on the Australian tour of 1965–6, when he was accompanied most of the time by his wife and two young daughters – then aged about three and one. It was a strange sight to see an England captain stepping down the steps of an aircraft to meet the awaiting press, carrying a baby, or sometimes even two, in his arms. It also meant that he had quite a few sleepless nights, not the best preparation for a Test match the next day.

As a player he will be best remembered for his performances for his county rather than his country. In Tests he scored 2,278 runs at an average of 31.63, with 3 hundreds and 4 scores out in the 90s. In all first-class cricket he averaged 41.84, making 39,832, including 69 centuries.

To sum M.J.K. up: a delightfully friendly person with his own peculiar dry sense of humour; not an easy person to interview, rather cunning and preferring not to give too much away. And a word of warning. Never have a bet with him on a cricket statistic – he has got in his head what Bill Frindall has in his books. But one thing I can guarantee. Ask any player who went on an MCC tour with M.J.K., and they will assuredly tell you what a *happy* time they had.

Bob Barber

There have been many discussions about the pros and cons of limited-over cricket, but one thing *is* certain. It turned a dull, rather dreary batsman into an opening batsman for England who attacked the bowling with glorious strokes from the start. Sometimes he came off, sometimes he didn't, but when he did he was a joy to watch.

'Ali' was a natural athlete – a climber, javelin-thrower, and a cricket blue for Cambridge in 1956 and 1957. From there he went to play for Lancashire as an amateur, and surprisingly was chosen to succeed Cyril Washbrook as captain in 1960 and 1961. He was not really strong enough to stand up to his committee who, incredibly, insisted that for away games he should stay in different hotels from his team. This was an archaic idea which may have been the custom before the war, but was totally unacceptable in the social conditions which existed afterwards.

40 Bob Barber

It meant that Ali led a lonely and unhappy life, and made good relations with his team extremely difficult. In his first year the playing results were good – Lancashire finished second in the Championship table and also beat Yorkshire twice – but in the following year they finished thirteenth and for 1962 he was replaced as captain by a club cricketer, J. F. Blackledge, who had never played first-class cricket. Lancashire had an even more disastrous season and finished one from last. Ali made his thousand runs but averaged only 27.51. He was, however, given a chance to develop his leg-breaks and googlies, but although he took 32 wickets they cost over 38 apiece. It was not therefore surprising that he decided to pack it in, and accept an offer from M. J. K. Smith to join Warwickshire.

He had usually batted at number four for Lancashire and continued to do so for Warwickshire, until the middle of 1964 when he began to open with Norman Horner, and he was especially successful in the Gillette Cup matches. The happy atmosphere of the dressing-room at Edgbaston and the friendly leg-pulling of Mike Smith completely changed Ali's outlook on cricket. He realised that it could be fun, and also discovered that he enjoyed playing attacking cricket. He found strokes which he had never played before, and also picked up 41 wickets at the low cost of 20.63. On the strength of this all-round ability and his excellent athletic fielding he was picked for Mike Smith's tour of South Africa that winter.

He had already played in one Test against South Africa at Edgbaston in 1960, batting at number eight. He was dropped for the next ten Tests, but then went with Ted Dexter's side to India and Pakistan in 1961–2. He still batted down the order, and had a moderate tour, but did score 86 when promoted to open with Geoff Pullar against Pakistan. He was, however, given a surprising amount of bowling and in the first Test against Pakistan bowled 60.5 overs and took 6 wickets in the match. In the third Test against them he also bowled a large number of overs (55) and took 4 wickets.

I have given these details about his bowling, because he was never given such a chance again. With more experience and encouragement he could have become a far better leg spinner, but in future Tests under Mike Smith he was sadly under-bowled. Mike was a fine player of spin himself, and not so good against the faster stuff, so he wrongly believed that it would prove too expensive to give Ali regular spells.

After Ted Dexter's tour there was a gap of twenty-seven Tests before Ali played for England again. He was called up for the fifth Test against Australia at the Oval in 1964. He was by then opening for Warwickshire, and at the Oval began his association with Geoff Boycott as openers for England. They opened together in fourteen Tests and should have made an ideal partnership – the right-handed anchor-man and the dashing left-hander – but strangely enough they only had two century partnerships, the great one being at Sydney in 1966, when they put on 234 for the first wicket. Ali made 185 with 19 fours, the highest score of his career. It was a magnificent innings of aggression and power and was watched by his father, Jack, amongst the crowd on the Hill.

In the last Test of the tour in Melbourne Ali sacrificed his wicket when Boycott called for an impossible single. Ali shouted 'no' loudly, but Boycott came on running regardless and actually ran past Ali at the bowler's end. Ali had never left his crease, so when the ball was thrown to the wicket-keeper's end he was technically not out, but in order to avoid a fuss he walked off to the pavilion when it became obvious that Boycott was not going to do so. Except for his 185 at Sydney, and a useful 48 at Melbourne he didn't make a lot of runs in the Tests, and only bowled 55 overs in the whole series with 3 wickets. He was only to play for England in three more Tests: two in 1960 against the West Indies, when once again he opened with Geoff Boycott and made 55 and 36; and his last was against Australia at Old Trafford in 1968.

Undoubtedly the highlight of his batting was seen in the four Tests he played in against South Africa on Mike Smith's tour there in 1964. His scores were 74, 97, 58 and 61, all scored in his typical attacking style. He didn't play in the fifth Test because of a broken finger, but also nearly missed the first Test at Durban. A fortnight earlier we had been in Port Elizabeth for the match against Eastern Province. We had a couple of days free before the match, and as exercise decided to have a game of football on the beach. He was the dashing centre-forward on one side, while I was trying to be a half-back on the other. Ali got the ball and was racing through to score when I stuck out my leg and accidentally (!) tripped him up. He lay there groaning and holding his ankle, which was badly swollen. I was of course in absolute disgrace and was cut dead by the team during the next two games, when Ali was unfit to play. Luckily for me he recovered in time for the first Test at Durban and he made 74 in a 120 partnership with Geoff Boycott, so I was forgiven. But there was no more beach football!

Ali retired to take up a business career and for those of us who were lucky enough to see him perform overseas, he will always be remembered as one of England's most *exciting* batsmen. Although he scored a thousand runs in a season seven times he never really reached his full potential, and because he was under-bowled England lost a valuable all-rounder. But the great thing about him was that, once freed from Lancashire, he really began to enjoy his cricket.

Fred Titmus

Ever since I kept wicket for my preparatory school, Temple Grove at Eastbourne, it had been my ambition to play out in the middle at Lord's – for England if possible, but if not any other team would do. I had been encouraged at Eastbourne by kind comments on my wicket-keeping by J. L. Bryan, one of the three brothers who played for Kent. The other two were G.J. and R.T.

41 Fred Titmus

J.L. was a brilliant left-handed bat who was the cricket master at St Andrew's School and so could only play for Kent in the summer holidays, but he was good enough to go on Arthur Gilligan's MCC tour of Australia in 1924–5, though he never played in a Test match. St Andrew's and Temple Grove were the two best cricket schools in Eastbourne, and all our matches were very competitive.

With my confidence boosted by J.L.'s encouraging remarks, I went to Eton, determined to play at Lord's in the Eton and Harrow match. But it was not to be. I was pipped at the post by an older and better wicket-keeper and had to be content with captaining the second eleven, or twenty-two as it was called.

So instead of playing out in the middle I had to watch from the Eton dressing-room, eating cherries from the huge wicker basket which Lord Harris always used to send up from Kent. As a companion I had the Eton coach at that time, the lovable George Hirst. He was a kind man and took me under his wing, and showed me all over Lord's, including the grandstand scoreboard and scorer's box. Perhaps this was his way of saying 'thank you' to me for something which happened just before Lord's. He and I were playing in a team against the first eleven, so there I was keeping to the great George Hirst, who was then a little round ball of a man, and bowled medium-pace left arm. He was still a marvellously inventive bowler and bowled a variety of deliveries. One of these was a faster ball outside the leg-stump – rather like Derek Underwood's. To my great joy he bowled one of these, and I achieved a leg-side stumping off one of the greatest all-rounders England has ever had. In the end I was rather relieved that I hadn't played in the Lord's match. Eton had two very fast bowlers – Page and Hanbury. Their direction wasn't always that good and the poor wicket-keeper, called Baerlein, let 35 byes. Goodness knows how many more there would have been if I had been behind the timbers.

Throughout the thirties and during the war no opportunities arose for me to play at Lord's, but in 1948 my dream came true. I had joined the BBC in 1946 and was the TV commentator for the Lord's Test against India. I used to go there regularly, not just to watch or commentate on cricket, but to play in the nets at the Nursery End. In fact when we moved to Cavendish Avenue in 1948 we were just eighty yards from the north entrance, and I used to walk down the road in my pads to have a net. Lord's became a second home to me, and after over forty years in St John's Wood it still is. I have been lucky to make friends with everyone on the ground, the pavilion staff and administrators, the ground staff and the coaching staff. And I must not forget the gatemen. Some visitors to Lord's – especially Don Mosey! – have found them unfriendly, obstructive and unhelpful. Happily they have never been like that to me, and since the 'local difficulties' at Lord's in 1987 I think even their worst critics will now find there's a new smile round the face at Lord's. My good relationship with the young ground staff who bowled at members in the nets was founded on a more commercial basis. It was the custom to put a bob or two on your stumps, and the bowler who knocked them down got the money. Over the years they made a small fortune out of me!

I was therefore especially pleased when Ronnie Aird, then assistant secretary, responsible for cricket, asked me to play for the Cross Arrows in one of their September matches. They are very much a Lord's club, with membership drawn from all branches of the staff, present or retired Middlesex players, and people like myself with a special connection with, and affection for, Lord's. They play some twenty matches right up to the end of September against club sides such as The Stage, Metropolitan Police, the Stock Exchange and so on. Most of the opponents are the same every year, though the demand to play against the Cross Arrows is so great that some have to miss out the odd year.

They now play all their matches on the Nursery Ground, but for some years after the war they had the honour of playing on the main ground. So I actually played on the hallowed turf, though admittedly right at the top end of the square, close to the grandstand. It was a great day for me. We changed in the Middlesex and England dressing-room, we drank the famous Hamptons drink at lunch (not unlike Pimms No. 1) and, best of all, we walked out through the little white gate on to the middle.

After this lengthy preamble you will no doubt be wondering where Freddie Titmus comes into all this. He was then aged sixteen, and had just begun his career with Middlesex. I remember him as a small perky boy with short steps and long hair – in fact, at that time Sir Pelham Warner told him to get it cut. Anyway, he was playing for the Cross Arrows in this match, and I kept wicket to him as he bowled from the Pavilion End. I have always kidded myself that I stumped someone off him down the leg side. I have checked in the Cross Arrows score books, and luckily they have not any of the score books as far back as that. So I can keep my dream!

So that was my introduction to Titters, as I have always called him – a chirpy, cheeky Londoner born in Kentish Town. He first played for Middlesex in 1949 at the age of sixteen, and played his last match for them in 1982 in his fiftieth year. For thirty-three years he was part of the Lord's scene, just as Patsy Hendren and Denis Compton had been before him, and Mike Gatting is today. Titters is one of Middlesex's greatest characters in all their history. Quiet and unobtrusive, maybe, to the spectator, but to his colleagues he was always cheerful, ready with a quip and a perfect example of what a professional and sportsman should be.

His record speaks for itself. The double eight times, a hundred wickets sixteen times. After two Tests in 1955 he did not play again for England until 1962, after which he played in fifty-one Tests, his appearances being interrupted by his bathing accident in Barbados in 1968.

I was on the beach at St James's when it happened. Penny Cowdrey was in a small round boat which had its rotary propeller underneath the centre of the boat, instead of in the usual place at the stern. Freddie went into the shallow water to push the boat out to sea, and as he got deeper his legs were sucked up underneath the boat. Blood oozed up and at first he thought that he had been stung by a jelly-fish, but when he came out of the water it was soon obvious that the propeller had made a clean cut of the four toes on his left foot. Luckily it had not gone right down to the nerves, just leaving four short stumps. As a result he remarkably never felt any pain at any time. He was rushed to the local hospital, who were warned in advance and had a team waiting for him. They did a marvellous job on cleaning and stitching everything up, whilst Titters kept cheerful and chatting away.

He was sent straight home for more treatment and, incredibly, with a specially made padded boot, was ready to play for Middlesex at the start of the 1968 season. This would never have been possible if the cut had been lower down, and had his big toe been touched, but luckily it wasn't because it is the big toe alone on which one balances. And now comes the pay-off. In the summer of 1968 Titters took 111 wickets and made 924 runs, only 76 runs off yet another double – incredibly considering that he had lost four toes. There's guts and determination for you – two assets of which he had plenty.

He had been well coached as a boy at Lord's, and was a correct and stylish batsman. He even opened the innings for England at Trent Bridge in the first Test against Australia in 1964, when John Edrich reported himself unfit on the morning of the match. Titters's partner was none other than Geoff Boycott, playing in his very first Test. They put on 38 for the first wicket but not without an augury of 'things to come'. Boycott called for one of his famous quick singles, and Titters loyally responded to what looked like an impossible call, but he collided with the Australian opening bowler, Corling, and fell to the ground. The ball was thrown to Wally Grout the wicket-keeper who, seeing what had happened, sportingly refused to break the wicket. I wonder if this would happen today.

A proof of Titters's guts was in 1974 in Australia, where against the devastating partnership of Lillee and Thomson at their fiercest and fastest he made a gallant 61 on the fast Perth pitch in the second Test. This was in fact his first appearance in a Test since his toe accident, and he was forty-one years old.

As a bowler he was everything an off-spinner should be – a few jaunty steps, a fine sideways swivel action, with the right arm high. He spun the ball, but not prodigiously. He relied more on extreme accuracy, flight and variation of pace. His faster ball was well disguised and gave J. T. Murray many a stumping down the leg side. He also perfected the away floater, which got him quite a lot of his wickets caught in the slips.

He captained Middlesex for three seasons, but I don't think he ever really enjoyed it and he resigned halfway through the 1968 season. He preferred to enjoy his cricket, chatting away incessantly in the slips with his two special chums Peter Parfitt and J.T.

One nice story concerned him and Percy Pocock. Surrey were playing Middlesex at Lord's, and when Percy came in to bat Titters noticed that he was wearing glasses. 'What are you wearing those for, Percy?' he asked. Percy, knowing that Titters was a bit deaf, replied: 'So that I can *hear* the ball better, of course.' Percy then took guard and was immediately clean bowled by Titters. As Percy passed him on his way back to the pavilion Titters said to him: 'You didn't hear that one very well, did you Percy?'

Titters now keeps a post-office-cum-newsagents in Hertfordshire. He leaves the post office business to his mother-in-law, but he himself gets up at dawn to sort out the papers for the delivery boys. He plays golf, smokes a pipe and in his 'old' age has become a selector. This he enjoys as it keeps him in touch with the game. It also ensures that there is plenty of humour around at the Test matches.

If only there were more Titmuses around in first-class cricket today, cricket would be a far happier game.

Six Aussie keepers

The first Australian wicket-keeper I saw was J. L. Ellis, who was the reserve wicket-keeper to Bertie Oldfield on the 1926 Australian tour of England. He wasn't needed for any of the Tests and in fact never played in a Test. I only remember him because he kept wicket against Gloucestershire at Cheltenham in 1926, which was the first time I ever saw the Australians play. I can see him now standing miles back to the fast bowling of Gregory, and remember that when he went to take one ball wide down the leg-side his left glove came off.

I then saw Bertie Oldfield at Lord's in 1930, a neat dapper little man, rather sparrow-like in his movements. He was a beautiful wicket-keeper to watch, quiet and immensely efficient as he stood right up behind the wicket with his large black gloves, which he kept rubbing together rather like Uriah Heep.

42 Bertie Oldfield
43 Ben Barnett

He was stylish in everything he did and had a perfectly balanced crouch – just up on his toes, hands pointing down in front of him. There is a wonderful photograph which shows him in this position with Wally Hammond just finishing one of his classic cover drives – and Bertie is still crouching down. What a lesson to young wicket-keepers. When standing back he was, like so many other keepers of the time, seldom if ever seen flinging himself about. Somehow he always seemed to get across to the wide balls.

In 1948 he joined our TV commentary team in the two London Tests, and with his high squeaky voice was a model of good-mannered criticism.

I visited him in his sports shop in Sydney in the sixties and there he was, bird-like and immaculate in white flannels. He sold me – at a *slightly* reduced rate, a pair of his wicket-keeping gloves, and I used these until I gave up playing. At the same time I met and talked to the gnome-like figure of Clarrie Grimmett at Adelaide. I asked him about Bertie, who of course got so many of his 130 Test victims off the bowling of Grimmett. He only played in 54 Tests, but even so his total of 52 stumpings beats everyone else, the second best being 46 for Godfrey Evans for 91 Tests. Bertie actually caught 9 and stumped 28 off Clarrie. I was singing Bertie's praises, with which Clarrie agreed but added with a mischievous smile: 'But he missed a lot off me too.' Bowlers are not the most grateful of people!

The next great wicket-keeper was Don Tallon, nicknamed Deafy because he was! He toured England in 1948 and 1953, and undoubtedly should have been chosen for the 1938 tour. Why he and Grimmett were not selected is still a bit of a mystery, especially as Grimmett had had a most successful season in the Sheffield shield. Ben Barnett came instead of Tallon, and F. A. Ward instead of Grimmett. Ward played in only the first Test, where his bowling analysis was 30–2–142–0. Barnett fared much better. He was a good wicket-keeper, not quite in the super class. Remarkably, in the four Tests played he got no victims at all in three of them, but made three catches and two stumpings in the fourth Test. He always remembered the final Test at the Oval when Len Hutton made the record-breaking 364. Poor Ben is said to have missed stumping Len when he had scored 34 – just imagine what he was thinking as Len piled up the runs. He was a charming man and settled in England after the war. He played for Buckinghamshire, and also in a lot of festival cricket, and turned out regularly for the Lord's Taverners.

Don Tallon was tall for a wicket-keeper, with long arms, and was a brilliant performer. I once asked Lindsay Hassett in the seventies who was the best wicket-keeper he had seen – and remember that Lindsay played for Australia before and after the war, so had the opportunity to either play with or see all the Test wicket-keepers from the mid-thirties until he gave up summarising for ABC in 1986. He unhesitatingly plumped for Don Tallon, and it's a judgement I feel one must accept in spite of Evans, Knott, Taylor, Grout, Marsh and so on. Surprisingly, Tallon only played in the first Test at Trent Bridge on Lindsay's 1953 tour.

As I've said, he was a bit deaf. When, one evening during the match, Australia were struggling against the superb bowling of Alec Bedser (he took 14 for 99 in the match), Lindsay said to Tallon as he went out to bat: 'Give the light a go, Deafy' – meaning appeal against the light. Tallon thought he had said 'give it a go', and proceeded to attack the bowling and make a lightning 15 before being caught off Tattersall when going for another big hit!

44 Don Tallon   **45** Gil Langley

For the remaining four Tests Gil Langley took over from Tallon. He was heavily built and rather podgy, and was the first of the modern keepers to stand back to medium-pace bowling. At the time it seemed a travesty of wicket-keeping to see him standing back to someone as slow as Slasher Mackay, but he wasn't just a stopper. He was most effective, dropped very little, and possibly made catches which he would not have held if he had been standing up. As proof of how effective he was, in only 26 Tests he bagged 98 victims and tops every Test wicket-keeper past or present for the best average number per Test – 3.769. He had a very short Test career – 1951 to 1957 – and when he retired he became a Labour politician in South Australia, finishing as the Speaker of the Parliament there. I can't off-hand think of any other Test cricketer with such a distinguished political career.

After Gil Langley came the great Wally Grout, who so sadly died from a heart attack in 1968 when only aged forty-one. His fifty-one

Tests were also crammed into the short time of nine years, and he was already thirty when he played his first Test. He was the epitome of what many people imagine an Australian to be. He was tough, gravel-voiced, hard swearing, and he enjoyed racing and betting. He had the will to win and played Test cricket the hard way, but, as we saw in the previous chapter, was always the complete sportsman. He will best be remembered for his partnership with Alan Davidson, off whom he caught 43 with Alan bowling his fast-left-arm-over-the-wicket and swinging the balls away from the batsmen. But Wally was also a brilliant taker of spin and was reponsible for many of Benaud's and Kline's wickets. I know that Richie places him very high in his list of Test wicket-keepers.

As I've said, he had a rich command of expletives, and it amused me when at the end of a dreary drawn Test match at Sydney in 1963, Wally publicly complained that Ted Dexter had sworn at him. The biter bit!

46 Wally Grout   **47** Rodney Marsh

My final Australian keeper is Rodney Marsh, with the incredible total of 355 Test dismissals in 96 Tests, way ahead of Alan Knott with 269 in one Test less. I saw him in his first Test at Brisbane against Ray Illingworth's MCC side. He was sturdily built, with a figure not unlike that of Gil Langley, but although there was a suspicion of overweight he was remarkably fit and had tremendous energy, flinging himself here, there and everywhere. At that time his enthusiasm outweighed his skill and he did not always take the ball cleanly. In fact he earned the name of iron gloves; this was rather unfair to a young 23-year-old and it not only annoyed him, but acted as a spur for him to prove himself. This of course he did and he was a regular member of Ian Chappell's successful side, becoming the vital apex of the Lillee–Thomson–Marsh triangle. I don't know how many catches he missed off this formidable pair of fast bowlers, but he certainly managed to catch 116 off them (Lillee 88 and Thomson 28). He also kept well when standing up to spinners like Mallett, Gleeson, O'Keeffe and Bright. So after his unfortunate beginning he can point to the records and rightly claim to be the most successful of all Test wicket-keepers.

On the field he was part of Ian Chappell's 'sledging' team, and it was lucky that in those days there was no microphone built into the stumps, as some of the language would have put the transmitters off the air! But although he played hard, he was always fair. You may remember his gesture in the Australian Centenary Test at Melbourne in 1977. Randall had been given out caught by him in answer to a universal appeal from the Australian side, but Marsh indicated to the umpire, Brooks, that the ball had not carried and Randall was allowed to continue his great innings of 174.

Marsh was fun to meet off the field, and I had an enjoyable evening sitting next to him at the English Centenary Dinner in London in 1980. I remember he left the table at one point to go and check on the final racing results. He was a keen betting man, and at Headingley in 1981 gladly accepted the 500–1 odds against England winning. They of course did so, and Marsh and Lillee won some money, if not the Test.

He was probably at his best during Mike Denness's tour in 1974–5. Lillee and Thomson were then at their peak, and were a terrifying combination for the batsmen to face. I saw Marsh having a net on the No. 2 ground at Sydney (now alas no more). I asked him how his hands were standing up to the pace of the dreaded pair, and he showed them to me; they looked sore and bruised. He said he protected them by putting plaster round the joints of his fingers. Quite a few wicket-keepers do this, but it is an awful bore having to bind all the tape round the fingers every time you go out to field. I told him that his fingers reminded me of an old radio comedy series back in England – 'Much Binding in the Marsh'. He looked at me blankly. He had never heard of the show! But always after that I used to call him Much Binders. He didn't seem to mind.

John Edrich

There must be something about the Norfolk air which produces small men with guts. It certainly produced Bill Edrich and his cousin, John, two of the bravest cricketers I have ever seen. John was born in the village of Blofield – not Blofeld, as in Blowers – and joined Surrey in 1958. He played for them for twenty years, and captained them for five seasons between 1973 and 1977. In that time he made 39,790 runs and hit 103 centuries, 12 of which were made for England in 77 Tests. For good measure he made 1,000 runs in 19 of his 21 seasons, and 2,000 6 times.

Mere figures don't, however, adequately portray his real value to England and Surrey. He was the opening batsman every captain dreams of. He was the anchor-man supreme, one of the best judges of line I have ever seen. He seemed to know to the nearest millimetre exactly where his off-stump was, and often had one's heart in one's mouth as he left a ball alone which just missed the stumps.

He was physically very strong and a superb cutter of anything short. He was equally strong off his legs, and when he drove a ball often hit in the air over the arc of mid-off to mid-on. He was also a quick runner between the wickets and a good judge of a run. He opened the innings for England with Geoff Boycott in thirty-two Test innings and was only run out twice! But on one occasion at Adelaide in 1971 it was Boycott who was run out – and was so annoyed that he flung his bat down. Funnily enough John – or Edders as I inevitably called him – often batted at number three – or even four – for England, especially during the time when Boycott had Bob Barber as his partner.

There were two Tests in which he showed the Edrich guts beyond the call of duty. In 1975 at Sydney, after scoring a brave 50 in the first innings, in the second he was hit a sickening blow in the ribs off the first ball which he received from Lillee. He was taken to hospital where two fractured ribs were diagnosed, but this did not stop him returning to the ground and nearly saving the game for

England against the might and fury of Lillee and Thomson. He was not out 33 when, with only $10\frac{1}{2}$ overs left, Geoff (initials G.G., hence nicknamed Horse) Arnold was out. Both he and Bob Willis had put up a brave resistance, the last two wickets adding 26 and 27. Edders had not recovered by the next Test at Adelaide but returned to make a typical 70 in the sixth Test at Melbourne. Incidentally, this is a good question for a cricket quiz. Did John Edrich ever captain England? The answer is yes, in this Sydney Test, when Mike Denness dropped himself due to lack of form.

48 John Edrich

The other battleground was Old Trafford against the West Indies in 1976. Edders was then thirty-nine, and he had made 37 and 76 not out in the first Test at Trent Bridge, where he completed his 5,000 runs in Test cricket. As a result of injury he didn't play at Lord's but was given a 'new' partner to open with him at Old Trafford – a 'young' man called Brian Close who was then aged forty-five. As I said on p. 87, this combination of eighty-four years withstood a terrible onslaught of short-pitched bowling from Holding, Roberts and Daniel for eighty minutes at the start of England's second innings. Neither of them flinched and both were prepared to offer their bruised bodies as a second line of defence. Talk of backs to the wall. This was fronts to the ball and displayed courage and bravery typical of them both.

In 1965 Edders made the highest score of his career against New Zealand at Headingley. His 310 not out is one of eleven triple hundreds made in Test cricket, and only the second by an Englishman in England. There was of course Len Hutton's 364 at the Oval in 1938, and only two others by Englishmen abroad – Wally Hammond's 336 not out against New Zealand at Auckland in 1933 and Andy Sandham's 325 against the West Indies at Kingston in 1930. But he, perhaps surprisingly for the type of player he was, scored more boundaries in his triple hundred than any of the others – 57, which comprised 5 sixes and 52 fours. An interesting comparison is with the highest individual Test score – 365 not out by Gary Sobers at Kingston in 1958. This contained only 38 fours – and no sixes.

As you might expect, Edders has made a success of his business life since retiring from first-class cricket in 1978. He is good-looking, with an engaging smile and a dry sense of humour. He also has a strong character and is not afraid to speak his mind. With his determination and guts he will be as great a success in whatever he tries as he was when facing the world's fastest bowlers.

Graeme Pollock

Graeme Pollock was one of those unlucky South African cricketers who after 1970 were prevented by politics from playing any more Test matches. By 1970 he was already one of the outstanding batsmen in the world and was still only aged twenty-six. What he might have achieved is anybody's guess, but he would surely have rivalled all the other 'greats' in terms of the number of Test runs and hundreds he made.

He was an infant prodigy, encouraged and coached by his father, who was a newspaper editor who played for Orange Free State. Graeme was also helped by his elder brother, Peter, three years his senior. Peter became a fearsome fast bowler who took 116 Test Wickets for South Africa. In fact I made one of my many unfortunate remarks about him. He came over to play for the Rest of the World side at the Scarborough Festival in 1968. He was on his honeymoon and brought his bride with him. We were televising the game with Denis Compton as summariser and myself as commentator. Peter ran up to bowl, slipped and twisted his ankle. He hobbled off and it was soon announced that he had a badly swollen ankle. 'What bad luck,' I said to the viewers, 'especially as he is on his honeymoon. But it will probably be all right in the morning if he puts it up as soon as he gets back to the hotel.' A perfectly innocent remark, but made to appear otherwise by the uncontrolled laughter of Denis.

49 Graeme Pollock

Back to Graeme. He scored his first Currie Cup hundred at the age of sixteen, and made his Test début at Brisbane against Australia three years later. At the age of nineteen he made over 1,000 runs on the tour for an average of 53.27, and scored the first two of his seven Test hundreds in the third and fourth Tests.

I was lucky enough to see three of his hundreds. The first was at Port Elizabeth against England on Mike Smith's tour of 1964–5. It was a superb innings and he became the only Test player other than George Headley to score three Test hundreds before the age of twenty-one. The second one I saw was even better. He made 125 at Trent Bridge the following summer in the second Test against England, off only 145 balls with 21 fours. South Africa had been struggling against the medium-pace seamers of Tom Cartwright, who took 6 for 94. They were 80 for 5 when Graeme was joined by his captain, Peter Van Der Merwe. They put on 98 runs together, of which Van Der Merwe's share was 10!

Graeme's innings was one of the best I have seen in Test cricket. The conditions were humid and there was dampness in the pitch – typical English conditions – but right from the start he dominated the bowlers, who besides Cartwright included John Snow and Freddie Titmus. I shall never forget the timing of his off-drives through extra cover, and the power of his back strokes and cuts off anything short. This was the first time many people in England had seen him in top form, and it was good that those not at Trent Bridge could see him on television.

People were soon talking of a second Frank Woolley. I only saw Frank in his later days: tall, willowy, stiff-backed, but my impression of him was that he was more effortless than Graeme. The ball went off his bat far and often high, but he appeared to stroke it, rather than power-drive like Graeme.

But there was better still to come – at Durban in 1970 in the second Test against Australia. Graeme made 274, his seventh and last Test hundred and the highest Test score for South Africa. He and Barry Richards slaughtered the Australian attack, vying with each other to see who could score the most fours. They put on 103 in an hour after lunch. I was commentating on radio with Charles Fortune and Alan McGilvray, and it was one of the most thrilling commentary periods I have ever had. Graeme finished with a 5 and 43 fours and the crowd at Kingsmead rightly went mad.

Graeme was fair-haired, over six feet tall, strongly built and had a slow shambling gait. I believe that basically he was lazy – at least he never seemed to hurry himself, whether batting or fielding. This was deceptive because, like all the great batsmen, he saw the ball early and had that much more time to play his stroke. He used a very heavy bat for those days, just under 3 lbs, which today of course is common enough. His technique was a perfect blend of power and timing, and not even Sobers could rival his crashing drives through the covers. Like Hammond he had a reputation for being primarily an off-side player, and not so strong on the leg side. In fact, on that 1970 tour by Australia in South Africa, Graham McKenzie and Alan Connolly both tried to concentrate on his leg-stump. Precious good it did them, though perhaps on occasions it slowed him down a bit. His scores of 49, 50, 274, 52, 87, 1, 4 help to show what a fine all round stroke-player he was.

Although not a fast mover in the field, Graeme was a safe catcher at slip, and he also liked to bowl the occasional leg-break. But they were only *occasional*, as his captains did not quite have the same high opinion of them as he did! How difficult it is for a batsman to persuade anyone that he can bowl. On the other hand, bowlers through necessity have every opportunity to show if they can bat. Whether they bat at number ten or number eleven, there is always the odd crisis when they can prove their mettle.

Graeme was also one of those people who succeed in any sport at which they try their hand. Even so, at one time he did have a spot of eye trouble and actually tried to play in glasses, but he soon discarded them and finished his career in South Africa in a blaze of glory. What a pity it is that so few cricket-lovers in England were able to see this blond giant play on the cricket grounds of England. They can justly say 'we was robbed'. It was also sad that MCC did not invite him as one of their many overseas guests to attend the bicentenary match at Lord's. Thanks to a sponsor in South Africa he did finally come, and we were glad to welcome and interview him in the commentary box. But I think MCC did their members – and the general public – a disservice by denying them the chance to welcome one of the greatest left-hand batsmen of all time.

Geoff Boycott

I cannot honestly say that I *know* Geoff Boycott, though he has always been most friendly to me. I call him Boycers and he and my Yorkshire-born wife get on like a house on fire. I covered four MCC tours which he was on, but never really got close to him as a friend. He is a complex character – an enigma – and seems to have a dual personality. I am often asked what he is really like. I always refer the questioner to England or Yorkshire players who have *played* with him. They can give a truer picture.

There is so much to admire in him and in what he has achieved. He was born and brought up in the mining village of Fitzwilliam and became a clerk in the Ministry of Pensions. He was pale-faced, wore glasses and looked an unlikely cricketer. He had been encouraged and supported by an uncle and the rest of the family, and when still a small boy showed a grim determination to become a great cricketer. Whilst other boys played and went to the cinema, he would practise – a word that was to become synonymous with him throughout his career.

50 Geoff Boycott

In 1962 at the age of twenty-two – he played his first match for Yorkshire and in his second county game was responsible for the first of the many run-outs for which he became famous. The following year he made a hundred in his first Roses match against Lancashire. In 1964 he played for England against Australia and scored the first of his twenty-two Test hundreds. It was an incredibly swift rise up the ladder.

It is a story of complete dedication, determination, self-discipline and single-mindedness. As the story of his life unfolds, it is sad to say that perhaps it is more accurate to substitute the word selfishness for single-mindedness. I have always felt that he could have been the perfect golf professional, where all these attributes are essential. He could have played for himself and would have relished the hours of practice necessary to reach the top.

From the start he had this love of batting. Nothing else mattered. He read, questioned, watched and copied to achieve a defensive technique which would prevent bowlers from getting him out. In this he was so successful that he became one of the greatest *defensive* batsmen of all time. Any schoolboy could copy him. Everything was right – sideways on, straight bat, head still, nose 'smelling' the ball. You'll notice that I have qualified my praise by using the word 'defensive'. I have never considered him as a great batsman, pure and simple. He was an insatiable accumulator of runs, but rarely tried to get on top of bowlers by *attacking* them. The only time I ever saw him take an attack apart was in the Gillette Cup Final of 1965 when he made a brilliant 146 against Surrey.

I once asked him why he so seldom tried to 'master' a bowler. He replied quite honestly that he was the best batsman on the side, be it Yorkshire or England. It was therefore essential for him to remain at the crease for as long as possible. Let the others take the risks and make strokes, whilst he slowly accumulated runs at the other end.

It was the same with his famous run-outs. Why was it always the other chap who was run out and not him? Again came the answer that he was the best, and that it was in the interests of his side for the other batsman to make the sacrifice. He has in fact been heard to call out to a young Yorkshire batsman with both of them stranded in mid-wicket: 'Sacrifice, sacrifice.'

There was a famous run-out during the Adelaide Test on Ray Illingworth's tour in 1971. Geoff called for a run on the off-side but the fielder hit the stumps at the bowler's end and he was given run out. He flung his bat down on the ground and stood with his hands on his hips, before being 'steered' towards the pavilion by Greg Chappell. Again I asked him about this and strangely he admitted to me that he *was* out, but he went on to say that he was only out by a few inches, and that the margin was so small that any umpire should have given the batsman the benefit of the doubt.

None of this made him popular with his fellow players, and was one of the reasons for so many young Yorkshiremen becoming discouraged and failing to live up to their early promise. But strangely enough the Yorkshire public seemed to be mesmerised by his runs. The more he scored, the more they worshipped him, and he always had a tremendous following wherever he went. Little did they realise that the *more* runs he made, the *less* likely were Yorkshire to win. He took so long about it. A perfect example was in 1971 – his first year as captain of Yorkshire. He had a wonderful season – for Yorkshire alone he scored 2,197 runs with 11 hundreds and an average of 109.85. And yet Yorkshire had what *Wisden* described as 'the worst season in their history'. They finished thirteenth in the County Championship, and had the longest sequence of seventeen matches without a victory which the county had ever known. They scored a lot of runs, but far too slowly, and only picked up 47 batting bonus points compared with 82 scored by Kent. Only three sides scored fewer than 47.

Against all this you have to set all the good things in Geoff's career as a batsman. His dedication has never been rivalled – he put in hours and hours of practice. On tours on the rest day of a Test others would play golf or go on the beach, but Geoff would be down at the ground batting against any young boys willing to bowl at the Master – and there were always plenty of them. To have bowled Boycott was the highest accolade.

Not naturally athletic, he kept himself wonderfully fit. He went to bed early, only drank the occasional glass of white wine, and never exposed himself to the heat of the sun. No lying around a pool for him. And on the field he looked a wraithlike figure: sleeves down, shirt collar turned up and sometimes a neckerchief round the neck. And always a cap. He may have worn a white floppy hat on occasions but I don't remember them. He was always neatly turned out, with immaculately white trousers, pads and boots.

It's not surprising that he became such a vast accumulator of runs. In five-day Test matches – especially abroad – he did a wonderful job opening for England. He seemed to revel in the good light and faster pitches. The latter seemed to help his favourite scoring stroke, which he executed so well – a square drive off the back foot on the off side, either side of cover. And of course he has some incredible figures. He averaged over 60 in eleven English seasons, and between 50 and 60 on six more. Twice – in 1971 and 1979 – he averaged over 100. And he just managed to pip Tom Graveney on the post as the most prolific scorer of post war batsmen. He scored 48,426 against Tom's 47,793.

Geoff has a deep knowledge of the game and its tactics, and has always studied the strengths and weaknesses of other players. He enjoyed being captain and one ambition, which he never achieved, was to be made captain of England. He did captain them in four Tests on the tour to Pakistan and New Zealand in 1977–8, but only as a stand-in for the injured Brearley. It would be untrue to say that he was a popular captain and he also suffered the indignity of leading England to their first ever defeat by New Zealand.

It was the same when he captained Yorkshire from 1971 to 1978. His tactics were sound enough, but it was not a happy period in Yorkshire cricket. There was no real team spirit, and they won no trophy in any of the four competitions in that time. A cricket captain has to be like the old cavalry officer who always saw the men and horses fed before he had his own meal. A cricket captain has to think of the other ten members of his side before himself. It became obvious that such a single-minded person as Geoff could never be a leader of men.

As a southerner – albeit married to a Yorkshire woman – I refuse to get embroiled in all the internal quarrels in which Geoff was involved. Suffice to say that controversy seemed to follow him wherever he played, ending with the sad finish to his Test career when he came home early from India after achieving his (then) record 8,114 Test runs.

He so often crucified himself. He played in no Test cricket between 1974 and 1977. It was a self-imposed exile because of his disappointment over Mike Denness being given the England captaincy instead of him. When one thinks of the number of Test runs he denied himself over this period, one must appreciate how strongly he felt. Needless to say, being Geoff, when he *did* return against Australia at Trent Bridge in 1977 he made a hundred. And just to show that he had lost none of his reputation for bad calling, he ran out local hero Derek Randall! He was I think unfairly criticised by Tony Greig, who accused him of lacking the courage to face the dreaded pace attack of Lillee and Thomson in Australia in 1974. His colleagues also felt that he had let them down and left them to face the barrage of bumpers, but I don't agree with Tony. Geoff has always had guts and I have never seen him flinch nor back away when facing a fast bowler. Discomforted he may have been, but he was always technically correct right behind the line of the ball.

He made himself into a good fielder and perfected his throw so that on the seventy-five-yard English boundaries at least, the ball would land plop into the wicket-keeper's hands right over the stumps. He was also quite a useful medium-pace in-swing bowler. He always bowled in a cap – like Ronald Colman in the film of *Raffles*. Once, in a big match at Lord's, he even reversed his cap with the peak over the back of his neck, like motorcyclists used to do. He did it just to amuse the crowd and it is worth repeating what a happy rapport he used to have with crowds all over England.

Nowadays, as one would expect, Geoff writes and talks very sensibly about cricket. However, two headlines from his pieces in the *Daily Mail* about England's tour of New Zealand did make me chuckle. It just goes to show how much easier it is to play in the commentary box rather than out in the middle. They read: 'Time we speeded it up' and 'Go-slow spoils perfect day'. He is an excellent summariser on either TV or radio, and I suspect that he will now try to devote himself to this in his retirement. I believe that he will mellow and that his dry sense of humour coupled with his expertise will gain the same rapport with listeners as he used to have with the Yorkshire crowds.

Let's hope too that he now has time to make friends. Surely the fight is over, and controversies a thing of the past. It is sad that, because of his devotion to his own career, he left behind so few real friends in the cricket world. His future is now assured after two highly successful benefits and his recent autobiography, for which he attended more signing sessions than even Ted Heath did for his!

Good luck, then, to Boycers. I wish him well as I finish with this apocryphal story. Geoff reported to St Peter at the Pearly Gates, who asked who he was. St Peter looked at a list which he had, and then said: 'I'm sorry. There's no Geoff Boycott on the list. If you are not on it, you can't come into heaven. So please go away.'

Geoff walked off very disgruntled, but after five minutes' thought went back to St Peter and said: 'Look, I don't think you realise who I am. Geoffrey Boycott of Yorkshire and England. 8,114 Test runs, 22 Test hundreds, 48,426 first-class runs. One of the greatest batsmen of all time. Please let me in.'

St Peter got very annoyed. 'I repeat, if you are not on the list, you cannot come in. For the last time, please go away.'

So Geoff reluctantly left and as he did so a small old man with a long grey beard came up to St Peter and, when asked his name, said: 'Geoffrey Boycott'.

'Oh do come in, Mr Boycott', said St Peter, 'we are delighted to see you. Please come straight into heaven.'

An old cricketer who was standing by said to St Peter: 'What's going on? You turn away the *real* Geoff Boycott, and admit this old man with the long grey beard who pretends he is Boycott but obviously isn't!'

'Oh,' said St Peter, 'we have to humour him. He's God and he keeps on thinking he's Geoffrey Boycott!'

Mike Procter

Not many people have counties named after them. Worcestershire was of course known for many years as Fostershire because of the seven Foster brothers – B. S., G. N., H. K., M. K., N. J. A., R. E. and W. L. – all of whom played for the county. So did H. K.'s son C. K. But the same honour was accorded Mike Procter during his sixteen years with Gloucestershire. Especially during his successful captaincy from 1977 to 1981, the county became known as Proctershire, so great was his influence and popularity. He was tall, fair, chubby-faced and strong as an ox. He bowled very fast off a prodigiously long run. He charged in at a terrific rate, hair flopping, ground shaking. He must have been an awe-inspiring sight to a batsman. He delivered the ball 'off the wrong foot' square on to the batsman, with a whirlwind arm action. As a result he bowled mainly in-swingers, but occasionally resorted to fast off-breaks. He only played in seven Tests, all against Australia in South Africa. In three Tests in 1967 he took 15 wickets and in 1970, 26 wickets in four Tests, making a total of 41 wickets – an average of a fraction under 6 wickets a Test – 5.85. This compares with Syd Barnes's average of 7.00 and just beats Clarrie Grimmett's 5.81. Otherwise Proccers beats all the other Test bowlers for rate of strike. Of course it's not really fair to compare his figures with bowlers who have taken 300, 200 or even 100 more wickets than him, but it does give some sort of clue as to what he might have achieved had he played in more Tests. It is difficult truly to assess his speed, but when fully fit he must have been as fast as any of his contemporaries.

He came over to England with his friend, Barry Richards, in 1965. Both intended to qualify for Gloucestershire and they both played in one match – against the visiting South African side. They didn't do too badly either. They were top scorers in a total of 279, Richards 59, Procter 69, and put on 116 for the fifth wicket in just over ninety minutes. *Wisden* reported that Proctor (sic) was the dominant partner. They finished that season as dressing-room

attendants at the Oval during the fifth Test against South Africa –
a useful way of absorbing Test match atmosphere.

51 Mike Procter

They both came back to England in 1968, Richards to play for
Hampshire, and Procter for Gloucestershire, and from then on until
he had to retire in 1981 due to bad knees Proccers was the mainstay
of Gloucestershire. Besides his bowling he was a magnificent field
anywhere, and as a batsman pure and simple would have been
worth his place in any Test side. He was a magnificent stroke-player
who scored at a very fast rate. Because of the amount of bowling
he had to do, he didn't achieve as much as Richards with the bat,
but I reckon there was little between them in actual technique. What
a difference in temperament, however. Richards, the casual rather
bored player who needed crowds and incentive to bring out his
best, and Proccers, who just loved to play cricket. He was a great
trier and never gave up, and he gave everything he had towards
helping Gloucestershire. And they loved him for it.

What's more, he brought success to W. G.'s old county. In 1976
and 1977 they finished third in the County Championship, only just
behind the leaders. In his first year of captaincy Gloucestershire
won the Benson and Hedges Final at Lord's. He was an inspiring
captain and cared for his players, who would have followed him

anywhere. A perfect example was in the Benson and Hedges Final. A young player called David Partridge had not made much impression in the match. He didn't get an innings and so far as I remember dropped a catch, and was looking rather out of things fielding under the grandstand balcony. When it became apparent that Gloucestershire were going to win, Proccers called him up to have a bowl. His three overs were expensive, and cost 22 runs, though he did take the valuable wicket of Alan Knott, but the point was that Proccers wanted him to have a share in the victory. A most thoughtful piece of captaincy.

Proccers performed some splendid feats. He scored 1,000 runs in a season nine times, and took 100 wickets twice. He did the hat-trick four times in county matches – in 1979 in two successive matches against Leicestershire and Yorkshire. What's more, in the Leicestershire match he also made a hundred before lunch! And there's more to come! In his hat-trick against Yorkshire at Cheltenham all his three victims were lbw – something he also achieved in his 1972 hat-trick against Sussex, bowling round the wicket at a tremendous pace.

As if all the above was not enough, he once scored six hundreds in consecutive innings for Rhodesia. So all in all a remarkable player who because of his skills, guts and keenness would always be *my* all-rounder in any world eleven – just so long as Gary Sobers was unfit to play!

Colin Milburn

Saturday, 24 May 1969, was one of the saddest days in my cricketing life. I was at Lord's to commentate on the annual Whitsun match between Middlesex and Sussex. About an hour before the luncheon interval BBC news telephoned me to say that the previous night Colin Milburn had had a bad car accident and had lost his left eye. Would I, as BBC cricket correspondent, please do a 'piece' in the one o'clock news. This was the first that I had heard of the accident and it was a tremendous shock. I immediately knew what a tragedy it was for Colin, whose whole life revolved around cricket. Not just playing it, but the whole way of life, the companionship and friendly atmosphere of the cricket circuit. He was a natural who had played cricket all his life, and was quite untrained for any other job. I realised that the future was bleak for him. It was even doubtful then whether the sight of his other eye could be saved – there were splinters of glass still in it. You can imagine how difficult it was for me to do my piece but I got through it somehow, though not without the occasional break in my voice.

52 Colin Milburn

A few days later I went to visit Colin in hospital in Northampton. I took him a bottle of champagne to cheer him up, but it was not necessary. There he was, smiling and as cheerful as ever. He later told me that several of the many visitors he had broke down in tears, and that he had to try to cheer *them* up! Luckily the sight of his right eye was saved.

So what sort of person is Ollie, as he is always called? He was – and still is – the Billy Bunter of cricket. Large, jolly, fat with a big frame and a tremendous appetite, he is always laughing and has always been the butt of jokes – both verbal and practical. But he takes it all smiling. He's rather like Charlie Naughton in the Crazy Gang. The rest of the gang, led by Bud Flanagan, used to play cruel jokes on him, both on stage and off it. If they didn't do something outrageous to him during a performance he would ask them after-wards what he had done wrong.

I was still doing TV commentary in the summer of 1969 and it was nice that we were able to ask Ollie to join our commentary team of Richie Benaud, Denis Compton, Peter West and myself. We had always had fun in the box, but with Ollie there it became even better. I shall never forget one Test match at the Oval, when in those days we had a small wooden hut on the roof of the pavilion. Somehow we all managed to squeeze in, even with Ollie, but he had to stand leaning against the door. It was a terribly windy day and when someone opened the door from the outside, the gale caught the door and blew it wide open, taking Ollie with it. He landed safely with a plump on the roof, and of course we all got hysterics. We were saved by the coolness and professionalism of Richie Benaud, who, although the summariser, took over the commentary while we recovered.

Since then Ollie has done much radio and TV cricket, usually as a summariser, and has proved himself a knowledgeable, fair and practical critic and a humorist, all in one. He always played for fun and enjoyed it, and this comes through in this comments.

Ollie is a Geordie, born in Co. Durham, and was one of the many cricketers to come south from there to play county cricket. He was immensely strong with a good eye and was always attacking the bowling. He was a particularly good cutter and hooker but could also drive immense distances, and for a big heavy man was remarkably nimble on his feet. He was an ideal opening batsman, who could tear the new-ball bowlers apart. He played fast bowling especially well and was very brave, however fast and short the bowlers bowled. Perhaps he gained extra confidence by knowing that his rolls of fat would cushion any blow received on his body! But for some reason the selectors were shy of selecting him, perhaps thinking him too big a risk, and also a liability because of his slowness in the field, but in fact he was a very good catcher close to the wicket, even if he didn't exactly *sprint* after the ball! As a result he only played in nine Tests, but made 645 runs with the high average of 46.71, and in county cricket for Northants hit 1,000 runs in a season six times.

His first Test was against the West Indies at Old Trafford in 1966. He opened England's innings with Eric Russell, but was run out for 0, slipping up when being sent back. However, he scored a splendid 94 in the second innings. He followed this up with 126 not out in the Lord's Test, and scores of 7, 12, 29 and 42 before being dropped for the fifth Test at the Oval, when John Edrich took his place. The following year he played in two Tests against India and Pakistan in England before touring the West Indies under Colin Cowdrey. He had a frustrating time, as with Boycott, Edrich, Cowdrey, Barrington, Graveney, D'Oliveira and Knott there was not much opportunity for him and he did not play in a single Test. However, back in England he made a fine 83 against Australia at Lord's, but then injured his hand so couldn't play for England again until the Oval Test. England won this with five minutes to spare after the famous 'mopping up' operation after a torrential thunderstorm, in which all the spectators took part, thus enabling the game to re-start and giving England time to win.

He wasn't selected for Cowdrey's tour of Pakistan that winter so went to play cricket in Western Australia, for whom he made a sensational 243 against Queensland at Brisbane. It was Ollie's highest score: he hit 4 sixes and 38 fours and made 131 runs in the two hours between lunch and tea.

It was shortly after this, when Ollie had returned to Perth, that he received a cable from Donald Carr at Lord's which said briefly: 'You will catch the next plane to Dacca in Pakistan'. This was an order, so Ollie had to travel a roundabout route to Dacca, arriving about two days later, short of sleep and rather bewildered by the whole thing. He didn't know that there were some doubts about Cowdrey's fitness, after he had made exactly 100 in the first Test.

Anyhow, the whole team and all the media went to the airport to meet Ollie. He was garlanded with flowers as he descended on to the tarmac, where he gave his famous rendering of 'The Green, Green Grass of Home' – his signature tune. Colin and the manager, Les Ames, explained to Ollie that unfortunately there was no accommodation for him in the team's very comfortable Inter-Continental Hotel, but they told Ollie that they had, with great difficulty, managed to book him into a downtown doss-house called The Shatbag Hotel, and they hoped he wouldn't mind too much if it wasn't all that comfortable. He was surprised and horrified when he was driven to The Shatbag, but was so tired that all he wanted to do was sleep. However, the good news was then broken to him and he was taken to the team's hotel.

He took several days to recover from his journey and wasn't fit enough to be considered for the Dacca Test, but he was selected for the third Test at Karachi which ended with a riot on the third day, and we all packed up that night and flew back to England. Not, however, before Ollie had justified his trip by scoring 139, reaching his hundred off only 163 balls. It was his last Test innings, though at the time we all thought that now at last Ollie would be certain of a regular place in the England team. This seemed even more probable when, on 17 May, he made 158 in only 77 overs with five sixes, and sixteen fours against Leicestershire. But alas it was not to be, as six days later he had his accident.

A proof of what a great character Ollie is, was the effect his arrival had on the MCC team when he arrived at Dacca. It had been a miserable tour, with politics and riots interfering with what should have been a few happy weeks, but as soon as Ollie came everyone cheered up and there was much fun and laughter. He has a very good voice and has a large repertoire (in more senses than one!). He and I have always sung two songs together – 'Underneath the Arches' and 'Me and my Shadow'. We even entertained the Pakistan team at one of the airports so much that their captain, Saeed Ahmed, went to the gift shop and bought us two very nice presents.

At one time after his accident Ollie continued to live in his flat at Northampton, where he was well looked after by a caring landlady, but later he went back to live with his mum at Burnopfield and has done a number of jobs, mostly connected with cricket. He hosts cricket tours abroad, he coaches at Butlins, he does after-dinner speeches and PR work, and is increasingly doing what he most loves to do – cricket commentary. The spate of phone-ins for the latest cricket scores has meant that when the BBC cannot use him he is fully occupied doing the commentaries for British Telecom. Not only does the caller get the latest score from Ollie, but they hear his cheerful voice as well, which makes the 38p a minute call well worth while.

At Trent Bridge during the first Test in 1988 I committed one of my gaffes. We were talking about Ollie and I said: 'That happened shortly after Ollie died.' Someone quickly pointed out that I surely meant 'after he had lost his eye'. Of course I corrected myself, hoping that Ollie's mum had not been listening. She is very fond of 'her boy'. But Ollie had been listening next door, and rushed into the commentary box saying: 'It's all right. I've been resurrected!'

Ollie has shown tremendous courage in overcoming his handicap. He never shows the disappointment and frustration which he must obviously feel, especially when he's commentating and a fast bowler bowls a short ball which just asks to be cut or hooked. How he must ache to be out there, but he is never bitter. Instead, he is the source of much fun and laughter and we love having him in the box with us.

John Snow

I don't know whether 'Snowy' ever did any acting when he was a schoolboy at Christ's Hospital, but he would have made a perfect Hamlet. He was moody and temperamental, and normally went round with a fierce dead-pan expression on his face. It was only when you knew him that he broke into a friendly smile. I suspect he put on this façade to promote fear in the hearts of batsmen, although it's true to say that he was genuinely anti-establishment and against any sort of authority. Quite why this should be I don't know, because his father was a Church of England vicar, but throughout his career he had brushes with committees, his captains and occasionally the press.

He was undoubtedly one of England's best fast bowlers, filling in between the Statham–Trueman era and Bob Willis. In 49 Tests he took 202 wickets, and it's interesting to compare this with Bedser's 236 in 51 Tests, Statham's 252 in 70, Trueman's 307 in 67 and Willis's 325 in 90. He was one of those fast bowlers whom it was a pleasure to watch, if not to play. He was wiry and slim and had a relaxed, loping, rhythmic run-up. At the wicket he was not completely sideways on, but near enough. He was not anywhere near as square-on as Bob Willis. He was probably not as regularly fast as Trueman, Statham and Willis, but could send down some quick and vicious deliveries. He had a good bouncer, but didn't over-use it. He was basically in-swing, though with movement off the pitch from leg to off. When in the mood he could be lethal, and here comes the crunch: there were too many occasions – even for England – when he didn't appear to be putting everything into it.

One cannot expect a fast bowler in between Tests to give his maximum the whole time for his county – although look at Trueman's figures for Yorkshire – but it is suprising that Snowy only took 100 wickets in a season twice, although on the Hove pitch he could prove devastating. It needed a Mike Brearley to make a study of him to find the best way of handling him. Ray Illingworth succeeded on his MCC tour in Australia in 1970–1. Prior to the first Test at Brisbane, Snowy didn't seem too interested in the State games. Perhaps he was keeping himself for the Tests, and he also had some skin trouble with his toes, but Ray decided to have a chat and made it quite plain that if Snowy didn't buck up, he would be dropped and possibly even sent home.

53 John Snow

It worked like magic. Snowy proceeded to take 6 for 114, and 2 for 48 at Brisbane with bowling which *Wisden* said 'filled the Australians with apprehension'. He went on to take 31 wickets in the series, which would surely have been more had he not broken a finger at the start of Australia's second innings in the final Test at Sydney. This was the match when Illingworth led the England team off the field, and as I was commentating at the time I think it is worth repeating how I saw the incident.

England made 184 in their first innings, and just after tea on the second day Illingworth took the new ball with Greg Chappell and Terry Jenner together and the score 180 for 7. The first two overs with the new ball were bowled by Snow and Lever with no suspicion of a bouncer. With the seventh ball of the third over Snow, however, did bowl a bouncer at Jenner who ducked into it, was hit on the back of the head, collapsed, and had to be carried off. The crowd naturally enough booed and shouted, roaring their disapproval of Snow. While the new batsman Lillee was on his way out to the wicket, Lou Rowan, the umpire at Snow's end, told Snow that he should not have bowled a bouncer at a low-order batsman like Jenner. Snow became incensed at this and asked Rowan in not too polite a way whose side he thought he was on. Umpire Rowan then seemed to lose his temper and in what appeared to be an emotional decision, promptly warned Snow under Law 46, Note 4 (IV) for persistent bowling of short-pitched balls. Then it was Illingworth's turn to protest at what he considered a wrong interpretation of the law. How could one bouncer come under the heading of persistent?

Unfortunately, in the heat of the moment, Illingworth also became annoyed and was seen by thousands on the ground and tens of thousands on television to wag his finger at Lou Rowan. What in fact he was trying to indicate was that Snow had only bowled 'one' bouncer. He was not trying to admonish the umpire. Amid a storm of booing – I've seldom heard such a noise on the cricket ground – Snow completed his over by bowling one ball at Lillee. He then turned to go off to his position at long leg. When he had got halfway there some beer cans were thrown in his direction from the small Paddington Hill to the left of the Noble Stand. Snow turned back and returned to the square, where Illingworth told the umpires that he would not go on playing until the field was cleared of the cans. The team sat down while this was being done by the ground staff. After a few minutes the ground was clear and Snow set off again for long leg.

I remember saying on the air at the time that I thought the whole incident was going to end happily, as members in the Noble Stand and people on the hill started to applaud Snow and a man stretched out over the railings to shake hands with Snow. Snow went up and shook hands, but a tough-looking spectator who had obviously 'had a few' then grabbed hold of Snow's shirt and started to shake him. This was the signal for more cans and bottles to come hurtling on to the field, narrowly missing Snow. Willis ran up and shouted something to the crowd. Then Illingworth came up, saw the bottles flying and promptly signalled to his team to leave the field. The two batsmen and two umpires stayed on the square. Then the two umpires made their way to the pavilion – the first time they had left the square since the trouble started. Rowan made it plain to Illingworth that if he did not continue he would forfeit the match and an announcement was made that play would be resumed as soon as the ground had been cleared, not only of the cans and bottles but also of a number of spectators who had clambered over the fence. This, in fact, took only ten minutes and Illingworth led his men back thirteen minutes after leading them off. In the remaining forty minutes the England side somewhat naturally seemed to have lost their zest, and Chappell and Lillee added 45 runs so that Australia finished the day 235 for 7 – a lead of 51.

That was the incident as I saw it, though it is true to say that opinions differ about what exactly did happen. I said at the time, and I still believe, that Illingworth was right to lead the side off. Not only was it becoming dangerous with bottles flying around, but this action so stunned the crowd that the throwing stopped immediately and play was very soon restarted. In other similar circumstances in the West Indies, the fielding side had stayed on the field and play had to be abandoned for the day. There was, of course, no excuse for Illingworth to argue in such a demonstrative manner with the umpire. He has since publicly said he was sorry he acted as he did, and also concedes that he should have gone back to the square and warned the umpires that he was taking his team off, but he had to make a quick decision and it is surprising that neither umpire left the square at any time to go to deal with the incident at the trouble spot. Illingworth and Snow have also been criticised for Snow's return to long leg after the first lot of cans had been thrown at him. There are two views about this. As captain, you either take the peaceful way out and give way to force and threats or you stick to your right to place your fieldmen where you like. Finally, Snow was criticised for going up to the fence and accepting the proffered handshake. Who can say what the reaction would have been if he hadn't? I apologise for dealing at such length with this unhappy incident, and now you must judge for yourselves.

It was in Australia's second innings, after Snow had bowled Eastwood for 0, that going for a high catch at long leg off Lever he somehow caught a finger in the boundary fence and broke it. He went off with the bone showing through the broken skin, and couldn't bowl again that Test.

Snowy enjoyed batting and in fact first went to Sussex as a batsman who could bowl, occasionally opening for them in one-day games. He played some useful innings for England and perhaps most enjoyed his last-wicket stand with Ken Higgs at the Oval against the West Indies in 1966. They both made their maiden first-class fifties and put on 128 for the last wicket, only 2 runs short of the world-record last-wicket stand of 130, made for England by R. E. Foster and W. Rhodes at Sydney in 1903–4. Snowy's share was 59 not out, and as the West Indies attack included Wes Hall, Charlie Griffith, Gary Sobers and Lance Gibbs he had every reason to be pleased.

This was not his highest Test score. That came in 1971 at Lord's against India, when he was top scorer for England with 73, but the match finished unfortunately for him. In India's second innings Gavaskar was going for a short single, and Snowy, following through, seemed deliberately to block his way and knock him over. In spite of an apology at the lunch interval, Snowy was dropped from the next Test as a disciplinary measure.

When trying he could be a fine fielder with a strong arm, but he did tend to lose interest in a game as he stood down at long leg. This is not just me being critical. He himself confirmed many of the criticisms against him by entitling his autobiography *Cricket Rebel*, but to soften this rather macho image, he also published two volumes of poems. One was about a butterfly and my son, Barry, tried to put it to music, but I'm afraid nothing came of it. Snowy was one of the first to sign for Kerry Packer, thus virtually ending his first-class career in this country. I still see him, and the smile always breaks through. So it should. He is happily married with two young daughters and has become a successful travel agent, concentrating especially on cricket tours.

He was a varying character both on and off the field, but when he was bowling at his fastest and best I always reckoned that his signature tune should have been 'There's no business like Snow business'.

Dennis Amiss

Twice recently when travelling by train to Birmingham I have met an old friend, immaculately dressed in pin-stripe suit, carrying an important-looking briefcase and smoking a pipe. In other words, a typical businessman with no hint that he had ever been a famous Test cricketer. It was Dennis Amiss, who even before his retirement in 1987 had joined a firm dealing in office planning and design. It was typical of his character that he had planned his retirement long before he played his last innings for Warwickshire.

54 Dennis Amiss

He was born in Birmingham and first played for them at the age of seventeen, and so was a first-class cricketer for twenty-eight uninterrupted summers. Dennis had a remarkable career of loyalty and success: 43,423 runs, 102 centuries and an average of 42.86. He played in 50 Tests, scored 3,612 runs, hit 11 centuries and had the high average of 46.30, but as I have said so often, mere figures don't give truthfully the real value of a player. Dennis didn't just make runs. He set a wonderful example of what a true professional should be, not just by his skills but by his behaviour and the example he set.

He had the air of a countryman – burly, pipe-smoking, with strong forearms and a rolling walk. Like Tom Graveney he was basically a front-foot player, but he had all the strokes and could adapt his style to suit the conditions. And like Geoff Boycott he had a rock-solid defence and great powers of concentration, which enabled him to play long innings.

He was probably happiest and most successful when opening the innings, which he did in 38 Tests for England, and from the early seventies onwards for Warwickshire. All his 11 Test hundreds were made when going in first, and in addition to them he made 99, 90, 86*, 82, 79 and at least 9 other scores in the 40s and 50s, but it's the size of his hundreds which reveal his concentration and ability to accumulate runs over a long period of time. Here they are: 262, 203, 188, 183, 179, 174, 164, 158, 138, 118, 112. Amazing figures really, and as I say all made when opening the innings.

It was not smooth going all the way, however, and he will always remember the torrid time in Australia in 1974–5 when, like other England batsmen, he was shell-shocked by the battering from Lillee and Thomson. He made 90 in the third Test, and 37 and 25 in two others, but finished with a hat-trick of ducks in the fifth and sixth Tests. Two years later he had to face some of the fastest bowling I have ever seen, when he played for MCC against the West Indies. I purposely sat sideways on to check on Holding's pace as he bowled from the Pavilion End. It was frightening just to watch, and on a darkish Saturday evening poor Dennis was hit an awful crack on the back of the head. He ducked to a short ball without keeping his eye on it, and one could still see the effect of Lillee and Thomson in the jittery state of his batting.

He came back to bat on the Monday with four stitches in his wound, but not surprisingly he only made 9 and 11 in the two innings and was not selected to play in the first four Tests; but he was averaging over 60 for Warwickshire and so was brought back for the fifth Test at the Oval. Whatever he felt, he didn't show it and with tremendous guts stood up to the pace of Holding, Roberts and Daniel and made a magnificent 203 out of 435. It was a triumphant return for him and must have done much to restore his confidence, as did the helmet which first Brearley and then he decided to wear. Dennis designed a model which was used by many of the players. It has been improved since then, and the modern helmet is stronger and tougher than his original, but they are hot and heavy compared to a cap and with protection for the ears and a visor to shield the face they must be very frustrating and uncomfortable to wear. There must be a feeling of being shut off from what is going on around you, and I am sure that quite a few run-outs result from the batsmen not being able to hear each other properly; but they have come to stay. Who am I – an ex-club cricketer and watcher from the safety of the commentary box – to criticise anyone who uses them?

Dennis's Test career was finished when he signed for Kerry Packer in 1977, otherwise I am certain he would have played many more Tests for England. But it was a decision he made for the sake of the future security of his family, and remember that until the arrival of Packer and the generous sponsorship of Cornhill, England players were undoubtedly grossly underpaid. It says much for his skill and fitness that he continued to be a highly successful batsman for Warwickshire, until at the age of forty-four he found the old legs feeling the strain of a long innings in the field. He had always been a good fielder anywhere and when he began playing bowled left-arm medium slow. It is as a batsman of the highest grade and character that he will always be remembered, however, and there was universal rejoicing when he finally scored his hundredth century against Lancashire at Edgbaston on 29 July 1986. He got it in the last twenty overs, thanks to the sportsmanship of Clive Lloyd, who allowed the match to go on even though a draw was certain. His hundred only took Dennis 114 minutes and so was probably the fastest of his career. He was to score two more before he finally retired at the end of the 1987 season. If you are ever thinking of planning a new office, give him a ring. One thing is certain. He won't let you down.

Basil d'Oliveira

Dolly, as he is inevitably called – was the innocent cause of international cricket's biggest crisis – surpassing even the furore caused by the Bodyline Tour of Australia. It resulted in South Africa voluntarily resigning from the International Cricket Conference and being ostracised from Test cricket. And it so nearly didn't happen.

In the winter of 1967–8 Dolly had had an unsuccessful tour of the West Indies under Colin Cowdrey. He was out of form and never seemed fully match fit. Perhaps he enjoyed the tempting mixture of rum and sun too much. Anyway, when he came back there was no question of him being considered for the first four Tests against Australia, nor, after his West Indies tour, would anyone have had him on their list for South Africa in the following winter, but then fate took a hand. Roger Prideaux was selected for the Oval Test after his début in Test cricket in the fourth Test at Headingley, where he made 64, but just before the Oval he declared himself unfit with bronchitis. Colin Cowdrey suddenly thought he needed a fifth bowler to support David Brown, John Snow, Derek Underwood and Ray Illingworth. He rang Doug Insole, chairman of the selectors, and asked for Dolly. It was an inspired choice

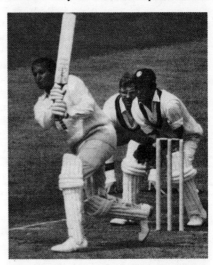

55 Basil d'Oliveira

because, although he was missed by Barry Jarman when 31, he went on to make 158. Furthermore, in Australia's second innings, when a draw looked certain after a rainstorm, he made the vital break-through when he bowled Barry Jarman. This paved the way for Derek Underwood to mop up the last 4 wickets and for England to win with five minutes to spare.

Then came the selection of the team for the winter tour of South Africa. Even after Dolly's performance at the Oval, those of us who had seen him on tour in the West Indies never thought he would be selected.

The selectors met in the MCC committee-room, and as the BBC's cricket correspondent I was waiting outside the glass door whilst they deliberated. The six o'clock news was due to come over to me 'live' as soon as the team was announced. There had been terrific speculation in the media as to whether Dolly would be chosen or not, and it is fair to say that most people thought that he definitely should be, after his fine 158 at the Oval.

The six o'clock news had already started when Billy Griffith, the MCC secretary, hurried out and gave me a list of the selected team. I asked the news to come over to me in two minutes' time, so that I could quickly analyse the team. In those days I frequently had to announce teams on the air and always read them out: captain, batsmen, bowlers, wicket-keepers and all-rounders in that order.

I quickly sorted out the names, and realised at once that Dolly was not one of them. When the news came over to me I announced them in my usual order, so that – but this was not intentional – anyone listening to hear if Dolly had been chosen would expect to have to wait for the all-rounders at the end. I remember including Ken Barrington as an all-rounder, which pleased him a great deal, though he said he had had the willies when his name was not among the batsmen.

The omission of Dolly caused an uproar in the press, and the selectors and administrators were severely criticised for bowing to South African pressure. But then once again fate stepped in. Tom Cartwright, selected as a bowler who could bat a bit, declared himself unfit, and the selectors' took the easy way out. They selected Dolly. When asked about Dolly after their original meeting Doug Insole said that they had considered Dolly, but only as a batsman. Now they chose him instead of a bowler and so upset the balance of the side.

This was enough for the South African government. Prime Minister Vorster said it was a political decision and promptly refused to accept Dolly as a member of the MCC team. There was nothing left for the MCC committee to do but to call the tour off. As a result, South Africa resigned from the ICC and haven't played England at Test cricket since.

That, briefly, is what happened in what became known as The D'Oliveira Affair, and it is important to emphasise how well Dolly behaved throughout. He acted with great dignity and restraint and never put a foot wrong.

He was a Cape Coloured born in Cape Town. In what year is not known for certain. *Wisden* originally had his birthday as 4 October 1934, but there was always some doubt about this and the question of his age became a bit of a joke. Later *Wisden* 'adjusted' his birth date to 4 October 1931, which is probably about right. Dolly played local club cricket in Cape Town and scored eighty hundreds. His reputation soon spread to England and in 1960, through the help of John Arlott, Peter Walker (himself a South African) and John Kay of the *Manchester Evening News*, Dolly came to England. At a salary of £450 he played for Middleton in the Central Lancashire League. Friends in Cape Town paid for his fare and expenses and for a year he had to leave his wife and children behind. It took tremendous courage to do what he did. It was a step into the unknown, but he knew it was the only chance he would ever have to play first-class cricket. After four years with Middleton he qualified for Worcestershire in 1965, having made a hundred for them the previous year against the Australians.

It is an incredible story of determination to reach the top, and by 1966 he was playing his first Test for England at Lord's against the West Indians. His first four scores were 27 (run out), 76, 54, 88. For the next six years he was to play 44 Tests averaging 40 with an aggregate of 2,484 runs. In addition he took 47 wickets and became England's regular all-rounder, batting at number five or six and acting as the third-change bowler. He bowled slow-medium, with a lovely sideways action off a short run. He swung the ball and moved it off the seam and soon gained a reputation as a breaker of stands.

As a batsman he was a hard hitter of the ball, but believed in playing himself in. 'The first hour belongs to the bowler,' he used to say. 'After that I'm in charge.' He was immensely strong, especially in his forearms, and had a remarkably short back-lift, but his timing was perfect and the ball would leave his bat at a rate of knots. In defence he was very correct, which speaks volumes for his ability to learn during his four years with Middleton.

A remarkable man, Dolly, coming from the background he did and at such a late stage in his life. He is always a good companion, with a delightful laugh rather like a hyena's. He is exceedingly gregarious and social and much enjoys a party. It's always better to argue with him before he gets 'warmed up', otherwise you are liable to be prodded hard in the chest as he tries to ram home his argument. He's a persuasive fellow too. I was so pleased that he was one of the many England players who came on my 'This is your Life'. Thames TV call the participants to an early rehearsal and there is always a long wait back stage. I believe they were called for an early lunch, had a brief rehearsal and then had to hang around until I arrived at about 5.00 p.m. Wisely, perhaps, Thames TV close the bar after lunch, but on this occasion they were 'persuaded' to reopen it by two very thirsty ex-England players – Godfrey Evans and, of course, Dolly. They were very cheerful when they finally came on to shake my hand, but of course behaved impeccably!

When he retired Dolly became the coach at Worcester, where his son, Damian, has profited from his advice. He always makes everyone welcome, with that distinctive laugh and the occasional prod in the chest. His is a fairy story with a happy ending, and I will always admire his successful efforts to rise from club cricket in the Cape to Test cricket for his adopted England.

Derek Underwood

I always call him Unders, but then I have never had to play against him. Those who have, call him Deadly. A very apt name, as anyone who has seen him wheeling away for the last twenty-five years will testify. I was lucky enough to see him as a seventeen-year-old in his first sensational season for Kent, when he became the youngest bowler ever to take 100 wickets in a season – 101 actually, and he took exactly the same number in 1964. But his third season was a comparative failure – he only took 89!

I always enjoyed watching him bowl in those early days. Fair-haired, fresh-faced and already with those large flat feet. His parents followed him around wherever he played, and I could always be certain of a good cup of tea and a bun during the tea interval, when I would join them at their car. They were intensely proud of him, and supported and encouraged him in everything he did. He was a unique bowler. There has never been one quite like him. He was near-medium pace and usually cut the ball rather than spin it. His main weapons were his perfect length and line, his flight and variations in pace. He also had a well-disguised 'arm' ball, bowled a little faster, and from which Alan Knott made many leg-side stumpings.

His accuracy frustrated even the best batsmen. They could never collar him, and it was extremely difficult to hit him over the top. He always liked to start with a maiden over, after which he would get in a groove and was quite happy to bowl all day. He just loved bowling. 'If you don't bowl you cannot take wickets,' he once said. As you can imagine, every captain enjoyed having him in their side. It meant that you could block one end, and experiment at the other.

56 Derek Underwood

On a rain-affected pitch he was practically unplayable, as in addition to turn he got bounce out of the pitch as well. Strangely, he was not quite so devastating on a dry pitch which was cracking up and losing its top surface. But he will go down as one of the greatest slow bowlers – only Wilfred Rhodes and George Lohmann were younger when they reached their 1,000 wickets. Unders did it in his seventh season at the age of twenty-five. His 297 Test wickets could well have been at least a hundred more had he not decided to sign for Kerry Packer and later go on the 'rebel' tour to South Africa. Like most of the others who did the same, he did it for the sake of family security, and gave himself a strong financial base. It is difficult to criticise anyone who puts his family before his own career, but I personally felt very sad at his decisions. He and Alan Knott were both sadly missed by England, though after the famous Packer law case, they were allowed to play for Kent during the English summers.

He enjoyed batting and became the automatic night-watchman for both England and Kent. He had a good defensive technique but loved to play his favourite scoring stroke – over mid-wicket's head. Not strictly orthodox but often effective. In his capacity of night-watchman he always showed tremendous guts against the fast bowlers, in spite of getting a sickening blow on the mouth (before helmets) from a Charlie Griffith bouncer in his first Test at Trent Bridge in 1966. Possibly his happiest moment was when he scored his maiden century at Hastings in 1984 at the age of thirty-nine.

He decided to retire at the end of 1987 and has been sadly missed by Kent, and even by his opponents. He is such a nice, modest person, with a hearty laugh, and real enjoyment of life. A final example of his love of and dedication to cricket was the way he made himself into a good fielder. With his flat feet he was not naturally athletic, but he was a safe catcher and had a good arm which he used effectively from his usual position down at long leg. Let's hope that someone somewhere discovers another Unders, with both his skill and technique and his lovable reliable character.

Clive Lloyd

It would be difficult to find a more unlikely-looking athlete than Clive Hubert Lloyd. Spectacles, drooping head – often covered by a white floppy sun hat – a round-shouldered figure with a shambling, gangling gait. As he walked to the wicket he would prod the ground impatiently with his bat. And what a bat! It was the first of the real heavies, weighing at least $3\frac{1}{4}$ lbs, possibly more. The handle was of double thickness, and once at Robertsbridge in Sussex, where the bats are made, I tried to get my hands round it and failed. I thought my hands were fairly big, but his are very large with long fingers.

He is six feet five inches tall and had immensely strong forearms which enabled him to wield his giant 'club'. He was one of the hardest and biggest hitters I have ever seen, and his favourite stroke was the lofted drive, when the ball seemed to 'sail' clean out of the ground. He was equally severe on anything short, hitting the ball off the back foot just wide of cover, or hooking it hard and high over the square-leg boundary. In contrast, he could defend as well as anyone if necessary, since his basic method was so correct.

Early in his career the England bowlers used to think he was a sucker to the ball just outside his off-stump, before he got his eye in, but in later years there was not much sign of this. His figures cannot portray the extent to which he could turn a match by his hitting, nor the number of times when, but for him, a high run-rate required for victory would never have been achieved. Even so, 7,515 runs (second only to Gary Sobers' 8,032) for the West Indies in Tests at an average of 46.67, and 31,232 first-class runs at an average of 49.26 do prove that he was one of the outstanding batsmen in post-war years.

57 Clive Lloyd

These figures do not of course include his performances in limited-over cricket, where he excelled, both for the West Indies in their two Prudential World Cup Final wins in 1975 (102) and 1979 (13), but also for Lancashire in their run of victories in the Gillette Cup Final. They did the hat-trick – 1970, 1971 and 1972 – and won again in 1975; and Clive contributed scores of 29, 66, 126 and 73 not out.

Not many batsmen have been reported to the police for aggression – at least not on the field! But once in a match against Kent at Dartford I saw him pepper a row of adjoining houses with a string of giant sixes. An elderly lady was so terrified that she dialled 999 and called the police for help!

Clive never seems to have been handicapped by his glasses, which he has had to wear since, as a young boy, he was injured in breaking up a fight. He did try contact lenses for a short time in 1973, but soon gave them up. Like other great batsmen such as Sobers and Compton, however, he did have great trouble with his knees, though thanks to several operations he was able to continue batting as well as ever, right up to the end of his career. Indeed, in May 1988, in a charity match against the West Indies touring team led by Viv Richards, I saw him make a swift 37 not out against their bevy of fast bowlers, with several sixes soaring over the boundary in the typical Lloyd fashion.

The knees did affect his fielding, however, and he was forced in the end to spend most of the time in the slips. He had been a superb fielder in the covers – as good as Colin Bland, and there is no higher praise than that. He was like a giant cat prowling about and would pounce on the ball with tremendous speed, hurling the ball at the wicket like a rocket. But although he was a great loss in the covers, he caught many good catches at slip, and in all caught 89 for West Indies, second only to Gary Sobers. To complete his all-round ability he occasionally bowled *right*-arm medium-pace, although of course he was a *left*-handed batsman.

Off the field Clive is a friendly person, gruff but with a good sense of humour, and is a surprisingly amusing after-dinner speaker. He became a British citizen in 1984 and is happily settled in Cheshire, where he does charity and social work, mostly connected with finding work for the young unemployed. He and his wife are also converting a house to become a rest-home for the elderly. He is a compassionate man who also likes to coach and encourage young cricketers.

He has a strong personality which, combined with his other qualities, made him a natural leader and a great captain of the West Indies. His record is remarkable. He was their captain in 74 Tests, a record for any country – the nearest to him was Greg Chappell's 48 for Australia. Of these 74 Tests West Indies won 36 and drew 26, and at one time they went 26 successive Tests without defeat, including 11 successive wins in 1984. And of the 18 series in which he was captain, only 2 were lost.

It's not just these results which made him such a successful captain, however. He had the ability – like Sir Frank Worrell – to weld together all the differences and rivalries of the West Indian islands, and inspired loyalty from what became a happy and united side. From the commentary box it often looked as if his captaincy was a 'piece of cake'. He just stood in the slips and rang the changes on his four fast bowlers, with the very occasional spinner thrown in. Of course it wasn't really as simple as that, but it would have been fascinating to see him captain a weak side and then judge his tactics and judgement.

He had one hiccup during his years of captaincy. In 1978 he had a disagreement with his board of control over the Packer affair. He was a leading player in the World Series cricket and resigned as captain of the West Indies at Georgetown just before the Test against Australia in March 1978. Ali Kallicharran took over the captaincy for the remaining three matches and went to India as captain in six Tests a year later, but by the end of 1979 all was forgiven and Clive was back at the helm in Australia.

There was one side of Clive's captaincy with which I didn't agree. *On* the field he could be ruthless, quite unlike the friendly figure *off* it. He seemed to tolerate the frequent bowling of bouncers from his plethora of fast bowlers, which brought a nasty smell of intimidation into the game. People go to watch batsmen playing strokes, not ducking and weaving to avoid injury. A perfect example was the Close/Edrich partnership at Old Trafford in the third Test in 1976, when they were both battered all over the body by Roberts, Holding and Daniel and had to duck and weave their way through a most unpleasant evening. Neither the umpires nor Clive did anything about it, though Bill Alley did warn Holding towards the end. Clive has always maintained that it was up to the umpires to take the necessary action allowed by the Laws. Technically of course he is right, but for the sake of cricket I still feel he should have stopped it. He later admitted that 'our fellows got carried away'!!

I also disagreed with his tactics in employing a slow over-rate. Unfortunately, all other countries have also been guilty from time to time, but I don't excuse them either. Clive used it in order to give his fast bowlers with their long run-ups a longer rest between overs. He somewhat cynically defended himself by saying that if they had bowled more overs in a day, they would have won their Test matches a day or so earlier! He also made the point that the crowds didn't seem to mind, as there were always big attendances at all the West Indian Tests. One thing he couldn't deny, though. West Indies' usual slow over-rate made it virtually impossible for any opposing side to have sufficient time to build up a big enough score to beat them.

In spite of these personal criticisms of mine, however, there is no doubt that Clive will go down in history, not only as a great batsman and fielder, but also as a man and captain who had a tremendous influence for good in West Indies cricket. I doubt if anyone will ever captain their country more times, and I wish this new British recruit a very happy and prosperous retirement.

Alan Knott

Knotty was responsible for me making one of my worst-ever puns – and that's saying something! At one time he used to play for Dartford, as did Derek Ufton, another Kent wicket-keeper. I was discussing which of them usually kept wicket for Dartford. 'Well,' I said, 'due to Knotty's commitments with Kent it was more Ufton than Knott!'

When he finally retired in 1985 – not owing to loss of form but to a dodgy ankle – cricket lost one of its great characters. He was not the usual run of Test cricketers. His health came before everything, so he didn't smoke, drank only the occasional glass of sherry or wine, and went to bed early. He was meticulous with his preparations before play, hence the fact that he was seldom ready in time and could usually be seen trotting out behind the others as they left the pavilion. He wore a shirt several sizes too big so that it didn't restrict his movements. Underneath he always wore a flannel on the small of his back to soak up sweat. Like his shirt, his trousers were baggy, not tight round the bottom as they are today. His gloves had always been well-broken-in, so they looked old and scruffy, but they were comfortable. And he always had a handkerchief sticking out of his left pocket (Wally Hammond's dark blue one was always in his *right* pocket) to make it easier to blow his nose. He thought of everything, and during a match interval would have a complete change of clothing after a shower. This did not give him much time for lunch, but he was a sparse eater. Once on the field he indulged in those strange exercises which became famous on television – swinging his arms, bending his knees and touching his toes. He had a genuine fear of stiffening up.

As a wicket-keeper he was for years the best in the world, far more consistent, especially for Kent, than Godfrey Evans. He was as agile as a cat, and brought off some incredible catches standing back to the fast bowlers. Just as Godfrey had been so brilliant standing up to Alec Bedser, so was Knotty when he stood up to Derek Underwood, who at his pace on a turning wicket was very difficult to take.

58 Alan Knott

My one 'quarrel' with Knotty was that he did not always stand up to medium-pace bowlers like d'Oliveira or Woolmer. He claimed that he was more certain to take catches standing back than up. For a wicket-keeper of his quality that seemed to me nonsense. I am a great believer in the pressure that a wicket-keeper exerts on a batsman, when standing close to the stumps. We used to argue about it, and this led to quite an amusing story. Knotty asked me if I would write something in his benefit brochure. I said I would be very happy to do so, but on one condition – that if Bob Woolmer came on to bowl in one of the Tests against the West Indies in 1976, Knotty would promise to stand up to him for at least one over. He promised to do so.

Sure enough, Woolmer came on to bowl at the Oval. To my delight I saw Knotty go up to the stumps, then look round at our commentary box and give the thumbs up. Next door my TV colleagues were speculating on some tactical ploy, possibly a leg-side stumping. The left-handed Fredericks was the batsman and to my horror Woolmer's first ball was wide outside his leg-stump – not an easy ball for a wicket-keeper to take. I thought, oh my goodness, here come 4 byes. But needless to say, Knotty got across outside the leg-stump and made a brilliant take. He stood up for the next five balls, and then stood back for Woolmer's subsequent overs – but he had kept his word.

It was very difficult to say whether Knotty or Bob Taylor was the better keeper. Bob certainly stood up more and was far quieter and more unpretentious, compared to the more spectacular keeping of Knotty. I think it's fair to say that they were both equal and that they both qualify to be compared with the best Test keepers ever.

Knotty was, of course, by far the better bat. He could play either game – defensive or attacking. When defending he was strictly orthodox, playing with a dead straight bat, but when on the attack he was the greatest improviser I have ever seen, not forgetting John Emburey of the modern players. He could cut and drive, and I saw him hit a six over extra cover in Auckland in 1971, but his favourite stroke was the sweep, played off the most unlikely balls, even those outside the off-stump. The most astonishing innings I saw him play was his 82 in the fourth Test at Sydney in 1975. Lillee and Thomson were at the height of their powers, and were a terrifying combination with their devastating pace and short-pitched bowling. When they *did* pitch the ball up he hit them through the empty spaces in the covers for four. If it was short outside the off-stump he would deliberately steer it over the top of slips' heads. In one hour after lunch he made 56, 33 of them in three overs against the second new ball. Lillee and Thomson were not too pleased, but how proud I was to have seen such a brave and brilliant innings. Remember, Knotty was a small man, but he was very quick on his feet and had tremendous guts. He didn't have that jutting-out chin for nothing!

His record in Tests would have been even more remarkable had he not signed up with Packer, and later had not gone on the 'rebel' tour of South Africa, but loyal as he was to England his family always came first and he was determined to set up a firm financial base for them. I see him only too rarely these days, but when we do meet the wicked twinkle in his eye is still there, his mischievous smile and his impish sense of humour. And when you see those piercing brown eyes you can understand why he was such a great wicket-keeper.

Keith Fletcher

Although he is five feet nine and a half inches tall, he has always been nicknamed the Gnome. I have hoped for years that the occasion would arise when I would have to ask him to direct me to some place or other. I would then be able to say, 'Show me the way to go, Gnome', after the famous 1925 hit song. Perhaps it's just as well that I have never been given the opportunity! But to get back to his somewhat strange nickname. He first played for Essex when he was only seventeen – a Trevor Bailey discovery. He was a shy, rather frail-looking boy, and no doubt appeared rather small compared with the likes of Trevor Bailey, Tonker Taylor, Jim Laker and Doug Insole – all playing for Essex at the time. Small he may have seemed, but even at that age his timing was so good that he could hit the ball further than most. He only played in a couple of matches in 1962, but in 1963 he scored a thousand runs in a full season.

He soon developed into a complete batsman who could attack or defend as the occasion demanded. I have always felt that if he had been more assertive and outwardly confident he would have become an even better batsman, but throughout his career he would walk out to the wicket in an apologetic way, head down and looking at the ground, not exactly apprehensive but certainly not in the confident manner of the great batsman. And yet he was good enough to take on the best. Like the other England batsmen he was shell-shocked by the battering from Lillee and Thomson on Mike Denness's tour in Australia in 1974–5. There weren't helmets in those days, and it wasn't just England who were shattered – the following winter Australia beat the West Indies by 5–1. It undoubtedly shook the Gnome's confidence, but he fought back with a fine 146 in the sixth Test at Melbourne, though one must admit that Lillee only bowled six overs and Thomson wasn't playing!

Because of his footwork and variety of strokes, he has always been especially good against spinners, either punishing the short ball off the back foot, or going out to drive the over-pitched ball.

In his early days he hit a lot of sixes, but sobered up a bit as he got older.

59 Keith Fletcher

He played in 59 Tests and averaged 39.90 with 7 hundreds. One of these was the slowest Test hundred ever scored in England, and also the slowest in first-class cricket. It was at the Oval against Pakistan in 1974, when England were fighting to save a follow-on after a Pakistan first innings of 600. Thanks to the Gnome it was saved, and his hundred took 458 minutes. He was finally run out for 122 in 513 minutes. He has been a prolific scorer for Essex and achieved 37,665 runs, with 63 hundreds. When he started he was a promising leg-spinner, but on the green Essex pitches, and generally in modern cricket, a leg-spinner is lucky to get on – even if he exists. The last regular leg-spinner in first-class cricket in England was Robin Hobbs, who in spite of the Essex pitches took over 1,000 wickets in his twenty-year spell with the county.

The Gnome has always been a good fielder, especially in the slips or in the covers, where he was a very fast mover. I remember in one match in Australia he came on as substitute and was put in the slips. The Australian captain objected on the grounds that this was the Gnome's specialist position, which in those days captains were allowed to do. So he was moved from slip to cover, where he proceeded to field brilliantly. But there was one occasion when the Australians were only too delighted to see him fielding at slip. This was in the Headingley Test in 1968, when he was included in the England side in place of Philip Sharpe, who was one of the finest first slip fielders there has ever been, and, incidentally, had a Test average of 46.23. The Yorkshire crowd resented this and barracked the poor Gnome unmercifully as he had the bad luck to drop two or even three fast low and wide chances off John Snow. They would have been very good catches, but the Yorkshire crowd believed (probably rightly) that Sharpe would have gobbled them up. It didn't help the Gnome when he proceeded to make 0 in the first innings, after an unkind reception from the crowd as he came in to bat. He has never enjoyed playing at Headingley since then, and in two later Tests there against Australia again failed with 5, 8 and 14. However, against New Zealand and Pakistan he did make 81 and 67 not out, but even so Headingley is not a tactful subject of conversation with the Gnome.

I have said that I think he could have been an even better player if he had a more aggressive approach, but this does not apply to his captaincy of Essex from 1974 to 1985, and then again in 1988 after two years of Gooch's captaincy. He is undoubtedly the best tactician on the county circuit at the moment, and rivals Ray Illingworth for his understanding of the game and his summing-up of his opponents' strengths and weaknesses. Even when playing for England he would often be consulted by his captain. In addition to his tactical skills he has the ability to be firm, but at the same time to have probably the happiest team in the whole country. The Essex dressing-room has always been a place of laughter and leg-pulling, and this has a lot to do with their recent successes.

Under the Gnome they won the County Championship in 1979, 1983 and 1984. They won the John Player in 1981, 1984 and 1985, the Benson and Hedges in 1979, and the NatWest in 1985 – not a bad record, and he must be given great credit for their performance.

His brief captaincy of England – six Tests in India and one in Sri Lanka in 1981 – was not such a happy experience, though I am one of those who think that he was harshly treated when dropped in favour of Bob Willis for the 1982 Tests in England. There were ostensibly several reasons for this. It was an unsuccessful tour, India winning the first Test, the remaining six being drawn. In the second Test he was given out, caught behind the wicket by Kirmani off

Shastri. He obviously thought he was not out, and in a fit of annoyance flicked off a bail with his bat, as he turned to go back to the pavilion. On reflection, this seems small beer compared with what went on in Pakistan in 1987. It was also contrary to his character because he had been careful to warn his side *not* to react to umpires' decisions, however gross they might be. Another possible reason why he was dropped was that in the third Test in New Delhi there appeared to be an over-rate battle between Gavaskar and Fletcher. India, with only one bowler over medium-pace, bowled 12.79 overs an hour during a day, with England not much better with 13.06, though they did have Willis, Lever and Botham with long run-ups. However, I believe in one hour England only bowled just over nine overs, and it would obviously have been far better had England scorned such tactics and, instead of copying them, shown an example and bowled a reasonable number of overs. But I must say that it is easy to say that away from the heat, umpiring and frustrations of a Test match in India. A typical frustration was in the third Test when the ball was changed *twelve* times, and on another occasion play was delayed for eight minutes because the umpires had lost the key to a cupboard containing the new cricket balls!

England played one Test against Sri Lanka on the way home and won it, so that the Gnome's record as England captain was 7 Tests, 1 win, 1 loss, 5 draws, and it was the end of his 59-Test career.

Although born in Worcester in 1944, because his parents had been evacuated from London, the Gnome is basically a lover of the Essex countryside. In recent winters he has been an oil salesman, dealing with farmers, and likes nothing better than a bit of rough shooting – preferably partridges, which do particularly well in Essex. I toured with him on Ray Illingworth's 1970–I tour, when his catch at silly point off Derek Underwood in the seventh Test at Sydney meant that England regained the Ashes and won the series 2–0. It was a great moment for him as he snatched the catch off Jenner's bat and pad. He is always great fun to be with and has a dry sense of humour. A highly successful county captain – modest, fair and a great credit to cricket.

Barry Richards

I have often been asked the nearly impossible question to answer: 'Who is the best batsman you have ever seen?' It is difficult to answer because there are so many candidates, and they have played at different times against varying strengths of bowling. Who can attempt to choose between Bradman, Hammond, Compton, Sobers, Hutton, May, Cowdrey, Greg Chappell and Viv Richards, to name just a few? They were all great and each had his own special style. So I normally play safe and reply: 'I will tell you who was the most perfect batsman technically, whose every stroke was an exact copy out of the textbooks. There may have been batsmen who were his equal, but you cannot be better than perfection.' I then, usually to the surprise of the questioner, nominate Barry Richards. Note *Barry* not *Viv*.

He had, and played, every stroke off both front and back foot. With a high back lift he played beautifully straight, and used his feet far more than the others I have mentioned, with the exception of Bradman, Hammond and Compton. He would even dance down the pitch to the fast bowlers, just like George Gunn used to do, except that George walked casually down the pitch, rather than dance.

Barry's technique was backed by his supreme confidence in his own ability, and an insolent contempt for all bowlers. Goodness knows how great his achievements would have been had he had the incentive of Test cricket, where he could match his skills against the world's best. Sadly, he became bored with county cricket – there was not sufficient challenge. I sometimes thought that he must have felt like a father playing against the boys in the parents' match. He was *that* good, and so much better than his contemporaries. It was all a sad waste of talent. He once said that he dreaded having to go down to the ground every day at 9.30 a.m. I remonstrated with him about this, and pointed out how lucky he was compared with so many other people like miners, office or factory workers. I pointed out rather pompously that he had been given these great gifts and should do his best to make full use of them, but it all came down to the fact that he needed a challenge from his equals and, robbed of Test cricket, he very seldom got it.

60 Barry Richards

In fact he only played in four Tests – against Australia in South Africa in 1970. He didn't do too badly either! 7 innings, 508 runs, and an average of 72.57. I was lucky enough to see all these innings, as Charles Fortune of SABC had kindly asked me out to be the 'neutral' commentator with Alan McGilvray and himself. Barry never once failed, and how's this for consistency: 29, 32, 140, 65, 35, 81, 126. That 140 alone was worth travelling all the way to South Africa. He reached his hundred in the first over after lunch off only 116 balls. There then took place one of the most thrilling partnerships I have ever seen in Test cricket. He and Graeme Pollock put on 103 runs in an hour, completely pulverising the admittedly not too strong Australian attack of McKenzie, Connolly, Freeman and Gleeson. It was not like most big partnerships, where one batsman does most of the scoring whilst the other plays second fiddle. On this occasion Barry and Graeme matched each other with four after four. It was thrilling to watch and I felt privileged to be there to see such perfect stroke-play. It must have given Barry a bitter taste of what might have been, although at the time the South African tour to England in the summer was still due to take place.

Barry is tall with fair curly hair, and good-looking with an engaging smile. I always found him a friendly person, but he could undoubtedly be temperamental, brought on I am sure by his frustration. In the end he decided to prove his greatness by selling his skill to the highest bidder. He was perhaps the first top cricketer to realise his true commercial worth, and this may have made him appear greedy and grasping.

He played, of course, with great success and panache for Hampshire after one experimental match for Gloucestershire. He went there originally because of his great friend Mike Procter. As I have mentioned, they were both given a trial and played in just one match – against the visiting South African side in 1965. Play was only possible on the first day, but the new boys managed to be the top scorers for Gloucestershire, Barry making 59 and Mike 69. They filled in part of the summer by acting as dressing-room attendants in the third Test against South Africa at the Oval.

Mike continued to play for Gloucestershire, but Barry did not make up his mind immediately what he really wanted to do. So it was not until 1968 that he began his ten years' career with Hampshire, and what a first season he had. He scored 2,395 runs, the next highest aggregate by any of the other Hampshire batsmen being 990 by Barry Reed. He scored over 1,000 runs for the county nine times before trying to sell his wares elsewhere, and played with great success for South Australia in 1970–1 when he made 356 runs against Western Australia – 325 of them coming on the first day. He returned to England to play for the Rest of the World in the five 'Tests' against England in place of the cancelled South African tour. Strangely enough he didn't really take advantage of this opportunity to prove his great talent, only averaging 36.71 with 257 runs from his eight innings. After he left Hampshire he signed up with Kerry Packer and was one of the successes in the World Series cricket.

In addition to his batting he bowled off-breaks off a short run and gave the ball an enormous tweak, and with only 77 wickets in his career was much under-bowled. He was a good catcher anywhere, especially in the slips.

I have seen him on my various trips to South Africa and interviewed him in our commentary box during the Lord's Bicentenary match in 1987. He was geniality itself and half admitted that he regretted not having enjoyed county cricket as much as he should have done. I felt that he was casting a longing eye out on the middle and would dearly have loved to have been batting out there against the likes of Marshall and Quadir. At the age of forty-two I reckon that he would still have shown them a thing or two and delighted the large crowd of cricket connoisseurs who came to the match.

Mike Denness

In 1962 I was commentating on the Kent *v.* Surrey match at Blackheath. This was the traditional venue for the annual match between these two near neighbours. Now alas there is no longer a Kent fixture at Blackheath. Peter Richardson – arch leg-puller – told me that he had a promising young player called Mike Denness. He was a Scotsman and played cricket for Ayr, but to do this, Peter told me, Denness used to bicycle two hundred miles every weekend from his father's farm way up in the Highlands. I thought this was a wonderful example of a young cricketer's keenness and gave it full play during my commentary. It was only later that I learned that Mike's father was *not* a farmer, that Mike was born and lived at Bellshill in nearby Lanarkshire, and that he had been at school at Ayr Academy, from where he played for Ayr. I have yet, after all these years, to get my own back on Peter.

Mike was the only Scotsman *born* in Scotland to captain England. Douglas Jardine had Scottish parents but was born in India, and Tony Greig was born in South Africa, though his father was a Scot in the RAF who was sent out to South Africa. Mike, surprisingly, was captain in as many as nineteen Tests, including two major tours in Australia and the West Indies. It was largely because of his selection as captain that Geoff Boycott opted out of Test cricket for three years.

Mike replaced Ray Illingworth, who was dropped after England lost two Tests in the three-Test series against the West Indies in 1973. It was unexpected because England had won two Tests against New Zealand in the same summer, but it was Ray's lack of form rather than his leadership which brought about the change. In the six Tests he averaged 20.08 with the bat, but took only six wickets at a cost of 75 each.

Anyway poor Mike got the short end of the straw. He started with a series in the West Indies which England managed to draw 1–1, thanks largely to Boycott making 99 and 112 in the fifth Test, which England won by 26 runs to square the series. In view of Boycott's feelings this was a bit ironical. However, he was to play in only one more Test under Mike before going into voluntary exile – the first Test against India. It was a comparatively easy and successful summer for Mike, England winning all three Tests against India and drawing the three against Pakistan.

61 Mike Denness

The following winter against Australia was a different matter, however. England found the combination of Lillee and Thomson at its fastest and best and lost the series 1–4. Mike's own form was so bad in the first three Tests (scores of 6, 27, 2, 20, 8, 2) that he took the unusual step of dropping himself from the fourth Test at Sydney, John Edrich taking over the captaincy. Captains have dropped out on a tour before this, but because of injury or ill health (e.g., Wally Hammond in the fifth Test in 1947 or Gubby Allen in the West Indies in 1947–8). I cannot remember any captain on tour being dropped for loss of form, or in this case possibly confidence.

Mike came back refreshed and rested for the last two Tests,

however, and scored 51, 14 and 188. This latter was a splendid innings and spoke much for Mike's determination and character. In fairness, it must be said that Thomson was not playing and Lillee only bowled six overs because of injury to a foot. Still, it acted as a tonic to Mike, who in the two Tests in New Zealand which followed made 181 and 59 not out.

There was no let-up for him, however. On returning to England there was the Prudential World Cup. England won their three group matches but were beaten in the semi-final by Australia, Gary Gilmour taking 6 for 14 on a typical Headingley pitch. Four Tests against Australia followed and Mike only captained England in the first at Edgbaston. He was then unceremoniously dropped. England selectors on the whole are apt to stay loyal to their players – too loyal sometimes, in these days when a player dropped loses a lot of money – but they do tend to drop their captains rather abruptly at short notice. The apparent decision to drop Mike was because of his disastrous decision to put Australia in to bat – the first England captain ever to do so at Edgbaston. It was said to be a team decision, Snow, Arnold and Old feeling that the overcast conditions would suit them. Sadly that was not so, and Australia made 359. Then came the cruel blow for Mike. A thunderstorm on the second afternoon after England had batted for just one over presented Lillee, Walker and Thomson with a rain-affected pitch. England made 101 and were all out for 173 when they followed on. So off came poor Mike's head, especially as he himself had only made 3 and 8, but he can also fairly be blamed for allowing his team to make up his mind for him.

I have the impression that he was never entirely happy as captain, either for England or for Kent between 1972 and 1976, although he led them to victory in all the one-day competitions. Kent beat Worcestershire in the Benson and Hedges Final in 1973, Lancashire in the Gillette Final in 1974 and won the John Player in 1972, 1973 and 1976. Not a bad record! But once again he suffered the indignity of being asked to leave. It was said that his relationship with the Kent players was not all that it should be. This is surprising to me because Mike was always a cheerful and friendly person.

He was an entertaining batsman to watch, and enjoyed playing an attacking game. He was very quick on his feet and was at his best against slow bowling, but he had all the strokes and a classical sideways-on stance, and ran very fast between the wickets – as befitted a more than useful Rugby fly-half. He scored 1,000 runs in a season 14 times, and scored 25,886 runs in first-class cricket with an average of 33.48. He also had a good average of 39.69 in 28 Tests, thanks largely to his 4 Test hundreds. Added to all this, he was a superb fielder, especially in the covers, where he moved with great speed. He ended his career playing four seasons for Essex, and also acted as their coach and captain of their second eleven from 1981 to 1984. He has acted as manager for Kerry Packer's World Series teams and busies himself with a variety of other jobs in public relations and so on.

I'm sure that looking back he will have enjoyed his cricket with England and Kent, though I think he will also be disappointed at not achieving more – he just missed it. But he remains as cheerful and friendly as ever.

Greg Chappell

I am sure that he will regret it until his dying day. It was a snap decision taken on the spur of the moment, which prompted an action totally contrary to the spirit of cricket. It happened at Melbourne on 1 February 1981, in the third of four Finals between Australia and New Zealand in the Benson and Hedges World Series Cup.

New Zealand had won the first match and Australia the second, so it was an important game to win. Greg Chappell was captain of Australia who batted first and made 235 for 4 off their 50 overs – just about par for a winning score. There was a controversy when Chappell – on 52 – refused to walk when Snedden claimed to have made a low catch at deep mid-wicket. The New Zealand team appealed vehemently to the umpires, who both gave it not out because they said they hadn't been looking! They were evidently both watching for short runs.

There was therefore some slight ill-feeling between the two teams, especially as Chappell went on to make 90. Thanks to a fine 102 not out by Bruce Edgar, New Zealand were only just behind the clock when the last over came, and they still needed 15 to win with 4 wickets in hand. It was to be bowled by Trevor Chappell, the youngest of the three brothers. The other bowlers had all completed their allotted 10 overs each. Richard Hadlee hit the first ball for 4, and was lbw to the next: 11 runs needed, 4 balls and 3 wickets left. The new batsman, Ian Smith, hit 2 twos before being bowled by the fifth ball. So in came Brian McKechnie with 7 runs needed to win, or 6 for a tie, off the last ball of the match. It was then that Greg did the dirty trick. He ordered his brother Trevor to bowl this final ball underarm all along the ground – in cricket parlance a 'sneak' or a 'grub'. McKechnie was no great batsman and would have been pushed to hit a six off a slow half-volley on this huge Melbourne arena. Even had he done so, Australia would not have *lost*. It would have been a very worthy tie with McKechnie a justifiable hero, but it was not to be. The grub made such a task completely impossible, and McKechnie made no attempt to hit the ball in protest.

All hell broke loose and Greg's decision must still haunt him. In a telegram to the Australian Prime Minister, the New Zealand Prime Minister accused Australia of cowardice. The whole cricketing world on television, radio and in the press mercilessly criticised Greg's sportsmanship – or lack of it. He later publicly regretted what he had done, but of course his reputation as a sportsman suffered irreparably.

This was a pity because his action was not really characteristic of Greg. Admittedly, he had a strong will to win and played the game harder than most out in the middle, but except for the unpleasant habit of 'sledging' which he had learnt from his brother Ian, when he was captain, he always played fairly. And later, when he took over from Ian, he appeared to become more relaxed and less aggressive. But he was undoubtedly a tough character; tall, dark and handsome, he sported a beard for much of his career and didn't smile too often. He could be petulant in his reactions. I remember seeing him once slap a streaker on his bare bottom with his bat.

As a batsman he must be among the top five ever produced by Australia. He had a good pedigree. His mother was Vic Richardson's daughter and she used to bowl to her three sons in the garden. Brother Ian was the loud, confident extrovert, while Greg was more reserved. He divided his playing time between South Australia, where he was born (57 matches), and Queensland (51). He was a tower of strength to the latter and restored an interest in the state side and improved their standard of play.

As a batsman Ian was the more aggressive and enterprising, and more willing to take risks and take on the bowlers, but Greg was the more correct. He had an upright style, was stiff-backed with a high back lift, and played with the straightest of bats. To start with, his main stroke was the on-drive between mind-on and mid-wicket – he played it as well as Peter May, and that is saying a lot – but as time went on he developed a repertoire of strokes all round the wicket.

62 Greg Chappell

I was lucky to see his first Test innings at Perth in 1970 against Ray Illingworth's side. He made 108 and immediately showed his class by the way he played the pace attack of Snow, Lever and Shuttleworth on the fast Perth pitch. He seemed to have plenty of time to play his strokes, the majority being on-drives. Towards the end of his innings he cut loose and completely dominated the England bowlers – his last 60 runs coming in only 13 overs, or just under the hour. So he scored a hundred in his *first* Test innings, and fourteen years later he scored 182 against Pakistan at Sydney in his *last* Test innings – the first Test batsman ever to do this double.

During this innings he also became the first Australian to score 7,000 runs in Test matches. He passed Don Bradman's total of

6,996 runs, but has always modestly disclaimed any relevance in this. He points out that he had 151 innings against Bradman's 80. It was also his 24th Test hundred, a total only exceeded by Gavaskar (32), Bradman (29) and Sobers (26).

Also in the Sydney match Greg caught his 122nd catch in Tests, passing Colin Cowdrey's previous record of 120. He was a fine fielder anywhere, but in later years fielded mostly in the slips, where he made so many of his catches. He always gave the impression that he was casual, and made no fuss nor showed any sign of elation when he took a catch, but he made many brilliant ones, plucking the ball out of the air in the manner of Hammond, Cowdrey or Sharpe.

As if all this was not enough, he was one of those invaluable change bowlers, who look innocent enough from the pavilion but are in the habit of picking up a vital wicket to break a stand. He was medium-pace and did a bit in the air and off the pitch, and undoubtedly learnt much about the art of bowling during his two seasons with Somerset in 1968 and 1969. His experience of the more difficult English conditions also did much to help his batting.

He also holds another Australian record by captaining them in 48 Tests. The only other Test captain to beat that was Clive Lloyd, who led the West Indies 74 times. Greg could have been captain in many more Tests and could have scored another 1,000 runs or so, had he not signed up with Kerry Packer, where he was a great success. I saw him play in three of the five matches in the World X I v. Australia series in 1972, and he batted brilliantly, scoring 425 runs at an average of 106.25 in the three matches.

Oh, I have forgotten, there is yet another record which he broke and now shares. In 1974 against England in Perth, he became the first non-wicket-keeper to catch seven catches in a Test. This was later equalled by Yajurvindra Singh against England for India at Bangalore in 1977.

So that is Greg Chappell, a superb player rivalling the best in all Test cricket. He was always pleasant and friendly to me, and is a far nicer person than his unfortunate action with the sneak at Melbourne would suggest.

Dennis Lillee

All games have their controversial figures – cricket perhaps more than most. And Dennis Lillee certainly qualifies as one of them. Off the field he was intelligent, friendly and normally well-mannered. I say normally, because he did once break protocol by thrusting a pencil and paper at the Queen for her autograph during one of those presentations in front of the pavilion. But as I say, he was friendly enough, and didn't seem to mind that, for obvious reasons, I used to call him Laguna.

What a change when he was on the field, however. With his longish black hair and moustache he was a ferocious and swarthy-looking person – rather like those gauchos in cowboy films. He was quick to lose his temper and often blasted the unfortunate batsman with savage verbal abuse. As a weapon he had a lethal bouncer which he didn't fail to unleash when he felt like it.

There were several ways of dealing with his temperament. You could keep quiet and disregard his abuse. You could – if you had the guts – taunt him, as Trevor Bailey would have done and Derek Randall did, especially in that great innings of his in the Centenary Test in Melbourne. Or – if you were good enough – you could challenge him and match your skill against his, as Ian Botham did on several occasions, but especially at Old Trafford in 1981. England were in trouble – 104 for five – when Botham came in at number seven. He played himself in for his first thirty runs, then Lillee was given the new ball and the fight was on. Botham proceeded to show Lillee who was the master. Lillee gave it all he got and bowled very fast from the Stretford End. He tried Botham with three vicious bouncers, which were all contemptuously flicked off his eyebrows by Botham, and went sailing over long leg for six. The battle was won, but perhaps only Botham could have won it in such a daring and devastating way.

Apart from his personality, what sort of bowler was Lillee? He was as fast as anyone else since the war, but like Lindwall learnt to conserve his energies and keep his really fast ball up his sleeve. He had a flowing run-up to the wicket and a perfect action, with a high right arm and his chin tucked in behind his left arm as he peered down the pitch. He could swing the ball and move it off the pitch; he cleverly disguised his variations in pace and his yorker was as lethal as his bouncer. It's impossible to say whether he was better than Lindwall or not, but without doubt he was one of the greatest fast bowlers of all time.

63 Dennis Lillee

I first saw him on Ray Illingworth's tour in the sixth Test at Adelaide, when he got off to a good start with 5 for 84 in the first innings in which he bowled in Test cricket. He was to take 5 wickets in a Test innings another 22 times, and 10 wickets in a Test 7 times. He impressed everyone at Adelaide, and the English batsmen realised what they would have to face for the next twelve years or so.

He always studied the art of bowling and took the trouble to learn about English conditions by playing in the Lancashire League in 1971. He was still only twenty-one years old, and his future looked assured when he took 31 wickets the following year on Australia's tour of England under Ian Chappell. But then tragedy struck. He suffered stress fractures of the lower spine and it looked as if his playing days were over – but he was saved by his character, determination, discipline and guts. For more than a year he had painful treatment and carried out demanding remedial exercises. He refused to give up, and it paid him handsomely. He came back to Test cricket against Mike Denness's team in Australia in 1974, and with Jeff Thomson devastated the England batsmen with some of the fastest, most ferocious and dangerous fast bowling I have ever seen. Lillee took 25 wickets in the series and would have taken more had he not bowled only six overs in the final Test, before he bruised his right foot.

He never looked back after that and took his Test total to 355 wickets, third only to Botham and Hadlee. He would – like Underwood and several others – have taken many more had he not been one of the first to sign for Kerry Packer after the Centenary Test of 1977. When 'peace' was declared two years later he returned to play in thirty-seven Tests, until a bad knee forced his retirement in 1983. But, being Lillee, he has come back again, playing for Tasmania in 1987 and for Northamptonshire in 1988. To undergo a busy season in county cricket after all his injuries and at the age of thirty-eight is proof of his determination and courage.

He was a useful batsman when he felt the occasion called for it. His highest test score was 73 not out at Lord's in 1975, and it remained his highest score in all first-class cricket. He came in at number ten with the score at 133 for 8. He put on 66 with Edwards, and a further 69 with Mallett for the last wicket. He hit three huge sixes and eight fours and batted for two and a quarter hours, which just shows what he could do. This was the match where a streaker ran on for the first time ever in a Test match. As he did the splits over the stumps at the pavilion end, Alan Knott, who was the non-striker at the Nursery End, said it was the first time he had ever seen *two* balls coming down the pitch towards him.

Lillee made four tours (1972, 1975, 1980 and 1981) of England and at the start of the 1981 tour he caught pneumonia and didn't play until the second Prudential match on 6 June. But he was fit by the time the Tests came along and took 39 wickets in the series. When he had his pneumonia he was treated by a lady doctor, 'Micky' Day, who looked after some of the staff at Lord's. She unwittingly encouraged Lillee to break the law, telling him that she would only declare him fit for play if he came in and changed his sweaty shirt after every bowling spell. So there was Lillee walking off – presumably with the permission of the umpires – and a substitute coming on to take his place. At that time the law stated that no fielder should leave the field to change his clothing or to have a rub-down. Nowadays they can do so, but no substitute is allowed on to take their place. So Dr Day caused a change in the laws.

I have earlier said that Lillee was short-tempered and became an aggressive character once on the field of play. There were two famous instances when his temper got the better of him. Both, funnily enough, occurred in Perth – perhaps the famous 'Freemantle Doctor' affected his liver! Anyway, in 1979 against England he came in to bat with an aluminium bat which a firm was trying to market. Both the umpires and Mike Brearley objected, and there was a ten-minute delay while Greg Chappell tried to persuade Lillee to use an ordinary bat. He finally agreed but flung the aluminium bat forty yards or so away in anger. This unfortunate episode caused another change in the laws, which now state that 'the blade shall be made of *wood*'.

The other incident occurred at Perth in the first Test against Pakistan in 1981. Javed Miandad was captain of Pakistan, and is not the most popular player in any cricketing country. He can be infuriating, and somehow got up Lillee's goat. Lillee deliberately tried to impede him when he was going for a run, and then aimed a kick at Javed's backside. Whether he actually connected I'm not sure, but Javed was so angry that he then tried to hit Lillee with his bat. With hundreds of thousands of young people watching on television, it is pathetic and unacceptable that two grown men playing for their countries should behave like this.

One final piece of unusual behaviour from Lillee was when, in the 1981 Test at Headingley, with Australia only needing 130 to win, the odds against England were 500–1 (these were assessed by Godfrey Evans, and proved rather expensive for Ladbrokes). As they watched England going out to field, Lillee and Marsh saw a friend going off to back England. Hearing the odds, they are said to have shouted: 'Put a fiver on for us.' I think it was more of a joke than anything else, with nothing sinister in it, especially as Lillee made 17 in a gallant stand of 35 for the ninth wicket to try to win the match for Australia.

Since his retirement from Test cricket Lillee has proved himself an astute businessman by putting money into the great Australian film success *Crocodile Dundee*. I am thankful that I never had to bat against him, but I am pleased that I saw him at his fastest and best, with his Australian crowds encouraging him as he bustled in on his long run-up to the wicket with shouts of, 'Lilleeeeee, Lilleeeeee.'

Bob Willis

The first time I met 'Big Bob' was in early December 1970, when he came out to Australia as a reinforcement for Ray Illingworth's side. He was only twenty-one, a tall gangling figure six feet five inches tall, with a mop of brown hair. Even then he had a rather lugubrious, unsmiling face, and spoke with a slow nasal drawl, but right from that very moment, underneath it all there was warmth and an engaging sense of humour. He has always been a friendly, welcoming person and I have spent many happy times in the Warwickshire dressing-room with him, Mike Smith and David Brown.

He was born in Sunderland but his father came south and worked in the BBC news-room at Broadcasting House. Bob used to keep goal in the winter for Guildford and played his first game for Surrey in 1969, when Geoff Arnold fell out through an injured heel. Bob played five matches that August and picked up 5 wickets against Notts and another 5 against Yorkshire. His pace and bounce in those matches surprised the batsmen and he took 17 wickets in all at 19 apiece. The following year he played in eleven matches and finished with 28 wickets, though they were rather more expensive (33.07), but the point was that he was definitely fast and most unpleasant to play. He didn't do much with the ball – there was no great swing or movement off the pitch – but, as he continued to do throughout his career, he always tried to bowl straight.

On the evidence of those two seasons with Surrey, Alec Bedser, the chairman of selectors, shrewdly put him on the reserve list for Australia. Alec knew that in spite of his lack of experience, Bob's pace and bounce would be effective on the harder pitches down under. As it was, Bob played in four of the six Tests and took 12 wickets – a good start. And, as befitted a goal-keeper, he also fielded brilliantly in the slips, or close to the wicket, though in later years his normal place in the field was at long leg.

MCC spent that Christmas of 1970 at Hobart in Tasmania. I

remember standing with Ted Dexter and watching Bob bowl. Ted had seen him in two earlier matches in Perth and Adelaide and as a result had given Bob some good advice. Bob, even then, had his tremendously long run-up and used to set off at a great pace like a cavalry charge, but by the time he had reached the stumps he had slowed up and Ted suggested that he reversed the process – i.e. a slower start building up to maximum speed just before he delivered the ball. Bob was a good learner and took Ted's advice. He was not a pretty bowler to watch. He had a knee-high action as he ran in, and had none of the smoothness of a Trueman, Holding or Snow. He just pounded in and as he delivered the ball he was square on to the batsman – none of the side-on action as recommended in the coaching manuals. But his arm was high, and with his height, great strength and the momentum of his run-up, he got a lot of bounce out of most pitches. (He even took 20 wickets in the 1976–7 series in *India*.)

He put a great strain on his body, however, which took a lot of punishment, especially his knees. He had various exploratory examinations and operations on both knees from time to time, culminating in the removal of both knee-caps when he returned home from the West Indies, early in 1981 without playing in a Test. Unbelievably, he was fit for that summer, when he took 29 wickets in the series against Australia. This included his best ever Test performance – his 8 for 43, which I have referred to when writing about Mike Brearley. It was certainly one of the fiercest and most aggressive pieces of fast bowling that I have ever seen. It is interesting to note that he had his greatest success against Australia. In all he took 128 wickets against them, including three particularly successful series of 27 wickets in 1977, 20 in 1978–9 and 29 in 1981.

It is worth comparing his Test figures with those of the other England fast bowler who took 300 wickets – Fred Trueman. Fred played in only 67 Tests and took 307 wickets at 21.57 apiece. Bob played in 90 Tests and took 325 wickets at 25.20. Both these are remarkable figures and rather support Fred's theory that, had he been selected for all the tours and Tests which he reckons he should have been (!), he might well have reached 400 Test wickets.

Of course, the main difference between them was on the county scene. Fred bowled his heart out for Yorkshire year after year, in spite of his many Tests. He took 100 wickets in a season twelve times and *outside* Tests took 1,997 wickets in nineteen years between 1949 and 1968.

Bob had three seasons with Surrey before he left them to go to Warwickshire. He felt that after his performance in Australia he deserved his county cap. Surrey thought otherwise, so he left them after the 1971 season, but he seldom bowled well for Warwickshire.

64 Bob Willis

He seemed to reserve all his energies for the Tests. Over fifteen years – four fewer than Fred – he only managed to take 353 wickets for Warwickshire and, remarkably for an England bowler, never once took 100 wickets in a season. The best he ever managed was 65 in 1978. So he was a really remarkable phenomenon – a big success in Test cricket, a comparative failure for his county.

He was always a worrier, and in Australia consulted a hypnotherapist who gave him some tapes to play which did virtually hypnotise him. Before a big match he would play them and hype himself up for the occasion. When he wasn't listening to these tapes, he would listen for hours to his beloved Bob Dylan, whose name he added to his own George by deed poll – hence Robert George Dylan Willis.

Because of his bowling action he suffered a lot from injuries but, especially later on in his career, he took a lot of trouble to keep fit, running many miles a day. Viewers of BBC TV will also remember how before a match he would stand on one leg with the other resting on the shoulder of Bernard Thomas, the England physiotherapist for so many years. This exercise is meant to stretch and strengthen the hamstring muscles, but you try it – it's jolly painful, though luckily Bernard was rather small so Bob didn't have to reach too high.

It may be surprising to learn that when he first attended Alf Gover's indoor school, Alf thought he had potential as a batsman! Well, he did score 840 Test runs with an average of 11.50. He played quite a few timely innings for England, either when runs were wanted quickly or, usually, when he was required just to hold his end up. With his height he had a long reach, and his main defensive stroke was a forward lunge at every type of ball, no matter what its length. It was not exactly orthodox but often proved effective – a perfect example being Headingley in 1981, when with Botham he added a vital 37 runs for the last wicket in England's second innings. Admittedly, Bob's share was only 2, but as England won by only 18 runs it played an important part in England's victory.

He was even more unorthodox in attack. He wound himself up and whirled his bat around in a circular motion. Occasionally this would result in a scorching cover drive, but more often it went high in the direction of the third man. His natural position in the batting order was number eleven, but he somehow persuaded Brearley to put him in at number ten above Mike Hendrick. Also, when he was captain he put himself in ahead of Norman Cowans, but otherwise he played number eleven.

He holds two unusual batting records. He was not out 55 times out of a total of 128 Test innings. This is far more than any other Test player, Lance Gibbs (39) and Derek Underwood (25) being the runners-up. He will rightly claim that it says something for the forward lunge!

The other record is even more strange and quite unique. He is the only Test batsman – or for that matter probably any batsman – to go out to bat without his bat! It happened after a tea interval in the Edgbaston Test against the West Indies in 1984. He actually reached the middle before he realised that he was batless, and I shall never forget the sheepish look on his face as he went back to the dressing-room to collect it!

He took over the England captaincy from Keith Fletcher in 1982 and was captain in 18 Tests with varying success (won 7, lost 5, drew 6). He was not an ideal selection. In my opinion no fast bowler is, though Gubby Allen may not agree, but both physically and mentally a fast bowler has too much to cope with already, without having to bother about changes of bowling, tactics and field placings. Bob concentrated so intensely that he often seemed oblivious to what was going on around him. At the end of one of his overs – sometimes more than six balls because of his no-balls – he always appeared knackered, and with head down would snatch his sweater from the umpire and walk off down to long leg. When he was not captain I have seen him do this regardless of the fact that Mike Brearley was trotting alongside him trying to say something, but Bob would just press on regardless as if in a coma. So when he was captain there was a kind of hiatus on the field. The bowler at the other end was often ignored and Botham and Taylor could be seen making field changes, though this never seemed to worry Bob. It undoubtedly made things difficult and led to England appearing to be a ship without a rudder.

When he was on top form, however, he led from the front with his example of effort and guts. He didn't say much to the team on the field, but in the dressing-room he encouraged and exhorted them and bolstered up their spirits, and was a popular captain.

Now that he has retired he can devote more of his time to his music and horse-racing, though the PR company he has set up with his brother David keeps him busy – so much so that he has had to move down to London. He also had a three-year spell as a summariser on BBC TV, and with his drawl and occasional dry wit made some very shrewd comments.

This only goes to show that captaincy, like batting or bowling, is far easier done from the commentary box. I'm sure too that Bob got a far better idea of what was going on than he ever did from long leg.

Imran Khan

As always seems to happen when I am travelling in a London taxi, the driver was talking cricket to me through his glass partition. With all the traffic noise it's not always easy to hear what they say, and it's necessary to shout back one's answers, but it is nice to know how many people *are* interested in cricket. What about Botham? Should Gatting have been dropped? Why don't we sack the selectors? The questions come thick and fast. On this occasion we were talking about the trouble that Gatting and Imran Khan were having with the authorities, over the books which they had written. 'I was in the City the other day, and there was a queue about two hundred yards long outside a bookshop,' said my driver. 'And do you know', he added, 'they all seemed to be women.' I wasn't at all surprised when he informed me that, on making enquiries, he was told that Imran Khan was inside signing copies of his new book.

He is certainly the most glamorous player in modern cricket. He is a dashing figure with striking good looks and 'come up and see me some time' eyes. He has a soft beguiling voice and, at thirty-seven years of age, is one of the most eligible bachelors alive. He comes from a well-to-do family in Lahore with strong cricketing traditions: two previous Pakistan captains, Javed Burki and Majid Khan, are his cousins, and as an added bonus his uncle was chairman of the Lahore selectors! This may have helped with his selection to tour England in 1971 when still only eighteen years old. He was already a tearaway fast bowler and a useful batsman, but it didn't do him much good. In the first Test at Lord's he was run out for 5, and although he bowled twenty-eight overs for only 55 runs he didn't take a wicket, was dropped, and did not play in the remaining two Tests.

From then on, however, he became Pakistan's pin-up boy and was revered and hero-worshipped by every cricket follower – and that means most of the population. Proof of his popularity came in 1987 when he publicly announced that he would play no more Test cricket, but by public demand – and, it is said, some 'persuasion' from the president, General Zia – he decided to go as captain to the West Indies. The result was a thrilling series. Pakistan won the first Test by 9 wickets, the second was honourably drawn, and the West Indies won the third in an exciting 2 wicket victory. Tony Cozier, the famous West Indian commentator and writer, headlined his report 'Imran's Triumphant Return', and he went on to say that Pakistan were inspired by the personal example and leadership of their captain. He has undoubtedly been an inspiration to Pakistan cricket, and perhaps because of his upbringing has always been a natural leader. He is highly intelligent, and as a result of his playing ability has always been able to lead by example. When he went up to Oxford for three years he was, unusually, elected captain in his *second* year, a tribute to his character. As Frank Worrell did for the West Indies, so has Imran been able to weld the different personalities in Pakistan into a close-knit team with tremendous confidence in their ability to win.

65 Imran Khan

As a player he is one of the great Test all-rounders. At one time he was possibly the fastest bowler in the world, but time – and the odd injury – have tempered him into a bowler in the Lindwall/Hadlee mould. He can still bowl as fast as most, but uses his speed less frequently. He is mainly an in-swinger, with a fine high action and an inexhaustible supply of energy. With a new ball he occasionally bowls an out-swinger, and can bowl a yorker and a bouncer as well as anybody. He has had various injuries, including a broken left arm as a boy, and a stress fracture of his left shin which kept him out of Test cricket for three years. Even so in 73 Tests he had by 1988 taken 334 Test wickets at the low average of 21.91, and 5 wickets in an innings 23 times. He learnt a great deal of his bowling skills during his six seasons with Worcestershire from 1971 to 1976. Since 1977 he has moved to Sussex, for whom he still plays, though rather irregularly. He enjoys the night-life of London, where he lives, and commutes daily to Hove for his cricket.

His bowling has rather overshadowed his batting, where he now bats at number seven. He is a powerful hitter who can still turn a game with his forcing strokes backed up by a sound defence. Perhaps he should have scored more than his 2,860 runs in Tests, but he put most of his energy into his bowling. Needless to say, with such a fine physique and athleticism he is a magnificent fielder anywhere.

Imran is very much his own man. He knows what he wants and usually gets it. He has had his occasional brush with the authorities – his option to play for Packer is an example – but his charm and good manners have made his path easier. He is an intensely proud man who likes nothing better than to fight for Pakistan with all the energy, guts and skill that he can muster. He has done them proud, and they reward him with fervent hero-worship. What lies ahead so far as cricket is concerned is uncertain. What is more certain is that he will eventually settle down to live in Pakistan, and select a Pakistani girl for his wife. And whoever catches the selector's eye will be a very lucky girl, and the envy of thousands of his female supporters all over the cricket world.

Bob Taylor

It is often said that wicket-keepers are born and not made. If that is true then Bob Taylor was certainly born to the job. He and Keith Andrew had the best pair of hands of any of the Test wicket-keepers whom I have seen. They were both quiet and undemonstrative, but wonderfully efficient, either standing back or up to the stumps. Others, like Marsh, Evans or Knott, were more spectacular, but Bob in his quiet way caught just as many of those impossible-looking diving catches. He was a perfect model for any young keeper to follow: left foot between middle- and off-stumps, crouching low with his eyes just above the bails, the fingers of his two hands pointing downwards as they gently touched the ground. He stayed down until the last possible moment, making absolutely sure of the line of the ball. Once up, he was incredibly quick to move either to the offside or, far more difficult, to the ball outside the leg-stump.

A wicket-keeper standing up is taking the ball blind outside the leg-stump. Here I am sure that instinct, as well as practice and experience, plays a large part. Again, when watching Bob, you can notice a slight 'give' in the hands at the moment of taking the ball, a sure safeguard against bruising when keeping to fast bowlers.

66 Bob Taylor

You will notice Bob's record of 1,648 career dismissals, 121 more than his nearest rival John Murray. Bob will tell you that it's not the number of catches and stumpings you make that matters, however – it's the number of misses by which a wicket-keeper should be judged. Had the records been kept I bet that Bob's misses would have been fewer than anyone else's. One of his assets was his consistency, day in, day out, no matter whether playing for his country or county. He was such a perfectionist that he gave up his short captaincy of Derbyshire because he felt it was affecting his concentration behind the stumps.

He was the ideal professional and an exemplary tourist – uncomplaining, cheerful, loyal and helpful to the other players. He had to wait for eleven years before he played in his first Test; he was in the shadow of Alan Knott, acting as his understudy waiting to go on stage. I was lucky to be there when he achieved his ambition. It was in New Zealand at Christchurch during Ray Illingworth's 1971 tour. Illy asked Knotty to stand down to reward Bob for his patience and loyalty. He had the pleasure of keeping to Derek Underwood on a sub-standard pitch which took a lot of spin. Unders took 6 for 12 and Bob got his first three Test victims. Knotty took over for the next Test at Auckland and perhaps to prove a point made 101 and 96! Bob could never compare with Knotty as a batsman, though I did see him play several useful defensive innings in Test partnerships, especially his top Test score of 97 at Adelaide in 1979.

I shall always remember Bob on the field with his white sunhat turned up in front. Godfrey Evans was famous for the way he lifted the morale of a tired fielding side, but, in his quieter way, so did Bob. You could often see him running after a perspiring bowler at the end of an over, just to give him an encouraging pat on the back.

Off the field, as I've said, he was a perfect tourer. He was at his best at the many official functions which a team *has* to attend. He earned himself the nickname of 'Chat' for the way he chatted everyone up, but what was so nice about him was that he would always volunteer for those private parties to which the team did *not* have to go. You could bet on Bob being there – the perfect ambassador for his country.

Sadly, towards the end of his career he became slightly dis-illusioned with the behaviour and attitudes of his younger colleagues. He retired in 1984, but had a remarkable if brief come-back against New Zealand at Lord's in 1986. The England wicket-keeper Bruce French had been struck on the back of the helmet when batting against Richard Hadlee. He was unable to field, so Bill Athey took over behind the stumps. Someone then had a brilliant idea, to which the New Zealanders generously agreed. Since his retirement Bob has become a very popular and efficient PRO for Cornhill, who, of course sponsor the Tests. He had been entertaining some Cornhill guests to lunch in the Cricket School. After seeing that they were all looked after, he started to have a prawn cocktail himself, but he was soon interrupted by a request from the pavilion to take over as substitute behind the stumps.

He readily agreed because he always keeps himself fit and plays regularly in charity matches, so he collected his gloves from the back of his car, where he always keeps them 'just in case'. He had to borrow from various people a shirt, boots and trousers, and of course a box! He had a marvellous reception as he ran on to the field – the same grey-haired figure in his white sunhat. And needless to say, although out of first-class practice, he kept wicket immaculately – as he always did.

Richard Hadlee

There are many arguments for and against overseas players playing in the County Championship. Those *for* say that it enables spectators in England to see great players from all over the world regularly in action every summer, instead of every four years or so when their countries tour England. The county secretaries say that the acquisition of a top overseas player gives every county (except Yorkshire) a better chance of winning one of the four competitions. They also claim that it gives our young players the chance of playing with and learning from the overseas stars.

Those *against* say that our young players are denied opportunities in their county team. The overseas player so often gets preference in the batting order, or is given the new ball which would otherwise be taken by a home-bred player. They also point out that many who come here are not already stars. They come here to *learn* their cricket under English conditions and then use their improved skills and experience to beat England in Test matches. Personally I am in favour of the present restriction on overseas players, which will eventually mean that each county will only be allowed to register one player not qualified for England.

All this brings us to Richard Hadlee, who by playing over here from 1978 to 1987 has benefited both his county and himself. In this period, under the captaincy of South African Clive Rice, Nottinghamshire became one of the top counties: they won two Championships and a NatWest Trophy, were finalists in the Benson and Hedges, and came second twice in the Sunday League.

As for Hadlee himself, he came here as a fairly ordinary tearaway fast bowler who had taken 89 wickets at 31.58 apiece. In November 1988 in New Zealand he passed Ian Botham's total of 373 Test wickets, but what happens thereafter depends on Ian Botham's recovery from his bad back and when Malcolm Marshall decides to retire from Test cricket.

The daily hard grind of county cricket forced Richard to adjust his methods. He cut down his run and learned to concentrate on swing and movement off the seam. He was nearly as fast as before and could still unleash a really fast ball which he used sparingly. Like Lindwall, Trueman, Lillee and Marshall, he simply relied on skill rather than speed.

67 Richard Hadlee

He is a dedicated cricketer, and is number four out of five sons of Walter Hadlee, the old New Zealand captain. So he was brought up in a cricket atmosphere and was soon taught the finer points of the game. He has always set himself targets, and with his sense of purpose and determination has usually achieved them. He is said to have a number of slogans, which he keeps repeating to himself as occasion demands – a sort of self-hypnosis. And how well they worked for him, Nottinghamshire and New Zealand. He did the double in 1984 (the first since 1967) and topped the bowling averages in 1980, 1981, 1982, 1984 and 1987, but his slogans let him down slightly in 1987. I am sure he had planned to do the double in his last season for Notts. He just achieved his 1,000 runs, but only took 97 wickets. Even so, only two other bowlers did take 100, Neil Radford with 109 and Jonathan Agnew with 101. But they bowled 150 and 186 *more* overs respectively than Richard.

So what makes him such a great bowler? He is tall (six feet one inch), lean and wiry with long arms and a whippish action – not unlike Brian Statham in build. He has a perfect sideways-on action and bowls from near the stumps. He swings the ball away from the batsman, and can then bring it back off the seam. His shortened run is about twelve yards, and he has a long raking stride. Because his arm comes over so high he produces a lot of bounce, and he keeps a good line and length with only the occasional short ball. Richard is a bowler whom any young player should copy to the last detail.

As a batsman he is a left-hander who used to go in at number eight or nine and then try to knock the cover off the ball, but he has gradually improved his defence without sacrificing his ability to strike the ball a long way, often high in the air. He has so much improved that he can now be called a genuine Test all-rounder. He has already made over 2,600 Test runs and in 1987 topped the Notts batting averages with 1,025 runs. (Needless to say, he also topped the bowling averages.)

His batting reached a peak in the NatWest Final at Lord's in 1987 against Northants. He made 70 not out in 61 balls, hitting 2 giant sixes and 4 fours. At one time Notts needed 51 off only 5 overs, but thanks to Richard and Bruce French this was reduced to 8 runs needed off the last over, to be bowled by David Capel. French was run out for a splendid 35 off the first ball. The next Hadlee hit for a towering six into the 'free' seats at the Nursery End. The third ball he pulled to the Tavern Stand for four, and Notts had won a thrilling game, coming from behind when all had seemed lost.

To complete his skills as an all-rounder Richard is a fine fielder anywhere, moving fast and with a good arm. What a chap to have on your side. He is always trying, is eager to win and as a bowler is feared by even the greatest Test batsmen. Ironically, he failed to pass Ian Botham's 373 Test wickets, when it seemed a racing certainty that he would after a highly successful tour of Australia, where he took 18 wickets in the three-Test series. This meant that he was equal with Botham at the start of the first Test against England at Christchurch on 12 February 1988. A big crowd had come to see their local boy make good – like Denis Compton at Lord's, Richard used to sell score-cards at Christchurch. But it was not to be. His analysis was 18–3–50–0 before he injured a calf muscle trying to stop a hard drive from Robinson. He didn't bowl again in the series, and whereas he might have retired from Test cricket if he had passed Botham, he decided to tour India with New Zealand on their short tour in November 1988.

So, like all cricketers, Richard has suffered his ups and downs, but he went out in a blaze of glory at the end of his time with Notts. Thanks to his fine all-round performance and the inspirational captaincy of South African Clive Rice, they won both the County Championship and the NatWest Trophy. They nearly did the hat-trick, finishing second in the Refuge Assurance League, only two points behind Worcestershire.

Both New Zealand and Nottinghamshire owe a debt of thanks to Wally Hadlee for producing such a magnificent all-round crick-eter, and such a thoroughly nice person as well.

Tony Greig

Six feet seven inches tall, fair-haired and good-looking, Tony Greig was the glamour boy of England cricket for a short period of five years. From 1972 to 1977 he played in fifty-eight consecutive Tests for England, before retiring at the early age of thirty-one. His father was Scottish and in the RAF, and was transferred on service to South Africa, where he married a South African girl. Twenty years or so later the blond bombshell burst on to the Sussex scene. He had been coached by George Cox, and it was he who recommended him to Sussex, who must have been pleased at their choice. In his first innings in county cricket Tony – not yet twenty years old – hit what *Wisden* described as a 'sparkling century'. The opponents were Lancashire, whose attack consisted of Brian Statham, Peter Lever, Ken Higgs and John Savage. Yet the new boy managed to hit twenty-two fours in his 156, and by the end of his first season for Sussex he had scored 1,193 runs and taken 63 wickets – not a bad start!

He became an outstanding all-rounder – in the Keith Miller class, though nowhere near so good a bowler. He was, however, a magnificent attacking batsman with a long reach and a penchant for searing drives over or through the mid-off to mid-on area. Because of his height and his gutsy competitiveness he had no fear of even the fastest bowlers, and treated them as savagely as the slower ones. Again, because of his height, he was the first to hold his bat in the air over stump high as he waited for the ball. It made him prone to the yorker, but his Test record of 3,599 runs, at an average of 40.43 with eight hundreds, shows how effective his method was.

As a bowler he was not more than fast-medium, coming in off a short, long-striding, prancing run. But he could get considerable bounce out of most pitches and, although his 141 Test wickets were comparatively expensive (32.20), he was never easy to play. He also used to bowl occasional off-breaks at medium pace and won the fifth Test for England at Port-of-Spain on Mike Denness's tour of 1974. He took thirteen wickets in the match with his spinners, including 8 for 86 in the first innings. His match figures of 13 for 156 are the best for any English bowler against West Indies.

68 Tony Greig

Another of his strengths was his magnificent fielding in any position, but he was perhaps of most value to England in the slips, where his large hands made a big percentage of his 87 catches.

On the field he was a flamboyant character and, like Keith Miller, enjoyed riling or amusing the crowd, but he carried his aggression and eagerness to win too far in his 'sledging' of batsmen. With such a strong personality there were inevitably one or two departures from perfection. In the first Test at Port-of-Spain in 1974 there was an unfortunate scene when he ran out Ali Kallicharran off the last ball of the second day. He was bowling to Bernard Julien, who played the ball slowly back to him. Ali was the non-striker and, thinking that it was the end of play for the day, began to walk up the pitch towards the pavilion. Tony, seeing him out of his ground, flung the ball at the bowler's wicket and on appeal the umpire, who had *not* called over, was bound to give him out. The success of the series seemed threatened by this gesture, which at its best could be called gamesmanship, but was definitely 'not cricket'. But luckily, under threats from a hostile crowd, the captains and administrators got together and the appeal was withdrawn. So next morning Ali came out to bat, and he and Tony ostentatiously shook hands and all was well.

It is worth noting that at the time the laws did *not* allow a captain to withdraw an appeal, but the 1980 code changed this and Law 27, Note 7 says: 'In exceptional circumstances the captain of the fielding side may seek permission of the umpire to withdraw an appeal, *provided the outgoing batsman has NOT left the playing area.*' So in spite of this change Ali would still have been out today, and the subsequent withdrawal would still have been illegal in spite of its logicality.

In 1975 Mike Denness captained England in the first Test at Edgbaston, and after putting Australia in and losing by an innings was dropped as captain. Tony Greig got the job and was captain for the next fourteen Tests, handing over to Mike Brearley after the Centenary Test at Melbourne in 1977. He was an enthusiastic leader, who led from the front and instilled a will to win in his side, but in his efforts to do so he over-stepped the mark in an interview at Hove at the start of the 1976 series against the West Indies. He boasted that England would make the West Indies grovel, a remark which the West Indians did *not* appreciate! It probably accounted for some of the short-pitched bowling which they employed during the series.

The saddest and most regrettable fall from grace, however, was Tony's behind-the-scenes activities on behalf of Kerry Packer, *whilst still captain of England.* By recruiting players for the World Series he knew he would be robbing England – and Australia and the West Indies – of some of their best players for the next two years, and so belittling Test cricket and the strength of the England side. There were undoubtedly strong reasons for changing the standing and pay of Test cricketers, but that was not an excuse for underhand dealing during the friendly and historic occasion of the Centenary

Test. All is – I hope – forgiven now, and Tony himself has stated that he now thinks money plays *too* big a part in the game, and that the endless sequences of one-day internationals are harmful to the welfare of Test cricket.

Anyway, he played five more Tests for England under Mike Brearley in the summer of 1977 against Australia and made useful scores of 91, 76 and 43, as well as taking 7 wickets. But that was the end of his Test career, and he and his lovely wife Donna emigrated with their children to Australia, where under the Kerry Packer banner he has become highly successful in the world of insurance, and has a lovely house in Vaucluse, the 'posh' part of Sydney. He has kept his contact with cricket through his television and radio commentaries. Viewers not only in Australia, but in Britain too, see his tall figure crouching down on the pitch before the start of every match. He gives his opinion of the pitch and its texture. He predicts what the temperature for the day will be and also the humidity or 'players' comfort' as he calls it.

One thing not generally known about Tony is that he suffers from epilepsy. By taking pills and getting the right amount of sleep he has managed to overcome this handicap, and kept it secret from the public for many years. It says a great deal for his courage that he did so, and when the news leaked out it was a tremendous encouragement to other epilepsy sufferers. If the captain of England could carry on and seemingly lead a normal life, so could they. I have always admired him for the way he overcame this problem, and to my knowledge only twice did his pills fail him in public. Once, a long time ago, when he was batting for Border in South Africa, and once at London Airport when returning from an overseas tour. This last occasion was due, I was told, to Tony not getting enough sleep on the plane.

Tony is always a friendly, welcoming figure whenever one visits Australia. He had his short but magic moments for England, and in a lesser degree for Sussex. He used to have a flat overlooking the ground at Hove. I sometimes get the feeling that he misses his old friends in England, and the fun and success which he enjoyed during his twelve-year stay.

Viv Richards

How great a batsman is Viv? The answer must be that he is one of the greatest ever, but from pure figures alone it is impossible to compare him with others like W.G. Grace, Jack Hobbs or Don Bradman. For example, the Don played in only 52 Tests over a twenty-year span from 1928 to 1948, which of course included the war years, and there was no Pakistan. There were also far fewer tours, and the Don himself never went to South Africa, New Zealand, the West Indies or India. On the other hand, over fourteen years from 1974 to September 1988 Viv has played in 99 Tests with 7,268 runs and an average of 52.66. The Don made 6,996 runs and averaged 99.94.

They had one thing in common, however. They were both head and shoulders above their contemporaries, and both imposed themselves on a game of cricket. They could win or turn a match by their outstanding individual performances. But in one respect Viv is an original. Most, if not all, of the great batsmen of the past have been orthodox with odd individual variations. A schoolboy watching their strokes could safely try to copy them, but in no way should a youngster try to follow or emulate Viv's method of batting.

He is immensely strong and uses a very heavy bat. He has a wonderful eye and mainly plays across the line of the ball towards the on side. This does not mean that he cannot cut, off-drive or even hit straight, but let's say that he favours the area between the bowler and the square leg. He is an immensely powerful hooker, and thinks nothing of pulling a ball from *outside* the off-stump over square leg for six. He is in fact a great hitter of sixes, which on the whole the likes of Bradman, Hutton, Compton, May, Chappell and Boycott were not. Gary Sobers, Clive Lloyd and Wally Hammond, on the other hand, did enjoy hitting the ball in the air.

Viv's other asset is his supreme confidence in himself. In fact he would probably have scored many more runs had he not been such an impatient starter, seldom trying to play himself in. He is an arrogant figure on the field, with a distinctive swaggering walk. He has never worn a helmet and shows the utmost contempt for the fastest of bowlers. He has always been most vulnerable against spin – possibly because he has so little practice against it these days.

69 Viv Richards

There is no doubt that if one were asked to pick the two outstanding destroyers of bowlers since the war one would unhesitatingly pick Ian Botham and Viv. They can both turn and win a match practically on their own, and both are inspired by the big occasion. Take Lord's. In 1979 Viv scored a century against England in the World Cup Final and in the same year another hundred for Somerset in the Gillette Cup Final. There followed a hundred against England in the 1980 Test, and in 1981 yet another in the Benson and Hedges Cup Final.

He made his first-class début in 1972 and was signed up by Len Creed for Somerset in 1974. There he acknowledges that he learnt much of his batting skills on English wickets from Brian Close. It helped that basically he has always been a front-foot player. Figures can be a bore, but I think his performance in 1976 is worth recording. In the eight months between January and August he made 1,710 runs in 11 Tests at an average of 90.00. His opponents included Australia, India and England. Enough said.

He has always been athletic and in spite of his height (five feet eleven inches) and his strongly built frame he has always been a brilliant fielder anywhere, with a devastating throw. Nowadays he is most often at first slip, where he makes the most difficult catch appear easy, and for the West Indies he has already 'pouched' more than 100. He is also quite a useful off-break bowler and can bowl seam at medium pace. With so many fast bowlers playing for the West Indies he has sometimes had to fill the spinner's place and has 28 wickets to his credit.

He took over the captaincy of the West Indies in 1985. He started by beating New Zealand and England, but then followed three drawn series against Pakistan, New Zealand and Pakistan again. There was talk of a West Indian decline and an end to their world dominance. Naturally the new captain was partly blamed, but he was learning the job and had the difficult task of following Clive Lloyd. Furthermore, the West Indies were gradually introducing new players into their team. By the time they came to England in 1988, however, they were right back on top with Viv very much in command. Admittedly, they were a far better side than England, and Richards's task with his battery of four fast bowlers may not have seemed too difficult, but in fact his captaincy was a revelation. On the field he was astute with his field placings and changes of bowling. He obviously knew the faults and weaknesses of the England batsmen. He also made sure that his side were one of the fittest I have ever seen. I watched one of their work-outs, which they did every day for forty minutes before each day's play. I was exhausted, just watching, but it meant that they completely outshone England in the field and I think were the best fielding side since Jack Cheetham's South Africans in 1955.

Off the field Viv was also a great success. In the past he had always appeared to be rather haughty and aloof, and there is no doubt that he is a very proud man. He was the first captain from the Leeward Isles and he has put them on the map so far as providing Test players is concerned. They have even displaced Barbados as *the* cricketing island. Anyway, off the field in 1988 Viv did everything right. His relationship with the media was excellent, and he made a point of mixing and greeting us all with a smile.

It was sad for him that he ended the England tour in hospital, and so missed seeing the last two days of their fourth victory in the series. He had had an operation in the West Indies during the winter, which meant that he missed the first Test against Pakistan. Perhaps he came back too soon. Anyway, the trouble recurred and he had to have a second operation. I am sure he will soon be back at his fittest and brilliant best. Except for some eye trouble a few years ago, and a bad leg, he has been remarkably free of injury – and remember he doesn't wear a helmet! He is still only thirty-six – he was born in Antigua in 1952 – and he should have several years more to captain West Indies and to delight crowds with his own unique style of batting. But don't try to copy him!

Mike Brearley

You would never have thought that he had captained England thirty-one times, and has been rated as one of the greatest of all Test captains. There he was on an autumn afternoon in the playground at Primrose Hill, pushing his young daughter on a swing. Curly grey hair, open-neck shirt, old jacket and jeans. A slow, welcoming smile of recognition – a quietly spoken voice: 'Hello, Johnners, how are you?'

Mike Brearley, possibly the most successful, certainly the most intellectual of England's captains. Under him they won six rubbers, halved three and lost one. As captain of Middlesex from 1971 to 1982 he led them to win four County Championships and two Gillette Cups.

He was a truly remarkable all-rounder. He took a first in Classics and a good second in Moral Sciences at Cambridge. To cap this he came top in the Civil Service examination in 1964 – a gateway to a top job in almost any occupation. He played cricket for Cambridge for four years from 1961 to 1964, and in that time made a record 4,310 runs, captaining them in the last two years. Just to prove his versatility, he scored two hundreds in the Varsity matches at Lord's, and was also their wicket-keeper on two occasions.

I first got to know him well on Mike Smith's 1964–5 tour of South Africa. Coming straight from his triumphs at Cambridge, Brearlers – as I have always called him – had an inexplicably unsuccessful tour. He had scored 2,178 runs in the summer of 1964, yet on the tour he played in none of the Tests, and scored only 406 runs at an average of 25.37 in the other matches. He started well enough with a couple of sixties, but the second half of the tour was a complete disaster for him. It was a tremendous test of his character, but he took it remarkably well. I never once heard him complain, and throughout he played his part in supporting Mike Smith and the team in every possible way.

70 Mike Brearley

You get to know people well over a bridge table, and that's how I got to know and like him. Charles Fortune, the South African broadcaster, and David Brown made up our four and we had some hilarious games. Brearlers was by far the best player, though Charles Fortune probably thought *he* was! Big Dave and I were 'instinct' players and didn't worry too much about conventions. We were rather like the very poor player whose erratic bidding had got his partner into terrible trouble. At the end of the game, the poor chap left the room to go and spend a penny. After he had been away for about half a minute, his partner said brightly: 'Well, for the first time this evening, I know what he's got in his hand!' I'm bound to say that it didn't seem to matter what Brearlers had in *his* hand. He always seemed to win.

His standing as a batsman is difficult to assess. He had the benefit of the easy Fenner pitches during his four years at Cambridge, but even so he scored a lot of runs elsewhere. He had a correct, pleasant style with sound defence and all-round strokes, and liked to open the batting. In fact, I wonder how many people realised that he actually opened for England forty times. Twenty of these were as Boycott's partner, without a single run-out! So he had plenty of chances to prove himself as a Test batsman, but never quite did so. His batting always showed character, however, and time and time again he came up with a useful score just when it was needed.

In the field he gave up serious wicket-keeping after his first two years at Cambridge, giving way to Mike Griffith in the last two years when he was captain. But he later proved himself a first-class slip catcher (52 catches for England), and was perfectly adequate in any other position. I saw him make one of the best catches that I have ever seen in the Prudential Final at Lord's against the West Indies in 1978. He was fielding at wide mid-on when Andy Roberts took an enormous heave at Mike Hendrick, who was bowling from the Pavilion End. The ball soared high in the sky towards the boxes in the Tavern Stand. Brearlers turned and ran fast in that direction with the ball coming from *behind* him. He was going at full tilt, looked up at the right moment and took a brilliant catch as the ball came over his shoulder. He had to suffer the indignity of being kissed by most of his side! But it emphasised his own skill as a fielder, which was an important factor in his success as captain. By his own example he was able to make the England side into a magnificent fielding machine, possibly the best it ever was.

On balance, therefore, he did not earn his Test place as a batsman, but was well up to standard in the field. Certainly, since I have followed cricket England captains have generally earned their place by their playing merit. Exceptions to this might be the old amateurs like Arthur Gilligan, F. T. Mann, Percy Chapman and, latterly, F. G. Mann. But, as Yorkshire proved for so many years, no matter how strong a team may be, a good leader is essential.

The secret of Brearlers' success as a captain was that he loved the job. Both for Middlesex and England he revelled in the many challenges. Cricket is a complicated art, and gives so much scope for thoughtful captaincy. A deep knowledge of the history of the game and its laws, tactics, field placings, study of opponents' strengths and weaknesses are all essential ingredients for good captaincy, but a 100 per cent pass in all these is still not enough. A cricket captain has not only to lead his team *on* the field but also *off* it. Cricketers spend so much time together during an England summer, or on winter tours. A great captain has also to be a father figure to keep them happy and help to solve their personal problems. This was Brearler's great strength. With his psychological approach he got to know and understand every member of the team. He studied each one separately and decided on the best way to handle him. (Stuart Surridge did the same thing in his five successful championship years for Surrey. He found that to get the best out of them he had to be gentle with Jim Laker, for example, but tough with Tony Lock.)

Rodney Hogg was quoted in Australia as saying that 'Brearley has a degree in people' – a very perceptive remark for a fast bowler! But Brearlers was deceptive until you knew him well. On the surface he was a gentle person, with his slow friendly smile, but underneath he was tough and strong-willed, and expected to get his own way. At the same time he supported his players and looked after their interests, especially where money was concerned. He wasn't exactly a barrack-room lawyer, but he always tried to see their side in any discussions or disputes.

I will end by showing how important to his success was his understanding of individuals. A perfect example occurred on the last day of the famous 1981 Test at Headingley, which England won so sensationally by 18 runs.

Brearlers had been recalled to the England captaincy for this third Test in the series. Under Ian Botham England had lost the first at Trent Bridge and drawn the second at Lord's where Botham scored a pair and then resigned the captaincy. Things didn't seem to be going much better for Brearley. England had to follow on 227 runs behind and then lost 7 wickets for only 135 runs, but thanks to a magnificent 149 not out by Botham and 56 and 29 from Dilley and Old, Australia were set 130 runs to win with most of the last day available to get them.

At the start of their innings, to our surprise Botham was put on to bowl downhill and downwind from the Kirkstall Lane End. Poor Bob Willis, aged thirty-two but still by far the fastest bowler in the side, had to bowl *up*hill and *up*wind from the Football Stand End. Botham took the early wicket of Wood, but came off after seven overs. Old replaced him for a few overs, and then at last Willis was switched round. He proceeded to bowl with tremendous speed and ferocity, generating high bounce from the pitch. He ran through the side – with a rest at the lunch interval. I have never seen him bowl better or with more fury, venom and bite in every delivery. He finished with 8 for 43 – by far his best Test analysis ever. Coupled with Botham's great innings, Willis was undoubtedly the cause for one of the greatest turn-arounds ever in Test cricket.

I asked him after the match why he had started uphill and upwind. He said the same thought had quickly occurred to him! So he went up to Brearley and said: 'Skipper, why am I bowling from the Football Stand End, into the wind and up the slope?' Brearley smiled his slow smile, 'To make you angry,' he said. How's that for captaincy?

Graham Gooch

In these days of helmets which hide players' faces, Graham Gooch is still an easily distinguishable figure. He is six feet tall, heavily built and has a rolling gait, like a sailor who has just come ashore, or a ploughman returning after a long day tilling the soil. Under his white helmet, which he always wears, he has a rather doleful face with a droopy Mexican moustache. But this hides his real personality. He has a good sense of humour, and with an unexpectedly high-pitched voice for such a big man he is friendly and amusing. At the odd function which I attended during his very successful benefit year, he also proved himself an entertaining speaker. He is a superb mimic of other people's bowling actions. His 'Bob Willis' was a classic and in a Test in India he actually bowled left-arm when imitating Dilip Doshi. As his two overs only cost 4 runs, he should perhaps have always bowled left-arm!

In fact he has been a much under-rated and under-used bowler. He bowls medium-pace out-swingers and can really move the ball in the air – with more practice and use he might well have taken many more than his 13 Test wickets, and have become a genuine all-rounder.

In spite of his apparent heaviness and slowness of foot he is an excellent fielder and a very safe catcher, especially at second slip, but of course it is as a batsman that he has stood out amongst his colleagues over the last thirteen years. This, in spite of an appalling start in his first Test in 1975 – it was against Australia and he bagged a pair. He was then only aged twenty-one, played in the next Test at Lord's, and was promptly dropped, even though he did make 31.

He didn't play again for England until three years later, when he reappeared at Lord's against Pakistan. For the remainder of the series he opened the batting, first with Mike Brearley and then with Geoff Boycott, but after two more Tests in Australia he was dropped down the order to number four, and in fact played another eight Tests before becoming a permanent opener for England.

71 Graham Gooch

He has never had the good fortune to have a regular partner such as Hobbs and Hutton had. There have been too many choppings and changes and he has often looked a lone figure at the top. He is similar in his approach to Charlie Barnett. If a half-volley comes along first ball, he promptly drives it for four. He is very powerful and hits the ball tremendously hard. It fairly rockets off his bat. He has a full repertoire of strokes and, using a very heavy bat, drives majestically through the off-side or straight. He is also strong off his legs and a good hooker.

He has followed the example of Mike Brearley and Tony Greig and holds his bat high over the stumps as he waits for the ball to be delivered. Somehow he manages not to sway or move his head, but to the purist it's not a pretty sight. One of his faults has been that when out of form he seems to get square-on and plays across the line of the ball. This has made him vulnerable to the ball which swings or cuts back late, and he is sometimes trapped leg before wicket. When he is in form, however, he oozes confidence and gives the appearance of being in total command of the bowlers, and when in full flow he is one of the best sights in cricket today.

For reasons which I will explain he has played in far fewer Tests than he should have done. He is very much a family and home-loving man. He can be obstinate and not easy to deal with. He dislikes long tours and being away all winter. He has also always had an eye on the future and it was purely a desire for financial security that made him accept the offer to captain the 'rebel' team in South Africa in 1982. He knew the risks he was running, but like most of us he was staggered when he was barred from Test cricket for three years, from 1982 to 1985, as a 'punishment'.

I personally feel that this was a most unfair decision. He and his fellow players were under no contract to the TCCB at the time, but were merely pursuing their lawful trade as professional cricketers. I am afraid that our authorities unwittingly succumbed to some of those cricketing countries who are determined to isolate South African cricket completely, in spite of the complete integration that has taken place in the structure of cricket in South Africa. The TCCB were scared that the West Indies – and others – would refuse to tour here again unless they took action. This to my mind is ridiculous. The West Indies especially *have* to come here — and to Australia – in order to finance their cricket. Their players also come over here in their droves to play for counties or in the leagues and, cynically perhaps, seem quite happy to play with or against South Africans. It doesn't really make sense, and as happens all too often in sport today money was the real cause of the ban. The TCCB feared – on behalf of the counties – that they would stand to lose too much money if the tourists refused to tour.

I'd like to make other points about the ban. Even murderers get something knocked off their sentences, but when the TCCB sounded out the possibility of their reinstating the 'rebels' after *two* years of the ban, they were quite plainly told that the other countries wouldn't stand for it. And I am also sure that had Graham and his colleagues taken the TCCB to court for restraint of trade, they would have won easily. But for the sake of cricket, and because of the large amount of money it would have cost, they decided not to be 'bloody-minded' and refrained from doing so.

So Graham was lost to England for three years, but during that time he continued to be in great form for Essex and did much to help them to their Championship wins of 1983 and 1984. He returned to Test cricket against Australia in 1985, and started off in great style in the three one-day internationals with a fifty and two hundreds. But in the Tests proper he had, for him, only a moderate summer until the final Test at the Oval, when he made his highest Test score with a magnificent innings of 196.

His happiness was short-lived, however. That winter he went reluctantly to the West Indies under David Gower. Graham is a very sensitive person and he had a miserable time. Because of his South African connections he felt he was unwelcome, and did in fact meet with a certain amount of hostility. He withdrew into himself and his gloomy appearance affected not only him but the whole team. As a result, when England so badly needed someone to stand up to the West Indian pace attack he was not at his best. Even so, he made more runs in the series (276 with an average of 27.6) than anyone else except David Gower.

In the summer of 1986 he made 443 runs in eleven innings against India and New Zealand – not bad, but still not Gooch at his best – but as captain of Essex for the first time (*when* he was available) he led them to win the Britannic Assurance Championship. However, soured by the West Indies tour, he declared himself unavailable for Mike Gatting's successful tour of Australia. The winter's rest did him no good and 1987 was a bad year for him. He just scraped 1,100 runs for Essex and as a result played in no Tests. His form was too bad to be true and he blamed it on the captaincy, which he gave up at the end of the season.

Once again Graham did not wish to go on tour and leave his wife Brenda and their twins back at home. So he only made himself available for the World Cup and the following tour of Pakistan, which meant that he would be back for Christmas with his family. His masterly 115 in the semi-final against India enabled England to reach the final of the World Cup, where they were beaten by Australia.

The summer of 1988 brought the disastrous series against the West Indies, who completely outplayed England to win 4–0. But Graham did manage to average over 45.90 with two splendid innings of 73 and 146 at Trent Bridge and a fighting 84 at the Oval. Here, no doubt to his surprise, as a result of Chris Cowdrey's injury, he found himself captain of England – the fourth of the summer. He may not have enjoyed captaining Essex, but he appeared to enjoy his responsibility as captain of England. He handled his bowlers well, and gave help and encouragement to the new boys in the side. He was captain again against Sri Lanka in the one Test at Lord's, where England won a Test match for the first time in nineteen Tests and for the first time for five years at Lord's.

Throughout the Oval Test there was speculation as to whether or not he would be selected as captain on the proposed winter tour of India. He had originally declared himself unavailable and had fixed up a contract to play for Western Province in South Africa. Once again he appeared to be the reluctant tourist, but when finally offered the captaincy he decided to accept and cancelled his South African contract.

It's really an extraordinary story. Here we have a reluctant tourist who dislikes leaving his wife, and – now – *three* young daughters. He has always said that the captaining of Essex affected his batting. And yet here he was at the end of the 1988 season going off on tour as captain.

I am not sure either that, in the two Tests in which he captained England, his form has not suffered. He has no longer appeared the dominant figure at the crease and has seemed unwilling to play his strokes. His 84 in the second innings at the Oval took him 7 hours 10 minutes, and even against the mediocre Sri Lankan attack at Lord's he seemed unable to bring himself to attack the bowling.

It is all past history now, but at the time I wondered whether it was a good idea to send someone to lead a side in India who would basically rather not go. It is a hot, difficult tour, where much patience and tact is needed. Graham has not got the charisma of Gower, nor the flamboyance and outgoing qualities of Tony Greig, two of our most successful captains of England out there. His naturally doleful appearance hides his friendliness, and he would have had to call on all his powers of leadership to keep his side happy, and to lead them to success in the Tests. Now that it has all been cancelled we shall never know whether I was right or not.

And finally, I must not forget the unique and farcical record which Graham holds. He played in a Test match for England in the morning, and in the afternoon of the same day played for his county, Essex. It all came about because of the four-day county matches which were tried out in 1988. Essex were due to start their game against Surrey at the Oval on a Tuesday, which happened to be the final day of the Sri Lankan Test at Lord's.

So Graham went in to bat at Lord's at 11.00 a.m. He was out for 36 at 12.23 p.m. with England still needing 24 runs to win. As captain he had to stay at Lord's until the finish, although Keith Fletcher had already included him in the Essex side at the Oval.

It all became quite ridiculous. Everyone – including Gooch – must have thought that it would all be over by lunch, and that he could then rush off to the Oval, where, remarkably, Fletcher had won the toss and put Surrey in to bat. This meant that he had to field with only ten men until Gooch arrived. But of course in this extraordinary summer the England batsmen continued to play like schoolboys. The Sri Lankan bowlers ranged from fast-medium to slow-medium and yet in the 'struggle' for victory England managed to lose the wickets of Barnett and Lamb, so that with one over to go before lunch 5 runs were still needed for victory.

Tim Robinson had been in all morning and had only scored 30. In the last over he drove Samarasekera for a straight four. There were three balls to go and the scores were now level. Unbelievably, especially as storm clouds were threatening, Robinson did not try to score off any of them. And so they went into lunch with England still needing 1 run to win! Whether Robinson misread the clock and thought that there was another over to go I don't know, but the whole thing was crazy. I wonder what Gooch said to Robinson in the dressing-room!

Anyway, whereas he had hoped to receive the winning cheque from Cornhill *before* lunch, he now had to wait another forty minutes, plus any time that England took to make the 1 run necessary for victory. In fact Robin Smith hit Ranatunga for four past cover in the first over, and England had won by 7 wickets. It would have served them right if it had rained all afternoon – the match would then have been a draw.

But wait. The Gooch saga was not over yet. The small crowd gathered in front of the pavilion to watch the prize-giving ceremony. An impatient Gooch was waiting to receive his cheque. It was then announced that the ceremony would be postponed for some minutes because BBC TV, wanted to broadcast it, and that popular Australian soap opera, 'Neighbours', was on at the time and had to finish! It did so at 1.55 p.m., and after the medals had been presented to all the Sri Lankan team and the umpires, Gooch was finally presented with Cornhill's cheque for £6,500. And then he still had to wait whilst the two 'Men of the Match' awards were announced and presented. At 2.07 p.m. he finally hurried off to his car, still in his flannels, and dashed off to the Oval, where he joined the other Essex fielders at about 2.40 p.m., and promptly took two catches at second slip. It gave us all a good laugh, but I am not sure whether it did the Test match image much good.

Michael Holding

One of the most graceful sights in cricket – so long as you weren't the batsman – was Michael Holding running up to bowl. He had a long run of about twenty-five yards and seemed to float in the air as he glided like a gazelle over the turf. He was tall, slim and athletic, as might be expected from a class 400-metres runner. He hardly appeared to touch the grass and it was said that the umpires could never hear him coming. For some reason he always nodded his head halfway through his run. Somebody once rather unkindly described him as 'Whispering Death', and someone else more aptly said that he could run on soft snow without leaving a footprint.

At his fastest he was undoubtedly the quickest bowler I have ever seen, though to be fair I was not in Australia to see Frank Tyson in 1954–5. I once sat sideways on to watch him bowl against MCC at Lord's in 1976. It was impossible to see the flight of the ball through the air – one had to wait to see it as it arrived at the batsman's end. In this case the main sufferer was Dennis Amiss. The poor chap had a torrid time, ducking and weaving to avoid the short-pitched balls, and finally had to retire hurt after receiving a nasty blow on the head.

Not only was he very fast but Holding was also a fine bowler, bowling chiefly away-swingers plus movement either way off the pitch. Because of his athleticism and fitness he was able to keep going for long spells. He had a vicious bouncer, which on the whole he used sparingly, but there were times, such as against MCC in 1976, when he overdid it and bowled unmercifully. Another occasion was in the third Test at Old Trafford in 1976, when with Andy Roberts and Wayne Daniel he bombarded Brian Close and

John Edrich with some quite unnecessary short-pitched bowling. And again in 1981 at the Kensington Oval at Bridgetown he carried out a terrifying assault on Geoff Boycott, whom he dismissed for 0 and 1.

Unlike Jeff Thomson, who admitted that he tried to hit batsmen, Holding once said that he never wanted *wilfully* to hurt anyone, but he did give himself the right to bowl a bouncer 'to make the batsman aware that if he gets on to the front foot he will find himself in trouble'.

72 Michael Holding

In his 60 Tests between 1975 and 1987 he took 249 wickets at a cost of 23.68 apiece. It is impossible to mention all his fine bowling performances, but one of the most outstanding was in the fifth Test at the Oval in 1976. On a slow, placid pitch he took 8 for 92 and 6 for 57 – a total of 14 in the match. As proof of what great bowling this was on such a pitch, compare his figures with the other fast bowlers in the match. Willis and Selvey for England, and Roberts, Holder and Daniel for the West Indies took a grand total of 5 wickets *between them*! And they all did plenty of bowling as it was a very high scoring game, with the West Indies making 687 (Viv Richards 291) and England 435 (Dennis Amiss getting his revenge with a courageous 203).

Holding seemed to enjoy the Oval. When he returned there eight years later in 1984 he had for some time been bowling off a shorter run, but in England's second innings he reverted to his longer run and took 5 for 43.

He was a magnificent fielder, especially away from the wicket, when his speed over the ground saved hundreds of runs and batsmen were wary of taking risky runs to him, so good was his arm. He could also hit the ball mighty distances as a batsman, coming in at about number nine. I remember especially two innings of his on the 1984 tour of England. He made 69 in the first Test at Edgbaston, and in the third Test at Headingley he actually hit Bob Willis for 5 sixes in an innings of 59 out of a stand of 82 with Larry Gomes.

Finally I come back to the Oval, where he was concerned in one of my most quoted gaffes, though I did not realise what I had said at the time. After the match I received a letter from a lady who said how much she always enjoyed listening to my commentaries. 'But, Mr Johnston,' she went on, 'you must be more careful what you say, as we have a lot of young people listening to "Test Match Special". Do you realise what you said when Michael Holding was bowling to Peter Willey? You said: "The bowler's Holding, the batsman's Willey." Really, Mr Johnston, you must be more careful.'

Ian Botham

There have been many *great* Test players, but very few who merit the classification of being a colossus. I can think of only three: W. G. Grace, Sir Donald Bradman and I. T. Botham (Guy the Gorilla or Beefy to his friends). The dictionary defines a colossus as 'more than life-size, a gigantic person standing astride over dominions'. W.G. *was* cricket in Victorian times and dominated the game throughout the country. Don Bradman brought a new concept into the art of accumulating runs and was head and shoulders above his contemporaries. And lastly there is Ian Botham, who for eleven amazing years hit the world's headlines, either with his remarkable performances on the field or his equally remarkable behaviour off it! Is there a common factor between the player and the man? One word comes immediately to mind – aggression. So let's take the player first.

His figures in themselves clearly show him to be one of the greatest ever all-round cricketers, perhaps sharing the rostrum with Gary Sobers alone. In eleven years between 1977 and 1987 he played in 94 Tests, made 5,057 runs, took 373 wickets at 27.86 each, caught 109 catches and took 5 wickets in an innings 27 times, second only to Richard Hadlee (32). In comparison Gary Sobers played in 93 Tests, made 8,032 runs, took 235 wickets and also caught 109 catches.

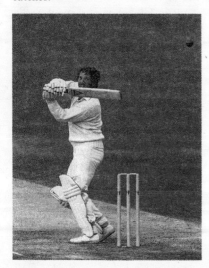

73 Ian Botham

Like so many modern Test cricketers, his figures for his country are far better than those for his county. There are several reasons for this. Test bowlers, especially fast ones, cannot be expected to give continuously of their best whilst taking part in three one-day internationals and six Test matches. With fewer Tests and no one-day internationals bowlers like Trueman and Bedser did manage to take 100 wickets regularly for their county, but in those days they had the spur of big crowds. No great players – like 'great' actors – enjoy playing before an empty house. They are only fully inspired and give of their best in front of big crowds or audiences. It may be unfair on the counties but it is understandable.

Ian is quite simply the best hitter of a ball that I have ever seen. He is physically immensely strong, powerfully built in forearms, thighs, legs and bottom (important for a fast bowler). One of the main reasons for his success is that he hits the well-pitched-up ball *straight*, most of his sixes going in an arc from wide long-on to wide long-off. To anything short on or outside the off stump he strikes a tremendous blow off the back foot through the covers. In addition to his enormous strength and wonderful eye he has always used a heavy bat, well over 3 lbs., which means that he has never been able to produce a genuine cut. This may be his excuse for the occasional reverse sweep, which so shocks the older generation like myself!

Anything short of a length on the wicket or outside the leg-stump he hooks to square or long leg. He can never resist a challenge. If a bowler places a man at deep square leg, then Ian will try to hit the ball over his head for six. It is his competitive spirit, combined with his aggression, that makes him such enormous value to a side. He must always try to come out on top. I shall never forget him at Old Trafford in 1981. Dennis Lillee had just taken the new ball and bowled Ian three bouncers, which Ian promptly hooked off his eyebrows for sixes over long leg. This was perhaps the best exhibition of hitting I have ever seen in a Test, better even than his remarkable 149 not out in the Headingley Test a month earlier. He – as *Wisden* put it – 'plundered' 118 in 123 minutes with 6 sixes (a record in England and Australian Tests) and 13 fours. It is worth noting that he played himself in, his first 28 runs taking 70 minutes. He then went berserk and in only 53 minutes made the remaining 90 runs. This proved that he is not just a hitter. With more concentration and patience he could play Test cricket again as a batsman pure and simple for several years to come. Not for nothing was he on the ground staff at Lord's, where young boys are taught all the right techniques. This means that he has a correct and sound defence, but there will always be the matter of his temperament. How long is he prepared to allow a bowler to dictate to him? Not for long I fear. He just has to prove himself top dog.

It should be easy to assess a Test bowler who in eleven years has taken 373 wickets. When he started he was a lively fast-medium, bounding in off a longish straight run with a high knee action. Once at the wicket he got sideways-on and, because of the pivot of his body, was able to bowl devastating out-swingers. Over the last five years or so, however, his action gradually altered, owing largely to the development of his figure – though looking back it may also have been the beginning of his back trouble which handicapped him. He ran in more slowly, without the previous bound and energy, and bowled more square-on, but remarkably he continued to take wickets, quite often with bad balls (though a bad ball becomes a good ball if it takes a wicket!)

Even when he had lost some of his bounce, pace and swing, however, he continued to bowl short with two deep legs, and defy the batsman to hook him for six. Many fell for the trap and perished – none more so than Hilditch and Wood on the Australian tour here in 1985 – but to me it was rather sad, and a fall from the high standards of his early Test career.

One of his troubles was that he was such a competitor that he wanted to bowl all day, which he often seemed to do, especially when David Gower was captain. David found it difficult to prise the ball away from him, when he obviously wanted to take him off.

There was, however, one famous occasion when Ian actually did *not* want to bowl. It was during his golden year of 1981 in the fourth Test at Edgbaston, following England's amazing win by 18 runs at Headingley. In their second innings Australia needed 151 runs to win. It was the fourth day of the Test – a glorious Sunday afternoon. It seemed plain sailing for Australia, who were 105 for 4, needing only 46 more runs when Border was out caught off his glove from a surprise lifter from Emburey.

Brearley had been about to bring Willis back, but suddenly changed his mind and in a moment of inspiration turned to Ian. He had only taken one wicket in the first innings and none so far in the second. He seemed tired and dispirited and suggested several alternatives to Brearley – anyone but himself. But the captain insisted and 'ordered' him to bowl. The result was unbelievable. Ian proceeded to take 5 wickets for 1 run in 28 deliveries and Australia were beaten by 29 runs. So the great all-rounder had performed yet another miracle.

To complete his all-rounder tag Ian was a magnificent and unique fielder at second slip. He caught many brilliant catches, standing about two yards in front of first slip. He saw the ball so quickly that he made catches off balls which would not have reached him had he been standing in the normal second-slip position alongside first slip. But I would not recommend mere mortals to copy him, nor to stand with both hands on the knees as he did, as the bowler ran up to bowl.

As if his all-round performances were not enough, Ian also

captained England twelve times. He took over from Mike Brearley in 1980 for the first Test at Trent Bridge against the West Indies. The West Indies just won this match by 2 wickets and the other four were drawn. He then captained England in the drawn Centenary Test at Lord's, followed by four Tests on the controversial West Indies tour, when the second Test was cancelled because the Guyanan government refused Robin Jackman an entry permit. The West Indies won the first two, and the other two were drawn. On top of all this Ian suffered a severe blow when Ken Barrington so sadly died at Bridgetown. So it was an unhappy tour, and a some-what chastened Botham returned to captain England against Aus-tralia, who won the first Test at Trent Bridge. England managed to draw the second Test at Lord's, where Ian suffered the embar-rassment of making a pair. This was too much for him. The media had already been after his blood and he promptly resigned the captaincy just before, so it is said, Alec Bedser could tell him that he had been sacked.

So the story of his captaincy is not a happy one. Perhaps he was too young (twenty-four) and inexperienced. It was certainly asking a lot of such a vital all-rounder to have the extra strain and worry. He always protested that it did not affect his performance as a player, but it certainly did not help his batting. In twenty-one innings he only averaged 12.09, with 57 his top score, but he did take 34 wickets at 32.3 apiece, about 5 runs a wicket more expensive than his Test career figure. Finally, he had the bad luck to be captain against West Indies in nine of his twelve Tests. Funnily enough, however, I believe that if he were ever asked to captain England again he would leap at the chance.

So much for the player. Now for the man – a complex character if ever there was one. Aggressive, courageous, loyal, compassionate and larger than life. Wherever he is, whether on the field, in the dressing-room or at a party, his strong personality and mere physi-cal presence outshines everyone else. He is able to influence some of his fellow players, not always for their good, and has a slightly warped sense of humour. Never stand near a swimming pool at an outdoor party if he is anywhere nearby. Be prepared for leg-pulls and practical jokes, all done in a boisterous friendly way, so long as you don't object. After a few drinks he can be a dangerous man to cross or argue with. His whole career has been blighted with brawls and fights in bars, hotels, airports and even in aeroplanes.

He is seldom contrite afterwards, and usually blames the media for the publicity. The same applies to the many accusations of his drug-taking and sexual exploits. He finally admitted the former after suing various newspapers, but he would blandly stand in front of the TV cameras and deny everything – always blaming the media.

And here one must be fair. I went on ten tours from 1958 to 1973 as a commentator and saw plenty of off-the-field activities by players which would have made news today, but my colleagues and I were there to report *cricket*, not personal conduct. Nowadays, however, the editors of the tabloids send special reporters to stalk and spy on the players in their off-duty hours. Hence the headlines. Whilst not excusing some of the excesses reported, I deplore the gutter press paying large sums of money to anyone – especially beauty queens – who is prepared to reveal all.

It is something which Ian has brought on himself, however, and he has to learn to live with it. What he has needed all his life is strong but friendly leadership, and he has not often had it. Whenever he has, however, he is a different person. His friends have not always helped him and he has been tempted by large sums of money to do some extraordinary things, such as being groomed to become a Hollywood star.

There is of course another side to him – the family man who loves his wife Kathy and his three children, and likes nothing better than living in the country with them and his dog, and rough shooting. There's also the fishing, where he overcomes his natural impatience and enjoys a long fight against the salmon. He will try anything so long as it offers a challenge, hence his learning to fly and his notoriously fast driving. And of course there's the compassionate man who believes in action rather than words – as proved by his walk from John O'Groats to Land's End and his journey over the Alps. Though often in pain and great discomfort he never gave up, and through his courage and determination made millions of pounds to help fight leukaemia. And finally there's his loyalty to his friends, as when he resigned from Somerset when he thought Joel Garner and his special friend Viv Richards had been unfairly treated.

As I write, he is still fighting his biggest fight, after his major back operation in the early summer of 1988. I am sure he will win the fight and be back to live another day in the Test arena – probably not as a regular bowler but as a hard-hitting batsman who has learnt to have the patience to build up a big innings.

I am always a sucker for anyone who is nice to me, and Bothers has always been that. So I wish him well and hope that the only headlines which I read in the future will be of his prowess *on* the cricket field, representing England again.

Mike Gatting

I shall always remember a strange incident which happened at Lord's in 1978. It was during the annual Whitsun match between Middlesex and Sussex. Mike Brearley was captain of Middlesex and fielding at mid-off. Imran Khan was one of the Sussex batsmen. For some reason, which I have never discovered, he and Brearley began to have an argument. From the commentary box it looked quite heated and there was a face-to-face confrontation, with the odd wagging of fingers.

To my, and I imagine everyone else's surprise, a squat rather tubby figure trotted up from wide mid-on. He went up to the two contestants, said something and started to pull Brearley away. Brearley tried to brush him off and was obviously annoyed with the 'mediator', to whom he appeared to address some sharp words, but at the end of the next over he had second thoughts. He went and put his arm round the 'mediator' as if to apologise, and presumably to say thank you.

You will, of course, have realised that the 'mediator' was Gatters, then only aged twenty-one and still a newcomer in the Middlesex team (he first played for them in 1975 and gained his cap in 1977). In view of events in Pakistan nine years later, it *is* surprising that he acted as he did, but it reveals the true side of his character. He is basically a sportsman who likes to 'play the game'. He may be obstinate, slightly quick-tempered and not afraid to speak his mind. He may be naïve – especially in his relations with the media and the public – but he has tremendous guts, both mental and physical, and is a terrific competitor. When he walks out to the wicket you can see his determination. He seems shorter than his five feet ten inches, and with his short, now greying beard, and his stocky chunky figure, he looks every inch an Elizabethan sailor, out to repel an invader. You know, whatever happens, that he will fight and not be intimidated.

He is extraordinarily athletic and quick on his feet in spite of weighing at least fourteen stone, partly a result of his voracious appetite. It's lucky for him that he plays at Lord's, where Nancy presides over the kitchen which provides food for the committee and their guests, the players and officials and, it must also be admitted, the 'Test Match Special' team. She sends us up a supply of sandwiches, biscuits, tea and coffee, and for many years now has made me her own special beef sandwiches. Anyway, she makes sure that Gatters has a second breakfast of bacon and eggs when he arrives at the ground, and supplies him with nibbles and meals throughout the day.

74 Mike Gatting

Gatters is an all-round games player, but unlike his brother Steve, who played football for Arsenal and then Brighton, chose cricket. He is a very good fielder anywhere, and an especially safe catcher at slip, though as captain of England he sometimes had to field in the deep – not ideal for a captain – because at least two of his side had bad shoulders and couldn't throw. But he's equally happy anywhere, short leg or mid-on, where he made a brilliant catch in the 1981 Headingley Test, running in fast and picking the ball up at his toes. He is also quite a useful fourth- or fifth-change medium bowler, who can sometimes break up a partnership.

As a batsman he can be correct and play straight with all the orthodox strokes. He is a strong cutter and punches the ball hard on either side of the wicket off the back foot. He is quick on his feet and drives the ball beautifully through the off side or straight, but in limited-over cricket he is often tempted to try the *unor-thodox* – backing away to give himself room, or even that ghastly reverse sweep. Both have brought him runs, but they have also proved fatal at vital moments in a match.

He had two bad habits which he has tried to cure. When he first started he used to bang his bat up and down on the popping-crease as the bowler ran up to bowl. He used to take his bat up high to do this, and often was bringing it *down* just as the bowler delivered the ball. This meant that he was late in bringing it up again to play the ball.

The other habit still occasionally haunts him. He is apt to pad up to a ball just outside the off-stump with bat high in the air. I must remind you that unless a batsman plays at the ball, even if the part of his body hit is *outside* the off stump, he can be given out if the umpire thinks the ball will hit the stumps. There was the famous occasion at Lord's in 1984 when in both innings he was lbw to Malcolm Marshall padding up in this way. Malcolm can bring the ball back sharply from the off, so it is a dangerous thing to do. But exactly the same thing happened in 1988 in the third Test at Old Trafford. Gatters had returned to the England side after not playing at Lord's and was lbw to Marshall for 0. I have rarely seen a more unhappy man as he returned to the pavilion, hitting his pad with his bat as a sign of how annoyed he was with himself for having done such a thing.

He played his first Test in 1977 against Pakistan in Karachi, but it was not until 1984, in his fiftieth Test innings, that he made his first Test hundred. He scored 136 against India in Bombay, quickly followed by 207 two Tests later at Madras. In that series he made 527 runs with an average of 87.83 in the Tests, and at last established himself as one of England's leading batsmen and an indispensable member of the side. One of the reasons for this long-delayed success was that he was never picked on a regular basis, and was always in and out of the team. And then, when he *was* picked, he was moved up and down the batting order like a yo-yo.

He became captain of Middlesex in 1983, and of England in 1986, taking over from David Gower after the first Test against India at

Lord's. He has had his successes and failures and his record as captain of England is: played 23, won 2, lost 5, drawn 16. He has had better luck with Middlesex, winning the Britannic Assurance County Championship in 1985, the Benson and Hedges Cup in 1983, 1986, and the NatWest Trophy in 1984, 1988. His high point with England was the Australian tour in 1986–7, when England won the Test series 2–1 and then completed a hat-trick by winning the Benson and Hedges special challenge, and also the World Cup series. Gatters was then on top of the world, but since then nothing has gone right for him, except for reaching the World Cup Final in Calcutta in 1987. England lost to Pakistan 0–1 in the summer of 1987 and this was followed by the disastrous and infamous tour of Pakistan immediately afterwards. After a dull no-result series against New Zealand came the Trent Bridge incident which lost Gatters the captaincy.

It is difficult to assess him as a captain. To start with, except in one day internationals, England during his captaincy have lost two series against Pakistan and one each against the West Indies, New Zealand and India. To be fair, so far as playing skill in Tests is concerned, England are now probably bottom of the Test match countries, except for Sri Lanka. So it is difficult to blame his captaincy. He has always liked to be in the game, and enjoys the tactical side. This has tended to make him too fussy in the field, with innumerable field changes and endless conferences with the bowlers. But he is a good motivator on the field and always leads from the front, and with both England and Middlesex has always had 100 per cent support from his players. He has not been an ideal captain, because inevitably – rising from the ranks as he did – he is too close to the players and therefore finds discipline *off* the field far harder than *on* it.

There have been glaring incidents of poor behaviour by any cricket standards, but he has probably inwardly sympathised with the culprits and therefore has not been a tough enough disciplinarian. As a result there was the disastrous tour of Pakistan, culminating in the infamous Shakoor Rana incident.

There were plenty of *reasons* for this. But there was no *excuse* for an England captain to be involved in such a confrontation with an umpire. The England side maintain that Shakoor Rana started it when he called Gatters a f—— cheat, and that Gatters reacted by losing his temper and wagging his finger at Shakoor Rana and giving as good as he had got. He had actually done nothing wrong. He warned the batsman, Salim Malik, that he was moving long leg round to deep square leg. As the bowler ran up Gatters raised his hand to the fielder – David Capel – to stop. It was then that the accusation of cheating was made. It is easy to be wise from so far away, without knowing all the frustrations and bad umpiring that had already taken place, but of course the correct thing for Gatters to have done would have been to walk off the field and complain to the authorities that he had been abused by the umpire.

As if this was not bad enough, there followed the Trent Bridge incident off the field, where Gatters invited a barmaid back to his hotel room, and she sold the 'story' – more than somewhat embellished, I suspect – to a newspaper. Whatever the rights or wrongs of the case, one can only say that it was unwise for an England captain to do that sort of thing in the middle of a Test, knowing that there are hungry reporters hanging around just waiting for such a story. Nor was it wise of Gatters to agree to the publishers adding a chapter to his book about the Shakoor Rana incident, even though he did not write it himself. It cost him £5,000 in fines and, looking back, it was all so sad and unnecessary. He is a thoroughly nice person – friendly, straight and honest. A somewhat naïve bulldog, perhaps. I just hope that the winter's rest which he is taking will enable him to put everything behind him, to live happily with his wife Elaine and two boys, Andrew and James, and that he will appear in the spring at Lord's fit and ready to do battle for England against the old enemy – Australia. At least Middlesex's victory in the NatWest Final will have helped – even though he himself was run out for 0!

Malcolm Marshall

Have you ever thought what it would be like to stand in the path of an express train approaching at 90 m.p.h.? I don't expect that anyone has ever done such a crazy thing, except possibly in films, but any batsman who has ever faced Malcolm Marshall at his fastest knows what it would feel like. He must be a terrifying sight as he sprints in at a tremendous pace off a twenty-yard run. He takes tiny steps and is going so fast by the time he reaches the stumps that there is no chance of an orthodox bowling action. He is more square than sideways on, and there is practically no swivel of his body. He simply brings his right arm over like a whiplash, and the ball hurtles towards the batsman at about 90 m.p.h.

75 Malcolm Marshall

Unlike most of the West Indian bowlers, he does not bring the ball down from a great height. He is only five feet eleven inches tall, and most of them are anything from six foot three to six foot seven. The result is that the ball tends to skid through at chest or throat height rather than bounce over the batsman's head. He has been called lethal and destructive, and when he is bowling at his fastest he is certainly both.

You can check with Andy Lloyd of Warwickshire, who in his first – and only – Test at Edgbaston in 1984 was struck on the helmet from a short rising ball. He retired hurt, suffered from blurred vision and did not play again in 1984. And that was *through a helmet*!

By now Malcolm has joined the band of great fast bowlers – Lindwall, Trueman, Lillee, Holding and Hadlee. He varies his pace from very quick to fast-medium, often off a shortened run. His main ball is the one which leaves the batsman, but he has also perfected the one which swings *in* unexpectedly. This gets him many lbw decisions, and among his eleven lbw victims in the 1988 series against England were Gooch and Lamb twice and Gatting once, padding up without playing a stroke.

He has always been a fitness fanatic and is said to do fifty to sixty press-ups a day – or sit-ups, as I think they are now called. During his ten years of Test cricket he has kept remarkably free from injury. He has boundless energy, and when not playing cricket plays tennis and golf. Since 1981 he has led a double cricketing life, playing for Hampshire in our summer, and for the West Indies during the rest of the year. He has worked wonders for Hampshire, and between 1981 and 1986 he was always one of the three top wicket-takers in the County Championship. In 1982 he took 134 wickets in the twenty-two match Championship, and this is still a record. Unlike so many of our modern Test fast bowlers, he has always given of his best for his county, and tried as hard as he does when playing for the West Indies.

I was in Barbados in February 1988 when there were rumours of him having knee and ankle trouble. Certainly, when I saw him bowl for Barbados against Guyana he only seemed to be at three-quarter pace, but in fact he started to bowl genuine leg-breaks and promptly took three wickets. I asked him afterwards whether this was going to be his secret weapon against England in the summer, but he said no. He was captain and thought the Bridgetown pitch might take spin. He had, he explained to me, begun his bowling life as a leg-spinner, and only took up fast bowling later.

After missing the first Test against Pakistan soon afterwards he regained almost full fitness, though he was troubled by a rib injury during the summer tour of England. Indeed, in the first Test at Trent Bridge he was forced to retire hurt in England's second innings. It is perhaps worth noting that this was the only Test out of five which the West Indies failed to win.

It was unusual for him, as he has tremendous guts and loathes giving up. This is what makes him such a great competitor. At Headingley in 1984 he suffered a double fracture of his left thumb, stopping a ball from Chris Broad in the gully, but this did not prevent him from going in to bat so that Larry Gomes could reach his hundred. He had to bat one-handed, and even so managed to hit a four. Better still – although his thumb was encased in plaster, making it difficult to use his left arm, he proceeded to take 7 for 53, including a two-handed caught-and-bowled to dismiss Graeme Fowler.

As a batsman he has improved so much that he very nearly qualifies as a genuine all-rounder. His method and style are correct and he hits the ball very hard. He has a top Test score of 92 (against India) and has also scored four hundreds for Hampshire.

It took him about four years to become a regular member of the West Indies fast quartet, and since then has been reckoned the fastest bowler in the world. His record is phenomenal. In 58 Tests he has taken 290 wickets at a more economical rate than any of the top eighteen Test wicket-takers. He averages 20.41, a fraction better than Joel Garner (20.97) and Freddie Trueman (21.57). What's more, he took 35 wickets in the series against England.

In spite of his continued success, he has let it be known that he wants to retire soon. He will play against Australia in 1988–9 and against India in the West Indies in the spring of 1989. After that, who knows? Like Richard Hadlee, he sets himself targets. I cannot therefore believe that he has not got his eye on passing some at least of the nine Test bowlers at present ahead of him. By September 1988, he averaged exactly 5 wickets per Test, so at that rate he only needed about sixteen more Tests for him to pass Underwood (297), Trueman (307), Gibbs (309), *Kapil Dev (319), Willis (325), *Imran Khan (334), Lillee (355) and *Botham and *Hadlee (373). Those marked with an asterisk are still playing so could add to their total, which makes it a tough task.

As a person he is reserved and not easy to get to know, but he is an immense enthusiast and trier. So long as he keeps fit and maintains his present form I would back him at least to pass 350 before he finally decides to retire. And it could so easily be 400!

David Gower

Few Test players have had as many gifts showered on them by the gods as David Gower: good looks, fair curly hair, charisma, charm, good manners, a sense of humour, intelligence. In addition he is athletic, six feet tall and moves like a gazelle with speed and lightness of foot.

As a batsman he has a wonderful eye, and a sense of timing which strokes the ball to the boundary. There is no brute force nor bludgeoning of the ball – everything he does is graceful and elegant.

Tom Graveney is the nearest living batsman to compare with him and, from what one has read, the two Palairet brothers, L.C.H. and R.C.N., were in the same mould. Of course, being a left-hander has helped him. To my mind there is nothing to beat a left-handed off-drive through extra cover.

76 David Gower

It all sounds too good to be true, and of course there are a few minuses. He has – rightly, I think – been criticised for being too casual, careless and irresponsible. He has earned himself the sou-briquet of 'Laid-back' both on and off the field, and he certainly is. This has both advantages and disadvantages. It means that, outwardly at least, he remains calm and doesn't panic. He accepts umpires' decisions without question and can ignore the pressures to which modern cricketers claim they are subjected.

This also gives him the appearance of being a non-fighter, however, and not seeming to care when disasters happen. It was the main criticism of his captaincy: an apparent air of laissez-faire, with insufficient attention paid to discipline, dedication and practice. He seemed to rely on everyone giving of their best, without the necessary encouragement or criticism. On his West Indies tour he gave the impression of preferring a day off on the beach or sailing, rather than a hard session at the nets. His natural talent may not have needed much net practice (Denis Compton was the same – he hated it), but lesser mortals *do* need continuous practice, to keep the eye in and to iron out various faults in technique which crop up from time to time. In this respect cricketers could take a lesson from the star golfers and tennis players – who never seem to stop practising.

It must be said on his behalf that in his twenty-six Tests as England's captain he had the bad luck to play ten of them against the West Indies, and lost them all. But he did have a successful tour of India in 1985 when after losing the first Test, he managed the difficult feat on India's slow pitches of fighting back and winning the series 2–1. And in the same summer he beat Australia 2–1 in England.

Like Norman Yardley, he may be too nice and not ruthless enough ever to be a great captain. His handling of Ian Botham is a case in point. He often seemed to have difficulty in taking Ian off, even when he was bowling badly and a change was clearly needed. I won't say that Ian refused to give the ball up, but it looked jolly like it!

David lost the England captaincy in unhappy circumstances after the Lord's Test against India in 1986. They won by 5 wickets and, following immediately on the five defeats in the West Indies in the winter, his fate was sealed. Unlike Ian Botham, who, after the Lord's Test against Australia in 1981, got in his resignation *before* he was sacked, David had the news of his sacking broken to him by Peter May after Mike Gatting had already been appointed in his stead. Sacking anyone is never easy, but in the case of some past England captains (believe it or not there have been thirty-two from 1946 to 1988) it does seem that some of them have been dismissed rather abruptly and unfairly. However, after seeing all the traumas and dramas of Mike Gatting's brief captaincy, David must be relieved that he was sacked when he was. Funnily enough, though, he enjoyed his captaincy, and if he were ever to be offered it again, I bet that he would take it.

He has undoubtedly played far too much cricket during the thirteen years since he first played for Leicestershire in 1975, including 100 Tests and goodness knows how many one-day internationals. He was rapidly becoming stale and played out and wisely took the 1987–8 winter off, thus missing the World Cup and the tours of Pakistan and New Zealand. In truth it didn't seem to have done him much good, and he had a run of poor scores for Leicestershire. Nor was his form against the West Indies up to his highest standards, and he was dropped for the fifth Test at the Oval. Even so, he did better than most of the others, with 211 runs at an average of 30.14. Only Gooch and Lamb did better. At least he had the satisfaction of reaching exactly 7,000 runs in 100 Tests, but he never really showed the determination, concentration and fighting qualities which are needed against the battering of West Indian fast bowlers.

Ever since, at the age of twenty-one, he scored 4 runs to square leg against Pakistan at Edgbaston off his first ball in Test cricket, he has been both a delight and a torture to watch. He is what I call a 'touch' player, relying on eye and footwork acting in perfect harmony. When they don't he seems strangely vulnerable. In his early days he was a sucker to the ball on his legs. Time and time again he has tickled it to a leg slip or short fine leg especially placed there, and sometimes to the wicket-keeper. At one time he appeared to have mastered this, though he occasionally half-drove a ball into the hands of mid-wicket.

In later years his footwork has let him down, and by not moving his feet he has tended to give catching practice to second or third slip. He sometimes appears unable to resist playing a ball wide of the off-stump which he should have left alone. It is as if his bat is attracted like a magnet to the ball. His supporters despair, and so does he, because no matter how he looks, he *does* care. On the other hand, when everything is coordinated he is still as good a batsman to watch as any other in the world today, except perhaps for Graeme Hick. His off-drive is perfection, and he wafts away anything short to the boundary. He also has the great asset of being a good judge of a run and very fast between the wickets. Some of what I have said may seem to be too critical, because after all to make 7,000 runs in 100 Tests means an average of 70 for every Test, and that can't be bad! So laid-back he may be, but the figures show that it has stood him and England in good stead. Furthermore, his fourteen Test hundreds contain several where he has been prepared to get stuck in and battle on after passing his century – as scores of 212, 173 not out, 166, 157 and 152 go to prove.

As a fielder his swiftness and ease of movement made him into a brilliant performer, especially in the covers. He used to have a fine arm, but then damaged his right shoulder so that he now cannot throw at all – a severe handicap. When he has chased a ball to the boundary he often has to run back with it quickly or give it to someone else to throw.

Oh, yes. As a bowler he has taken one Test wicket against India at Kanpur in 1982 – and he wasn't even captain! His analysis read: 1–0–1–1. He treasures that, especially as his victim was that fine all-rounder Kapil Dev.

If David had to give up cricket tomorrow he would be far less affected than most other first-class cricketers. He has so many interests. He loves travelling and could be described as a *bon viveur*, with an expert knowledge of wines and a special penchant for port. He likes music, is a keen photographer and at least for short periods enjoys lying on a beach in the sun.

He is a naturally active person, so enjoys sailing and water-skiing. His other love is winter sports, and each year he toboggans down the famous Cresta Run at St Moritz. He has also been a member of a bobsleigh team. Both sports must be terrifying – on the Cresta Run especially, when you travel head first within inches of the icy track at speeds of 60 m.p.h. or more. Last year I asked him how he thought that I would fare with my long nose. He replied that I would plough a deep furrow in front of me as I sped down the run. And apropos of this conversation, he must be one of the easiest people to interview of all Test cricketers. He never dodges a question, but fends the awkward one off with disarming wit and a smile. It was good news for England that he was selected for the India tour of 1988–9. Last time as captain he had a successful and a happy tour (they don't always go together!). His charm and relaxed style would once again have helped keep everybody happy, and to act as a calming influence in the event of any trouble on or off the field.

One final thought. He was born in Tunbridge Wells and educated at King's School, Canterbury. How Kent must still be kicking themselves for allowing him to slip through their net and escape to Leicestershire. It's just like the man from Decca who turned down the Beatles!

Allan Border

You can spot him easily on the field. He looks smaller than his five
feet nine inches and walks with tiny steps, bearded chin resting on
his chest, eyes down, green cap pulled over his eyes. Even when
captain he is an unobtrusive figure, and off the field quiet and
modest. He can also be emotional, as proved by his reaction after
England had beaten Australia at Brisbane on Gatting's tour of
1986. He has proved himself a good leader, however, and become
not only one of the great accumulators of runs in modern cricket,
but also one of the most correct players with immense powers
of concentration. A left-hander, batting usually at number four,
sometimes at number five, he has time and again rescued Australia
from early disasters. As I write he is sixth in the list of Test batsmen
with 7,343 runs, but it surely won't be long before he goes into
second place above Geoff Boycott (8,114) though still a long way
behind Sunny Gavaskar (10,122). He is a glutton for cricket, as
proved by his spending his Australian winters over here playing for
Essex.

When Allan first came over here in 1980 for the Centenary Test,
and then again in 1981, he was an unexciting player to watch –
placing, nudging and cutting the ball rather than hitting it – but
when he came as captain in 1985 he was completely transformed.
He had a wonderful tour, scoring a hundred in each of his first four
matches. He made more runs than any of his batsmen, both in the
Tests where he averaged 66.33, and in all matches, with 1,355 runs
at an average of 71.31. But it was his change of style which was so
noticeable. He had become a hitter of sixes and used his feet
delightfully to drive the bowlers back over their heads. In his first
hundred against Somerset there were 4 sixes, against Worcestershire
6 sixes, against MCC no sixes but 22 fours, and against Derbyshire
5 sixes. It was a complete transformation, and ever since he has
been a joy to watch. His defence is sound, and at thirty-three he is
strong and sturdy and scores with drives, cuts and strokes off his

legs. He is already Australia's top scorer in Tests and there is no reason why he should not continue to flourish for at least five more years. If he does, then he *will* pass Gavaskar. With 22 hundreds already, he should also pass G. Chappell (24), Sobers (26) and Bradman (29), and then try to challenge Gavaskar (34).

77 Allan Border

He has been a great success in his two seasons for Essex. He was signed by them to replace Ken McEwan, and got off to a terrible start, not reaching 50 until the end of May. But he then had a purple patch, scoring 1,287 runs at an average of 51.48 before returning to Australia in the middle of August. He fitted splendidly into the Essex team – always a happy one. He didn't act like a star Test player but was very much one of the boys, and when asked was helpful with his advice. He seems to play cricket non-stop, but returned again in 1988 as keen as ever to undertake the hard grind of county cricket and scored 1,393 runs, average 58.04.

He is an excellent fielder in the covers, mid-wicket or round the bat. He is also a more than useful slow left-arm bowler, who can pick up the odd wicket and break up a stand. He has formed an efficient partnership with Bobby Simpson as his manager, and together they shared the triumph of unexpectedly winning the World Cup in Pakistan and India in 1987. He is not the most glamorous of cricketers, nor the most spectacular personality, but his sturdy character and outstanding skill as a batsman make him one of the most successful Test cricketers ever.

Last over:
for better, for worse

I have always tried to be an optimist, so when I go to a cricket match I always tell myself that it's going to be a great day's cricket. Sometime it is; more often than not, it isn't. In my forty-three summers of broadcasting I have seen so many changes, some for the better, some for the worse. On balance I think it's fair to say that cricket today is not as good to watch as it was twenty to thirty years ago.

I must emphasise that I am only talking about the professional game. Although I no longer do so myself, I am sure that cricket in clubs and villages is as much fun to play as ever it was.

For better

1. Players today are generally far fitter and more athletic than in the past. They have extensive pre-season training under a qualified PT instructor. They have a thirty-minute 'warm-up' before each day's play. They carry out a complicated selection of what I call physical jerks. They do press-ups, sit-ups and numerous stretching exercises. They trot round the ground, every now and again doing an extraordinary sideways run. It exhausts me just to watch them. And what a contrast to the old days, when before a game, players practised in the nets, batsmen getting their eyes in, bowlers loosening up.

This may explain why today almost every fast bowler suffers from trouble with backs, hamstrings, knees and ankles. As Alec Bedser says, the only way to get fit as a bowler is to bowl. A bowler's sideways-on action brings a lot of unusual muscles into play. It's certainly significant that the likes of Bedser, Trueman, Statham and Bailey rarely broke down. Nowadays there's a constant procession of fast bowlers going back to the pavilion for repairs, and when they come to play for their counties after a Test, they are often too knackered to give of their best. Yet the Bedser brigade bowled hundreds more overs per season, and regularly took their hundred wickets. I think the whole thing was best summed up, as I have noted before, by the sight of Bob Willis standing on one leg before a match. His other was resting on the shoulder of Bernard Thomas, England's popular physiotherapist and father confessor for so many years. Big Bob looked just like a pelican!

2. The real benefit from the general increase in physical fitness is shown in fielding and throwing, which has become an entertainment in itself. I think the best fielding side I ever saw was Jack Cheetham's South African team of 1955. They sprinted after every hit, flung themselves at the ball to save a boundary and caught some incredible catches. Nowadays, almost every county can match this. The close catching may be no better – nor worse – but the extra speed over the ground helps to reduce the scoring rate. I once asked Charlie Barnett how he managed to get 98 not out before lunch against the Australians at Trent Bridge in 1938. 'Oh,' he said, 'we always used to run two to third man in those days.' It's not often possible to do that today, partly because throwing has universally become so much better. In the old days you could pick out the fielders with really good 'arms' – people like Hendren and Sandham in the deep, or Hobbs, Washbrook, Bland and Lloyd in the covers. Now everyone seems able to throw back accurately and fast to the wicket-keeper. Our seventy-five-yard boundaries do help, but except in big playing areas like Melbourne we no longer suffer in comparison with the Australians, as we used to do.

3. Field-placing has become far more scientific and professional. It doesn't help on the entertainment side, but it *does* restrict scoring. Modern captains study batsman's strengths and weaknesses far more closely and set their fields accordingly. They also give up trying to take wickets earlier than did past captains, and set defensive fields far sooner. Walter Robins told me that in the 1930 Test at Lord's, where Australia made 729, he was still fielding at silly mid-off right up to the end of the innings.

4. There are now far better playing conditions for the players. Thanks to the Players' Cricket Association, they now have a minimum wage and a pensions scheme. The minimum wage (£8,000 now but negotiating to increase it to at least £9,500) may not sound

much, but of course it is only for six months, and many of the players go abroad to coach in South Africa or Australia during the winter. The top twenty or so players on the Test circuit can of course earn far more money, with sums like £10,000 to £12,000 for a home series or a tour, together with bonuses, advertising sports goods, appearing on the media or 'writing' articles for papers or magazines. There is also the additional bait of a substantial benefit, which is generally given to a player by a county after about ten years' service. In the old days a player was given one match for which he had to pay all expenses and then took what profit was left, so he was very much in the hands of the weather. Nowadays a player can have collections at about six matches, which he can choose. He also has a benefit committee which organises dinners, golf tournaments, six-a-side pro-am cricket matches, raffles, etc., etc. Compared with the old days the amounts achieved are quite staggering. Anything under £100,000 is considered disappointing and £200,000 is the target for a really top player. And – touch wood – it's all still tax free!

5. Today's spectators are far better off, though the price of admission has gone up accordingly. But instead of spectators standing all day or sitting on the grass, most grounds now are trying to provide bucket seats for everyone, instead of the old hard benches. The crowds are also far better informed of what is going on, with excellent public address systems and electronic scoreboards. Before the war at Lord's a hand-cart used to be wheeled round the ground, supporting a blackboard on which was chalked details of changes in the teams and who had won the toss.

The armchair spectator at home is also far better served by television and radio. Television coverage now involves at least six cameras, whereas when we started in 1946 we were lucky to have three. I once even did a county match at Swansea with only one camera. There is also the action replay, which when properly used is a great asset. People have got so used to it that when they actually go to a match, and a wicket falls, they automatically look around expecting to see the replay. I cannot here resist telling the story of the Irishman who caught a brilliant catch at second slip but missed it on the action replay!

The one danger of the action replay is the effect it can have on umpires. They have to make an instant decision, and it is most unfair if an action replay is played again and again on television while commentators have a second, third or fourth look before giving *their* opinion. It is a big responsibility for the TV producers not to help denigrate or embarrass the umpires. Their decision must be final and not questioned, and for the good of the game it is essential that the players have confidence in them. That is why I am against the big screens used on some grounds in Australia, which play everything back to the spectators. It has certainly shown up some really bad decisions, especially with run outs. I have even heard the umpires booed after certain play-backs, and that cannot be good for the game.

Radio has developed 'Test Match Special', which means that the listeners hear every ball bowled during a Test – plus a good deal more between deliveries and overs, and during intervals! But the great improvement in radio is in its transmissions from overseas tours. Now that we have the Commonwealth Cable the quality of reception is superb. No longer does one hear the crackles and fadings of the post-war years, though some people miss them.

6. Grounds are now better equipped to combat bad weather. Covers are bigger and more efficient, and instead of the old mopping-up blankets there are new machines which suck up the water and which have intriguing names like waterhogs and whales.

7. Sponsorship and business entertaining in boxes, as well as the advertising round the grounds, has saved first-class cricket. Without them no county could afford to run a professional side, the yearly cost of which is anything between £500,000 and £1,000,000. I do, however, wish that the guests who are entertained by firms to lunch and tea would return to watch the cricket a bit earlier. There are often large blocks of seats empty in the stands an hour after the luncheon interval is over. The guests or clients then sit and watch for an hour, and then toddle off to tea. Those empty seats seen on television must be an annoying sight to the genuine cricket-lover who has been unable to buy a ticket.

8. Club and village cricket is flourishing, and more people are playing cricket than ever before. The various sponsored competitions have done much to foster the amateur game, with the great incentive of appearing at Lord's as the main prize.

For worse

1. The standard of batting has fallen throughout county cricket. Very few batsmen now play straight, and because of limited over cricket they have developed some really bad habits. They play across the line. They back away and give themselves room to try to place the ball on the off-side, by doing which they expose their stumps to the bowler. They steer the ball outside the off-stump through the empty space at slip, but when a Test match comes along this space is no longer empty. There are three or four slips ready to gobble up the catches. Because they use such heavy bats it is now very difficult to get on top of the ball and cut it as they used to do. The weight of the bat is also partly responsible for the stance at the wicket, with bat raised high above the stumps, which so many batsmen now use. This must make it difficult to keep the head and body still as the bowler delivers the ball.

There is also the reverse sweep, as used by Ian Botham, Mike Gatting and John Emburey among others. It was originally introduced by the brothers Mohammad – Hanif and Mushtaq. It is a fun stroke and should never be used on an important occasion. When it is used the ball must be pitched outside the off-stump, otherwise the batsman exposes his wicket to the bowler, but if it *does* pitch outside the off-stump why not cut it or drive it, depending on its length? The reason given for using it is to take advantage of there being only two or three fielders on the off-side.

I once saw it used in a club match, and it caused quite a furore. The Eton Ramblers were playing the RAF Halton just after the war. Colonel A. C. Wilkinson was batting for the Ramblers. He was a fine batsman who had played for the Army, and a very brave man who had been awarded the GC for clearing a minefield single-handed. He also had an impish sense of humour and a quick temper. He soon got bored batting against the RAF and found run-getting too easy. So he thought he would experiment, and proceeded to play a succession of reverse sweeps against their leg spinner. This infuriated the RAF captain, who was an Air Vice-Marshal. He thought it was an insult to his bowler and that Colonel Wilkinson was mocking him. There was an awful row between the two of them, so that at the end of the game everyone left in a huff without the usual after-the-match niceties. A few months later Colonel Wilkinson went to the Golf Ball at Grosvenor House. There were various sideshows, including a small putting green. As he passed this the Colonel saw a large figure stooping to pick his ball out of the hole. He quickly recognised his old adversary, the Air Vice-Marshal. So without any hesitation he went up and gave the AV-M a terrific kick up the backside. 'There you are,' said the Colonel. 'So far as I am concerned the incident is now closed!'

2. The quality of pitches – with one or two exceptions – has become universally low. Counties, anxious to get results, deliberately under-prepare them, or leave on too much grass to assist their seam bowlers. Without flat hard pitches where the ball comes through at an even height, batsmen stand little chance of playing long innings, so essential for Test cricket. It also makes things too easy for the bowlers. The pitch does all their work for them, when they should be learning how to bowl batsmen out on good pitches.

3. Partly because of one-day cricket and partly because pitches suit the seam bowlers, spin bowlers have in the last ten years or so become few and far between. If they do exist, captains seem reluc-tant to bowl them or even to select them in their side. Leg spinners have virtually disappeared, though in 1988, thank goodness, down in Sussex Andy Clarke has had a regular place in the side and has been given plenty of bowling. His figures for the 1988 season were 618–156–16.50–44–37.50. They may not be outstanding, and were rather expensive, but at least he was encouraged. In fact, only fourteen bowlers bowled more overs than he did during the summer. Up in Lancashire Michael Atherton – surely an England batsman of the near future – also bowls more than useful leg-breaks. And of course in Derbyshire there is Kim Barnett. But strangely, although he has been captain since 1983, he seldom gives himself a bowl, partly I suspect because of his undue modesty.

There are still – given the opportunity – some off-spinners or slow left-arm bowlers around. For too many years they have been given an over or two before lunch or tea, but seldom given a long bowl. In the last two years, however, things have been looking up. Spinners are being used far more both in first-class and one-day cricket, and captains at last seem to realise their true value – if given a proper chance. Slow bowlers take far longer to mature than the fast bowlers, and the great spinners have usually been at their best when well over thirty. But they will never improve unless they are given long spells of bowling. Too often they are told to bowl 'flat' and keep the batsman quiet, instead of to flight and spin the ball *to try to get him out*. But as I say, things do look a bit better and it is particularly encouraging to see the spinners also beginning to play an important part in NatWest and Benson and Hedges matches.

4. One of the bad effects of one-day cricket is that bowlers are encouraged to bowl defensively and keep the runs down, rather than to try to bowl the batsman out.

5. There are still too many bouncers bowled, though mercifully in 1988 the West Indies, except at the Oval, hardly found it necessary to bowl any. But short-pitched bowling does ruin the game both for the batsman and the spectators. The former cannot play the most attractive scoring stroke – the drive. So the spectator is robbed and has to endure watching the batsman spending much of his time avoiding getting hurt. It is all in the hands of the umpires. The Laws have given them the powers to stop it, but they often seem reluctant to do so.

6. Measures have been taken to cure the slow over rate in first-class cricket by imposing a minimum number of overs which have to be bowled during a day. This is 90 for Test matches and 110 for other first-class cricket, but this still means only 15 or 18 overs per hour. It's difficult to believe that 20 overs an hour was once the accepted target – and often exceeded – even for a few years after the war.

I'm afraid this is all part of the defensive techniques used by modern captains, and they get up to all sorts of tricks to slow the game down. Long conferences with the bowlers, constant changing of the field, complaining about the state of the ball and so on. Another reason for the slowing up of the rate is that nowadays most bowlers – especially the fast ones – field at either third man or long leg. Most bowlers used to field close to the wicket in the slips or at mid-off or mid-on. I think it was Doug Wright and Brian

Statham who first preferred to field away from the wicket. It means that the bowler has to trudge off to long leg or third man at the end of his over, and then trudge back again to bowl his next. It adds at least 30–40 seconds to the time between overs. Multiply that by 90 overs and, hey presto, more than 45 minutes is wasted during a day's cricket.

I saw one possible solution in a city square in Aden, of all places. The locals were playing cricket and bowled from the same end for half an hour or an hour. They then changed round and bowled from the other end for a similar period. This meant that the interval between overs was reduced to about ten seconds. The next bowler always fielded at mid-off or mid-on, and was immediately handed the ball. Meanwhile, the batsmen quickly crossed, and the next over began.

I cannot ever see it happening in first-class cricket, but it isn't a bad idea. And, incidentally, the best Law made since the war was Law 17, which rules that in the last hour of a match a minimum of 20 overs have to be bowled. That at least has robbed the captains of the chance of any time-wasting in the last hour.

7. It has been sad to see over the last few years a deterioration in good behaviour and discipline on the field. Admittedly, television picks up many of these misdemeanours, which may have gone unnoticed in the past, but the blatant showing of dissent at umpire's decisions and the incessant and unfair appealing are not part of cricket. After all the unhappy events of 1987 and 1988 both on and off the field, let's hope that the cricket authorities, and *most important of all the captains*, will insist on the sort of behaviour which was once taken for granted and which fostered the phrase, 'It's not cricket.'

8. There is undoubtedly too much cricket, and for the professional a lot of the fun seems to have gone out of the game. It has become a job – like going into the office every day – and involves too much travel and rushing about the country. No wonder they say that they don't have enough time to practise. Also, how often do you see a cricketer smile? There should be fewer tours abroad, and when they do tour there should be fewer one-day matches. The same applies in England. There are too many one-day games intermingled with three-day, four-day and Test matches. The poor player must be

bewildered as he has to change from one technique to another. At least the one-day competitions should be separated from the first-class games. No one can deny the good that one-day cricket has done to cricket's finances. It is also understandable that the modern spectator, who cannot, like commentators, go to all five days of a Test, naturally prefers to see a result on the one day he can go. But I feel that the amount of this type of cricket should be reduced.

9. There are now too many overseas players in county cricket. When they first came over they were usually famous Test players like Sobers, Lloyd, Barlow or Richards; but now they come here to learn their trade by playing in one of the Leagues, usually, and then being signed up by a county. By doing this they are taking the places of young potential England players. The overseas cricketer, if he is a batsman, get a favoured position as an opener or number three or four. As a fast bowler he will be given the new ball, thus robbing a home-bred player of experience. It also encourages counties to look abroad for players, instead of training, coaching and encouraging their own. Most counties now boast either a West Indian fast bowler or a South African batsman. Some even have two, although under present regulations only *one* player not qualified for England can play in a county team. By signing a reserve, they spend unnecessary money which could go to add a thousand or more pounds on to the present basic salary.

The counties' excuse for signing so many players from overseas is that today a county can only keep alive if it wins one of the four competitions from time to time. This is perfectly true. Where would Somerset, Lancashire, Derbyshire, Nottinghamshire, Hampshire, Surrey, etc. be today without their overseas stars? It explains why Yorkshire, a team consisting only of players born in the county, now win so little. The general standard of counties has improved so that no match is a walk-over. Pre-war Yorkshire would back themselves to beat the likes of Glamorgan and Somerset in two days.

I think the solution should be that a county can only *register* one overseas player, and in an ideal world that player would already have had to have played for his country. I don't know whether this is likely to happen, but it would prevent comparative novices coming over here to learn their techniques at the expense of our own young players.

10. People say that there are fewer personalities in cricket today than there used to be. I suspect that every generation has said this, though there is perhaps more reason for saying it today. You may find that strange in view of television and the tremendous exposure it gives to the modern cricketer, but how can you be a personality if you look like a zombie shrouded in a helmet and a visor, so that the spectator cannot see your face and reactions. Would Denis Compton have become such a folk hero if he had always worn a helmet? I very much doubt it.

11. There has been a big decline in cricket played in the schools. This is a result of many things. Term times and exams have been altered in the summer, so there is less time to play. The comprehensive schools are so large that it is more or less impossible to organise enough cricket. There aren't the pitches, and there isn't enough time in the tight curriculum. And in most schools there are not sufficient teachers qualified or prepared to give up their time to coach and organise the games. From the letters I get I know that there are many dedicated cricket-lovers in schools who do their best – but it's an uphill struggle.

However, things are not all that bad. The county associations and clubs now run cricket for boys in the holidays. Sponsors like Texaco, Wrigleys and the Lord's Taverners organise competitions. And the National Cricket Association and bodies like the England Schools Cricket Association do a wonderful job in promoting cricket for those boys who *want* to play. That is an important point. When I was at Eton you could either play cricket or row. You had to do one or the other, so about 550 boys were Drybobs and 550 were Wetbobs, but of the 550 cricketers probably only half really wanted to play. The rest were just a nuisance and ruined the game for the others. Nowadays at Eton you can take your choice. You can play tennis, golf, do athletics, swim or other such activities. Only those who really enjoy cricket now play, and the result is better games and higher quality cricket, though the number playing has dropped considerably.

I think it is fair to say that in most parts of the country a boy, even if starved of cricket at his school can, if he is keen, go to his local club or county cricket club and find that he will get some coaching and organised games. There are now so many good people trying to help boys to play cricket that I honestly believe that any really *talented* young cricketer has a better chance today of being discovered than he had in the past.

Last Ball

On reading through what I have written I am afraid that the 'for worse' team has easily beaten the 'for better'. I must seem like a moaning old codger, but I love the game so much that I can't bear to see some of the things that are wrong with it today. And remember that I am talking in general about the first-class professional game, not the club and village variety. But all its wrongs won't ever stop my love of cricket. I have always tried to 'sell' it and put it across the air in the best possible light. I remember that in the fifties, when I was the staff TV cricket commentator, I felt it my duty to get the game as much coverage on television as possible. Paul Fox, now the managing director of BBC TV, was then running 'Sportsview' and 'Grandstand'. I had to work hard to persuade him to include a cricket item in either of the programmes. When I saw I was losing the argument I used to say to him lamely, 'Well anyway, it's a lovely game.'

Sometimes he laughed and let me have my way, but in fact he didn't know *too* much about cricket. He was directing 'Grandstand' one Saturday afternoon, and we were televising the Roses match. We had been on the air for about twenty minutes when I heard him through my earphones say to our producer: 'OK, at the end of this over tell Johnners to cue over to the Athletics. We'll be coming back to you later. Let me know when it will be and we'll come over for the fall of the next wicket!'

Even if *he* doesn't *I* still think 'it's a lovely game'.

Index